WHAT THE DEAD CAN DO

WHAT THE DEAD CAN DO

A NOVEL

PETER ROSCH

NEW YORK

Books should be disposed of and recycled according to local requirements. All paper materials used are FSC compliant.

This is a work of fiction. All of the names, characters, organizations, places and events portrayed in this novel are either products of the author's imagination or are used fictitiously. Any resemblance to real or actual events, locales, or persons, living or dead, is entirely coincidental.

Copyright © 2025 by Peter Rosch

All rights reserved.

Published in the United States by Crooked Lane Books, an imprint of The Quick Brown Fox & Company LLC.

Crooked Lane Books and its logo are trademarks of The Quick Brown Fox & Company LLC.

Library of Congress Catalog-in-Publication data available upon request.

ISBN (hardcover): 979-8-89242-183-6
ISBN (paperback): 979-8-89242-280-2
ISBN (ebook): 979-8-8924-2184-3

Cover design by Meghan Deist

Printed in the United States.

www.crookedlanebooks.com

Crooked Lane Books
34 West 27th St., 10th Floor
New York, NY 10001

First Edition: August 2025

The authorized representative in the EU for product safety and compliance is eucomply OÜ Pärnu mnt 139b-14, 11317 Tallinn, Estonia, hello@eucompliancepartner.com, +33757690241

10 9 8 7 6 5 4 3 2 1

To Bodhi

Men are prostrated by misfortune; women bend, but do not break, and martyr-like live on.

—Anna Cora Mowatt

PART I

1
TAG

They were together. That's all that mattered.

At thirty-five thousand feet, Tag found this sentiment pedestrian and no match for the one-two punch of the *CRACK* and shudder of the cabin cradling his family above Nevada. The passengers around them gasped in unison, their palpable unease and the escalating turbulence setting Ethan off into warbled, panicked cries. Tag's wife Amanda embraced their two-year-old tightly, murmuring comforting words in his ear, but it did little to quiet their son. Even so, no one in the rows ahead turned back to glare at them for the outburst.

As the plane lurched forward, Tag studied the profiles of other flyers across the aisle. Save another child not much older than Ethan, every face looked like his felt: grave and uncertain, teetering toward alarmed while holding their breath for a return to smoother skies.

It was their first trip since Ethan's birth, one Amanda deserved for so many reasons. They'd swung big: Hawaii. Amanda had pitched him on a stay in Kukuihaele. Thirteen hours in the air, a three-hour layover, rides to and from airports, and the hubbub of travel was a lot to ask of a toddler, even one as calm as Ethan. The unexpected was to be expected.

Any other time, the passengers' ambivalence to Ethan's fit would have been welcome, but this turbulence was . . . different. Tag had experienced "nightmare trips" before. Real doozies, he might have said. What a laugh. He wasn't laughing now, though. His stomach sank as the cabin dropped.

This felt like a true disaster.

He swallowed his fear, then met Amanda's tearing eyes, hoping his offered comfort. "I'm sure it's nothing," he whispered.

The corners of her mouth started to lift, but a sudden, violent bump stalled the smile.

He felt an urgency to memorize her face. Tears or no tears, the green in her eyes hit him like the first time he'd seen them from across a crowded bar. The bar had a name he usually remembered but couldn't remember now.

As casually as he could, he cocked his head over his shoulder to find the flight attendant, hoping her expression might bolster the flimsy "it's nothing" assertion he'd made. She was strapped to her jump seat in the back, hands folded on her lap. Just as he caught the attendant's relatively composed expression, the plane leveled. It still struggled as if the racing clouds had turned into a cobblestone road, but at least it was no longer pitched nose to the mountains below.

They were seated halfway between the exit row and the rear lavatories. A good place to be, given Ethan's vocal ire. Tag had selected that location purposefully. The bathrooms were close by, but, more importantly, his family was surrounded by the 93-decibel rumble of the engines on either side. A child's diaphragm is a hearty organ, but few can pitch a fit at a volume that will rise over the rolling thunder of aviation physics for very long. Ethan began to settle, his face eerily at peace—even when the 737 MAX resumed a steep forward tilt toward the ground.

In the months leading up to the vacation, Tag had taken care of the planning, hoping it would mollify Amanda. The destination had been a no-brainer, given Amanda's "gentle" insistence that, on the whole, no island they'd ever visited in the Atlantic had come close to matching the beauty of Hawaii; his main focus was to make the trip as effortless as possible for her and to minimize Ethan's impact on other flyers. Travel magazines said plenty about how to calm crying babies in flight, too, which fed his anxiety about keeping Ethan steady. Every thought, every purchase, and every memorized how-to tip had been about protecting and caring for everyone who might be put out by Ethan's tempest.

Maybe, Tag had thought, a perfect family holiday would help Amanda forgive his affair.

There was a second *CRACK*. The vibrations were now on par with a violent quake. The possibility that his family in row 27, seats A, B, and C, could collide into the mountain below and walk away from the crash entered his mind.

Unlikely, but it was possible. People survived such things.

There was hope to be had.

He'd once seen an infographic that demonstrated theories of seat locations within a crashing plane that would give the highest probability of surviving the impact. Little cartoon passengers ahead of the wing were crushed within the fuselage. The seats behind the engines? Safest bet. The article said the wings had strong structural components, which helped that part of the plane withstand a crash.

"Heads down! Emergency position! Heads down! Emergency position!"

From behind them, the flight attendant had been repeating the commands for a while, but this was the first time her orders penetrated Tag's thinking about a more optimistic outcome.

Gravity had ahold of the plane now. The passengers to his right had their bodies bent and heads pushed against the seatbacks with their hands at either side for protection—in some cases, heads tucked fully between their knees. Despite the noise and thrust of the plane's descent, which made hearing difficult if not painful, Tag homed in on one flyer's voice, an aged woman speaking out a prayer in between her pained sobs:

"Guide me, Holy One, on this final journey . . . Your hand pointing the way, Your loving eye upon my face . . . As I seek my new dwelling."

Amanda had made a protective shell over Ethan. It was a struggle, but Tag laid his body on them both. Under a cacophony of passenger screams and last pleas to various gods, he repeated, "I love you, I love you," while staring at what was visible of the left wing through the nearest window. It looked stable. Solid. Unaffected by the growing mechanical snarl.

Faith is daunting, sure, but like a muscle, it can be trained.

Tag had sound scientific reasons to remain optimistic.

He managed to find Ethan's tiny hand, which was buried under the weight of Amanda's forward lean. He took it in his.

"We're going to be alright," he said.

In the final moments before impact, Tag squeezed his son's fingers for the very last time.

THE TEXT | SECTION ONE

WELCOME, TAGGART!

You will likely have questions about:

- WHY you are here,
- WHAT here is, and
- what CAN or CAN'T be done while you inhabit Second Plane!

    No one text can contain everything you need to know or the answers to these questions. What you experience here will be UNIQUE TO YOU.
    There will be shared encounters, but what residents see while inhabiting this space is up to the residents themselves. EXCITING, isn't it? You'll be creating and conjuring, but let's not get ahead of ourselves.
    This text, commonly referred to as "The Text," was created to give you some basic knowledge around topics deemed most necessary to address with new residents. Your best possible transition from PRIOR PLANE starts with a GOOD ATTITUDE and this text. The content within will stimulate an immediate and more coherent dialogue with your mentor.*
    THE PANIC YOU MAY FEEL RIGHT NOW IS ONLY A MIMIC OF THE ANXIETY YOU ONCE KNEW.
    If at any point you and your mentor develop irreconcilable differences, your mentor is obligated to inform the council. With TIME, with WILLINGNESS, with CURIOSITY, the relationship you develop with your mentor will serve you well.

---

*All residents are assigned a mentor from inception here. You will find their name and instructions on how to MAKE CONTACT on the back cover. All mentor/mentee relationships assigned are final.

2
MATTHEW

There's no margin for error with this one.

The thought first appeared after Matthew received word his best friend's plane had crashed. Three weeks ago. A pest of a thought, on par with "Out, damned spot" in Matthew's opinion, and one that had assaulted his conscience ever since they took Tag's boy in.

Who'd formally broken the news? He had no idea. The voice on the other end of the line said Ethan had somehow survived, but Tag and Amanda were dead—all 184 passengers and the seven crew members had perished, except for the boy. The boy was in Nevada. The boy was alive! Now, the boy was at Matthew's kitchen table in a pink high chair, picking at Cheerios.

There's no margin for error with this one.

Doubts about raising a child not his own were natural, but he craved a reprieve. Through a tired haze, he looked away from the two-year-old and into the living room, hoping some prized possession with a memorable backstory would push his thoughts elsewhere.

The keepsakes his wife had hung or shelved around their apartment over the years offered no intriguing histories. That made sense. He and Nicole had rarely left Brooklyn since the birth of their daughter eleven years ago. The flavorless décor made it easy to remain in one's head, and Matthew couldn't shake his troubled thinking about raising Ethan or how off-the-rails their first few weeks as Ethan's new parents had been.

Flight 2332 was a national tragedy a divided citizenry could get behind. If you watched the evening news, you knew about Matthew and Nicole's new son, knew him by the moniker sensationalism had provided, "The Miracle Boy," and likely learned about it all before Matthew had heard it himself.

"Not a scratch," the rescue team had told him. Talking heads on all the channels said that, too, and said it often. Even if Ethan hadn't survived, a crash of that magnitude would've been broadcast on cable 24/7 until a bigger, better catastrophe came along. "The Miracle Boy" was the icing on the cake, and journalists of all stripes crawled out from every nook and cranny of an international media ecosystem to find the lone survivor's new family.

"We must spread the joy our reeling nation deserves," a network exec told Matthew over the phone on day one. "This is a drama that writes itself and could be lucrative for your family."

A reality show—thank God Nicole hadn't taken that call. "Get rich quick" was one of her many temptations. She hadn't always been that way, but she hadn't always been an addict, either. Thinking about Nicole and his preteen daughter Emily's frequent toe-to-toes going public on Bravo made Matthew sick to his stomach. He shuddered, which thankfully kept the bile at bay.

As if on cue, four firm knocks rattled the front door. The third visitor that day.

"Uh oh," Ethan said. "Who dat?"

When anyone came looking for a scoop, silence was Matthew's preferred strategy. He gently put his finger to his mouth, and sadly, Ethan understood the ask completely. The boy nodded and went back to choosing bits of cereal with a heartbreaking focus on doing so quietly.

"Mr. and Mrs. Shultz . . . if you're home, I'd love to have a word with you," a pleasant enough female voice said. "My name is Katrina Polk. I'm a reporter for *The Epoch Times*."

A bold admission if there ever was one, Matthew thought.

The curtains were drawn across all the windows of their street-level unit except one—the kitchen window nearest to them. That would only be a problem if, like the first journalist that morning, Katrina used the rear alley entrance into their tiny backyard and tried to conduct her interview through the small pane over the sink. Matthew decided on a plan of sit-still-and-see. Most reporters—at least the decent ones—went away if he said nothing for long enough.

Katrina knocked again and said, "Matthew? I know you and your new son are home."

Using his first name was a common tactic.

Insisting she knew they were home was a first.

Matthew stood, put a light hand on Ethan's shoulder, and eyed the brand-new baseball bat leaning in a corner at the front of the house. On credentialed journalists, stern verbal warnings had been enough, but the Saturday prior, around dusk, a different sort of curiosity seeker had caught him off guard.

The stranger had come down the steps at them suddenly, right as Matthew was rolling Ethan in his stroller across the threshold to their home.

"Sorry. I'm not here to cause any trouble," the man had said before Matthew had a chance to turn around. "Just came to see the Miracle Boy for myself."

Matthew pushed Ethan into the relative safety of their foyer, then spun one-eighty to confront the stranger who'd already set one foot into their home.

The man was of average height and built like any other Midwestern chucklehead Matthew had seen on the trips he occasionally made in that direction, except for his eyes. Above their dark bags, they were decidedly unimpressed with the threat Matthew had fashioned. Instinct, not intention, had Matthew's fist up, cocked to his right, and ready to swing.

The man took a calmer than expected step back onto the patio and said, "Take it easy, now. I'm not here to cause a fuss. Some miracles you have to see with your own eyes to believe. News makes up all kinds of phony lies these days, you know?"

Matthew considered his next move. Fortunately, he didn't need one.

"Appreciate your time," the stranger said. "I see that the boy *is*."

The elongated emphasis he put on "is" sent a chill down Matthew's spine.

"For I know the plans I have for you, declares the Lord . . ." the stranger said in that way that those who quote the Bible do, pausing for Matthew to perhaps recognize the verse. When he didn't respond, the twinkling anticipation in the man's eyes went dim. "Well," he added with censorious disappointment, "I guess I'll leave you to it."

Matthew bought the Louisville Slugger the very next day.

The bat was a necessity now, but as disquieting as that incident had been, opening the door to Katrina with a weapon in hand seemed like poor form.

"We aren't interested," he said. "And my lawyer has informed me that what you've just said about knowing we are home can be considered a threat in a court of law. Please leave."

It was a bluff. They'd considered hiring a lawyer, but only if these types of incidents persisted. He was impressed enough with the faux-legal lingo he'd concocted on the fly to sit back down, though, and he said nothing more for the two minutes it took Katrina to respond.

"OK, Mr. Shultz. I'm leaving my card at your doorstep," she said. "If you change your mind, give me a call. I apologize for popping by. I hope you and Ethan both have a great day."

He removed the putty from the peephole a moment later to ensure she'd gone. She had, but it was the first time Matthew wondered if he should be looking into a gun.

"Lady go bye-bye?" Ethan asked as Matthew returned to the seat next to him.

"Yep, buddy. Lady go bye-bye."

The crash, the phone call, the press, the boy, *Nicole*, and Em. Thus, the badgering thought: *There's no margin for error.*

Grieving the loss of his lifelong friendship with Tag would have to wait. Reminiscing about back patio barbeques or the vacations the four of them took before Em was born wasn't practical. Besides, his most vivid recollections were of recent family get-togethers, where his energy was spent managing Nicole's consumption of alcohol. There was a point of no return with her intoxication, but he'd always had his friends out the door before things got crazy. They wouldn't have kept Nicole and him in their wills as Ethan's legal guardians otherwise.

He'd agreed to raise Ethan should his friends die. Both of them. And at the same time. As apparently, they had. What were the chances? One article he'd found estimated that 1.5 million children in the United States lost one or both parents before age fifteen, but hours more searching on the internet had not unearthed any certain statistical probability of losing both at once.

Matthew didn't think of himself as a spiritual person. He had vague ideas of what Heaven and Hell might be, but all of those images had been formed during his adolescence when his mom and dad bussed him to a neighbor's Baptist church to get him out of the house on Sundays.

As an adult, he'd done well at avoiding the types of people who had regular conversations about religious beliefs. Had anyone ever asked him about death, and to the best of his recollection no one ever had, he'd have said, "When you're dead, you're dead. End of story."

But if an afterlife existed, he imagined that in the few weeks Amanda and Tag had been there, they had absolutely regretted their decision to name him and Nicole as Ethan's guardians.

It'd been a three-ring circus so far. Nicole wasn't built for it.

No margin for error.

He had two fingers against his forehead. The circle he'd rubbed had turned painful, but he pushed deeper.

We should try harder to make this living room into something.

That thought wasn't new either, but at least it didn't sound so clinical.

To the right of their front door, Em's black rubber galoshes towered over a smattering of more colorful, but equally muddy sneakers. Was there even mud in Brooklyn? None Matthew could remember. Maybe in Prospect Park. He wondered if Nicole had saved the smaller galoshes from when Emily was Ethan's age, but doubted any of his daughter's old clothes still lived with them. Storage was scarce. He vaguely remembered Nicole once asking if he was the kind of person who needed to keep everything their child ever wore, made, or had an attachment to. He might have been that kind of person had they had the space.

Any other boots he might find later today would be in the boxes that Ethan's grandmother had begrudgingly given to Matthew when he picked up the boy from her sprawling property in Jersey two weeks ago. A half dozen medium ones that Lucinda had insisted were packed to the hilt with Ethan's things, though, according to her, she had not done the packing.

Taking Ethan off her hands had been an ugly affair, so he didn't push the older woman for many details about how the rest of Tag and Amanda's estate was settled. She'd been understandably standoffish, but right before he got in his car to drive home with Ethan, Lucinda had calmed long enough to present Matthew with a small suitcase, one that she *had* packed. The blue roller bag had a vibrant *Paw Patrol* graphic printed on one side. "This is enough to get you started," she'd said. "And then some."

He guessed she'd been right because, for better or worse, Nicole had Ethan living out of that suitcase. The boxes had stayed packed and were living quietly in their bedroom—on Matthew's side of the bed, no less—just one more thing on Nicole's infamous list of things she meant to get done since he'd brought the boy home. But Matthew found it difficult to get angry at Nicole for not having already inventoried the boxes' contents. After all, even with all the distractions, he'd had ample time to unpack them himself.

It threatened to pour that day, and Pepper needed to be walked. Surely boots were in those boxes upstairs, and if they weren't, so be it. Squeezing in a trip to the playground down the street was one of the few activities Ethan seemed to enjoy.

Of course, even if Ethan's boots *were* in one of those boxes, they could be the wrong boots. In Park Slope, nothing you did with your children, and nothing you did parenting your children, went unnoticed or escaped being picked apart. To your face, or in a more passive-aggressive manner on the neighborhood app—a forum where busybodies posted everything from what they were doing better than you to what you were doing worse than them.

No margin for error.

That thought birthed another: *So, you're saying there'd been a margin for error with Em?*

Zero errors were an impossibility. They'd made plenty while raising Emily so far, but Em was doing fine. Their little girl was evidence enough to disprove that nurture deserved equal billing in the nature/nurture debate.

Still, it meant they hadn't screwed up that bad, right?

The microwave's clock flicked to 2:55 PM.

Nicole had left to pick up Emily from school an hour ago. His anxiety was the most unhinged when he was alone with Ethan.

It made no sense that his wife's absence had this effect.

He was the better parent—always had been. Hands down. She'd spent more time with Emily over their daughter's eleven years, but it was quality, not quantity. Also, Nicole had the unfair advantage of having made herself unemployable for the past five years. He'd taken unpaid leave that his boss granted on short notice to help Ethan get accustomed to his new home, but more so to help Nicole come to terms. Thank God he had, too.

His worrying turned to self-gratification as he imagined how poorly Nicole would've managed the onslaught of journalists, bloggers, and Jesus-nuts that wanted interviews, pictures, and chances to see—or sometimes to touch—the Miracle Boy. Hell, he'd thwarted three already today. Smugness wasn't a long-term solution, but it felt good to rise above his worries.

He might've gone on spiraling out, but Ethan's silence was too professional.

Matthew hadn't had eyes on his new son for a good five minutes. He wasn't choking—big phew—still just picking at Cheerios from his bowl. The boy seemed indifferent to his panic.

Long silences from Ethan were common, at least around Matthew and Nicole. That made sense, given what he'd been through. Only Emily could get him really talking, and when the boy did, he was surprisingly articulate for his age.

Maybe it was time to settle on how he'd refer to the boy: son, stepson, adopted son, godson—there were a handful of choices. He was leaning toward son but had yet to use the word aloud in front of Nicole, who so far had only called the child Ethan or "Tag's kid."

His *son* liked dry cereal. Not an irresponsible snack if it's the right cereal.

The bowl wasn't fun, though. No cartoon animals or colorful shapes lived on its surface. It was a ceramic bore, glazed in a color that could be called Meh. His placemat was no better. Totally lessonless. No solar system or human body circulatory diagrams, just plain white and in no way stimulating. The untouched spoon to the placemat's left was metal and adult-sized, which was reason enough for Ethan's tiny hands to have ignored it.

The snack time Matthew had thrown together was neither educational nor thought-provoking. When Emily was Ethan's age, stimulation was thought to be important, too, but Park Slope parents today made it out to be paramount. Not that long ago, Tag had said as much over the phone to Matthew while frantically searching for the perfect educational place setting in the aisles of a Target. If pressed about the boring placemat, Matthew could justifiably say he'd been a bit scattered, or he could dig in and insist it'd still been an opportunity for his son to work on his hand-to-mouth dexterity. Ethan put one Cheerio into his mouth as if on cue, then grabbed at five more using his hand like a bulldozer to excavate the surface of the pink high chair's tray.

Despite their apartment's lack of storage space, Em's old high chair had survived *Tidying Up with Marie Kondo* for no good reason.

Matthew had had a vasectomy when Emily turned four. The decision to have the surgery had been his. Plus, a vasectomy was reversible, TV said so, which would only have mattered if anything ever happened to Em.

The decision to focus on Emily had been a mutual one.

Publicly, he'd say their choice to only have one child was due to climate change, and that was fine. In Park Slope, a solid fear of the dystopian future adults were leaving their children was very popular.

Privately, he knew he'd been snipped because Nicole couldn't handle two kids.

Either way, finding the high chair at the back of their bedroom closet was a lucky break, or maybe a lazy break. The chair had brought no joy, he knew that. Marie Kondo would have, too. Hadn't he been put in charge of giving it a good home? Things like this had to cost more now than they'd paid over a decade ago.

Tag and Amanda had left them funds to offset the cost of raising a second child. Mid five figures wasn't anything to sneeze at, but it wasn't the windfall Matthew had been expecting and certainly not enough to have dulled the miserly rush he'd gotten when he found the high chair.

He grinned at Ethan, or maybe it was an affection meant for the chair, but it didn't do anything to stop Matthew's cursed thinking from bubbling back up.

There's no margin for error with this one.

Tag and Amanda hadn't outlined their dreams for their son, nor made a list of expectations for Matthew and Nicole to follow. There'd been plenty of legal paperwork but no notebooks, journals, or "If you're seeing this, it means we are dead" videos providing instructions. What the boy loved, hated, could or couldn't do, or needed was a mystery. Maybe you don't make a list like that for fear of tempting fate.

What had Tag and Amanda been hoping for when they picked Matthew and Nicole?

The day he had picked up Ethan and all those boxes waiting upstairs, Tag's mother, Lucinda, asked Matthew the same question. "What in the hell were they thinking picking you two?" she had asked. "I'm his paternal grandmother, for Christ's sake." That made good sense.

Initially, Lucinda had flown straight to Nevada and taken Ethan from the authorities herself. Matthew didn't believe her intent had been malicious. It was what any good grandmother would do. Plus, that first week after the crash had been hectic for all parties involved. The opportunity to pass Ethan's guardianship to a blood relative—an upstanding, well-off relation at that—was there. As Matthew understood it, he and Nicole were under no legal obligation and could decline. On paper, Tag's boy was a headache Matthew knew his family didn't need. No promise had ever been made aloud, but it had been implied, and breaking it felt like a dereliction of duty that far transcended what was or wasn't required of him by law. Via the executor, the *t*'s and *i*'s were eventually crossed and dotted. Tag and Amanda's wish for him and Nicole to serve as Ethan's guardians was legally clear, their reasons not so much.

Matthew had arrived at Lucinda's house ready to give her the slack she needed for a peaceful exchange. The woman was an intimidating silver-haired force. Former collegiate athlete, former CEO, former-anything-respectable really, and, in Matthew's opinion, plenty alert and physically capable at age sixty-five to raise her grandson. She was a widow, but didn't that mean she'd have *more* time to focus solely on Ethan? More than either he or Nicole would have.

"It's outrageous," Lucinda said. "I don't care what the law says."

Matthew had tried for a sympathetic smile and decided to stick to mostly nodding.

"It makes zero sense. ZERO!"

He nodded.

"Do you have any idea how much money I have?"

He nodded.

"I don't know you well, or your wife, but I remember how drunk she was at Ethan's first birthday party. I was there—not that you'd remember. Maybe she was high. Maybe both! I have a sixth sense for fuck ups like your wife and zero empathy for them."

He still nodded, but his smile dropped, and the heat in his face was plenty visible.

"What possible reason could Tag have had for wanting his son to live out his childhood with *you* two? You are virtually strangers to Ethan. Two nobodies. Tell me, Matthew, tell me how it makes one damn bit of sense?"

The older woman hadn't reached out since. Through Tag's lawyer, Matthew learned Tag *had* told Lucinda that he and Nicole were to be Ethan's guardians should anything happen. She'd known, and they'd told her their reasons, but Matthew wasn't angry she'd said otherwise. She was a mother, and no mother is equipped to believe they'll outlive their child. It's a passing thought, never a belief. It's easy enough to shrug off the probability. Or it's a biological imperative to hide the possibility in the furthest recesses of the mind in order to stay the course.

Lucinda was well-connected, though, friends with the types of power players who lived for a white-collar fight. Huge legal teams could be working on the case right now, biding their time as they waited for him and Nicole to screw up in a huge way, giving credence to a news-worthy suit.

Or, maybe Lucinda had made peace with the arrangement and was missing in action only because she needed time to lick her wounds. Regardless, Matthew wasn't looking forward to constantly having to prove to Lucinda that they were up to the task of raising her only grandson.

"More O's, please," Ethan said, and Matthew obliged.

Right in that moment, his new son was the spitting image of Mrs. Lucinda Littlefield.

Matthew blinked a few times to erase the resemblance. Ethan blinked back, matching the intensity and pace. It was simple mimicry but Matthew smiled for the second time that day. For a moment, the challenge of raising a boy who'd come from somewhere better and been through so much shrunk into a more manageable task.

They *had* done a good job with Emily, and that's what Tag had known—that's why they'd picked him and Nicole. It had to be the reason Tag had been so calm when he'd phoned him earlier that year. It had to be.

* * *

"Sorry to bug you at work, brother."

"No worries," Matthew said, barely engaged while entering numbers into a spreadsheet. "What's going on?"

"We're adulting—or parenting, I guess—and, well, some things can't wait, you know?"

"Sure, sure . . . hit me with it."

"Would you be cool—I mean, would you *and* Nicole be cool with us naming you two Ethan's legal guardians in our will? You know . . . in case anything tragic befalls us both?"

The ask pulled Matthew away from his work completely. This wasn't a conversation to half-ass his way through. He wanted to be sure he'd heard correctly. "Anything tragic befalls you both?" He'd also repeated the phrase in a bad English accent.

Tag laughed. "Feels less likely when you say it that way."

"I'm glad to hear you're making a will. You two are way ahead of the curve. Or maybe I'm telling myself that so I don't feel like we had been well *behind* the curve when we finally made our plans. Which, if I'm being honest, was done via LegalZoom. Not surprised you two—"

"This is all Amanda, brother," Tag interrupted.

"Amanda doesn't fuck around," Matthew said. "You're lucky about that." He didn't like the way that'd sounded. But he was nervous. This call was a big deal.

"Yeah, that's mostly true," Tag said, sounding somewhere between wounded and ambivalent. "Her way or the highway, I guess. Could be worse."

Matthew left the line silent for too long as he pondered whether he needed to say something like "You know what I mean" or "Just screwin' with ya" to soften what he'd said.

"If you aren't into it," Tag said, "we'll figure out something else."

If felt like an opening to decline.

"Nothing is going to happen to us, I'm sure, but . . ."

Matthew hadn't audibly agreed to the ask yet. He'd spaced out. He'd insulted his friend's wife and made him ask twice now if they'd be willing to be Ethan's legal guardians.

"Are you kidding? Of course, Tag. We'd be honored."

"Don't you think you should check with Nicole first?"

"She adores Ethan, are you kidding me?"

"Yeah, still—"

"I've always wanted two kids, you know that. Shit, man, we'd be honored."

"Thank you, Matty!" Amanda said.

"Am I on speaker?" Matthew asked. "Hi Amanda, not even a problem!"

"Nah, but you are loud," Tag said. "Listen, thank you. We're over the moon you two would agree to do this."

"Do we need to sign anything?"

"Don't think so. I'll hit you back if that's not the case. Let's get together this weekend."

"For sure. Ping me later," Matthew said.

"Will do."

"And Tag?"

"Yeah."

"It means a ton that you'd think of us for this." The sentiment felt too thick. It didn't match Tag's nonchalance. Matthew tried for a joke. "I mean, you two have to know we'll be scheming ways to get rid of you both, so we can have Ethan to ourselves, right?"

There was no response.

"Tag?"

Tag laughed the huge laugh anyone who knew him loved to hear. He recovered more quickly than normal, then said, "Yeah, that'd occurred to me. We're wily, though—killing us won't be easy."

Matthew gave a strained chuckle. "I was just—"

"Kidding. Obviously," Tag said. "Love to the fam, brother. I'll hit you up later."

After they hung up, Matthew had been too amped to get back into the work on his screen.

It was weird, but being chosen felt validating.

The hypothetical deaths of his dear friends aside, it would be incredible to have a little brother for Emily, who would no doubt be an amazing sister, too. Another opportunity to do a few things better than they'd done the first time around. Maybe even another Yankees fan in the house—finally. Matthew continued speculating on what having Ethan join the family would look like. He daydreamed of a future that included a son until it made him uncomfortable.

There was something insidious about the joy he was feeling; obviously he wanted nothing bad to happen to his friends.

He wished like hell he hadn't cracked the joke about scheming ways to kill them. Overcome with nausea, he grabbed his phone.

Yo. Sorry I said that last bit. I'm NOT planning to kill you.

That was text enough, but when no response came back, he dug the hole deeper.

We love all three of you and are up for the task!

He waited for a thumbs-up or any reciprocation, then kept typing:

Should it happen. I've said enough. TTYL

He added a sunglasses-smile emoji out of habit and hit send.

Typing indicator bubbles appeared then disappeared. Matthew waited, but no response ever came.

* * *

Until today, Matthew's brain had done a bang-up job of forgetting that call.

"Such a dumbass thing to say," Matthew said, and Ethan's eyes went up.

"Dummass," his son said plainly. "What dat?"

"Don't say that. Sometimes I say bad words, Ethan. I'll try to do better."

Ethan nodded in agreement.

No margin for error.

Though his earlier attempt had failed, Matthew put his fingers to either temple and rubbed at the thought again. Ethan, still grinning in uncertain awe of a foul word that he probably couldn't yet label a curse, put his fingers against his temples as if he, too, was suffering a pang of guilt for fuck-ups yet to happen, rubbing at them while trying to match Matthew's pace.

There are going to be mistakes.

From age nine on, Emily hadn't been shy about pointing out his gaffes. She went lighter on him than Nicole, and he was grateful for that. The verbal assaults his little girl piled onto her mother were relentless. It wasn't daily, not even weekly, but her observations were hued in truths that routinely left Nicole asking Matthew in a wine-washed whisper, right before bed, if she was a good mother. He hadn't stopped saying yes.

There'd been a time when he could tell himself she was doing her best.

Truthfully, Matthew thought that her best back then had been better than most. But now? At a minimum, he felt his parenting was in line with the parenting of other couples they'd known in the past decade. But what was he really measuring against? Maybe an outline or list of goals might help better define Ethan's future.

He reached for the notepad that Nicole kept at the center of the dining table.

He opened it and grabbed the pen inside. Only the first page had any scribbles. They were indecipherable, mini-Rorschach-like blobs that reminded him of two things:

1) The book itself was swag from a boutique hotel in Manhattan. A three-night romantic getaway that had been anything but. A staycation that was hardly any more affordable than it would've been had they traveled to Bermuda, not that the location would have helped.

2) He still hadn't gotten around to asking Nicole to consider getting help for her drinking.

Before they'd made that trip, Matthew was putting twice the number of wine bottles in the recycling bin than the year prior, a few vodka bottles too. Other than the one time he'd gotten sick on vodka as a teen, he never drank the clear spirit, and the amount of wine he allowed himself to enjoy in a week had rarely deviated from four or five glasses.

"I want to draw too!" Ethan said, pawing for the notebook.

"Are you done eating?"

Ethan threw one hand atop his other and over the bowl, protecting the cereal while shaking his head. A definitive "no." It made Matthew laugh aloud, giggle even, and to be doing so refreshed him.

"I see. When you're done, we'll draw together."

Ethan's nod was reluctant but agreeable.

Matthew drew the number one in the top left corner of the second page and circled it. He tapped the tip of the pen to its right, stuck in the consideration of a good first parenting goal.

DON'T HALF-ASS IT.

Before he could think better of his only entry, he underlined it a few times, then went ahead and drew a circled two underneath it. The second entry stayed blank.

They chose us because they never thought anything would happen— because they never believed they'd die at the same time. Statistically, simultaneous deaths must be very rare. A commercial airline crash couldn't have been high on their list of what-ifs. We were the "just in case" couple, not the "they'll do a wonderful job that no one else could ever do" couple.

CRACK! The sound of ceramic busting into pieces jerked Matthew from his thoughts. There were enough Cheerios on their dark hardwoods to feed five kids. They had exploded in every direction and surrounded the table like a tiny army amidst the fragments of the bowl.

It'd startled him, and his reaction put Ethan on edge, but Matthew managed to recover quickly with an "uh-oh." He forced his eyes into surprised saucers to complement the bright pop in his voice. It was the very same affected "uh-oh" he'd used to make with Emily.

"Uh-oh," Ethan parroted. "Uh-oh."

Matthew bent over to grab the three broken pieces of the bowl from the floor. He pinched his index finger and thumb around the less aggressive edges of each shard, then grouped those pieces on the table well out of the boy's reach.

"Want to see a magic trick?" he asked.

"Yes!" Ethan said.

"Do you know how to cover your ears?"

Ethan nodded excitedly, as only little ones can when they know for sure they've done something they had seen grown-ups do.

"Great, let me see that. Let me see you cover your ears."

His son cupped his ears as he closed his eyes tight.

"Shut eyes are key to muffling bad noises," Matthew said, grinning yet again. Then, with four fingers in his mouth, he whistled.

Ethan frowned as the hiss of the command echoed around the kitchen.

Before its reverberations faded, the huge thump of sixty-five pounds of dog jumping from the bed upstairs shook the ceiling.

"I'm sorry, bud," Matthew said. He put a hand on Ethan's. "I'm sure a lot of what can and can't happen around an *almost* three-year-old will come back to me. Don't worry." Getting the age right had already proven to be very important to Ethan.

Ethan smiled, put his hands down, opened his eyes, and looked toward the sound of four paws overdue for a nail-trimming thundering down the wood stairs. The scratch was grating.

"Here we go. I call this trick the a-bra-ca-clean-up!" Matthew said.

He pointed toward the scattered cereal on the floor.

"Come 'ere, Pepper! Come on!" Ethan shouted, eagerly twisting his body within the high chair for a better view. "Snack time!"

The mutt came into view—mouth at the floor, nostrils working feverishly to find and start with the Cheerios in the shadows underneath the loveseat against the room's wall.

"C'mon on, Pepper, here, good boy!" Ethan cheered.

The child's affection for the animal was contagious.

"Get 'em all, boy," Matthew added. "C'mon. Eat 'em up, big guy!"

Hansel and Gretel had nothing on the dog's ability to track each piece as it worked its way toward the kitchen. It licked up one after another on its way there.

"C'mon, boy! More in here!" Ethan said, tapping his tray to draw the dog closer.

Suddenly Pepper looked up from the living room floor, ignoring two dozen bits of cereal waiting for him. The dog set its gaze on Ethan, then stared hard to the boy's left, over his shoulder and beyond him. At what? At nothing, best Matthew could tell. A small spider hung from a ceiling corner in that direction, but their dog had never minded those before. Pepper's ears dropped flat as he raised his withers, every hair on the haunch was standing tall neck to tail, his teeth bared tight, and his guttural snarl was only the precursor to a barrage of barks more wild than domestic.

Ethan spun toward Matthew with enough force to pick the right side of the high chair up off the ground. He reached for Matthew with all he had.

Pepper gnashed and growled. The dog held his ground as his mouth snapped the air and his snout pointed toward nothing and then more of nothing.

Matthew plucked Ethan from the chair, and the child burst into earsplitting hysterics.

"Pepper! Cut it out!" Matthew said as he hugged Ethan into his chest. He searched the kitchen for the source of the dog's ire. "Shut up! Dammit, Pepper, shut up!" he shouted.

His demands for obedience only intensified Ethan's wailing.

Matthew shuffled toward Pepper as Ethan buried himself into his neck.

The dog kept his stare pointed at the back of the kitchen.

Matthew looked for anything unusual but came up empty.

"No!" Ethan shouted. "No! No! No!"

"It's going to be fine, Ethan. Calm down."

Matthew edged closer to the dog until he was able to squeeze himself between all its ferocity and the pocket door's frame. With his back to Pepper, he hurried into the family room to set Ethan down on the loveseat, but Ethan wouldn't let go.

"Ethan, I'm not going anywhere, let me just handle the dog."

Matthew tried to set his son down again, but Ethan put every bit of what an almost three-year-old can into ensuring there was no way Matthew was leaving him on the couch.

"Ethan, you're going to be fine, let me just—"

A short, sharp yelp interrupted Matthew's pleas for cooperation. The sound was followed by a thick silence.

He kept Ethan in his arms. The boy tried hard to get his tears under control, sucking up his fright in short inhalations that sounded like choking. Matthew tightened his embrace around his son as he turned to see why Pepper had gone silent so abruptly.

The hairs on the dog's back were half-energized, erect but settling. Pepper entered the kitchen completely, had his mouth and nose back to the floor, and was huffing and licking up the cereal that remained there.

"I'm going to set you down," he told Ethan. "See, it's just Pepper being a dumb old dog."

Between uneven breaths, Ethan responded, "Oh . . . kay."

Matthew set the boy down on the sofa and stepped into the kitchen.

The dog continued its hunt for cereal along the baseboards.

There was one window, over the sink, no bigger than two stacked shoeboxes.

As Matthew stared out the pane into the space his family sarcastically referred to as their backyard, his skin went cold and the hairs rose on his neck. Maybe reporters breaking into the alley to score an interview was the latest wrinkle, a new normal for him and Nicole. No privacy at all was to be expected now—at least with the wackos who called themselves journalists. He found himself hoping that if he *did* see something—did see some*one*—it would be Katrina. All things being equal, she had at least sounded relatively harmless.

He moved toward the sink to get a better look, and as he stepped to the counter, he heard the distinct crunch of ceramic underneath his shoe.

He lifted his foot. It was one of the pieces of Ethan's cereal bowl.

The other two were still on the table, where Matthew was certain he'd left all three.

THE TEXT | SECTION TWO

WHY YOU?

Many of you arrived here long before you imagined you would. Most of you have arrived alone, but some residents come as couples, and fewer still come as families.*

Even if you are one of our more elderly arrivals, you probably didn't see it coming, at least not the *exact* moment. If a fortune teller "predicted" even a rough approximation of your passing on to Second Plane, it was a coincidence, we assure you! THERE IS NO GREAT MYSTERY TO SOLVE. THERE IS NO CONSPIRACY. Your time was your time but not by any grand design.

It sounds odd, but you must allow yourself to not care. This is key to finding traction with residency. THAT SAID, if you choose to spend any of your stay here thinking about a galactic meaning for your removal from Prior Plane, so be it. HAVE FUN! But know that the tranquility you feel from such speculations is just a mimic. REMINDER: you are here now. Not there. So, GO FORWARD!

---

*Please see page four: "The Children."

3
NICOLE

Nicole's reasons for a nip here, a swig there were plentiful—obvious even, if only to herself. Her excuses for drinking during the day weren't necessarily logical, and wouldn't look good on paper, but she hadn't ever claimed them to be. Besides, like so many rationalizations made to self-approve self-destruction, the value of one reason or another for a tug on the bottle was relative. Or moot.

The point is, she had *her* reasons.

Her problems weren't illegitimate, but to date, no friends or family members had bothered to ask what her problems were. She had to pay for someone to ask. And she had a therapist, so technically, she was. Therefore, any evaluations, judgments, or condemnations made by those same people not asking squat about her issues or her self-medication techniques amounted to bupkes as far as Nicole was concerned.

She'd snuck a quick sip outside of MS 51 plenty of times. She stood there now and had been taking the tiniest little swigs of vodka since arriving. Nicole didn't particularly care for the spirit, but wasn't it said that vodka was the drink of choice for the smartest drunks committed to conducting necessary and public business?

Like every other day she'd gone to pick up Emily, not one parent on the sidewalk outside the school expressed a "gotcha" or an "I saw that." Not verbally nor silently, not subtly nor using overt contortions of smug facial features.

Oh shit, was she buzzing already?

Nicole knew she wasn't the first mom in the history of momming to carry a quarter-pint bottle of booze in her bag. In fact, "Mommy Juice" culture was real—acceptable even, perhaps honorable—but she was loath to declare herself part of the trend or become a card-carrying member of the Wine Mom club. She was a drunk. The rest of them? Pretenders.

Covertly sneaking the drinks she needed was even more important now that Ethan was in the picture. She had to be ninja-like. A sauced expert in stealth boozing. Being busted drinking while under the watchful eyes of journalists would do no one any good. She wasn't a monster, though, not by any definition she'd ever read, but she didn't want to compound her problems.

But the reporters—goddamn, the reporters—were all looking for any excuse to keep Ethan's story more sensational than it already was. It wasn't enough that he was the *only* survivor of Flight 2332. No, the vultures needed those clicks, needed those eyeballs to pay the bills, and no twenty-first century anyone cared about anything for very long. The parents of all the kids that had been gunned down in the United States over the past decade could attest to that.

These fuck-sticks were practically begging her to be piss-drunk at all times. They wanted her to be supremely inebriated so that she *would* screw up. The journalists themselves were just another reason *to* drink. Definitely an issue worth drinking over, should anyone ask.

And they loved her, didn't they? Not just a mom now—at least not just Emily's mom—but the newly anointed mother of the Miracle Boy. Could there have been a better story than one in which Nicole fucked over his life worse than the plane crash had, by being an irredeemable drunk?

No one had to have known Amanda personally to compare her to Nicole. Amanda's mothering would remain forever perfect now that she was dead. And the looky-loos were comparing Nicole to their own A-plus parenting, too, she was sure.

After the crash, the press was on Ethan's story light-switch quick. They found Nicole's family even before the Miracle Boy was there and did so as easily as if there'd been a giant spotlight parked on their stoop. He was headed their way, a new mom, a new dad, and though they'd asked, no one could tell them how the press had caught wind of that fact before his residency in Nicole's home had become a reality. She suspected Lucinda had leaked that information to derail their guardianship before it could begin, and oh boy, how she wished the older woman had succeeded. It wasn't a crazy thing to think, even if Matthew had said so.

Those first few weeks, the reporters knocked, phoned, texted, emailed, and even sent letters. Matthew's nonstop refusals to grant the networks an interview with the Miracle Boy didn't stop the news from creating stories. There were cameras on all of them at all times.

Who could roll sober with that scrutiny?

NBC, ABC, FOX, CNN, and the others had packaged, promoted, and aired their multiple exposés on the probability of Ethan's inexplicable survival, yet the harassment hadn't ended. Because while the mainstream media had moved on to some high-stakes congressional standoff, the underbelly of America hadn't.

And the underbelly of that underbelly never would. Any knucklehead with a phone had taken it upon themselves to get the "real" story. They didn't care the crash was under investigation by the NTSB. Few of the oddballs that approached Nicole and her family actually asked for permission to record videos, take pictures, or ask questions. They did as they pleased.

The amateur interview requests came from every direction at all hours. If Nicole walked Ethan to or from the park two blocks from their home, the weirdos were there. Turn a lamp on at dusk—oh, wonder who's that banging at the door? Some had lists of questions that rivaled a receipt from CVS; others were content to snap a quick shot and run.

One influencer from New Hampshire had claimed in a multipart post that Nicole and Matthew had been chosen by the Devil to raise his own son—the next Child of Disobedience, the poster had called him. All the signs were there, this little fucker had said. He colored

red lines from the crash site in Nevada to their home in Brooklyn as two points to a pentagram drawn over a screenshot of North America from Google Maps.

There were so many theories.

But there was no silver lining to being saddled with a miracle toddler if you weren't going to profit from tending to him. If you weren't going to let his inadvertent fame fill your coffers while it could.

It felt yucky to feel like that, and Nicole hated herself for thinking that way, but hating herself didn't make the notions go away.

In Ethan, they had an opportunity. She and Matthew were broke—no drink or drug could obscure that fact—with no reason to believe their finances would change for the better. Maybe not *broke*, but scraping by, and what had Matthew done about it? Sure, he hadn't pinned his firm's failure on her outright, but he didn't have to. She could read between the lines.

They had been given a chance at real money. Cosmic shit, really, one in 11,000,000 odds. Even only a few appearances would have netted serious bank. At least, that's what Matthew had indicated at one point, but then, out of nowhere, he'd decided it felt unethical. There'd been no conversation about it, just his proclamation of *his* decision. Nicole might have been angrier at him had she not been secretly terrified about performing like a perfectly sober doting wife and mother, a have-it-all who could do it all for the cameras, hosts, reporters, and public.

She was a self-described anxious sort. Everybody knew so. No prescription cocktail removed her anxiety completely, which reminded Nicole that she needed a new therapist, but she couldn't be bothered to reach for her phone to add it to her list of things to do.

Bottom line: If they couldn't make bank, everyone needed to leave her the hell alone.

Of course, it could have been worse.

The face of a two-year-old, even one recently ordained a miracle in headlines and cable chyrons alike, just isn't that recognizable. They are cute, in their own way, but all look the same. You've seen one towheaded toddler, you've seen them all. Thank God for small favors.

In time though, Ethan's visage would resemble that of his dead biological parents'. The boy would grow up to be as handsome as Tag or as stunning as Amanda, or his face would be some amalgamation of them both. Nicole was sure of that.

Ethan would grow up a gene-pool lottery winner, and Ethan the teen would be instantly recognizable—maybe a model. Would anything he earned be available to her? Not likely. Plenty of producers, publishers, or anyone else who didn't actually have to raise Tag and Amanda's son would get wealthy off the boy's improbable story someday. But not them, not her.

It was quiet on the sidewalk that afternoon, though. Nicole realized she hadn't been bothered on the way to pick up Emily, and hadn't been that morning either. Was interest fading? Maybe it was the economy, maybe it was a new virus, maybe the news had finally figured out a way to make people care about UFOs—she couldn't say. But she had to admit, the random street interruptions were happening with less frequency, as good a reason as any to celebrate with another quick drink.

She grabbed the bottle from the bottom of her oversized satchel and, without pulling the booze into view entirely, gave the cap a quick turn. Then, under the shadows of the maples overhead, she brought the glass ring to her lips.

The heat of the liquor was quick; dopamine went to work at quelling her worries, though ridding herself of her dissatisfaction *with* herself would require more than the bottle had left to give. Hopefully, the Xanax she'd popped before leaving her apartment would do the trick.

She swallowed the rest, then dropped the quarter-pint back to the bottom of her bag.

Nicole felt like she might float away—and it was welcome. She'd rise high above the other parents, none of whom appeared any wiser about her impending flight or acted any more aware of the reason for the takeoff.

Her euphoria was short-lived.

"For fuck's sake, Nicole!" her daughter yelled. "If you're going to be picking me up again, which, I might remind you, I don't need—*at all*—do me a favor, will ya? Hit the bottle back on Seventh Ave. If you wanna be a drunk, at least be a smarter drunk."

Now the other adults *could* be bothered to make eye contact with Nicole.

Emily stood as firm as she probably thought her slick burn required, phone in one hand, with a neon-blue backpack slung over one shoulder. The heat in her daughter's eyes was similar to the same scorching hate Nicole often saw burning in Matthew's, but under her daughter's rainbow bangs, the ire seemed to burn even brighter.

Worse yet, Nicole didn't have to look down to see Emily's disappointment. The girl's height came from her father. At that moment, Nicole felt smaller than the word *petite* was meant to suggest.

None of the parents said anything. Nicole appreciated their silence as much as she had hated them for it when she first arrived at Emily's school.

Those parents had their own ridiculous reasons to be there to pick up their kids, but not one had bothered asking Nicole why *she* was picking up her daughter again.

Maybe they knew her situation, maybe they were scared they'd put their foot in their mouths, or maybe they were just self-centered dipshits who could go fuck themselves. The latter seemed most likely, but explaining any of this to her daughter wasn't going to move the needle.

Nicole tugged the strings on her gray oversized hoodie, which had become the top half of something close to a uniform. Her pants, too, were better suited for a lineman. She wanted those clothes to swallow her whole. To some extent, she'd succeeded. After all, she'd been left alone the whole day. Not one question, not a single picture snapped—the uniform had done its job.

Emily didn't say a word to mock how Nicole had recently chosen to hide herself. She didn't have to—her disapprovals had been cartoonishly large of late, a byproduct of what? The internet maybe, some TikTok challenge. Nicole deserved her daughter's disrespect, but not publicly. Even so, she let Emily's outburst slide, hoping to move past being caught and on to something less Nicole-centric.

"Em—"

"Save it," her daughter said. "Anything else you say is gonna make it worse."

Emily set out ahead, ignoring Nicole in favor of the texts that came up all at once when her phone booted up. When she was half a block away, she stopped but did not turn around. "You coming, Nicole?" It sounded like a dare, if only for its volume. "Please tell me you didn't crawl all the way here just to let me walk home alone." Then, her daughter resumed her escape.

Nicole didn't want to, but she launched into a speed walk, because she *had* to.

"I don't know what you think you saw," she said to Emily when she'd reached her, "but you've no right to talk to me . . ."

Nicole's anger lacked conviction. The liquor-Xanax fix-all was wreaking havoc on her tone. She raged on to the best of her ability, but Emily kept going. Her daughter didn't even bother with tilting her gaze from her phone as she pulled one hand off the device to extend a high middle finger. The gesture hung steady for a few steps, then her hand went back down to text a message she'd already started with her other.

Her fluidity was impressive, but Nicole decided that admiration needed to remain secret.

She pushed the range of her natural stride in order to keep up. "I need you to know that I know you don't need me to pick you up," Nicole said. She'd sounded as kind as she'd hoped to. "It isn't about you. It's about the fucking weirdos who won't leave us alone."

"There's nothing weird about people wanting to better understand how a child, and *only* that one child, survived the worst plane crash in years, Nicole."

Emily hadn't needed to leave the conversation at her fingertips to carry on with this one. Her skills impressed less this time; in fact, her apparent nonchalance to the whole affair thus far had heated Nicole's already red face.

"Maybe so, but what gives them the right?"

The kind-voice angle, a higher-pitched sing-songy thing that Nicole had started with in an effort to reason away her drinking fauxpas was no more, but it didn't faze Emily.

"Nothing. Or maybe everything. We're all complicit," she answered with the same holier-than-thou tempo her father employed when he felt he was making some unique observation, a steady-volumed bit of logic that left Nicole's eye twitching, even when drunk.

"How so?" Nicole asked.

Emily kept at her text. "What do you read online?"

"Well, I'm not on there looking up insane plane crash theories, I can tell you that."

"Sure, but I doubt it's the *Wall Street Journal*," Emily said.

Enough. Nicole took two stretched steps forward and put herself in Emily's way.

Her daughter rooted herself to the sidewalk with a bring-it-on posture that amplified Nicole's minor sway. Neither made an effort to step aside to make it easier for the other foot traffic. Nicole set her hands on Emily's shoulders, hoping to ease Emily out of the standoff. A deep breath provided some respite from her self-medicated haze, but her poise remained fragile.

"I won't need to pick you up from school forever. Interest in Ethan will stop. It's fading already. Until then, can't you and I try to enjoy these walks?"

"Newsflash: Much worse weirdos approached me before we had Ethan," Emily said. She removed Nicole's hand from her shoulders as her almost military bearing let up. The hate in her daughter's eyes downgraded to an uncomfortable frustration.

"What are you saying?" Nicole asked, sensing civility was possible.

"The ones interviewing me about him should be the least of your worries."

"So, they *have* been bugging you?" Nicole said with immediate regret.

Emily shook her head. "That's not what I said. You're a horrible listener. The worst in all five boroughs."

"You should talk. Are you texting with a stranger now?"

Emily swung her phone behind her back, then shoved it snugly into her jeans pocket.

Nicole thought her daughter's pants were too tattered to be intentionally so. If it weren't her daughter, she'd have pitied the girl in front of her, who obviously had a mother who couldn't be bothered with taking her daughter shopping for better intentionally destroyed pants. The two of them didn't brunch, they didn't share secrets. Nicole wasn't the mother she'd set out to be.

Her chin dipped to her chest. The Xanax had her zoning out, or maybe her shame was the culprit—likely, it was both.

"Earth to Mom. Mom, are you there?"

Nicole wished that she wasn't there. Maybe even wished she simply *wasn't*.

"No one's bugging me," Emily continued. "I answer a few questions, and they're on their way. They're not criminals. Dipshitism isn't a crime."

"What kinds of questions?" Nicole asked. When Em didn't respond immediately, she forced her heavy eyelids to part for wide open eyes. "I *said*, what kinds of questions, Em?"

"The same ones you and Dad have answered hundreds of times: How's Ethan doing? Does he remember the crash? Have you seen his dead parents lingering around? Any paranormal activity? Did your baby brother tell you what it was like to wake up next to his dead parents?"

"Please, God, tell me you're joking," Nicole said, swallowing the shaky break in her voice. It was gut-wrenching, but she wanted to stay angry. Pissed off was her comfort zone.

"I'm paraphrasing, but does it matter? Answer the questions and the weirdos move on. Put off answering their questions, and they'll just keep pestering you. Not rocket science."

"This is why I need to be here for you," Nicole said. "You're too young for this shit."

"I take offense to that. My answers are very adult."

Nicole stifled a smirk quickly in favor of maybe having a moment. "Oh really, adult how?" Her question came out even kinder than she'd planned.

"Like, I just tell them he's not even three. What in the hell do you think he's said?"

Her daughter could hold her own. On some level, Nicole knew that and Em's independence frightened her more than the weirdos ever could. Still, she needed to sound like a mom, needed to make her disapproval clear, not stan her daughter while under the influence.

"I'm supposed to feel better because you're telling me you're smart-assing strangers?"

"I'm just saying, I've got this. You've got your own . . . stuff," Emily said. "And Ethan being here has made it worse. *You* need help right now, not me."

Before Nicole could fire back, tires screeched bloody hell into a stop behind her. She turned and found the cab that had caused it. They readied themselves for a familiar inconvenience.

"Excuse me, O-M-G, you guys," a young woman said while jumping out of the taxi. She was made-up like a Kardashian but blonde, hair perfectly coiffed, and wearing a tight white T-shirt featuring a face that Nicole thought might have been the woman's own. "Aren't you baby Ethan's mother? And you're Emily, right? His new sister? Tell me I'm right."

The woman pulled her phone out and started recording.

Another twenty-something brunette came around the back of the cab. Save the color of their hair, the two women could've been twins. This second stalker's phone was already in hand, pointing at Nicole and her daughter. As the two nuisances scanned all around, presumably for Ethan, their eager faces looked like they might pop from zeal.

The cab's window went down and the driver leaned out. "Yo, you gotta pay before you get out of the car," he said. "This isn't an Uber."

Angry horns started in, then passing dogs upset by those horns started barking.

Neither rider many any effort to pay the cabbie.

"I'm Claire!" the blonde shouted over the traffic, holding out a hand to shake Nicole's. "At Claire Bear Original on TikTok and Insta, maybe you follow me?"

Nicole looked at Claire's outstretched hand. "Can't say that I do," she said, then hoicked her shoulders back and subtly increased the width of her stance, claiming her authority of the space between her daughter and Claire Bear Original, whose camera hand couldn't seem to decide where to direct the lens. One second it was pointed at

Nicole, the next on Emily, the next it was spun backward and filming herself or the angry cabbie.

The proximity of the two intruders, who were circling a bit while flailing their limbs as if gorillaing had become acceptable street introduction etiquette, was a clear violation of personal space. A short enough distance for Nicole to wonder if either smelled the vodka on her breath.

"What about you, Em?" Claire asked as she leaned left then right to circumvent Nicole's blockade. "Can I call you Em? *You* know me. Every girl your age knows me."

Nicole bobbed and weaved to match the woman's movements, but preventing Claire from making eye contact with her daughter dizzied her, and it was an angry kind of spin. "Look, I don't give a fuck who you are or if my daughter knows you. Now isn't the time. Get back in your cab and piss off."

"Hell no," the cabbie added. "Just pay me so I can get going already!"

"I have *two million* followers," Claire said, ignoring their suggestions. "This could be huge for you, Nicole—for both of you . . . or you three, or four. How many of you are there in the family now, anyway? You have a dog, too, right? Pepper, I think I read."

"Bitch, even if I believed you hadn't paid for all of your fans, we have nothing to say to you." Nicole turned to punctuate her displeasure by eyeing Claire's friend. "Or to you either."

"The lady is right, no one here gives a fuck," the cabbie said. "And I really don't wanna get out of my cab to collect that fare. So—"

"Ethan is not with them anyway," Claire's accomplice said. "He's not, right?"

The woman pushed her phone closer to Nicole's face. "Where are you keeping that little angel?"

Nicole slipped her hand into her bag. Her fingers found the empty vodka bottle and wrapped tightly around its stubby little neck. She committed to a firm grip, even if she didn't one-hundred percent know what a grip like that was for.

Claire suddenly put her phone down to her side.

"It's OK if Ethan isn't with you—better really," said Claire. "Personally, I wouldn't have him out this soon after the accident."

"Oh, are you a mother?" Nicole asked.

It wasn't a big backward step, but Claire retreated, got quiet, and appeared wounded.

Seeing the woman cower started a curl at one corner of Nicole's lips. Her mind momentarily found the focus that had eluded her for most of the day, emboldening her. The opportunity to provoke their stalker—to hurt her—was one Nicole could not let pass by.

"*Are* you, Claire? Are *you* a mother?"

"No, no. I'm not," Claire replied, her face instantly flushing.

What exact chord Nicole had struck didn't matter, she'd pulverized it.

By now, twenty cars were stacked up behind the cab. The first driver in that long line was practically scraping her vehicle around the obstruction to make it to the intersection before the traffic lights cycled. When her car's fender raked the taxi's fender, the cabbie finally gave up.

"Fuck you, cunts!" He went back to the wheel as his eyes took in the stack-up in his rearview mirror. "Fuck this place, too."

The cab darted back into the fray, dragging the traffic away with it.

"There went your ride," Emily said.

"She speaks!" Claire mockingly rejoiced.

Emily had stepped to her mother's side, but Nicole only just noticed.

Claire's camera hand was headed back up toward their faces. Nicole took her daughter's hand but left her other hand in her bag.

"Emily, maybe you could convince your mother that it'd be bene—"

Emily squeezed Nicole's hand gently, but the unexpected affection came too late.

The empty quarter pint came out of Nicole's purse in a flash and slammed into the woman's fake grin. The crack of the glass connecting to upper incisors gave way to Claire Bear Original's shrill scream. The bottle caught and chipped her canine tooth, too, and it hadn't needed to shatter into pieces to tear open the cheek and skin at one corner of the woman's mouth either.

There was blood. There was cursing. Emily was cursing loudest of all. Then, there was genuine concern, spoken at a volume below a shout—a rarity in the city—from approaching voices Nicole did not recognize.

Then, there was no one. Only silence. Nicole had blacked out.

* * *

Later that evening, Nicole woke, fully clothed between her bed's comforter and the sheets. In those first few conscious seconds after her eyes opened, she experienced a deep but phony relief.

It'd been just another normal day, hadn't it?

Hers was a relief any alcoholic and addict understood—one where a drunk like Nicole could wake anytime, anywhere, somewhere between how they'd fucked up and its consequences.

It was a moment that never lasted. Memories wake eventually, too.

In her case, the first recollection was the sound of her vodka bottle slamming into Claire's mouth. Red-tinged details arose thereafter, still buried in brain fog and a bit obscure, but the fuzzy, warm feelings—that oh-too-quick charade of normalcy—ended abruptly.

And just in time for her daughter to come barging into the bedroom uninvited.

"You really messed up this time," Emily said. She shoved her phone's screen in front of Nicole's face.

"What the hell, Em? At least let me sit up." She snatched the phone and managed to scoot into a lean against the headboard.

The things Nicole hadn't yet had time to remember—the blood, Claire's cry, the promise the woman made while hysterical, and even Nicole's blackout and collapse to the sidewalk—all of those gory details were there, looping over and over, at full volume, with over 250,000 likes so far. The throbbing in her head strengthened with each replay of the assault she'd waged.

This won't end well, Nicole thought.

The first comment under the video suggested as much.

THIS CUNT SHOULDN'T BE ETHAN'S MOM! CPS, ANYONE?

IG FAM . . . DO UR THING!

The consequences awaiting Nicole were big. Easy to imagine, even hungover.

Still, she couldn't help but marvel at how expertly she'd been able to swing the vodka bottle from her purse and into Claire Bear Original's big, fat, but not really fat at all, mouth.

Next to her, Emily's face was almost sprightly. The fire in her eyes was different, maybe even a twinkle and not a fire at all. She seemed . . . excited.

Was it possible that Em wasn't entirely put off by the spectacle still looping before them?

She hoped so.

She loved Em, she needed Em, she'd let her down for far too long.

If bashing some deserving shit-bag that they'd left to bleed on the sidewalk had earned her Emily's respect, even just the tiniest bit of it . . .

Well, it was a start.

No regrets.

At least, none about the assault on Claire.

THE TEXT | SECTION THREE

YOUR PAST.

You may observe the PEOPLE, PLACES, and THINGS of your past. It is not uncommon to visit your previous existence frequently at first. FACT: visits (AKA observations) impact you and you only.

Though it runs contrary to your feelings, observation has no effect on the living. Any direct eye contact is coincidence. Direct address by the name you had is to be expected but is not a sign. Observation itself provides neither safety nor comfort to your formers, nor does it serve as an indication that you are there. YOU ARE HERE. Affecting any item, being, or phenomenon in your former plane is an impossibility.

Residents who stay in Prior Plane too long report feelings that mimic the nausea they knew while living. "Too long" has no definition here (see the section labeled "Time"). The nausea-like sensation is prohibitive for most residents.

It is recommended that you make, and stick to, a plan to say a FINAL GOODBYE. Go, see, and recite well-wishes for those you still hold dear. THIS IS YOUR CHANCE TO BE A POET! FUN!

Couples should make their final few trips independently. Your last observation should be made alone. Then, commit to never returning.

It is recommended that visits made deep into residency are shared with your mentor. Find solace in the idea that those you feel compelled to watch will join you here—but only when it is their time.

With commitment and a plan, a FINAL GOODBYE serves you best.

4

AMANDA

Following a heated exchange with her mentor, Rebecca, Amanda returned to Prior Plane, going straight to the room Ethan shared with Emily. That observation—her fifth in the last twenty-four hours—began shortly after midnight. If The Text was to be believed, maybe Amanda was overdoing it with observations. Still, she found herself existing in the galley-like strip of space between his and Emily's twin beds no worse for wear, except for being dead, of course.

Her vision of the surroundings was adequately clear. That was not always the case, and she let out a sigh of relief as she took in Ethan's sweet face, peacefully asleep.

The sister he had never asked for was sound asleep in her bed, too. Save for the faint tick-tick-tick of Matthew pecking away on his laptop downstairs, the house was quiet. Undoubtedly, Nicole had already passed out, which seemed to be her MO. "Dead to the world," so to speak, and for the moment, that effect of Nicole's substance abuse was just fine by Amanda.

Since her son's move there, Amanda visited him every night around that same time. In her experience as a deceased observer, Ethan's new home was rarely this still for more than a few hours. Her late-night visits had become routine. She made them alone only after she and Tag had already visited to wish Ethan a good sleep while Matthew or Emily put him to bed.

Although Amanda and Tag weren't on any earthly clock, he always seemed put out after that "sweet dreams" visit with their boy. She didn't mind making the extra trip alone—she honestly preferred it—and if Tag had a problem with her solo visits, he hadn't mentioned it.

It seemed to her that she had been born—or perhaps had died—better equipped than her husband to endure the nausea that accompanied lengthy observations. It was a jumbled sickness of their current form, which, as far as she could surmise, was a kind of energy. Though the pain must have been entirely mental, that nausea compelled most residents to exit their observations when they had overstayed. Tag found it harder to return to Prior Plane immediately after a visit, but Amanda experienced no such difficulty. Not much of a surprise there. At least, not for her, because when it came to tolerating discomfort and pain, whether mental or physical, she had always been the hands-down winner. While alive, her husband could have been the poster boy for "Man Cold." Back then, his temporary inability to rise from bed or the couch to help or engage in family activities annoyed her, but she didn't mind his absence now.

She hadn't meant to be, but she was just staring at the rug on the bedroom floor. A ratty and worn thing featuring a giant prancing unicorn, stained and no longer pure white. Still, the zeal on the animal's face suggested it was living its best life within the rug's tattered borders. Like her, the mystical creature was a fanciful fiction, grinning and bearing it while caught in the perpetual act of an escape that Amanda feared would never come true for either of them.

From what she had gathered about Matthew's daughter, even Emily must have come to hate the rug by now. However, Amanda also understood that money in that household was tight; perhaps money for frivolous things was all but nonexistent. She supposed she should be grateful that Nicole hadn't rushed out immediately to buy a fresh rug for Emily—or anything else for the basic-bitch home the woman kept—using the money Amanda and Tag had left them to help care for Ethan.

She glanced up from the rug she had not chosen for her son and looked around the room. There was an unplayful nightlight, just a sickly yellow piece of rectangular plastic shielding an old-school mini-bulb plugged into the wall. Though the light in the room was dim, every other irritation was easy to spot. Preteen hobbies and a young girl's collections—not a young boy's toys—were stored in an open cube shelving unit that had seen better days. It held Scrabble, Boggle, and other word games, dozens of YA books, and an array of solid, angular trinkets and baubles that could not be snuggled, let alone played with by a boy Ethan's age, not without risk of causing harm. Amanda had taken in this disappointing farce of a young boy's room before, of course, but it was no less painful now to see that the real estate in the room still mainly belonged to Emily.

"Matthew and Nicole are dealing with a lot; give them time," Tag had said last week.

They'd had time, hadn't they? The problem was they couldn't see fit to *make* time.

Amanda's disappointment with their laziness consumed her and made it feel as though they'd had years to unpack Ethan's boxes—boxes she had tried like hell to unpack. She hadn't been able to open them, let alone poltergeist Ethan's shark-shaped bedside lamp into his room. His adjustment to having a whole new family could have been made less fraught with one or two of the things she'd once picked out for her son. It wasn't a lot to ask.

"They'll get to it. I promise. You'll see."

Logically, what Tag had said made sense, but she wasn't so sure they ever would. The media attention would eventually fade, but even when it did, everything she'd watched and learned about Matthew's family so far made it clear: While they had Ethan and were technically housing Ethan, her Silly Boy would never be a priority. He would never feel at home.

Intrusive thoughts had become the norm for Amanda. "Grief," Rebecca had stated firmly, "can be a real son of a bitch." It was the only time her mentor had cursed; perhaps it was the woman's best effort at trying to relate, Amanda thought. Rebecca probably believed the curse word necessary to break through to residents who'd once lived left or right of the Midwest. Her mentor's suggestions provided no relief, and neither had The Text's or Tag's. Not that she had yet dared to go into detail about what exactly her ill thoughts had been, and still were, with him.

Her recollections from going down a maternal filicide rabbit hole one day during a brutal bout of postpartum depression had not been helpful. As dark as parenting had seemed for her back then, she had still hated those women. Some were mothers with names the whole world knew. Their circumstances didn't matter—they had killed their children.

She remembered wanting those moms, dead or alive, to burn in hell with every fiber of her being. However, despite The Text's insistence on feeling nothing, she had developed a genuine empathy for their persecutory delusions. Did a fate worse than death await *her* son? She couldn't say, but it hadn't stopped Amanda from having horrible, headline-worthy ideas about how to end her grief, all of them unbecoming of a mother.

Her innermost wishes included dark plans and spectral hypotheticals she knew she could never voice to another resident. Those thoughts threatened to take hold of her again. It would have been wise to leave for Second Plane right then, but instead, she quickly moved her form to sit on the edge of Ethan's bed, hoping her proximity to him would blunt the hypnotic grip of her dark ruminations. On other nights, that closeness to Ethan had helped, at least a bit.

There was no way to seat her mind or energy—or whatever it was that she had become—upon Ethan's mattress. But she could *exist* beside him, and like her other late-night visits before, she began to hum Ethan a lullaby, even before settling still beside him. It was a simplified version of a soprano aria from an opera Amanda's mother Debbie had always loved: "*O Mio Babbino Caro.*" Debbie sang it to Amanda when she was a baby, and years later, Amanda sang it to Ethan while changing his diaper or guiding him into a nurturing sleep. She hummed the song now, hoping against hope that Ethan would somehow hear it—would somehow hear her.

In her last months of living, she'd often argued with Tag about whether their son was ready to be in a bed instead of a crib. She'd insisted he hadn't been. Now, she had to admit to herself that, then and at present, her Silly Boy was not that far off from being ready for that very transition. Even so, she knew that if it'd been *her* to take in a friend's toddler after his parents had died, she'd have had the boy sleeping in what was familiar, at least for a while.

The first night they found Ethan in the twin bed, Tag said, "See! I told you he was ready." Then her husband repeated something Ethan had said to them often: "Big boys get big beds." She remembered. Her son's overly exuberant declaration had started around two-and-a-half, and it played loudly, again and again, in her mind now. Amanda would have shed tears right then, but no matter how hard she tried as a resident, the tears never came.

She stayed near the bed and next to Ethan late into the night, fighting the pull of Second Plane the whole time, and did so until the hurt of being among the living was too much to bear. She guessed even she had limits. No matter. She popped into Second Plane, then returned to Ethan immediately, where she went back to humming, picking up right where she'd left off.

Return trips to Prior Plane made on the heels of another could be blurry, like trying to watch life unfold through six feet of pool water. Other times, the world appeared to Amanda as rudimentary as an eight-bit video game. Either version—and more cryptic variations—came as a shock, even when she'd gone into a repeat observation expecting those flaws. Still, to be anywhere but with her son was a nightmare, one even worse than the charged ordeal they'd created for Ethan.

On this particular return observation, Prior Plane projected as normal: clear and detailed. That occasionally happened with return trips, too, and Amanda was thankful this time was one of them. That said, she would've stayed even if what she saw had looked like an original Pollock.

Eventually, she heard Matthew put himself to bed. Not long after that, she heard the family dog slump itself against Ethan and Emily's door, which had become habitual for the mutt.

The Text said nothing about animals. Odd. Did the dog know they were there? Had Pepper been barking at her and Tag that afternoon in the kitchen? Though she wasn't sure why, Amanda wanted to believe the dog had caught them observing almost as much as she wanted to believe that she'd willed Ethan's bowl of Cheerios to fly to the floor. But it was equally possible, and infinitely more likely really, that Pepper was just a dumb dog and that her Silly Boy was still working out coordination issues like any child his age. Coincidences, like The Text blabbered on about. Still, she hadn't seen Ethan do it, and she'd been looking right at him; it felt like her doing, but she'd not been able to replicate anything like it since. And that was fine . . . for now.

Typically, this was the time of night when Amanda's musings over her son's dire situation went pleasantly wonky. With Ethan sleeping so soundly by her side, her potent mix of desperation and deceased naivety dragged her thinking toward an outlook where everything could be OK for her son in Prior Plane, maybe even tolerable. Not tomorrow—no way—but Matthew and Nicole weren't bad people. They weren't sociopaths. And somewhere down the road, if Nicole sought help, Ethan might yet flourish. Some small part of her wanted to believe that a bright future was still possible for Ethan. She'd asked herself how she could hope for anything less. But the foundation on which that lesser desire was built was fragile.

Under the right circumstances, hope, especially when tenuous, could quickly give way to horrific despair, like a tired hand gripping a stone to prevent a freefall to the bottom of a canyon. A situation where even a tiny ant bite is all that would be required to seal your doom.

As she studied Ethan's delicate features, a horrible retching shattered the little hope Amanda clung to. She heard what had to be Nicole vomiting into the toilet in the bathroom. Not hers and Matthew's, but the tinier one with the tub where Amanda hadn't once seen Ethan bathe in anything resembling bubbles. Nicole upchucked with reckless abandon in the kids' bathroom, which was situated next to Ethan and Emily's bedroom, with only a thin wall between the two spaces. It was a loud, barking evacuation Amanda swore rattled the whole brownstone, one made with no concern about who her sickness might awake . . . or *what* it might awake.

Emily stirred in her bed. Her clutch on her phone relaxed, and the device dropped to the floor. Its muffled thud didn't wake the girl, but Ethan's face squinched after its impact. Goddammit, Nicole. Amanda hummed louder, but what was the point? The sound of Nicole's hurling was violent and, more importantly, real. Thankfully, neither child awoke. However, the dead did *not* need sleep—the phrase "I'll sleep when I'm dead" was laughable, Amanda thought—but children needed theirs, and they needed it badly.

Ethan sighed, and his face returned to a peaceful sleep.

Underneath Amanda's nose, even in that horrible tactless wash of yellow light, Ethan looked every bit like a cherub, buoyed by what remaining baby fat still existed. Her son . . . her *sun*. Since her death, being near Ethan in the evenings had been all that could warm her, but she was ice cold now. Frozen and furious, yet only slowly becoming aware of how much damage Nicole's thoughtless interruption had done to her psyche. Nicole's vomiting—her selfish as fuck self—had awoken something in Amanda, or at least steeled it. Each dry heave poked at it and then stirred it into something buzzing and black and angry and unknowingly irreversible. Those intrusive thoughts—Amanda's secrets, Amanda's desires—weren't just back. They'd cemented.

Then there was silence. *Silence.*

Tag. Where was he? There was no excuse not to be there.

Enough.

Enough with acting like nothing could be done.

ENOUGH.

She would return to Second Plane and tell him, "We need to do something."

She would ask, "What do you think about bringing Ethan here?"

She would try to put it delicately unless a sensitive approach to what was required of them didn't work. Then, she would put a foot down, one she didn't have, and demand his cooperation. "I know it makes me sound horrible, Tag, but I wish our son were dead. I want him dead. And if you won't do that for me, I'll do it myself. Ethan belongs with me."

Too far? She didn't think so; it was exactly how she felt, but for a moment, she wondered how she might communicate the gist of what she planned to say to him in a softer, gentler way. But there was no time to correct the phrasing of what she would say to Tag because right then, the toilet flushed for the third time. Its whoosh did not wake Ethan, but when Nicole closed the bathroom door a second later in a manner more suitable for daytime—BANG—he awoke. His eyes immediately filled with tears, a precursor to the pained crying that followed.

Amanda heard Nicole walk past the closed bedroom door. Though it sounded like she might have tripped on the dog, there'd been no long pause between steps in the hall. Then the stairs creaked. Where the hell was Nicole headed?

By now, Emily had risen and rushed to Ethan's side to help calm him. The girl picked Ethan up and started to rock him, telling him, "There, there, you'll be alright. You'll be alright."

The nausea of inhabiting the children's room for so long was heavy by now. It was the first time the pull back to Second Plane felt truly inescapable.

Then, it happened: between two diminishing sobs, Ethan quietly cooed, "I want Mama."

Those three words denoted Amanda. She fought to remain in her observation—but to do what? Help Emily soothe her son? Even with knowing it'd have been of no use at all, under different circumstances, Amanda might have stayed to assist Emily or at least make sure the girl succeeded. But as it was, Amanda wasn't holding back her exit to Second Plane to uselessly try to comfort Ethan. No. She was fighting the pull because she was hellbent on fucking-up Nicole, and she moved like a gunshot.

As Nicole finished her drunken traipse down the stairs, Amanda punched at her, slapped at her, kicked at her face, and tried to jump on Nicole's back as she rounded into the kitchen. But in the end, her violent efforts had been fruitless. Once more, the energy her faux assault had exerted had given Amanda little choice but to return to Second Plane. As the pull found her again, disintegrating her form to bring her back home, all she could do was watch as Nicole reached for a bottle of vodka, then slugged some down, only to chase it with what was left in a bottle of wine. The last thing Amanda heard before disappearing was her son still crying upstairs.

THE TEXT | SECTION FOUR

WHERE YOU ARE.

The space around you is what you want it to be. A resident only sees what a resident chooses to see. See A LOT, see A LITTLE, see NOTHING. The choice is yours!

When with others, what you conjure (we aren't witches, but there's no better word) around you will not be what the others are seeing. Many find great joy in affecting their space with objects they create. If elements of a setting morph into objects you never encountered while living, DO NOT BE ALARMED. Simply pause, reset, and go again. After all, THERE IS NO NEED FOR ANY OBJECT.

Eventually, Second Plane will feel less and less familiar. Most items, décor, and indications of habitat will naturally cease to exist. Isn't that grand? OBJECT OBSOLESCENCE should be your aim.

There are some residents who have chosen to focus on the memory of just one object at all times, so the details stick, and report having kept that item intact within their space in perpetuity. NOT ADVISABLE, but no less remarkable!! WELL DONE. But do try to inhabit your space without any care for what is or isn't within it.

5
TAG

So far, Tag had met with his mentor, Donovan, every other day. Or what felt to him like every other day. Days didn't exist. He was on his way to see him now, moving through Second Plane in the way he'd decided: walking down a city sidewalk at a leisurely pace.

He'd been told by Donovan that most newcomers give up keeping track of minutes, days, weeks, and years pretty quickly. They stop adding up totals of this or that experience, too.

The past was living, and life was over. Something akin to the notion of a future only happened if a resident actively participated. *Now* was king.

Tag was familiar with the concept of living in the present. The people he'd known back home preached the virtues of nowness when selling sneakers or yoga, or coaching kids to ignore an upcoming big game in order to focus on the one they were playing that day.

In Prior Plane, *now* was only a style of living. Here, the present was an absolute.

There was no night unless you thought it into existence.

There was no daylight from sunshine unless you wanted it and made it happen.

No one in Second Plane ever said it in this way, but keeping track of time was also a pain in the ass. Time was a thought you had to hold onto all by yourself.

Tag had conjured the clocks he'd once known to assist him, but when he stopped thinking about them, they stopped ticking. The details blurred within the shapes of the timepieces. Sometimes they disappeared altogether.

He'd thought hard about lined paper to leave himself notes, too, and he'd strained his focus to hold onto walls he'd produced to draw vertical lines on, counting days as a prisoner might in a cell. But most objects and items only existed for the time spent thinking about them.

Keeping thoughts on inanimate objects was tiresome and dull. It saddened him to realize how much time he'd spent thinking about cars, boats, and eighty-six-inch TVs while alive. It was freeing not to need those things, but even more liberating to not have to *think* about those things.

Truthfully, he only had an idea of how long he'd been a resident because of the trips he and Amanda made to see Ethan. The Text called them *observations*, and they'd taken several to Prior Plane already—many times a day. Going by the timeline there, he'd been dead a few weeks.

Of course, even that tally of time would only be accurate if he and Amanda weren't accidentally observing something that had long since passed.

Early on, Donovan had warned him that sometimes an observation might actually be of a moment in the past. "What we were once can drag us back to what we knew," he said. "And sometimes we don't even realize we aren't following the chronology of what has been."

It was cryptic, but Tag understood the gist.

Amanda had called "displaced observation theory" horseshit. She didn't care about anything Donovan told Tag any more than she cared about the information her mentor told her about Second Plane. Tag agreed with Amanda that their observations had been in sync with the present in Prior Plane, but maybe only because to think otherwise would have been crippling.

Here, Tag had conjured a sidewalk for this stroll to see Donovan. He knew it wasn't necessary, but seeing something underfoot suggested gravity and helped him feel pointed toward a particular destination. "To think is to be there" is how The Text put it, but he was still attached to the idea of having to put physical effort into an action.

His mentor had also explained that no matter what distance Tag created to travel, the length would not impact the timing of his arrival. "You know what they say: time is blah blah blah," Donovan had once said with a chuckle, clearly believing his ambiguity was clever. Tag hadn't laughed but he got the drift.

Maybe at some point, Tag would stop walking. Maybe. Walking forever was an option, too, because speaking frankly about Amanda's mental state with Donovan promised to be uncomfortable. But sharing the disquieting and dark thoughts she had shared with him was the whole reason he'd asked Donovan for that connection. Even if he did decide to keep walking, Donovan would find him eventually, if he wanted. The agreement to meet was binding.

The city blocks he'd walked so far were identical to one another. Looping what he'd created for the first block was easier than conjuring variations to the scenery after every intersection. Besides, the walk was mostly a stall and he knew that. Even so, Tag intended to walk a dozen more.

The soundtrack was faint; his thinking was centered on his concerns, but if he focused, the volume of the running motors rose.

Under increased scrutiny, Tag recognized the avenue's shortcomings: The asphalt had long yellow dashes down its middle, but the street wasn't wide enough to allow vehicles to travel in both directions. The curbs themselves were off, two inches high if that, and if he let them, those same concrete restraints undulated with the whoosh of cars unseen.

It made him wonder how many details he'd fully acknowledged on walks before his death.

Tag considered adding a passing car, or cars, to make sense of the sounds. But the act of widening the road for them to exist on seemed like work. To *have* the road there at all, at any size, was work too, but he decided to leave it. Instead, he let go of the vehicular racket.

Birds chirped, but only on every tenth step. He attributed a low hum to other running machinery and electronics like air conditioners, traffic signals, and instruments of refrigeration.

Trees were captive by tiny fences meant to make it harder for dogs to shit there. Some trees disappeared before he could reach them. On others, the leaves were stock-still, except for one: a towering maple much taller than the rest. He'd put it half of a football field ahead. He had no recollection of its broad canopy hovering over the iron-cast entrance of a small park tucked between brownstones—a park he'd known for a short while before the end of living. Where had this maple come from?

As he approached the park, everything behind him vanished. The road, the buildings, the sky, the clouds, the curbs, all gone. The sounds of playing children mixed with the sounds he'd carried there, and, without effort, those noises faded too.

His space now was the park, the playground within it, and the lone tree.

The tree looked like it'd grown ten stories taller since he last glanced up. The leaves were rustled violently from its quaking limbs as if caught in their own storm, yet everything before him was shadowless.

The playscape was unoccupied. The benches were empty. What little grass and mulch surrounded the plastic climbing structure was still. The adolescent laughter he'd settled upon moments earlier grew louder, but there were no actual children at the park.

The intensity of his stare agitated the landscape, similar to the rippling of the curbs from before. Everything in front of him was like an antique TV set incapable of landing a signal: an image that was there but threatening not to be.

The whirr of the wind turned up to a volume wholly unnatural.

Then, one voice at a time, the laughter of each invisible child turned into sharp screams, forming a demonic chorus all around Tag that inexplicably put the first seconds after Little Boy went off over Hiroshima into his mind's eye for just a flash.

Was he doing this? Tag tried to think it away, but could not end the sounds or scenery.

Then, in the white sky above, the nose of Flight 2332 materialized. In a blink, it tore through the tree's canopy overhead and buried itself deep into the playscape. The ground swallowed every detail: the noise of the engines, the crack of wood, the explosive impact, and the screams—those of the children and those of the passengers who'd fallen with the piece of aircraft from above. Every new sound, even the few bird chirps that had mistakenly returned, were drawn into the inversion of the ground along with every visual feature of the scene itself.

When nothing was left to be swallowed, Ethan appeared. He was alone, hovering cross-legged a few inches above the white landscape that was left. His scream was deafening.

* * *

"Are you alright?" Donovan asked.

Tag opened his eyes and was startled to find Donovan at arm's length in front of him. He wasn't sure if he'd completed his journey by thinking himself to his mentor or if the man had found him first. Being found hadn't startled him; Donovan's form had. Although they had connected a dozen times, Tag had yet to get used to the body that Donovan presented. There was a lot of Santa Claus in the man's appearance, but he dressed as if he were on safari, at least in the way that type of adventurer was often portrayed in films. His all-white beard was trimmed much shorter than Santa's, too, and the hat he wore was stiff, brimmed, and beige, not at all something Tag would call jolly. "What you see is who I was," Donovan had told him at their first meeting.

"Tag? Are you alright?" Donovan repeated now.

"I'm good," Tag finally said. He was slow to adjust the confusion on his face to sell it.

"You don't seem good," Donovan said. "But I try to take everyone at face value, even when that resident has chosen not to show a face to me at all."

He left Tag the space required to laugh, but Tag didn't fill it.

"OK then, Tag. Tell me you're fine, and I'll run with that."

Tag took a deep breath. It was biologically unnecessary, but the idea of deep breaths remained an excellent way to mull over what he wanted to say or not say to Donovan next.

"Is it possible for scenery you didn't choose to appear?"

His mentor shrugged, but his eyes roamed their shared space, seemingly scanning for a hint of what Tag might be getting on about. "Anything is possible, I suppose. I've seen things I didn't *think* I'd conjured. Then again, part of our subconscious is always conspiring against us."

Tag felt dumb for asking. He looked to his left for Ethan, but his son was no longer there. There was no reason to keep his focus on the vast nothingness in that direction, but he did. It was easier than staring dumbfoundedly at a messenger he suddenly wanted to shoot.

"What are you visualizing around us now?" Donovan asked.

"Nothing."

"No such thing as nothing. Not really."

It was true. There were faint lines to the location. A box-like shape housed them. This had been Tag's default scenery as a resident, but only then did he realize it'd been his doing.

"The space around us looks like the room where Wonka shrunk Mike TV."

The comparison lit Donovan's eyes over his knowing grin. "See? Not nothing," he said. "Definitely something. An excellent film, by the way." Then he took one step closer and held out his chubby hand. "I know you like to walk. Shall we?"

The first time Tag met Donovan, he was put off by holding hands with the man, a stranger, a being of some sort that he'd been assigned. Maybe it was the Santa-ness of his mentor, but it left Tag feeling a bit like a child. Beyond that, it was a kind of physical connection that felt claustrophobic, even when remembering there wasn't a true physical connection happening.

> *Eventually, you will no longer feel compelled to use the physical form you once knew. Prior anatomy isn't necessary to exist here. The anatomy you choose to use when interacting with others is YOUR DECISION, just as the anatomy they choose to use is theirs. The use of any former physical representations is unnecessary. Intimacy without biological composition is perfectly acceptable, though no resident should ever frame their invisibility as a goal.*

Tag took Donovan's hand. As he did, he couldn't help but reintroduce the sidewalk he'd taken to get there. It appeared beneath their feet. He added only that detail.

He took a cautious step forward to align himself with Donovan. Then, they started toward a vanishing point on the zenith up ahead.

"Do you want to tell me what it is you saw?" Donovan asked. His tone was welcoming, but it always was. Whether that was something authentic to the man he'd been or a part of how he'd chosen to mentor his pupil, Tag could not say. "Or don't," Donovan added. "It's up to you."

"It was the plane."

"You put yourself inside of the plane?"

"No," Tag said. "I couldn't do that." He was hardened in declaring so because, in his mind, it sounded like just about the dumbest question anyone could have ever asked him.

"Couldn't or wouldn't?"

"My memory of our descent is minimal," Tag said, unsure why he'd lied. Remembering those final moments of violence that shredded the plane into bits as if it'd been constructed of tinfoil was easy. Perhaps even conjuring that same destruction in Second Plane, note for note, would be a breeze. In truth, what he was loath to remember from their plunge to Earth was how hard his love for Ethan had hit him—unpolluted, unspoiled, filling and grand, and immense enough that had the crash not killed Tag he was sure that the explosion of his heart would have. It was a feeling he didn't enjoy revisiting, and even if he did, it was an abstract, undefinable emotion that he felt compelled to keep secret from Donovan . . . and even Amanda.

"A foggy memory, eh? That's probably for the best," his mentor said, though he sounded more like he was letting Tag off the hook than as if he believed Tag's recollections were faulty.

"Why?" Tag asked, partly because he wanted to know and partly because Donovan's answer would distract him from that very feeling of love for Ethan he had worked hard to avoid.

"Some residents dwell in the final moments of the life they knew. If we choose to do so, we can hold onto the details of how we left for a very long time. Playing them back and forth, the way a quarterback might watch the film from Sunday's game on a Monday morning, convinced that if we had just made a move to the left or a dash to the right . . . or if we'd just stopped smoking the year before, who knows? The what-ifs are as varied as the events that pulled the plug on us. There's no such thing as madness here, I don't think. But I can't imagine the pain of getting lost forever playing a game of What If."

"I wasn't playing a game of What If—"

"I'm not saying you were, but I *am* advising against it."

The bird chirps were back. Tag was positive he'd had nothing to do with it.

"Are you advising me on this so that I might tell Amanda?" Tag asked.

"From what I've heard, Amanda doesn't spend any time looking back," Donovan said.

It sounded accusatory. Tag released his grip from his mentor's hand. "Heard from whom?"

It was one thing for him to have enmity toward his wife, but who else did? Had Amanda's mentor, Rebecca, been gossiping with the other mentors? Rumors were frowned upon here, but so was dishing dirt in the Prior Plane circles Tag ran in. It hadn't stopped people there.

"You, of course," Donovan said. "I didn't mean to insinuate anything."

He *had* told the man about his wife's tenacity, that was true, but that had been about it.

Prior to Tag and Amanda's most recent connection, she had only dropped troubling hints about what she hoped might happen to Ethan, and Tag hadn't shared those with Donovan. By now though, she'd been brutally forthright with him about what she wanted, and Tag wondered if coming here to chat with Donovan was a mistake.

"What observations have you taken thus far?" Donovan asked.

The sudden change of subject did nothing to quell Tag's unease. "Alone?" he asked.

"Alone or with Amanda."

"Every trip we make is to see Ethan."

"I see. So, neither of you has been visiting the investigation?"

"Of the crash?" Tag asked.

"Is there another investigation of interest to you?"

Buildings returned, rising on either side. But these weren't the same as before. The structures were triple the height and made of too much plate glass and steel to still be Brooklyn.

"If you've spent time watching the NTSB investigate Flight 2332, I wouldn't blame you. I had no son, but if I had, I'm sure I'd have returned to watch 'experts' spitball theories."

Tag's attention was firmly on thinking the buildings away. Straining made no difference.

"Surely you and Amanda have traveled elsewhere to observe other people or things."

Donovan's loose accusation was overshadowed by the formations Tag discovered.

Landscaping filled in the greenspaces in front of the buildings and on the medians between the roads, perfectly detailed. Leafy shrubs with colorful flowers at their ends, bright and in complex shapes foreign to Tag. The streets had the correct dimensions, too, with cars traveling comfortably in both directions. It was a city—somewhere from the Northwest. Washington State, maybe. The Space Needle appeared at the same time as a monorail raced over their heads.

This was not Tag's doing. He'd never been to Seattle. Wasn't Donovan from there?

"Are you seeing what I'm seeing?" Tag asked.

He knew the answer would be no but hadn't expected Donovan to take offense.

"Of course not," Donovan said. "I can't see what you see. You can't see what I see. I can't hear what you hear. You can't hear what I hear. We exist to one another within the personalized spaces we create. I know that you know *at least* this much."

His mentor's tone was condescending—a first. Though unthreatening, it was still jarring, and the entire town around them fell into nothing. Even the sidewalk, Tag's creation, was gone.

He hadn't realized he'd stopped walking until Donovan spoke. "Is something the matter, Tag?"

It was a sincere question, but it startled Tag. For no good reason, he felt caught. "All my observations have been to see Ethan. I don't know what else to tell you," he said.

Donovan dropped his head as he scratched behind his right ear. "Honestly, Tag . . . maybe I wish you and Amanda *were* observing the investigation."

"Why?"

"Or anything else . . . it doesn't have to be that."

Tag started forward again, on a sidewalk he wasn't sure he'd brought back, and into nothing but the idea of an all-white box. Donovan joined but didn't extend a hand this time.

Tag's gut told him he could re-see downtown Seattle if he chose to, not because he could create or envision it himself, but because he believed that maybe Donovan still was.

"You want me to stop observing Ethan," Tag said. "Say my 'Final Goodbye.'"

"Eventually, yes. That is The Text's suggestion, but right now, I'd settle on you at least—I don't know—hitting a Knicks game or dropping in on the Oval Office. Get inventive."

Their walk thus far had made Tag uneasy about sharing anything important. He'd made the connection to talk about Amanda—about something that could get her in big trouble, maybe.

"If I break from seeing our son, it doesn't mean Amanda will."

"I'm sure her mentor is making the same suggestion," Donovan said.

As if that mattered. Since day one in Second Plane, Amanda questioned The Text, the council's existence, and her mentor's advice. Tag's eager-beaver attitude toward assimilating took them both by surprise. Still, he understood the origin of his new preoccupation: Nicole ignoring an inconsolable Ethan was last-straw stuff, or close to it. When Amanda had told Tag about it, his unease with Nicole had turned personal. Her drinking and drug use unearthed a deep-rooted resentment for his father, a wicked drunk in his own right. He hadn't lost all hope as Amanda had, but he could no longer vehemently disagree with her. That's what scared him.

But what could he and Amanda do about that now?

"I'm worried about Amanda . . . worried she is going to do . . . something."

Donovan stopped walking as if the act itself added gravity to his vague concern. "You'll have to be more specific."

Tag had heard a rumor about a fate beyond this residency. A place where residents in violation of affecting the living were "even more dead." That's how it'd been put.

He'd connected with Donovan to see if that rumor had merit. He didn't know the man. Not really. For all Tag knew, his mentor could be on the council. He considered Donovan to be trustworthy, but only because he'd taken the man at face value, too. He hadn't traveled to their previous plane of existence to investigate if Donovan had been who he said he was.

It was the first time Tag realized anyone there could be anyone they chose to be.

In fact, a resident of Second Plane could claim to have been anything they wished to have been. A doctor, a lawyer, a banker, a caring person—there was no heaven or hell. No separation of the bad from the good. Liars and honest people died and arrived. Even with nothing material to gain, the pathologically dishonest ones probably still got off on their deceits.

He'd been eager to do well there—a distraction, sure—but he'd also been naïve.

Donovan hadn't waited for the specifics that he'd requested. Tag spotted him standing at the edge of a park that ran parallel to what looked like a bay.

"No rush on my end," Donovan said. He hadn't shouted and yet his voice sounded so close—as if he was standing in Tag's head. "Share your concerns when you are ready."

"She wants to bring Ethan here," Tag said, soft enough to wonder if he'd only said it to himself. "She misses him. We both do."

Suddenly Donovan was back at Tag's side. He appeared almost pleased.

"That's not something worth worrying about," he said.

"She's not going to let this go," Tag said.

"Of course, she's grieving, but—"

"Honestly, that's putting it mildly," Tag corrected himself. "She's obsessed."

"What are you afraid of?" Donovan asked.

"That she's going to kill our son. I don't know how—"

Donovan's laugh was inappropriate for the moment.

From the periphery of their space, a wash of every material that made up their scenery, broken and in pieces, raced toward them. It was accompanied by a thunderous rumble. In the days before, Tag might have let the explosion bowl him over out of habit, but he stopped the infrastructural shrapnel from burying them both simply by thinking it into stillness.

Maybe his face gave his consternation away, or maybe Donovan had seen the chaos and realized he'd crossed a line. Either way, his mentor had stopped laughing.

"I'm sorry, that was insensitive," Donovan said.

Tag gave no indication to suggest forgiveness.

"There's simply nothing Amanda could do," Donovan added as he put his hand on Tag's shoulder. "It's pretty cut-and-dried."

"She's heard differently," Tag said, then added: "And you don't know what she's capable of."

"She's heard gossip, old wives' tales—mistruths are rampant here. Sometimes I think we'd all be better off if comingling with other residents wasn't allowed—connections should be made with mentors and relations only, at least for any residents less than a year dead." Then, Donovan pulled him closer and lowered his voice to a whisper. "Not everyone who resides here is decent. And some of them have unfinished business."

Donovan let him go, took two big steps back while looking around as if other residents were within earshot, and continued talking in a raised voice, almost like he hoped to be clearly heard by someone other than Tag. Was the council listening? Were they omnipresent?

"If she's sharing these desires with her mentor, let them work it out—" Donovan interrupted himself by putting a finger to his own lips as if that were required to stop speaking. "That sounds dismissive. Let me try again: just like in the life you knew before, there are things a loved one will only listen to—truly hear—and abide by when a neutral third party suggests them. Give her time, Tag, and you'll see." Then he smiled, too wide and too toothy to be reassuring.

Donovan's semblance began to fade, indicating he was done with this connection, whether Tag wanted it to be over or not. But before he vanished completely, Donovan put forward a reminder:

"You've read The Text, so I know you know this already, but please remind Amanda—children who arrive here don't arrive as children at all."

THE TEXT | SECTION FIVE

YOUR CHILDREN.

There are no children here, young or otherwise. Offspring that made the journey with you, for any reason, arrived here as adults through a process some residents call Age Acceleration. COOL, RIGHT?

THIS IS NOT A SPACE FOR KIDS. A child's mind, even into their late teens, struggles with the absence of a setting. YES, your child was "very intelligent," or "so imaginative" but WE PROMISE, he or she or they would struggle to exist here permanently as a child.

If you are a parent who arrived here with one or more of your progeny, know the adult versions are being mentored JUST LIKE YOU. Anger, grief, despair, and confusion mimics are to be expected. On the other hand, to arrive here without your children is a blessing. Who among us would wish our youth to be deprived of the experience of living? Good, bad, or indifferent.

The mentors of parent-residents who arrived without their child have been coached to mimic empathy for their plight, which may or may not help. HINT: You have to let it. Parent-residents who have left children behind are common, and group connections among parent-residents are available as a means of support. Ending observations of your child quickly is the best way forward.

There is no accurate way to calculate their ETA. If you have left a child behind, TAKE SOLACE—they will arrive eventually too!

Again: There are NO CHILDREN here. It is not a misfortune to have arrived here without your own.

6
TAG

When Rebecca, Amanda's mentor, arrived to speak with Tag, he quickly learned she'd been born in the 1950s and had died by suicide in the mid-'80s. She'd hanged herself, and tossed that fact into otherwise benign pleasantries as gleefully as if she was sharing a recipe. That detail could have made their conversation awkward, but she spoke fast and bubbly—her whole vibe was the epitome of "I never saw it coming."

He was glad to hear that her residency had begun without her children, and without her husband, Henry. Neither her kids nor her "one true love" had joined her yet, and though she claimed to have given up tracking the passage of time since her arrival, she said, "Henry is meant to be joining me soon in Second Plane. I'm confident about that."

Then she ran the conversation right into her concerns about Amanda.

"Tag, I'm sure while living your wife was utterly pleasant..." Rebecca said, letting the start to the subject hang in the air, perhaps to gauge his reaction to where their talk might head. "But when I first met Amanda—which was hardly long enough after her inception here to have read much—she asked when she could see your son. First question, right out of the gate, and her only question," Rebecca said, raising her eyebrows as if that alone meant bad things.

"Is that so odd for a grieving parent?" Tag asked, and he wondered why he hadn't done exactly the same. In hindsight, reading The Text before searching for Ethan felt shameful now.

"No, I suppose the question itself wasn't strange, but the energy about her was. Anyway, I told her we could go immediately, if she was ready, or later if she was not." She paused a moment to study Tag head to toe. "As I'm sure you already know, there are no restrictions on observations. Go now. Go never. Think where and be there, it's not hard."

Tag nodded in agreement.

"But I don't think your wife is looking for company or step-by-step instructions. She didn't mean what she was asking. Do you understand what I'm trying to say?"

His wife had asked to *see* their son, a routine question in early residency, according to Donovan. Tag understood Rebecca was trying to communicate a deeper meaning, but having just met her, he wasn't comfortable admitting that he understood exactly what she was getting at.

"She probably hadn't read The Text," he said. "You just insinuated as much. I'm sure she meant *observe*—"

"Oh sure, not many do read it right away," Rebecca interrupted. "Did you?"

"Pretty much. Front to back."

"Well, that is indeed admirable. Good for you!"

Hearing that unprovable fact felt good. He hadn't been seeking gold stars, but something about embracing his new situation in full and then being praised for it gave him the comfort of at least believing he had some type of control over his new existence.

The current state of his and Amanda's relationship might have been better if, like her, he hadn't read The Text. If he had shirked the responsibility instead of diving into it so desperate for anything outside of his thinking, he wouldn't have known anything about the age-acceleration process that children undergo before becoming residents. Maybe then, he'd be fantasizing about having Ethan there with them, as Amanda was.

"She's really having trouble letting go," Rebecca said. "My words, not hers."

"We haven't been here very long. She just needs more time."

"That's true for most," Rebecca said. It didn't sound like she believed it to be the case with his wife, but he didn't move to defend her. "I've been doing this a while, Tag. Long enough to know that a small percentage of parents who arrive without their children don't ever come to terms with leaving."

"Understandable."

"Maybe, but not practical," she said. It came off like a warning.

"No. I suppose not."

"The worst offenders have one thing in common."

"And that is?"

"Their child was young. Too new to say goodbye to."

It might have been his imagination, but it felt like her eyes were sizing him up.

"And if the child had no siblings... well, I can't speak from experience, but maybe when there are no brothers or sisters left behind for that younger child, the thought of leaving your only son or daughter isn't something someone *can* let go of."

Tag suddenly felt queasy, sick to his stomach that he must not care enough about his son. He found himself trying to gauge his level of despair. Should he be wishing for his son to die an accidental death? Should he be running to any resident who would listen, asking hushed questions about what was and wasn't possible in Prior Plane, as he knew his wife had been?

"I miss my son, too," he said. "Terribly."

"I've no doubt that's true. But you've read The Text, and you are doing what's suggested. You are moving forward, and Amanda..." Her arms went up in lieu of vocalizing her accusation.

"Yes?" Tag said. Calm was a difficult position to hold at this point.

"It's a hunch, but my hunches have always served me well. Do with this information what you will."

"You've said nothing concrete," he said in a tone more piercing than he'd meant to and found he had to look away from Rebecca just to stop himself from saying something worse.

"Do I have to?" she asked. He looked back at her. The huge smile she had used to punctuate the question was infuriating. "I get the sense you already know why I'm here, Tag."

He had never punched anyone while alive. Had it been possible now, he might have.

This was the love of his prior life they were talking about—and still the love of his second life, though no one seemed to refer to residency in that way. But he also knew, better than anyone, what it looked like or felt like when Amanda set a goal and got after it.

If she wanted to bring Ethan to Second Plane, she would do it. And if Rebecca was actually worried about that, then Donovan had been lying to him, and The Text was wrong.

"Residents can't affect anything in Prior Plane," he said. "Or are you saying that's *not* true?"

"I have no definitive proof any of us can do anything other than observe," she said.

"So, what are you driving at, Rebecca? Tell me."

"You might want to lean on her to start taking the suggestions more seriously. Existence here can be pretty miserable for residents who refuse to accept death. I'm not talking about being caught in the previous plane like some ghost that can't find its way into the light. We are in the light now. I'm sure you've already experienced how difficult it is to spend more than a few hours in Prior Plane, am I right?"

The observations he'd made with Amanda had been taxing, ending like a DVD player had detected a scratch large enough to spit out the disc—and he was the disc. You could go back in right away, but what you saw from there on out didn't make as much sense as it had before.

"Yes. I've felt the pull back, I guess I'd call it."

"Residents are here until they are not—"

"And?" he asked. "For fuck's sake, say what you've come to say."

Tag didn't want to be angry at Rebecca, Text or no Text, though, he was pissed.

"I'm sorry," he dialed back the frustration in his voice, unsure if his façade followed suit. "I guess I don't understand why you've connected with me today."

"Just look out for her, Tag."

He shook his head, frustrated. "What's the worst that can happen? She's can't actually affect anything in Prior Plane, right?"

After a brief pause, Rebecca said, "No." But she left no time for him to feel relieved. She started a shrug but did not finish it. "So says The Text."

She stayed but offered nothing more, and Tag found it difficult to fill the void. He looked down only to discover he'd stopped projecting anything below the knee. He was startled by the sight but recovered, then said, "Fine, I'll keep an eye on her. I'll go with Amanda to Prior Plane more often." But until Rebecca spoke again, Tag wasn't sure he'd said what he'd said aloud or if it had been a promise that he'd made to himself in his head.

Rebecca's tsk finally broke her silence. "Your wife asked for a new mentor," she said. "She's seeking an answer to a question no decent resident here will answer—but believe me, there are plenty of foul residents, too. I think you know the question. You know the answer she wants to hear. I'm sure you do. Don't ask me to repeat it, Tag. Because I won't."

THE TEXT | SECTION SIX

WHO YOU WERE, WHO YOU WEREN'T.

While visiting Prior Plane, HEED THIS WARNING: you will observe behaviors from people—even close friends and family—that you hadn't witnessed while living. After all, YOU ARE NOT THERE. They do not know you are watching, and we can only hope that *all* you see is dancing. SPOILER ALERT: it won't be.

"I see dead people," is a quote from a film. If you hear someone say it, there's no reason to follow them home.*

Remember who *you* were around people and who you were when you were alone. Can you honestly say that you were your authentic-self twenty-four-seven? There is a public persona and a private persona, though technological advancements in Prior Plane increasingly seem to be blurring the line between the two concepts.

Be kind. Empathy—not the feeling, but the psychological construct—will serve you well. BEST BET? Don't visit Prior Plane.

---

*This section of The Text was added in 1999 and will remain a part of the full version of The Text until the phrase and its origin are dust.

7
EMILY

The not-too-toasted waffle under Emily's nose remained untouched. The strawberry slices had been cut as thin as she was capable of, and instead of syrup, she'd dusted hers in powdered sugar. It smelled delicious because it was a waffle and waffles often do, but hers had that extra aroma of culinary independence. It was her creation, made in exactly the way she liked, and on her schedule. Even cold, it'd be very satisfying for those reasons.

But so far, she'd spent most of breakfast time trying to coax Ethan to eat his.

And that was only when she wasn't responding to text messages from friends who'd seen Nicole's assault video—because who in the world hadn't—and had written to say things like:

Holy shit! UR mom is a BEAST!
My dad says you guys better lawyer up.
R U OK?
And, *WAY TO GO NICOLE!*

It was a mixed bag. Had been for two days. She put her phone to the side, hoping to keep her focus on Ethan. Maybe even set a good example.

In her opinion, getting a toddler fed first thing was important. Nicole and Dad hadn't made Ethan's breakfast a priority. She had plenty to say about it—some absolutely crushing zingers—but why bother? As it turned out, mornings were the only time she had alone with Ethan, and she really enjoyed it. Had Nicole or Dad been paying any attention at all, they'd have been as surprised as she was with how quickly she'd developed a fondness for her baby brother.

He wasn't really a baby, though, was he? Not technically. Give it a couple of months and he wouldn't be new either. But for now, new baby brother is how she thought of him.

They shared a bedroom. It wasn't ideal, but she could visualize a future where they would stay up late, maybe planning a great escape or, at a minimum, formulating a plan to convince their dad to take the whole family snorkeling in Tulum.

Every other kid on her block had been to at least Mexico.

If she expected anything to ever change around her house, she needed an ally, even a young one. In due time he'd be his own force, she guessed, but until then, bedtime was no time to be shooting the shit. Or the poop, as it were. She didn't even like to think-cuss around Ethan.

Out of nowhere, Ethan roared. Emily recognized it as his best T-Rex impersonation. That sound usually meant food was about to be eaten, so she had come to tolerate those frequent growls—she may have even roared a few times herself in the past week.

"Oh no," she said. "Not a T-Rex!" And went warm on his grin.

Emily had recently learned more about dinosaurs than she'd ever hoped to. With her help, Ethan's pronunciation of their scientific names remained far from perfect but scary good for his age. Dino-everything hadn't been her thing when younger, but talking therapods and sauropods with him was more comfortable than the few conversations they'd had about "Dead Mommy" and "Dead Daddy." Those were the names Ethan had chosen himself. However, she suspected his decision to use the word "dead" had been heavily influenced by what her brother had heard spoken by insensitive adults, the prying journalists, and maybe even her own damn parents while poor Ethan was in earshot. As an alternative, she suggested preceding adjectives like "Other" and "First" but didn't want to force the issue. A quick bit of research she'd done into the matter on the internet had suggested she was right to let his decision be.

Ethan was vocal; she didn't know if vocal equaled bright, per se, but he liked to chat if you had the patience to listen. She had that patience, but it certainly wasn't genetic. Though her brother used those names for Amanda and Tag, it'd been readily apparent to her that he didn't truly understand what dead meant. She had only mentioned the plane crash once, asking him, "Do you remember why Other Mommy and Daddy aren't here anymore?" The question hadn't stopped him from playing intently with his Legos, and though it felt unkind to ask again, she did. After a beat, he said, "Oh, I 'member." But when that brief conversation ended, Emily believed that Ethan had only acted like he knew what she was talking about to please her, which tracked with another run at Google that she'd made to get a better sense of all things toddler.

Her recollections felt heavy. She stared at him and then at the waffle. Ethan liked the waffles she made, too, which were just the frozen kind, sure, but he was polite and sweet, and his appreciation for something so ordinary was addictive. Even before she'd landed on a decorated version he'd happily devour, his pleases, thank yous, and the giggles in between were reason enough to leave for school in a better mood than the one she woke with.

After some trial and error over the first week, the Ethan Special had been born: a single waffle smothered in soft butter, drowning in syrup, with one shake of rainbow sprinkles, at least for as long as the shaker-bottle of cake topping she'd found in a kitchen drawer lasted. And all that mess was then topped with a smiley face made from Reddi-Wip.

Was it healthy? The box said the waffle was wheat, so maybe so. "Good job, Ethan!" she said. "That was a big-boy bite."

Even with the perfect concoction, if she didn't cheer Ethan on, he could take a good hour to finish. Which would have been fine with Emily, if she wasn't someone with somewhere to be. Or someone who had people expecting her to be somewhere, as was the case with her teachers.

"More syrup?" Ethan asked, grabbing for the bottle she'd placed out of his reach.

"If I were to put any more syrup on that thing, they'd arrest me," she said as she moved the syrup just a touch further away.

She couldn't remember when her dad had said it, but she knew she'd stolen the joke from him. It fell as flat on Ethan as she imagined it had on her back in the day.

"Let's just focus on—"

The apartment buzzer rang so harshly it felt connected to Em's brain. The jolt rattled her body and shook the glass in her hand, spilling half the orange juice onto her perfect creation. Powdered sugar soaked up what it could, but the waffle quickly turned into a perfect little island standing alone in a pulpy, orange sea. Ethan's sweet laugh punctuated the unfortunate sequence.

"Jesus Fucking Christ," she slipped.

He hadn't registered the cuss, not really, but her physical accompaniment—arms high and waving tragically—managed to turn Ethan's laugh up to a level more . . . pack of jackals.

"I'm glad you're amused," she said as she reached for her phone. And she meant it.

It was five past seven. Reporters typically waited until nine to jumpstart the chaos.

Their unit's street-level entrance had always seemed convenient, but now it meant if no one answered, visitors could shout questions from the very front door Emily had her eye on. That proximity had always felt invasive, but as of late, the pop-ins by news crews had given the buzzer's trilling extra gravitas.

Dad had recently banned her from greeting the press, legit or otherwise, but two Tuesdays ago, she *had* opened the door. On that day, Em had made no formal invitation, but by the time she closed the door, an overcaffeinated twig of a blonde woman and her cameraman had set up shop in the family room.

"Now is not a good time. My parents aren't home," she'd told them, unnerved but trying not to show it. "We've said all we have to say." How the reporter had thwarted those polite refusals was a blur.

When Nicole came down the stairs to find a TV crew asking her daughter questions, her already hungover expression was the perfect launch pad for a conniption. The reporter left with ample footage of a half-dressed, irate drunk detonating expletives, one who'd recently been put in charge of caring for a traumatized toddler.

That was the last "official" interview.

Since then, Emily had overheard talk of hiring counsel or even a PR agent—even *she* knew they couldn't afford it. Putting together a restraining order that might make it a crime for anyone from the media to approach her family was an idea that got floated, too.

It was no surprise to her that Dad and Nicole hadn't followed through on any of it.

Their ineptitude was habitual.

She wasn't supposed to open the door now or even communicate through the intercom. That was the fix and the only real adjustment they'd made to keep the grinning vultures at bay.

The buzzer rang a second time. Apparently, the reporters hadn't gotten the message.

Emily looked at the ceiling, hoping to hear the gallop of parental feet. There were none.

The water was running. It was probably Dad in the shower, and it was easy enough to imagine Nicole was enjoying a prescription sleep. In light of Nicole's assault, Matthew had decided from here on out, only he would be walking Emily to and from school. Her mom never needed extra incentive to stay in bed, but that decision had given her extra permission to laze.

Whoever was outside, they didn't wait long to ring the buzzer a third time.

It was the same ringing sound as the first two but somehow ruder. Emily shook a bit in her chair. She shoved herself away from the table, not to answer but to have a peek, and crept with a cat-like stealth toward the door to keep the floorboards from creaking. An arm's length away from the door, she remembered the wood putty Dad had put over the peephole.

The intercom rang again and kept ringing for many seconds longer than before. Its elongation made the noise shrill, and behind her, Ethan started to cry. Emily turned to see his dish and half-eaten waffle in midair as it fell to the floor. The clatter of the plate's destruction came right after the buzzer's tone had ceased. Its impact silenced Ethan, relative to his previous wailing. "Not me," he said, sucking on dry sobs. "No do it." Emily's frown came on too quickly to reverse, but thankfully, her disappointment did not set off Ethan again. He went quiet, almost like he understood. For a moment, only the water running through the pipes could be heard.

Then, a tight series of meaningful knocks were made on their door.

Where was Pepper? He never had any reservations about greeting guests and typically knew someone was outside before they had a chance to use the intercom and its bell.

She looked to the rear of the house for the mutt and might have even shouted for him had she not remembered Dad had boarded Pepper the day before without consulting with the family.

Just until things calm down a bit, he's been acting off. With sudden changes, dogs can go off-kilter, just like humans—I've read it.

Their dog would have been a nice thing to have at that moment. Wasn't this very scenario why they'd all gone to the shelter years ago to adopt the dog in the first place?

As Em turned back to the door, she caught sight of Ethan in her periphery. He was standing with his right foot dangling in the air in search of a rung to guide him down from her old high chair. A rung that didn't exist. These attempts to free himself were nothing new. She wished she'd ignored Matthew's stupid insistence that Ethan always be put in his high chair when at the kitchen table. He didn't need the damned chair.

"Ethan, sit down!" Her demand was as stern as it could be without giving away their occupancy. In lieu of approaching him to physically force him back into his seat, a tactic that had never gone well to begin with, she widened her eyes into saucers and said, "I mean it."

"No. I help," Ethan said. "My mess."

"Ethan. Sit back down," she said, adding a one-foot forward warning to fake a walk toward the table, which had been all that was required to bring her brother to heel other times.

"No. I help," he repeated.

The chair swayed as Ethan sought balance by shifting his weight from one leg to another.

"You're going to get hurt. Sit down!" she said. Her shout had all the volume required to give up their position unequivocally. "Or no more yummy waffles made by your favorite sister." Did he think of her as a sister yet? She wasn't sure. Her threat had just come out that way right before she started a *real* step back to help him stay put, but—

KNOCK! KNOCK! KNOCK! Deep thuds this time. She froze in her tracks.

"Mrs. Shultz, is that you?" a voice asked. The question was followed by three even harder pounds. KNOCK! KNOCK! KNOCK!

Ethan lifted his left leg off the seat to give more length to his other limb, which was already stretched to its max over the front of the tray. That final shift was all the favor gravity needed, and he and the high chair collapsed to the floor, crashing together to create a thud that sounded far worse than the collision appeared.

Her brother's crying may as well have been an ambulance.

She ran to him, knelt beside him, and angled the chair to pull his tiny leg out from underneath it. Despite the gentle care of her effort, his bawling got louder.

Steps finally boomed, one after another, rattling the ceiling above her.

"Em! What the hell is going on down there?"

It was Dad, skipping at least two steps at a time while he repeated his question louder.

When Dad rounded the corner, Ethan was crying, the visitors knocked again, and Emily realized she was bawling, too. She held Ethan tight to her chest. It was hard to say whose tears were whose.

Her father's brow furrowed, and his mouth puckered tight, no doubt holding back the additional inquisition on his tongue as his eyes locked in on the voices from the other side of the door.

"Mr. and Mrs. Shultz, we can hear you. I'm with the Administration for Children's Services. I must insist you open the door. We'd like to come in to talk with you. Could you open the door, *please*?"

It was the least polite "please" Emily had ever heard. "Should I open the door?" she sobbed. She pulled Ethan closer to her chest, trying to calm him. "I'm sorry, Dad," she said. "I should have come up and gotten you sooner."

Her father was wearing only a towel around his waist. "One minute," he said to the door. "I just got out of the shower." He knelt on the floor next to her. "For Christ's sake, Em. What happened here? Give him to me."

Emily's arms went tighter around her baby brother.

"Em, give Ethan to me. Now."

The gasps between Ethan's weakening wails were painful to hear. She worried the fall might have broken a bone.

"Just answer the door," she pleaded. "I'll tell them it was my fault. That's the truth. It's my fault he fell—I'll swear to it."

His deep breath indicated he was considering the plan, and then Nicole shouted from upstairs. "What's going on down there? It's way too early for this shit."

There was a good chance the tenants in each building on either side heard her.

"Mrs. Shultz, you're home too. That's good," the voice said, teetering between kind and urgent. "My name is Tamira Johnson, and I'm with the Administration for Children's Services."

No one inside the home immediately responded to her introduction.

"One of y'all better open the door. I've got my phone out. I don't want to involve the police, so don't make me. This is just a visit. Very basic, very routine, but that courtesy isn't a lifetime offer. I can promise you that."

The woman's voice had dropped a full octave. Emily was glad it had.

Matthew looked shellshocked, and Nicole's move from bedroom to living room was no longer pending. Her mother's much lighter pattering was evident through the ceiling.

Emily couldn't stop her first thought from escaping. "They're here because of her," she whispered to Matthew, nodding toward the ceiling and then toward her phone. "Because of what she did to Claire."

She was surprised to hear she sounded like she hadn't been crying at all. Her voice was resolute, and Emily thought that should have troubled her more than it did.

Nicole entered the kitchen, eyes practically gone Terminator, and locked right on her.

Emily decided to finish telling Dad what he had to already know, no longer in a whisper. "*She's* the reason we're going to lose Ethan, Dad! What are you going to do about it?"

THE TEXT | SECTION SEVEN

TIME.

There is no time like the present.
The time is ripe.
NOW is the time.
Time is a construct.

ID=8
# TAG

The consequences of Nicole's assault on the nosy influencer had come quicker than Tag had thought possible, but for all of social media's ills, it did sometimes throw gasoline on the right fires.

Ethan's fate was in Tamira the ACS case worker's hands now.

As he and Amanda continued observing the situation unfold, he thought Tamira's arrival could be a good thing to happen or a bad thing. That was the way with almost anything in Prior Plane. A hammer can build; a hammer can destroy. Sometimes it destroys something old to build something new, something better. In his experience, that was especially true of broken homes.

Upon entering Matthew's home, Tamira had been calm and pleasant. The woman could have come in swinging, but even with Nicole, who was struggling to part from her defensive posture and had cursed a few times in a low mutter to herself, Tamira came off more understanding than foreboding. She'd introduced her coworker Curtis to the family as Matthew took their coats.

Though The Text said it wasn't possible, Tag felt optimistic.

On the other hand, Amanda had gone silent the minute Matthew opened the door for Tamira and her coworker. Even now, her face gave nothing away. As the four adults in the room exchanged meager pleasantries—you have a lovely home, sunny day but a little chilly out, and even an apology to Ethan and Emily for interrupting breakfast—Amanda remained unmoved.

Tag had heard in Second Plane that stoicism was an easy thing to achieve if you were a resident who'd already accepted that any emotion you were feeling wasn't real. He doubted she'd made progress on that front, but he couldn't read her thoughts.

Was she hoping Tamira's arrival there was a blessing in disguise as he was? Not likely.

Help. That was the key word, one Tag overheard Tamira and Curtis use a few times as Matthew worked to settle the children on the couch before joining ACS and Nicole at the kitchen table. Though they'd not been there long, it was clear to Tag that Tamira and ACS were there to help steer Ethan's new family through a storm he felt he'd inadvertently caused. That had to be a good thing.

"If this is about yesterday, I'm sorry . . . but that bitch had it coming," Nicole slurred.

Matthew winced, but Tamira and her professionalism didn't miss a beat. "Matthew, Nicole . . ." she started, her face unclouded to match her ethereal calm. "Your situation is unusual, I get that. I wouldn't wish it on my own worst enemy. The press can be nasty, and that's me being kind. Little pitchers . . ." Then she nodded toward Ethan while eyeing Nicole, perhaps to suggest Nicole specifically would do well to stop cursing for the remainder of the conversation.

Amanda's mouth pursed at Tamira's civility.

"We appreciate your understanding," Matthew said meekly from across the table. "It has been rough." He probably should have left his assessment there, but he added, "For all of us."

Though Tamira politely nodded, she made no verbal confirmation that she agreed.

It was possible the woman's empathy wasn't authentic, that Tamira was a proficient actor using an agency script dictating language and tone, and her whole vibe had been directed—Curtis's, too. There's no room for improv when telling parents an investigation into their child's welfare has been opened. Nicole's abrupt outburst hadn't deterred Tamira, at least not yet.

But this was Act One stuff—it wouldn't be wise to pretend otherwise.

With the power granted to her by the state, Tamira could turn into a wrecking ball as part of Act Two. Tag had read more than one article about by-the-rules citizens losing their kids to the system because of a misunderstanding with the agency and sometimes because of a misunderstanding with the world.

There was no misconception here.

By then, Tag and Amanda had seen Nicole's sidewalk incident secondhand. Once while Matthew reviewed the clip on his phone and several other times when Nicole had done the same.

Tag had enjoyed watching Nicole clock the shit out of Claire Bear Original—she definitely deserved it—and he wasn't the only one siding with her. The public response was easily fifty-fifty. Tag had read over Nicole's shoulder as she had scrolled through the comments underneath the influencer's post, reveling in the ones where strangers said they'd have done the same, if not worse. At a minimum, Tag felt the assault was understandable even if Tamira, in good conscience, couldn't.

"The assault was certainly the impetus," Curtis said. Tamira's eyes seemed to give her coworker permission to go on. "But possibly it was just a symptom of a much larger issue."

So far, everything had been said kindly, but it was all business.

"Christ, let's get on with it already," Amanda said, laughing as she did. "Amateurs."

Tag was happy her apparent ambivalence had cracked, but her mirth was disgusting—and it hadn't felt like a mimic either. She soured again just as quickly as Curtis patiently explained what he'd meant by "symptom." Had Amanda left Tag alone in the observation right that second, it wouldn't have surprised him.

As if on cue, Tamira asked, "Have you had anything to drink this morning, Nicole?"

Matthew bristled at the question, and Nicole somehow increased her slump in her chair, rolling her eyes as she did. "Oh, here we go. This isn't about Ethan at all, is it?" Nicole asked.

Until that moment, Tag hadn't noticed the two empties sitting to the left of the kitchen sink: one with only a sliver of red wine at its bottom, the other a Grey Goose bottle. There were many more liquor bottles piled into a blue recycling bin tucked tightly against the end of the lower cabinets, too. Over the past three weeks, Tag had indeed observed Nicole drinking a lot and often. He hadn't liked snooping on Nicole or Matthew as a dead person any more than he would have as a living person, but he'd seen her drug use, seen the drinking.

Still, Tamira's question felt like it'd come out of nowhere—until a particular scent hit Tag: an odor of booze and sweat that had often wafted from his father, a smell Dad's body released sometimes a full twenty-four hours after the man's latest bender. Tag was unsure he'd truly smelt *anything* as a dead man so far. Ideas of scent, maybe, the fabrication of molecules and aroma compounds he once knew, but nothing so pungent and certain as what Nicole smelled like now. There was no way to know if Tamira and Curtis smelled it, but he thought they must.

"Don't play naïve, Tag," Amanda said, reading him too easily. She waited for a beat before continuing. "Oh, wait . . . you weren't here the other night. You didn't get to see Nicole creep down the stairs with God knows what pills in her hand, ignoring Ethan the whole time, frantically searching for what was left of the vodka she'd already nearly polished off while giving zero shits about your son."

That was true. He hadn't witnessed it firsthand, but Amanda *had* told Tag all about it. She had relayed the whole incident to tee-up some incredibly troubling demands of him, but before Tag could respond, Nicole shouted at Tamira, "What fucking business is it of yours?"

"Do you normally carry liquor in your purse?" Tamira asked, still calm.

"Is that a crime?" Nicole asked, her voice begging for a fight.

"No, just a question," Tamira said. Her continued commitment to a civil tone was impressive, especially in the face of Nicole's fidgeting, which was bordering on looking like it could give way to an even bigger mistake than she'd made with Claire. "I don't mean to be presumptuous here, but as a recovering alcoholic and addict myself, I can assure you: I'm not here to judge you. I'm here to help you." Her eyes found the kids on the couch. "To help all of you."

"She's a drunk," Matthew said as he stood up. "But I'm doing my best. It's just—"

"Who wouldn't be wasted all the time, married to you?" Nicole said, but she was unable to stand. What she said after that barely registered as a sentence, let alone English words.

"Real swell family you picked, Tag," Amanda said.

"I'd like to ask both of you to calm down," Tamira said, holding up a low hand just above the table to signal Curtis to stay put. Under the threat of this meeting going off the rails, Curtis suddenly reminded Tag of the muscle working the door of a Russian nightclub he hit once in Brighton Beach. Nicole and Matthew exchanged profanities with each other, but Tamira and Curtis remained dutifully seated. "Please, now," Tamira tried, with only the slightest crack in her repose, "You've got to calm down."

Ethan started wailing from the family room, and Tag quickly looked at Amanda, catching her struggling to contain the subtle curl at one corner of her lips. The smile her son's distress unleashed was an abomination. He could only assume she thought the tragedy before them would convince him to help her bring Ethan to Second Plane.

"Enough," Tamira said sternly. "Good lord, it's not even eight o'clock. Enough!"

Matthew finally sat back down. It wasn't lost on Tag that neither his friend nor Nicole, who had gone surprisingly quiet, had bothered to excuse themselves from the table to care for Ethan. Only Emily had tended to his crying son.

For a moment, the four adults sat in the uncomfortable aftermath of the argument.

"I'm not going to lie," Tamira finally said, sounding exasperated—no, sorrowfully resigned—for the first time since she'd walked through their door. "This doesn't look good. For you and definitely not for your children. Can either of you say any different?"

Matthew shook his head, but Nicole said nothing. Tag watched his friend's fingers squeeze Nicole's knee lightly under the table—to no avail.

Her face wasn't calm at this point so much as checked-out. It was likely she'd popped a couple of Xanax before coming down to investigate the commotion. He'd observed her routine.

"What I'm going to say next is required of me. We are well beyond this formality, but I hope you'll listen," Tamira said before exhaling deeply. "Our job is to tend to the children. This is the first of maybe only a few visits, or maybe many. The number of times you see us will depend on how cooperative you are as we move forward with your case. ACS will make some suggestions, but your next steps will be your own."

"That makes sense," Matthew said. "I think you'll find us agreeable."

"Oh great," Amanda said. "An enabler and an oblivious dummy to boot. Who the hell are these people? Not the Matty and Nicole I remember. But hey, what's done is done, right?"

Tag ignored her hostility. It sounded rhetorical, but even if it wasn't, he wanted to remain focused on listening to Tamira, not try to defend his friends or go into detail about the fragility of the human species. His wife was looking at Ethan only now, watching closely as he played with Emily in the family room while the adults in the kitchen continued talking. Tag studied Amanda's gaze. If eyes were the windows to the soul . . . he didn't finish his thought but shuddered nonetheless and felt what must have been a mimic of revulsion. For the moment, he let his wife be.

"We want to be sure that Ethan and Emily are being well-cared-for, no matter what extenuating circumstances you might claim," Tamira said. "Does that make sense?" She paused as if she expected that alone to reignite Nicole. It didn't, and she pressed on. "You've been handed a difficult situation, but I have to tell you: You are damn lucky that Claire Reynolds, the woman you assaulted, didn't press charges."

When that didn't animate Nicole either, Tamira's voice cracked just a bit.

"I've seen the footage and I can't say I would have extended you that same courtesy."

Matthew squeezed his wife's knee again, nodded, and said, "Understood."

Amanda turned to face Tag. "Was everyone this fucking dumb before we left? Tag? Hon?" She tugged at him. "We *need* to help Ethan. We can't leave him with any of them. Not our friends. Not ACS."

Then she turned away from him, putting her whole focus on their son again, watching as Emily used two of Ethan's favorite stuffies to help guide him back to giggles and his sweet smile.

Tag prayed right then—to a God he now knew didn't exist—that his wife wasn't expecting an answer or a solution because nothing comforting came to him. He couldn't remember any time while they were alive when she'd sounded so desperate, so lost.

She didn't turn back to face him, but she wasn't done. "We just can't. We've left my Silly Boy in a nightmare. We just . . . I don't know . . . majorly fucked up."

She sounded as adrift as he felt. He reminded himself that whatever he thought she might be ruminating on at this point wasn't urgent. She'd never be capable of causing an accident to happen to Ethan. What she wanted to pull off was impossible. Donovan had said as much. Amanda's mentor, Rebecca, had said basically the same thing. Or had she?

By now, the nausea of the observation was wearing Tag down. He'd kept his eyes mainly on the conversation between Tamira and Matthew the whole time, but his mind hadn't really been there. He looked at Amanda and then turned to stare at Ethan with her. As he did, everything Rebecca had told him the other day came to a head, and he decided to try and get some answers from his wife before they both slipped back into Second Plane. Some part of him suspected this would be the last time he saw her again, at least for a while. Amanda had forgiven him for plenty over the years but had rarely cut him any slack for not having a plan.

"Why are you seeking a new mentor?" he asked.

Amanda responded but never looked away from Ethan. "Turns out there's no actual rule against changing mentors, hon."

He was pretty sure there was, but not surprised she'd decided it didn't apply to her.

"And why wouldn't I want to hear from multiple people instead of just one? How can you be so content to only connect with a single soul instead of many? If you moved to London and knew you were going to be there forever, you wouldn't ask just one person what their favorite restaurant was, would you? No. You'd ask a handful of people, at least."

That made good sense, but he wasn't about to interrupt her to say so.

"Why in the hell are we supposed to let The Text and *suggestions* from one new friend guide us into eternity? Honestly, how are you OK with that, Tag? It's like you've given up on everything that made you *you,* and I guess that's fine—but I've told you what I want, and you don't seem ready to do anything about it."

"That's because you don't know what could—"

"Ooh, there's a fate worse than death? Oh no! I'm scared." She waved her hands at him like she'd just seen a shit ghost on a haunted hayride. "It's bullshit, Tag. Fear tactics. And when I have what I need to *prove* to you that it's bullshit, trust me, you'll be the first to know."

She turned and stared at him—with black irises now—and left before he could respond.

His first instinct was to chase after her; something akin to adrenaline raced through him, and he could feel Second Plane's pull. This observation had been a long one for Tag, but he fought the physics of a return and managed to stay put.

Stand in Amanda's way when she wanted something? Bad idea.

This was their *son*, not a new title or career move, not a seat on a neighborhood board. She would figure out a way to get to Ethan. Nothing he said was going to matter, and continuing to chase Matthew's family all over Prior Plane to observe some bit of good news he could share with her to change her mind seemed like a fool's errand. But he loved her, and he hoped she just needed the space to see things more clearly. For her sake. For all their sakes.

Tag hadn't realized how blurry ACS's conversation with Matthew and Nicole had become—he'd pushed the observation time to its limits—but then, Tamira's partner, Curtis, said something that recrystallized it.

"There are many great drug and alcohol treatment programs available within the Tri-State area," Curtis said. "But you can't do this for your family, Nicole. You have to do it for yourself."

"We understand this is a lot to drop on you on our first visit," Tamira added. "You don't have to give us an answer today, but I'd encourage you to think hard about what next steps you'll take to help us help your beautiful family. In my opinion, rehab is a step in the right direction."

With her hands to her face, Nicole nodded.

"We're here to help you. We're here to fix this."

Tears escaped from between Nicole's fingers. She barely made a sound as she cried.

The whole room stayed quiet. Tag looked for Ethan, but his son and Emily had left.

"I'll go," Nicole finally said. "I'm sorry . . . I'll go. If it means Ethan gets to stay, I'll go."

She sounded sincere, but his own father had always sounded sincere when he'd said the same types of things after a week-long bender.

I'm going to nip this thing in the bud, Taggart, you'll see.

In Tag's experience, an alcoholic's promises were flimsy until they hit a bottom they could no longer climb out from with their cons. He'd had a handful of friends achieve sobriety when they were ready. In the case of his dad, cirrhosis of the liver hadn't been "bottom" enough for him to ever make a promise that stuck. He died still making empty promises on his deathbed.

Still, Nicole's willingness to try rehab was good news. Her cooperation was a development that Tag could share with Amanda.

He let Second Plane claim him back, cautiously optimistic or foolishly so.

He had hope, and he felt hopeful—even if The Text said that he could not.

THE TEXT | SECTION EIGHT

LOVE.

Be advised: That which bound you in life can still bind you here.

That said, your space here can be lonely, even when inhabited by another resident you knew in Prior Plane. IN FACT, you may have arrived with a significant other, but that doesn't always mean you're meant to continue your journey together.

Not surprisingly, the most frequent reasons for COUPLE-ARRIVALS are particularly intense: accidents, murder-suicides (YIKES!), or being at the wrong place at the wrong time in tandem.

Any prior legal document defining your relationship is NULL AND VOID here. Free of distractions, fragile relationships forged on earth can fray quickly. Strong relationships have grown stronger here, too.

HINT: The privilege to exist here is not well-served by lingering suspicions, forced interactions, or resolutions to remain with another resident predicated on prior beliefs, religious or otherwise.

Like all resident interactions, any communion made here between the formerly coupled is only possible when both residents agree to have a connection.

Only blood relations are excluded from making a mutual commitment for a connection to occur. You may ask why, but the only answer we can offer is that it's never not been this way.

What you are here only *starts* with what you were.

9
EMILY

Though she and Ethan had been left behind in the waiting room, it wasn't hard for Emily to hear the video of Nicole's assault on Claire playing or the therapist's good-lord reaction.

When Nicole started crying, Emily pressed even harder on the filth between the carpet fibers under her fingers. The floor was years removed from its original beige and held biology native to a Manhattan sidewalk. Even if it had once been brand new, the color had been a poor decision.

The crying was more sincere than the wailing her mother had managed during the ACS visit to their apartment a few days ago. Authentic or not, Emily didn't think Ethan should have to hear it.

A toy that made a noise capable of hiding Nicole's sobs would have been a big win, but the collection scattered between them consisted of mostly oversized plastic blocks in bright primary colors, two generic rag dolls, one of which had been given a black marker mustache, and a Fisher-Price Noah's Ark set that was missing all but two elephants and a zebra. None of it was electric or played music, and the dolls made no squeaking sounds when she squeezed them.

The toys indicated parking kids there was common. "Wait here, honey, Mommy has to go spill her guts." Adults, it seemed, loved getting it all out in front of what basically amounted to a stranger. Nicole was one room over, doing just that. Emily hated her for it. Add it to the list.

Given the condition of the doll still between her hands, Emily decided the number of children that had visited the room was in the high hundreds. Or maybe the therapist bought a box of hand-me-downs from Goodwill the week prior. The "doctor's" clothing had that eclectic thrift-store look but Emily knew that didn't mean the woman had actually gone thrifting.

She quacked unexpectedly to distract Ethan from the tempest on the other side of the double doors. Two blackwood slabs that proved less thick than they'd originally appeared.

Nicole had never cried like this. It sounded painful, or pained, but more than that, it rang out like she imagined only legitimate capitulation could. The phony white-flag whimper her mom routinely offered up to Dad was very different. Emily didn't doubt Nicole had remorse each and every time she messed up—some tiny bit of guilt anyway—but no single instance came to mind in which her mother had cried in a way that felt that broken or defeated.

She wondered what an adult was *supposed* to sound like after being cornered.

It wasn't the blame-gaming her mother played. She knew that.

It couldn't be the way Dad pretended he never lost his shit, either.

Over the last few years, it was possible the only entity in the house that had ever expressed their true emotions was Pepper.

Good God, her mother's sounds were ugly—embarrassing, even. Emily felt the flush of her mother's repentance in her own face, and that hardly seemed fair.

"Wait here for a bit," Dad had said. A bit? He hadn't fooled her.

Their trip there to talk about long-term treatment had already surpassed two hours. And that was a good thing, Emily guessed, because at least Nicole hadn't left in the first five minutes. She decided it was actually a huge win, especially when considering that Nicole had insisted on seeing the same woman she'd seen for years and years—the same doctor who'd done fuck-all besides writing most of her mother's prescriptions.

Up until that point, the civil back-and-forth between her mother, father, and therapist had rarely crystallized beyond more than bumbling murmurs, but some words *were* intelligible now:

... drugs ...

... useless ...

... not fair ...

... drinking ...

... unhappy ...

Nicole was blame-gaming again, belting out familiar refrains in between horrible gasps:

"Not My Fault."

"You Don't Know What It's Like."

"You Put Too Much Pressure on Me."

She sounded like a harpooned seal or ten and a mess Emily was glad she and Ethan had been barred from seeing at least.

Ethan was doing a banger job of ignoring it all. Those damn blocks were serving their purpose. His focus on stacking them without causing them to tumble was precious to watch, but as Nicole threw out some last-ditch pleas for more time to sober up on her own, the residual heat of the shame Emily felt jumpstarted a new rage. It was insane to have brought her, let alone Ethan.

Before they'd left home, she suggested she was old enough to babysit Ethan. Dad hadn't dismissed the idea immediately. He looked around the apartment as he stuffed a jacket and umbrella from the closet into an already overflowing duffle bag he was packing for Nicole. His eyes went squinty, almost like he was deeply suspicious of what the apartment itself might do to them if he left them alone with her in charge. Real or imagined, he didn't find whatever it was he was looking for—and if it'd all been a stall to simply craft a believable explanation, it'd failed.

"You're coming," he said. "And no phone. I want your eyes on Ethan at all times."

No phone was fine. It hadn't stopped pinging since Claire's video. She welcomed a break from her friends' overenthusiastic support and her frenemies' cruelties.

"Of course, you're old enough, but I need your help, Em. Grab Ethan's stuff and get in the car."

So far, she'd been no help at all, but she kept quacking for Ethan nonetheless.

Deep moans avalanched through the walls. Nicole's sorrow felt intimate now. Her mother's remorse had either become legitimately more genuine than before or had simply gone on for so long that it'd tricked Emily into believing it.

Quantity of crying over the quality of it. That was a stunt Emily used to pull as a child, too.

As a *child*.

Nicole was still a child, really.

Nicole was the brat she always made Emily out to be. Emily didn't have the scientific term to describe it, but it seemed to her Nicole's brain hadn't aged past seventeen. Maybe she'd married too soon. Maybe she'd had Emily too soon, too. These were things adults blamed their failings on routinely in movies.

The guilt Emily sometimes felt years ago for having done as little as she had to help Nicole stung her stomach. She swallowed the vomit as skillfully as she did back then. It was the first time in a long time she experienced anything resembling empathy for Nicole. She'd gotten used to bending her worry into the seething anger she now preferred: an emotional obfuscation hard enough to weaponize against Nicole. It was a hate that had come easy, but it was hard to imagine the drubbings she was capable of would be of much help with Mom today.

Mom.

The last time she remembered calling her Mom, she'd been six.

By six, Emily had already seen a lot:

Mom passed out.

Mom vomiting in the hallway toilet on a Tuesday away from the ears of Dad.

Mom unwilling to do even the most basic parenting tasks because she was too tired or too mad or too upset to burn and butter some toast for her.

Those incidents were the tip of the iceberg.

These types of things in repetition suggest the adult is sick, maybe even has cancer or some other condition Emily had heard spoken of in hushed tones by other adults. Words not necessarily understood so much as felt because of how they sound when they enter a conversation in that secretive way. It didn't matter the adults weren't talking to her—what they said landed like a brick to the head. Her parents' quiet arguments always made Emily feel like death was around the corner, her mother's, or her father's, maybe her own.

She had once worked up the courage to say she thought Nicole drank too much.

That was quite a big deal for a girl who was only seven, in Emily's opinion, but Nicole only took the sickness she had and buried it deeper. She put makeup on it and added excuses and hid herself from the family more frequently. Nicole had made the disease—and herself—as forgettable as possible.

Dad, of course, had been all high eyebrows and spit takes, feigning disbelief—not ready to accept that his daughter was aware something was wrong and always insistent she shouldn't worry so much about her mother.

Her parents' charade, uncooperative and unrehearsed as it was, dulled the edges of Emily's fears, but only a bit. In the past four years, she'd lost countless hours of sleep to internal conversations, trying to convince herself that her dad must be doing something behind the scenes to help her mother and that she simply never saw any of it. As of late, though, it was just a lot easier to be mad at Nicole than it was to be scared for her or believe either of them gave a damn.

Our little girl is so fiercely independent.

Mom and Dad hadn't said that about her much in the last couple of years, but between seven and ten, they used the backhanded compliment often. As a brag to their friends. As a brush-off punctuation to any action she took to ensure her own survival in a home fraught with tension and disorder. It was a catchall to end any observations she made on their dysfunction.

The way Nicole used to love gloating about how amazing it was that Emily took care of herself, was thinking for herself, was her own person—it was sickening. A sorry attempt at keeping some mother–daughter bond from breaking irrevocably. It hadn't fooled Emily, but secretly, she relished the recognition and attention from her mother. It'd be a lie to say otherwise.

Emily was surprised that Ethan hadn't become upset once so far during Nicole's breakdown, though it did seem like Nicole's crying was finally diminishing.

Maybe her brother didn't think of Nicole as a person to be worried about yet.

He'd also quite literally lived through worse, even if he didn't have the vocabulary to explain the impact the plane crash had on him. Or maybe any child surrounded by that many building blocks can't hold the space to care about anyone or anything else at all.

He was only just about to be three. Still a little cherub-faced know-nothing, really. By the time Ethan consciously decided to care or not care about Nicole, their mother could be shiny and new or bloated and buried. Either way, it'd be his choice to make.

Emily remembered the day *she* made the decision to stop asking Nicole if she was OK.

It'd been afternoon on a Thursday, and her mother was still in bed. The only thing she'd said to Emily that morning was, "No school today. Isn't that fun?"

It was the second week of third grade, and Emily didn't remember her new teachers mentioning anything about a holiday, but maybe it was true, and staying at home, even with her mother basically absent, still held some allure.

Dad's office was walkable, something she'd heard him call a shared workspace, but it may as well have been in China. He never popped by on days like these. Sure, there were texts and calls, but her mother's responses to his check-ins were mostly lies, and at the top of the list:

"Of course I'm capable of picking up Emily from school today."

Earlier, Emily had made toast for herself, buttered it, and put her dish and knife into the dishwasher after she'd eaten it. There was a slice for Nicole, too. After two hours of cartoons and not so much as a toilet flush from upstairs, Emily decided she would bring her mother the toast. Breakfast in bed. That was a fun thing to do! She thought she could carry a plate and juice, and maybe a sliced apple on a tray up the stairs if she really, really focused.

Cutting the apple with the largest knife in the kitchen drawer proved to be more difficult than it'd ever looked when watching Dad do it. Still, it was an apple with some slices through it. The effort should have counted. Adults always said, "It's the thought that counts!"

Her thought that day didn't move her mother. Quite the opposite, really.

As she entered the bedroom, the presentation of the fine breakfast Emily had made, one she had managed to transport from the kitchen to her mother's bed without so much as a spilled drop, did nothing to add any life to Nicole's bloodshot eyes.

"I made you breakfast!"

"Mommy's not hungry."

"You have to eat to get better, silly. Everyone knows that a healthy—"

As Emily got older, it became easier and easier for her to believe that Nicole hadn't meant to swat the tray from her hands. But there was no way to pass the effects of processing that possibility back to her eight-year-old self. As it was, the tray had flown in the air, the food with it, and whether Nicole had swatted the tray on purpose or by accident was moot.

"Jesus Christ, Emily. Look at this mess! If I ever need your help, I'll ask for it."

What her mother said to her that day looped in her mind as she looked at Ethan.

The words were significant.

That day was officially *the* day Emily decided, consciously or subconsciously, that she'd done all she could to help her mother because nothing she did had ever amounted to anything. And Nicole had never asked for her help, anyway.

Ethan's smile dropped. He'd been so preoccupied with placing a final block delicately atop a stack of others. He gave up on the tower, set the block aside, and stood as tall as possible.

Nicole's crying was soft now.

"Your mommy sound hurt," he said, moving within the room to investigate with no confidence in his direction. "She OK?"

Emily considered lying, but hiding the truth was the reason they'd arrived at this moment to begin with. She'd heard enough to know Nicole was going away for a while.

"Rehab."

A word plenty of kids her age in her neighborhood knew and knew well.

She felt certain she was going to be left to mother Ethan alone for a while. Even if that arrangement was temporary, her new role needed to start with something other than another lie.

"No. She's not OK," she said.

"She fall down?" Ethan asked.

"Something like that, yes."

Emily stood, too, and reached for Ethan's hand. As they faced the double doors together, the child squeezed it tight, as if he believed doing so would squash the remaining indecipherable stanzas of her mother's misery. Emily didn't think their position in front of the exit would be received well by any of the adults, and she decided to walk Ethan over to the couch.

It was covered in a floral print that looked nothing like flowers at all. Whoever had picked it out must have believed vivid colors were all it took to change fates. Unlike the other furniture in the waiting room, the couch was still bright, almost like no one prior to Emily and Ethan had ever decided to sit on it at all.

They weren't much farther away from the din than they'd been, but the new distance would lend itself well to ensuring the adults believed they'd gotten what they wanted by leaving her and her brother in this room. Two ignorance-is-bliss tagalongs that wouldn't be causing any more trouble than Nicole still might cause herself.

Emily sat, then patted the available cushion to prompt Ethan to join.

"You will help your mommy?" Ethan asked as he climbed next to her.

Emily sighed. "Adults don't want kids' help."

"I help my mommy lots."

"With little things, sure. They like it when you set the table or feed the dog, but when mommies and daddies have real problems, kids like us can't do anything about it."

The door opened, and Matthew poked his head out. He searched the floor for them, looking dazed, and it took longer than it should have to register that she and Ethan had moved.

"Oh, there you are," he said. "Sorry, Em. I don't think we'll be here that much longer."

"It's OK, Dad."

"How are you doing, Ethan?"

"Em's mommy fall down?"

"No, she's fine, buddy."

Emily wasn't sure what the contortion of muscles under the skin on her face had put together expression-wise for her dad to see, but he did see it, and it had an effect.

"She's *going* to be fine, I mean," he corrected himself.

His correction was enough to set her face back to its baseline of complacency. She stared at him and said nothing. Matthew took her inaction as permission to leave them again.

"Just hold tight, guys," he said as he closed the door.

On the heels of the latch catching, Emily heard her dad say something that sounded like, "Enough already. It's time to go." Was it what he'd said or what she'd wanted to hear?

It *was* enough already. Enough. FUCKING ENOUGH. Let's get on with it, Nicole. There's no one left to blame, no drug to make it better quickly. It's time to own this shit. If not for Dad, if not for your own daughter, then for Ethan. Not blood, not family until recently, but a kid who sure as hell didn't deserve to be saddled with this situation after losing his parents.

The empathy that steered her mood earlier was gone.

Time to home in on pity. Pity would be a better vibe for all concerned.

"When my mommy cry, I hug her," Ethan said.

He offered his solution so softly it threatened to slow her heart, which was beating quickly. She was too angry at Nicole for his sweetness to have the full effect, though. It was time to remain cold, time for icy and unmoved—impenetrably over it for when Nicole came out.

"When my mom *cried*, I *hugged* her," she corrected him.

She regretted righting him before she'd even finished and hoped she'd said it as softly as he had spoken to try to soothe her. Maybe he hadn't really heard her, or if he had, she hoped harder still that he couldn't interpret the slight or realize just how off-putting the timing of her language lesson had been.

She might have apologized had he not responded so quickly.

"I hug her every day. Mommy so sad now."

THE TEXT | SECTION NINE

PAIN.

You are no doubt aware that when someone from the Prior Plane loses any part of a limb, they can experience a phantom itch, tingles where that part of their person used to be. As a resident, what you feel of your emotions and how you experience your perception of yourself is a similar process.

Few residents arrive already aware of something called Embodied Cognition: In Prior Plane, cognitive processes were deeply intertwined with your physical body. Like the missing limb example, you may feel you have a body because it used to be there. BUT BE AWARE: Seeing a body on another resident or presenting one of your own is a choice, but there are no bodies here. Not real ones. As such, there are no feelings here. Not real ones.

Want to be pain-free? Accept that you already are. Want to leave sadness behind? Accept that sadness is behind you. Want to be happy? Believe that you are. Contentment as a resident is not dependent on a physical feeling.

Like pain? Knock yourself out. Pretend it's there all you like. For the rest of us, though: If PAIN-FREE had been an option in Prior Plane, wouldn't you have taken advantage of it?

No resident in Second Plane can be defined by their emotions, because the emotions themselves do not exist.

10
TAG

It had been five weeks since ACS's initial visit with Matthew and Nicole. During that time, Amanda had left every invitation Tag had made to connect in Second Plane unanswered.

> *Like all resident interactions, any communion made here between the formerly coupled is only possible when both residents agree to have a connection.*

It was a good bet that, like him, she'd still been taking observation trips to check in on Ethan or Nicole's progress in rehab. There was no way to know for sure that she was still visiting, only hearsay from other residents that Tag had been introduced to through Donovan.

He could have gone on watching Nicole, Matthew, Ethan, and Emily—who was picking up the slack in a big way—for a lifetime. Their lifetimes anyway.

It wasn't his plan to do so, it was not advisable, The Text said, but he could.

He'd just returned from watching Emily read Ethan a bedtime story. His plan was to recharge in Second Plane before traveling back to take in Nicole's evening group therapy session at the rehab. The text said nothing about recharging. It was possible the energizing effect of a figurative sit was his fabrication. Even so, it'd given observations in bulk an HD-like clarity.

They'd hidden so much from him. *Matthew* had hidden so much from him.

He hadn't known Nicole was a drunk—or an addict.

Addict? Was that the better thing to refer to her as?

During her participation at the rehab the past three weeks, it was the word du jour.

Nicole seemed better so far, and though Matthew and Emily had spent a lot of time wondering aloud if she was going to leave her program early, she hadn't. That was progress. And progress, not perfection, was what the alcoholics liked to push. It was not terribly different from some of the suggestions the council made for residents, a similarity that wasn't lost on Tag.

Had Matthew been keeping secrets from him, too embarrassed to lean on Tag, or was it authentic denial? In Matthew's case, Tag decided it'd been the latter—a defense mechanism of a sort. That made sense. Considering the other two options meant accepting that their friendship had never been as strong as Tag had always assumed.

After all, he was familiar with denial, too.

He'd compartmentalized misdeeds while in Prior Plane. Too many times to count.

And to be fair, it's not like he'd gone to Matthew to seek guidance about navigating the aftermath of cheating on Amanda. Doing so would have destroyed the illusion that Tag's family was off to a perfect start—the type of go at a family that he'd coveted when Matthew and Nicole had started theirs.

Christ . . . had he had the guts to tell his friend about the affair, maybe booking the trip to Hawaii wouldn't have felt so urgent. He'd spent an unhealthy bit of time imagining what his future might have held had he and Matthew shared their problems with each other. A lot of different futures other than the ones they were living seemed possible.

He'd asked so much of Matthew when he'd called his friend that day with the lawyer.

Be our son's everything if we kick the bucket, will you? Great. Thanks.

He didn't know if Amanda had thought deeply about that decision before and when and after they'd made it, but he knew that prior to their deaths, he'd barely thought about it at any point at all. The odds of him and his wife dying at the same time and leaving Ethan behind hadn't seemed that good. He still didn't know what the *actual* odds of that happening even were. Maybe if he saw the odds of that type of accident coming to pass, then or now, he'd understand even better how flippant he'd been in assigning Matthew the responsibility willy-nilly.

At this point, his friend was doing his best to keep the household together, including working overtime to cover the costs of Nicole's treatment.

Leaving Ethan with Matthew had created a pit in Tag's stomach, an uncomfortable void in an organ he no longer had but that no amount of mental gymnastics had removed.

Guilt. Shame. Empathy. All of it, *mimics* of the feelings rather than actual ones, mixed thick.

But on the other hand, it seemed to him that having Ethan dropped in their laps unexpectedly was maybe what Matthew's family needed. The best possible existence they had left, whether that was weeks, months, or just days, might have depended on his and Amanda's deaths. Taking on Ethan forced their hand, and the results for their family could be better than they would have been if the crash hadn't happened. It was a theory Tag created that had offered some relief. At one point, he ran his optimistic nonsense by Donovan, who wasn't willing to agree or disagree. "I suppose that's possible," he'd said. "And even true . . . if you believe it."

The biggest surprise so far—one he hoped Amanda was seeing firsthand—was that an eleven-year-old girl was proving to be a better Mom than the one they had left Ethan with.

Emily is being a better mom than Amanda is capable of being right now.
The thought was ugly, but if his wife was feeling the same, it was worth considering.

Amanda had never been the jealous type—but he could no longer assume that any good quality she possessed in Prior Plane would be indicative of her character here.

In denying him a connection, one in which he could ask her questions directly or see how she was progressing with The Text and her mentor, she'd left him little choice other than to put more stock in rumors and the concerns of strangers than he ever would've while living.

Mistrust. The word sounded odd, but it was the right word—for his wife, for this place, even for Donovan now.

After possibly witnessing a version of Seattle that Donovan had conjured, Tag believed he had also seen, in fits and starts, what other residents had created. Those glimpses were infrequent, and he had no proof, mainly due to his unease about verifying what he had observed with those same residents. The Text stated that such a thing was impossible. Still, there was a nagging thought in his mind: What if the rules that governed civilization in Second Plane, The Text's suggestions, were only as concrete as a resident wished? It remained to be seen which of these were absolute truths and which were falsehoods, or at least malleable.

A week ago, one woman in particular had plenty to say about that, and the warning she gave him was a good part of why he'd been observing Prior Plane far more than recommended.

Martha, the name she had given Tag, had extended an invitation to connect to share information he "absolutely needed to hear." She had arrived at his space in the form of only *thoughts* he could converse with. No body, no face, and even the whiteness of nothing subtly framed by grayer whites that had become his baseline went absent. This woman—he'd decided she was a woman based on her name—conjured nothing visible to moor his interest to.

Her voice didn't sound old, young, female, or male. Her tone wasn't low or high, Tag didn't hear her as if she had been a smoker or as if she'd walked the earth talking to people with something hack writers might call silky smooth. Her words just existed, that's it. It was as if she wasn't using a mouth to speak to him at all. And that made sense. His body was fake, his mouth was imagined. No resident needed any of it—so why had he decided to cling to forms?

Martha was present but not present, and perhaps that gave credence to what she had come to tell him. She was there to discuss something forbidden in Second Plane, and maybe her connection to him as a conversation with no visual representation provided her some plausible deniability should the council find out.

"It *is* possible, you know? Possession in Prior Plane."

He'd expected directness. Nonetheless, her assertion caused an electric-like sensation—not a mimic of fear but more a mimic of anger. Of late, he hadn't felt much like defending his wife's good name, but Martha's opening felt like a personal attack, even if she hadn't yet said Amanda's name or claimed that this was Amanda's plan. That she hadn't had to for him to understand softened his rage.

"You're the only one I've heard say so," he said.

"I'm not sure why hearing others say so would make it any more true."

It was difficult to return fire at someone who wasn't pretending to be there. Her words floated around the body he'd drawn up for himself, a more angular version than he had at death, a muscular, thin physique he knew he'd been capable of if only there'd been time to hit the gym.

"You might tell me about a resident who's done it, but why should I believe you? We've never met," he said as he spun himself, trying to locate her breathing, which he thought maybe was a sound he'd added and not Martha breathing at all. "You're not really here now. If that—"

"I'm not a voice in your head. A head you don't have, I might add."

True, though he supposed he could have made her up. A ghost of his own concoction, there to start a conversation he'd been hoping to hear, a conversation he needed—if just to have a damn good reason to keep observing Ethan.

Imaginary Martha made more sense than her being a Good Samaritan who felt obligated to tell on his wife—whom she knew *how*, anyway?

He debated the realness of Martha unabated. "Are you still here?" he finally asked.

"I am."

"I don't think you are a voice in my head," he told her, though he still wasn't certain. "But possession seems improbable."

"It's complex, sure."

"And mentors don't mention possession as a possibility because?"

"Your mentor, maybe," she said. "Cowards die every day, Tag."

"And you? You're one of the brave ones, I suppose?"

"Yes, I am."

"And why is that?" It felt good to argue again. He hadn't argued a lot while living, but he wasn't immune to the dopamine hit that came with a good verbal volley.

"Because I have nothing to lose," Martha said.

"We're all dead—we've all already lost everything, haven't we?"

"You could still lose Ethan—in a much bigger way—but maybe I've misjudged you." It sounded as if she was threatening to leave. "I feel my coming here was a mistake."

Without a face, it was hard to tell if she was there enough still to stop her. "No, no. Please stay," he tried. "I'm sorry."

There was no answer. He thought she'd left, until she quietly said, "I accept your apology. And I understand your frustration."

"Thank you."

"I didn't say your wife was going to pull it off."

Tag paused. "But others have?"

"Yes. A few residents have performed successful possessions."

"What did those residents do?"

"Some had messages they felt they had to deliver—important information that justified the risks: hidden wealth or guns they worried might be found by grandchildren they'd left behind. There's no way to make those things known without taking over a body that has either a set of pipes or at least hands to write those messages down."

"So, these are people who pulled this off to perform something good."

"Well . . . one resident was motivated enough to perform his possession just to fuck again," she said, with a bit of clutching pearls. "Not exactly altruistic. Inane, even."

She waited for his reaction, but her example hadn't shocked him.

"In the end, the one thing they all had in common, no matter their reasons, is they were motivated. Motivation is key, best we can tell."

"We?" Tag asked.

"Rebels, outlaws, terrorists . . . What civilization hasn't had a segment that questions the authority it's been born into? Some of us are willing to risk punishment by pulling the veil back here to see what really *is* possible. It doesn't make us bad people—just bad residents."

"How often is possession successful?" Tag asked.

"Not often. I'm only here to say it's possible. Nothing more. Tell anyone I said as much, and I'll deny it."

"Fine. So how do you possess a body in Prior Plane?"

"It has to be someone you know and truly understand."

"I see. Like a friend or family member."

"Sometimes, but not always. But you have to *know* them well enough to realize they're in bad shape."

The people you knew were, on occasion, people you didn't know at all.

That was patently true with Matthew.

"Bad shape?" he asked.

"Best way I can say it: You must catch the soul somewhere between depressed and dead."

Tag considered that. "Someone who is suicidal, you're saying?"

"Many adults live a lifetime in this state without offing themselves. It's this emotional state, not a desire to be dead, that makes them susceptible. And it's a difficult mood to pinpoint."

As he let everything Martha had said sink in, he realized he had no idea where Amanda was with everything, no idea who she was in death, and, if he was being honest, maybe even no idea who she'd been in life. What had she decided to show him of herself versus what she was really made of? He had to admit he had no real idea what she was capable of.

"Of course, the *who* is just a part of it. I know nothing about the mechanics to it."

"What is it you think my wife wants, Martha?"

"Amanda isn't the first resident to consider killing a loved one before their time to reunite with them sooner. The situation with her, though, is a touch more troubling."

"How so?" He knew why it was more dire but had asked just the same—to help bolster his own disapproval, maybe, or to leave no more room for making excuses for her behavior.

"I'm told your son is not even three years old—"

"He'll be three in eight days," Tag said with the same excitement Ethan would have.

"Well . . . so there's your answer. I connected with you because she wants to do a despicable thing. I've never connected with your wife but from what I've heard, she sounds like that kind who succeeds: unafraid to seek the truth, even if it's to her own detriment."

"Motivated," Tag said, understanding.

"Frighteningly so."

THE TEXT | SECTION TEN

IS HERE IT?

That is a valid question, indeed. Based on your new personal experience with "death" and all that Prior Plane science had been unable to prove, you might assume the answer is no. Is there a THIRD PLANE? Unfortunately, we must PLEAD THE FIFTH!

In lieu of providing our own black-and-white answer, we are excited to be able to offer the relevant poem below, printed here with permission from the poet* herself, an exemplary Second Plane resident since 1886.

My life closed twice before its close—
It yet remains to see
If Immortality unveil
A third event to me
So huge, so hopeless to conceive
As these that twice befell.
Parting is all we know of heaven,
And all we need of hell.

Unlike Prior Plane, *here* can be "it," the last stop, if a resident adheres to best practices. Lean into the suggestions, spoken and unspoken, those written within The Text and those never bound into any book. What comes after Second Plane is not for the faint of heart. Confused? WORRY NOT; your mentor and other residents will likely not be so coy about Third Plane. CHEEKY DEVILS.

When you've achieved a solid footing here, so to speak, feel free to ask your mentor about any possibility—but don't be surprised if the answers you get, if any, are told in whispers. SHHHHHHHHH.

---

*By request of the poet, please do not attempt to connect with her. Thank you.

11
TAG

An hour into observing nothing—not like the nothing that existed in Second Plane when Tag didn't bother to conjure anything, but the nothings of the living: street signs, mopeds, fashionable shoes, and cheap jewelry behind plate glass—everything inhuman no longer held meaning. Through repetition or because they'd never meant much to begin with.

People-watching was OK, and there were hundreds of live bodies to choose from, but eyeing new strangers up and down and wondering where they might be headed had lost its appeal twenty minutes in. What strangers were up to, on their way to, or dealing with was a game for the living, not the dead.

He and Amanda had made three dozen passes by Ethan's pediatrician's office so far, never straying from West Fourteenth Street and walking only the block between Seventh and Eighth Avenues, back and forth. As streets in Manhattan went, Fourteenth was anemic. Maybe he'd always thought so. And if things went as he'd planned and he made his Final Goodbye, then that uninspired artery of the city would be his last glimpse of the life he'd known. He paused to take in the street again as a whole. What a horrible spot for a last look at the splendors of the world.

There was one bright spot. Despite the inconvenience of a trip from Park Slope to Manhattan, Matthew had decided to keep Ethan's doctor, the family pediatrician that Amanda had handpicked after months of research, instead of switching to a more convenient clinic in Brooklyn. It was a thin hope, but if that decision had scored any points with Tag's wife, she had yet to say so.

They were only there because, after several weeks of total silence, Amanda extended an invitation to connect, which Tag had eagerly accepted. His anticipation of their reunion caught him off guard because, during that same period, which included Ethan's birthday, she'd flat-out ignored the invitations he'd sent her. The birthday party had been only Matthew, Emily, Ethan, and Lucinda. In truth, it wasn't much to miss. Emily had made sure Ethan enjoyed playing with his gifts, away from Matthew and Tag's mother, who had struggled to keep their chit-chat civil between bites of the cake Lucinda had brought. Still, it had angered Tag that Amanda hadn't connected that day to share the moment and celebrate their son.

Although he'd suspected his mentor might know how Amanda had been faring, any time he asked, Donovan only suggested Tag reread the section of The Text titled "Our Only Prayer." It'd been maddening—both Donovan's repetitive suggestion and the prayer itself, a cryptic bit of nonsense that Tag had tried dutifully to take to heart.

Right when that damned prayer might have started to stick was when Amanda reached out. She wanted him to join her on an observation of Prior Plane. It was unexpected, but less so when she brought up Ethan's three-year checkup.

"It's happening a full week late, by the way," she had said. That was true, but only because Matthew had rescheduled Ethan's original appointment while putting Nicole into rehab and getting his home without his wife settled. Settled enough, anyway.

Amanda wanted Tag to observe the appointment with her, and he did not ask for her reasons. Their son's health and weight and height and dexterity or any other metric were sure to be par for the course, but Tag knew she was hoping to hear bad news.

He had agreed, but only on the condition that they let the exam happen in private—just Matthew, Ethan, and their doctor. He would accompany her to the location if they waited outside the doctor's office or took a walk while the checkup happened. The results would be the same no matter when they learned of them, and the day before,

Tag had overheard Matthew tell Lucinda that he'd be sure to call her with an update right after the exam. It'd be easy enough to hear the news from him—after the appointment was finished. Amanda's acquiescence to his demands did not provide him with any comfort. And as their time walking together moved into a second hour, he remained surprised by her compliance to his ask.

She'd said little to him the whole walk and kept her eyes on the front door of the pediatrician's office, craning her head 180 degrees when their backs were to it, which, real or not, was an unpleasant spectacle to behold.

The silence between them left his mind open to obsessing over the conversation he'd had with Martha about his wife. He needed to be smart about this and assume the worst.

Amanda was seeking an answer to a question no good resident would ever answer: How can I bring my son here? If possession were possible—and it was in Ethan's best interest for Tag to start believing that it was—then she already knew that.

They both knew people in Prior Plane who were on edge, sad, and even desperate, but she couldn't ever know just how dark it was inside their heads.

What would her deadline be for trying to retrieve Ethan?

She wouldn't give up without a good reason.

And he couldn't hope for Ethan's aging to slow Amanda down.

Still, trying to inhabit the bodies that belonged to souls that were sad or even clinically depressed—but didn't quite exist in that black space of just shy of dead—didn't strike him as something his wife would bother with. It was a guessing game. He doubted Amanda would fully commit to taking over a body unless she was certain that body was going to work. It had to be the right time and right place as it pertained to their desperation—a black space in one's thinking that made possession a possibility, that was how Martha had described it.

Tag wasn't a psychologist, but he wanted to believe that type of deep melancholy wasn't a constant for most of the living, not with all the prescription drugs everyone was on these days.

At best, possession would be a moving window of opportunity for his wife.

He shook his head. That was exactly the type of naivety he was trying to buck. Because if she succeeded at possession—even for only a short time—she would never quit trying. She might be capable of hurting Ethan once she had firm control of a body . . . *No. Stop it.*

He'd come into this observation with a plan, but the heavy intentional silence Amanda had insisted upon suggested that no matter how eloquently he spoke about Nicole's progress in rehab, that plan would fail.

Begging wouldn't work—it never had with his wife.

And innuendo about what might happen if she didn't practice the suggestions from The Text wasn't going to cut it either.

He thought about how Martha had ended their connection days ago, perhaps sensing his unease with the task.

* * *

"You have to be blunt about it," Martha had said. "For her, for Ethan. Do you know about Third Plane, Taggart?"

He did. He'd read The Text cover-to-cover, after all.

Unlike Prior Plane, here can be "it," the last stop, if a resident adheres to best practices.

He'd enjoyed the poem, too, but he hadn't thought too much about Third Plane, because surely it wouldn't apply to him. He took the suggestions very seriously. "Yes," he said, "I know about Third Plane."

"Does Amanda?"

He had no idea what Amanda did or didn't know. "I imagine she's already read and heard about Third—"

"Not from you, she hasn't. You have to warn her. If she keeps this up, nothing good will come of it."

Nothing good. He realized right then that what Donovan had told him about Third Plane had been just as vague as The Text. But knowing more wouldn't necessarily make it matter.

He scoffed at Martha. "I'm flattered you think she'd still listen to me, but I don't agree."

"So, what then? You'll just hang back and hope for the best for your son?"

Martha, the soul or the woman, was still invisible, but her anger was not. As she spoke, huge chunks of his pristine white sweep opened up into dark gaping holes, ragged at their edges.

"Isn't that basically what The Text wants of us?" he asked.

After a pause, she replied, "I've underestimated you."

"Perhaps twice," he admitted.

By now, there was more darkness than light. And though it made little sense, it felt as though the blackness she was wielding might be able to tear through him. "Those caught possessing a soul in Prior Plane will be punished by the council!"

Tag was still there, floating in the absolute darkness that she'd created, awkwardly unable to alter his space or add anything to it, no matter how hard he tried. He no longer wished to know what Martha looked like. Her last shout had rattled him, and when it finally rang out, he spoke.

"Punished how, though? I need to know what the punishment is. Help me."

"A life in Third Plane is no life at all. No observation. No residency. No community."

"I don't think that's going to sway her. She hasn't exactly loved—"

"It means it won't matter if Ethan is dead or alive, in Prior Plane or a resident here—once Amanda is in Third Plane, she will never have an opportunity to see him again. Or you. Even if you both eventually ended up there yourselves. And well, I'm hoping that still matters, too."

* * *

It wouldn't be long before Ethan's appointment was done. Tag would tell Amanda what Martha had told him to and then also make his final farewell to their son. If the threat of Third Plane didn't work, he held out hope that seeing him deliver the goodbye might be the tipping point she needed to come to her senses. With luck, it would be the last observation for them both.

He moved himself in front of her to stop her and make eye contact—if that kind of thing even mattered anymore—but she moved right through him. When he tried again, she turned away from him and headed back toward the pediatrician's office. And so, he didn't tell her. Because it occurred to him at that moment that doing so would have meant he'd also be saying, "Yes, dear, possession of the living is possible. You can do exactly what you have wanted to do . . . so long as you don't give up." To have faith in the punishment that Martha laid out was the same as having faith in the action of possession itself. One truth could not exist without the other, could it? And that was only if Martha was to be believed.

All of a sudden, it felt as if he was part of a conspiracy against his wife.

He was spiraling out. Exhaustion was kicking in, and soon he'd be returned to Second Plane no matter how hard he fought to stay.

Why in the hell was Ethan's appointment taking so long anyway?

Tag found a digital marquee in the foyer of a bank ahead. Even accounting for the routine delays of being seen there or in any city, Matthew and his son should have been out by now.

He studied Amanda.

If possession *was* possible, it was also possible The Text was wrong about a resident's ability to move things in Prior Plane.

He threw himself in front of Amanda again. "This is my last observation," he told her. "I'm going to say my final goodbye to Ethan. It's what's best for him."

She stopped and for the first time since their arrival on Fourteenth Street, looked back at Tag instead of at the office door that his son and Matthew had still not exited from.

There was dark swelling around her eyes, and the irises framing her pupils were no longer colored. If he held her stare long enough, the whole of everything between her eyelids went black. Tears were thought to be an impossibility, at least according to some parts of the literature, and she was shedding none now, but Amanda's face looked as if it'd had no break from crying for days. An authentic sadness, imprinted, and impossibly hard to believe she'd have conjured any of it intentionally when she could look any way that she wanted.

"I'm as far gone as I look, Tag. Do with that what you will."

"You chose to look this way?"

"Does it matter?"

It did matter.

Though their time away from each other had been short relative to the decades they'd lived as a couple in Prior Plane, Tag suddenly realized it'd been far too easy to stop holding empathy for what his wife was going through. And easier still to let his own grief turn into a vile malice, almost like he'd been wishing something bad would happen to her before she could make something bad happen to their son. She might have chosen to look the way she did to manipulate him, he knew that—she'd always been capable of it—but *that* didn't matter.

"How many times have you come here without me?" he asked.

Amanda started walking back toward the pediatrician's office as she answered. "I'm always here," she said. "Except when I'm not."

He imagined Second Plane, the power it wielded over the dead, having to fight to drag his wife away from their son. Her essence, molecules or atoms or space dust, all trying to hang together for as long as possible until it could completely defy the pull back into residency.

For a moment, he felt a beaming sense of pride for Amanda's newfound resistance to authority. She had always been the rule-follower: no deviations from recipes, no using shortcuts, a real by-the-bookism she had prided herself upon. She didn't bend the rules to her advantage, and she wasn't comfortable calling on favors, even when favors were due. She had never cheated at games or worked the system, at least not intentionally. She'd never been unfaithful or sinister or hell-bent on revenge. Tag certainly couldn't say the same. All this was moot now.

They were both fighting for their son. Just in very different ways.

As he caught up to her, she made a sudden movement to the left to get out of the way of a living pedestrian walking in front of them. It was odd.

According to Donovan, ethereality was not invisibility—they were seeing the street projected into their consciousness, but weren't physically there on Fourteenth Avenue, inhabiting the space in some cloaked way. They couldn't impede the living's momentum.

Yet Amanda flinched like she could bump into the living if she wasn't careful. The concern for her that had rekindled in Tag extinguished. She wasn't worried about hitting someone; she was a raptor testing the fences, hoping the right move at the right time would have some effect. She still thought she had something to do with that fucking cereal bowl.

"Is this really your last observation?" she asked. She stopped walking but kept her attention on the clinic door. The sweetness in her voice, one she often deployed to get her way while living, left Tag briefly believing she was reconsidering her plan. "If you are truly done visiting, I hope you know I won't find you to report back on Ethan's adventures."

He reached for her hand, and she allowed the union. "This isn't the best way forward, Amanda."

"Spare me," she said. She cast his hand back to him hard enough for it to cease existing momentarily. "Hearing you, of all people, use new-age babble like that is the pinnacle of cringe."

"So where does it end for you?" he asked, hating that his tone had sounded desperate.

"We're already dead, Tag. Newsflash: It ended."

"Exactly," he said. He held off on sharing what he'd learned about Third Plane. "We're dead. Ethan is not."

"Not yet."

"Do you even hear yourself? Jesus Christ." His anger at her was so intense it pushed the edges of his face in all directions—a true conniption—but he managed to recover his façade before it popped.

"Apparently, the son of God is no such thing."

"Seriously, Amanda. I get it—I can try to get it—but there are rules."

"So now we're calling them rules?"

"Suggestions. Whatever."

"Tell me you know we made a grave fucking mistake," she said.

He had no pulse that could race, but the energy within whatever he'd become would have passed easily for such a thing. He'd never hit her, and couldn't technically now—still wouldn't even if he could—but thought about it nonetheless. She had gone fucking mad.

"Admit it, and maybe I'll move on."

"I'm not going to tell you that," he said.

"Why not?"

He managed to dial his frustrations back and took a chance on a tone more logical. "Because where you see failure, I see progress. I see friends fighting with all they have to make sure he is cared for. They fucked up. We fucked up. Everyone fucks up. The key is owning the fuck-ups you make. That's how you move forward. Matthew and Nicole are moving forward the best they can. And Emily is a delight. She loves Ethan—surely, you've seen it."

"I need to hear you say you know *you* fucked up." If not for the forthcoming report on Ethan's health, he'd have left right then. "You left our son with an addict!" Her voice boomed like the God many people die expecting. Perhaps she sensed she was pushing her luck and was at risk of having him flee because, for a moment, she caged her ire. "And who can blame her, right?" Her question was sarcastically sweet. "She's married to a loser, her daughter's a twat—everything about them was and is phony as fuck. They weren't poor actors, I guess I can say that."

Tag chose to keep quiet until he was certain she was done.

"Say you fucked up, and I'll leave you alone. You can pop off and go full kumbaya with the other residents. You. Fucked. Up. And now our son's life is a tragedy. Just say it!"

Dozens of pedestrians had come and gone and were still passing them by, but none stopped to butt in. Tag wondered if they would have even while living.

"We made the decision together," he said, almost too quiet to be heard.

"Bullshit. My parents were my first choice, but no. Too old, too risky, you said." She was grasping at straws now.

"You need to talk to Rebecca."

"Not happening."

"Fine. Find someone else—"

"Not happening!" she repeated.

"Even if you *could* bring Ethan to Second Plane, he won't be the little boy you love. He'll be our son, sure, but older, age-accelerated. It's all in The Text."

"It's not true." She shook her head.

She walked briskly toward the pediatrician's office, directly to the front door, as if she intended to dishonor their original agreement to stay outside. Even so, he didn't follow her.

"What part of your childhood was so entirely fucked up that you would deny Ethan his own?" He instantly regretted shouting at her. Shouting had never worked before.

She turned back to look at Tag, her face tight with anger. "There *are* children in Second Plane."

Tag rolled his eyes. "You've seen kids, have you?"

Just then, the door swung open. By reflex, Tag thought himself between Amanda and the clinic door. He didn't really believe she could do anything, did he? But he couldn't afford to take any chances.

"No, but I know they're there," she said with a certainty that made Tag shiver.

Ethan emerged, bouncing on his feet. He licked a shiny red lollipop in one hand and held a green one in the other, still wrapped.

"What are you talking about?" he asked, his voice edging toward panic as he walked backward to stay in front of her, not that it would make any difference. The dead could be anywhere they wanted to be while observing. Just think herself there, and poof. Still, it felt better to present himself as an obstacle. "What are you doing, Amanda?"

Matthew stepped out of the clinic and collared the boy gently by the shoulder.

Amanda's momentum hadn't slowed.

Nothing physical can be done, felt, or made to happen.

Donovan's assurances meant even less now.

"I can feel the children there, Tag. I can hear them."

"You're delusional." Tag said. He wanted to hit her where it hurt. Always composed Amanda in Prior Plane wilted at any thought of being ungrounded—Tag knew this, knew her well enough to push her buttons. He wanted, more than anything, to throw her off course. "My question is," Tag said, practically spitting the words, "were you always?"

Matthew and Ethan turned to head in the other direction, their backs to them now.

"Some residents have their children with them, as children, not as some bullshit accelerated version of their children. I can hear them. If I can prove it, what does it matter?" she asked.

She stopped her approach. He was afraid to know why.

Behind him, Matthew walked Ethan by the hand, his phone to his ear. Tag and Amanda were missing the call to Lucinda—missing the results of the check-up.

He stepped into Amanda's form and let weeks' worth of building frustration explode, hoping like hell that the energy of his anger might short-circuit her back to Second Plane.

"Talk to a mentor. Talk to the residents. Fucking read The Text. You can't prove it. There aren't any children in Second Plane. I'm not having this conversation. I'm done."

But he wasn't done.

In light of what Martha had told him regarding possession and the existence of Third Plane, a life after their current life after death—a life worse than death—The Text might be all lies. But he feared investigating any further. He'd already faced so much uncertainty in Second Plane, dealing with any more threatened to break him. He knew it. It was easier to put blind faith in The Text, listen to Donovan, and move forward from the life he knew. He wanted to process his grief and stop clinging to the pain of wanting to hug his son one last time.

But in that moment, there on the street, the pain of yearning was too great. A hope that he might get to see Ethan's eyes light up at seeing him again, the way Ethan ran to hug him by the door when he came home after a long day at work, it was a temptation too great to ignore. His grief got the better of him. He missed Ethan badly.

What if there was a chance to see him—really *see* him—again?

For a moment, he must have felt what she'd been feeling. It was intoxicating. A beautiful high built on hope—no, desperation. An ugly and selfish desperation. He managed to shake it.

"If kids are in Second Plane," he said, "they belong there. But you are trying to *kill* Ethan. Trying to kill what is beautiful about him, his life! And if that weren't bad enough already, whatever this god-forsaken world is, it's fucking forbidden. We don't know what comes next. You need to know that if you were to succeed, the council is going to—"

A screech bled into the air, followed by a handful of taut screams.

One car after another went front end into the bumper of the last. When the din of the collision was over, Tag located Matthew and

Ethan. They were frozen in their tracks, Ethan clinging halfway up Matthew's body, mere feet from the collision.

Relief. Tag felt relieved. It was not a mimic.

The joy he felt when Matthew eventually coaxed Ethan down and then turned to walk his son away from the crash was real, too.

Tag turned to find Amanda, but she was gone.

He spun back around to see if she'd caught up with Matthew and Ethan. She wasn't with them, either. They were walking down the street, holding hands again, and Ethan had resumed his work on his lollipop, already behaving as if the crash and its consequences weren't still unfolding behind them. Somewhere in the corner of his mind, Tag heard himself remark, "Already a true New Yorker." The lightness of his passing thought led to no smile, but he decided to catch up with them anyway.

Through Matthew's phone, Tag heard his mother ask, "Are you sure you two are alright?"

Then, Ethan started on lollipop number two, even though he hadn't finished the first. He stuck both into his mouth at the same time.

"Give me a moment," Matthew said into the phone. "It's dangerous enough to walk with one lollipop in your mouth, let alone two, little guy!" He took both of them out of Ethan's mouth, and before the sour on his son's face went sonic, he pointed toward a park not far up ahead.

"You can have them both back in just a moment. I know the perfect bench for eating two lollipops. It's only a little farther."

Second Plane was pulling Tag back now, it had its hooks in, and that was fine.

Part of him wanted to follow Matthew and his son to the park to speak out the words he'd prepared, to say goodbye, and to tell Ethan one last time how much he loved him. But snooping on them—especially after Matthew's promise of that "perfect bench" had put a smile on Ethan's face—felt like a betrayal. He wouldn't want some ghostly buttinsky, former relation or not, following *him* to a park with Ethan, not if he ever had the chance to make those kinds of simple father-to-son promises again.

Although leaving right then may not have been his decision, Tag exited Prior Plane—believing it would be for good—and he did so without delivering his Final Goodbye.

THE TEXT | SECTION ELEVEN

OUR ONLY PRAYER.

I am, but I am NOT.
I did, but I am DONE.
I will while also WON'T.
I KNEW but know not.
I lived, and I am at peace with those still living.
My toil is for an eternal and peaceful existence here.
I am not my brother's keeper.
(SAY IT ALOUD)
I am not my brother's keeper.

12

AMANDA

Amanda conjured a hard wooden stool to sit on. A rectangle seat bolted atop black metal legs, barely big enough for an average adult butt. She conjured a second stool, and another. Only one other resident was expected. Even so, she placed many more stools along a bar long enough to host a second last supper. The stools looked painful, modern for modern's sake, modeled after the mass-produced homespun furniture that had dominated Prior Plane cafés for over a decade.

Floor-to-ceiling plate glass windows framed total blackness. The blackness was her default canvas for Prior Plane and apparently an uncommon baseline for an existence there, according to her first mentor, Rebecca. Windows like that, the smoothness of the glass, the exact measure of all three being precisely uniform, was quite a mental accomplishment.

She lit the void on the other side of those windows with a bright sun, then added a dirty city street and people. The bustle of human life was easy to fake when it wasn't meant to be the focus. Any resident who said it was difficult was lazy or inept. Rush hour in the city was simple enough if one made the time to practice.

Time wasn't something any resident was supposed to believe in anymore.

But if you don't bother hanging out with the mentor you've been assigned, one who refuses to answer your questions, what then?

If other residents refuse to answer the simple question you ask, what then?

If you aren't interested in rereading The Text or reading The Second Text that's been promised to you for showing good discipline in observing the suggestions from the first, what then?

You had time, that's what. And you practiced perfecting your scenery.

From her stool, she added books, colorful vases, and tiny statues to the store's decorative shelves. As she filled the gaps in between those, the clutter of baubles on each became redundant. She'd inadvertently conjured the cheap box-store trinkets from the cafés she'd frequented in her first year as a mom, but she wasn't inclined to start over.

She'd never set foot in corporate-owned cafes before having Ethan. Her loyalty to the coffee shop she and Tag visited daily, Lyla's Brooklyn Beanery, had been unbreakable. They'd called it "our spot," which was a goof more than anything. They hadn't first met there. He didn't propose there. She couldn't recall anything special happening there unless you counted comfortable silence. "Our spot" was simply easier than the mouthful "Lyla's Brooklyn Beanery."

I'll meet you at our spot in ten, Babe.

I'll meet you at Lyla's Brooklyn Beanery in ten, Babe.

Maybe there wasn't much difference at all.

She took in her handy work. The café had some of Lyla's allure.

Lyla, the owner, once told Amanda she'd spent fifteen years amassing her collection of chairs, eclectic trinkets, mismatched tables, and the rare artwork on the café's walls.

In honor of Lyla, who was very much still alive, Amanda placed a porcelain figurine of a woman reading a book on the nearest shelf. An older matriarch in her rocking chair next to a fireplace. The tiny reader had a black cat, too, curled up by the flames. Its tail was precariously frozen under one of the rockers, which threatened to crush it in the hollowest way possible. Tag had thought that statue was hysterical, had remarked on it far too often, but Amanda left it.

In addition to the doomed cat, there were other Lyla-like baubles, but it wasn't "our spot." The furniture she conjured was uniform, the countertop had never been used, and the abstract geometric animal art she'd hung on the walls was inoffensive. The collection looked like it'd been focused-grouped to ensure no patron ever noticed it and, therefore, never complained.

It didn't matter. This café would have to do.

Only Amanda would know she'd inadvertently put a Central Perk mug next to the register. The Text said so, and she *had* read some of it. She'd added a few props from *Friends*—so what? Pulling tchotchkes from her memory was harder than she'd thought, and in fairness to herself, she hadn't been to Lyla's since before Ethan was born.

Ethan was an excellent napper, but only when she was on the move. Put him in his crib, and no nap for him, no nap for you. It wasn't a unique problem to have. A child's ability to take a nap was a mommy small-talk staple. You rolled your kid to the coffee shop two miles away just to get him to sleep, then spent a fair amount of time bragging about how easy it'd been to put your child down to the other mothers that you'd only met because of having to walk so damn far.

A year into motherhood, Amanda knew a dozen routes of an hour or more. Snaking mazes that were miles long and charted to provide healthy stimuli, all with the same finish line: adjoining neighborhoods that'd lost the keep Brooklyn *Brooklyn* battle.

Locally owned java joints were some of the biggest casualties, but coffee is a convenience drug, and residents fell in line quickly. Her own capitulation to chain cafés of no note had been a necessity. The desire for healthy, healing sleep for your child was on par with the importance of hydration.

It was like the planet had gone Mad Max way ahead of schedule. Sleep and water. Only after those two topics were exhausted did one maybe move on to a conversation about future schooling. In a blink, neighborhood gossip had been neatly replaced with napping secret hearsay.

A month before they boarded that stupid flight, Amanda had asked her mother if sleep, water, and school were the topics she and her friends had talked about in her days as a mom.

"First off, we drank Taster's Choice. At home. And we drank it alone," her mother had answered.

The choice for taste . . . is Taster's Choice.

That tagline had lain in wait in Amanda's brain for some twenty years to resurface.

"Did you sleep a lot? Hell no," Debbie continued. "And yes, of course you drank water. From the tap. From a hose. These days, you lot have your babies connected to H^2O as if hydrating your child is the most heavily weighted category in some mother-of-the-year pageant."

Given her mother's recent mental lapses, Amanda was caught off guard by her quick responses. It was a welcome diatribe, so she decided to sit back and let her mother roll with it.

"Does Ethan pee all the time? How many diapers are you and Tag going through in a week? Aren't landfills of some importance to you and your generation? And if you are one of these couples who are diaper-free potty training, I don't want to hear about it. Do you remember Charlene? They used to host the Fourth of July block party—it doesn't matter. She was over at her daughter's home the other day, and the poor ol' gal spent more time cleaning up her granddaughter's piss and shit from the hardwoods than she did playing with the child. Don't think that's going to be me, by the way. I'm a grand*mother*, not a grand-janitor."

Amanda missed her mother and hoped her mom missed her, too, but she'd had no luck in gauging if she did just by studying her mother's vacant face in Prior Plane. Not every observation Amanda had taken was to see her son. She had gone to see her mother and had to admit, Tag had been right. Debbie and her father, Frank, would have made horrible legal guardians.

* * *

Amanda knew her mother couldn't hear her or see her or supposedly sense her, but during her last observation of Debbie, she'd told her mother what it was she hoped to pull off. "I'm going to bring Ethan home," she'd said. There'd been no point in beating around the bush.

Her mother's body was frail now. She'd always been petite, but at this point, it looked like a stiff wind might carry Debbie over a road as easily as it would with a tumbleweed. The mental decline was more evident than it'd been before the crash. She used very few words when speaking to Frank, who only came to their bedroom to feed her, to change her, to haul her to doctor's appointments, or to sleep next to her—but only on some evenings.

There were occasions when Amanda had seen her father come into the room just to cry, but her mother knew no difference. When Frank wasn't doing those things, he was glued to Fox News as if the answers to his prayers—prayers he made before bed—were hidden in the TV.

"Can you hear me, Momma? You'd have done the same, right?"

Debbie's eyes remained closed, and her fingers, pinky or otherwise, didn't quiver or move when Amanda asked the question, like you see with a patient in the movies. No resident or mentor in Second Plane seemed to truly understand her grief. This was an opportunity to unload—maybe even talk herself out of murdering Ethan. Before she could think better of it, the torment she'd hidden, a good deal of it even from Tag, spilled over her mother's sickbed.

"I can't be without him. Yes, you outlived me—but it's not the same. Not because you're sick, Momma. Please don't think I mean it like that. I suppose you'll see when you get here. If I haven't succeeded, we can go visit Ethan together. Oh, it's so painful, Momma. I can't bear it."

Amanda sat in the folding chair Frank kept next to the bed and placed her hand over her mother's.

"Where I live now, they want me to stop seeing Ethan. They don't say it that way, but it's what they want. And Tag . . . well, I know you always adored him, and I still love him—I do—but the feelings I had and maybe still have for him are of no use."

In the past, any time Amanda spoke negatively about Tag, her mother tended to disregard it. It bothered Amanda, but only a little bit, because a lot of what she complained about had been as trivial as her mother said. As if almost in an effort to finally get her mother to side with her—to side with her on going after Ethan—Amanda blurted, "He cheated on me, you know."

It felt ugly to have said it for the reasons she'd said it, but also freeing.

"Jesus. By the way, there isn't one—a Jesus, I mean. Not like people think, anyway. I didn't realize how much I needed you to know."

Her father coughed in the other room, and it startled her. For a moment, Amanda had forgotten she wasn't physically there with her mother. Remembering that she was just an apparition only intensified the heat in her gut, which she no longer had. She screamed with everything she could—releasing a sound both violent and thick with despair. If she'd been present in Prior Plane, the moan alone might have been enough to have her committed.

Second Plane would claim her back soon. With her mother, she had nothing to lose.

"Have they even bothered to bring Ethan to see you since taking him in? Or to visit with Dad? I suppose it's possible, but I haven't witnessed it, and I'm down here a lot."

Three photographs were scotch-taped to her mother's antique vanity table mirror. Amanda moved closer to see who or what was in the pictures. The first was of twenty-something Debbie and Frank, a classic or maybe tired pose of her mom shoving their wedding cake into Frank's face. The second was of baby Ethan sitting behind a cake decorated to look like a UFO that Amanda made to celebrate three months. She'd even crafted Martians using icing and jumbo marshmallows that she'd carefully tucked into the silver frosting on one side. Ethan was smiling back then, but not on demand—but in this photo his toothless little grin was huge. The last photo was of a group shot taken at the end of the fiftieth birthday party Dad threw for Mom. Half a decade of life was a huge milestone, but it still struck Amanda as odd that her mother had selected that one for the mirror. Maybe her mother had picked it because it'd reminded her of who she'd been once: attractive, active, and living a life where she could count on being surrounded by family and friends. There were at least twenty adults and five kids in the photograph. Given the distance the photographer had to stand at to fit all the revelers into the shot, the faces were small, but one stood out: Amanda's best friend, Vicki.

Tag never told her who it was that he'd slept with while out of town on business, not forty miles from her hometown. And, of course, Vicki had sworn up and down that it wasn't her—but Amanda had never stopped believing that her best friend, a forever flirt who always laid it on thick anytime she and Tag went to visit her parents, was exactly who he'd fucked.

"I'll be honest with you," she said as she turned back toward her mother. "I don't think you have much time left here."

She tried to get closer to her mother, but Second Plane was pulling hard now. She finished her thought as her parents' bedroom started to fall apart, becoming fuzzy and dark.

"Once you go, it's a good bet Dad will pass in the months after. You have always been everything to him. I'm not looking for permission—but if you can hear me at all, I want you to think about how magical it'll be when it's you, Dad, me, and Ethan. Love you, Momma."

* * *

Amanda didn't want to keep thinking about her mother. She hadn't built the coffee shop, or three-quarters of a coffee shop, to sit in it alone on a shit chair, thinking about Debbie. She wasn't sure she wanted to keep thinking about Ethan either.

As Tag had suggested in week one, it would be a lot easier if, when they'd arrived, their memories had been erased in advance, leaving no traces of whom they had known, what they had accumulated, or how they'd lived. As it was, ignorance about your life in Prior Plane was something a resident had to work for.

In her opinion, the suggestions in The Text and those made by mentors were trying to engineer complete and total ignorance, sometimes affectionately referred to as bliss. A beautiful little fool. *That's the best thing a girl can be in this world, a beautiful little fool.* The same might be true in Second Plane, too. Her mom loved *The Great Gatsby*.

Hadn't she decided to stop thinking about Mom?

Where was Gabriel? Her patience was running thin, but Gabriel knew something.

It's about your son, Ethan. His invitation to connect rang in her head.

Admittedly, it was not a lot to go on. She'd never met Gabriel before, but no other stranger had ever reached out to speak about Ethan. In fact, by then, Amanda's connection invitations to other residents had gone unanswered. She imagined she had gained quite a reputation, tainted by her asking questions that made most residents there uncomfortable. Now, she hoped her infamy might work in her favor.

No more rumors, just truth.

No more innuendo, but facts.

A legitimate way to affect the living was what she was after. Did Gabriel know how to do that? She couldn't say for sure, but starting a conversation angry could screw things up royally.

They'd never met, but his tardiness was already a massive strike.

To calm herself, she turned to the damn porcelain cat with its too-long tail about to get squashed under the rocker being piloted by the old lady with her piggy-little nose buried in her damn book. "Our spot" exploded into her thinking and threatened to never let go.

Our spot.

Our spot.

Our spot.

The coffee shop she'd created had a purpose. The music was cheery, the oversized pastries behind the curved glass were cooperatively amusing, and though it was entirely unpeopled, it was a decent representation of a *very* public place. It was the kind of location where a person could agree to meet someone else to spill their dark secrets. Secrets pack less punch simply for having been spoken in parallel to an all-piano cover of "Smells Like Teen Spirit." Amanda wanted to discuss an unthinkable thing: possession. But even something as sinister as that would lose a bit of gravitas when uttered under commercial fluorescents.

Connecting with residents rarely includes any sense of the passage of time.

The Text was utter bullshit. Gabriel was tardy and no clock was needed to know it.

Amanda was irate, but couldn't decide if it was at the stranger or at herself for just how desperate she'd become. Yes, she'd heard rumors of possession, and yes, Gabriel had ominously reached out about her son—*but this?* she thought while surveying the whole of her creation. This connection no longer qualified as a hunch. At best, it was a broken woman, grasping at straws.

She stood, then walked behind the counter. The whole idea of concocting a "safe space" to learn about something strictly forbidden was suddenly laughable. If she was going to vanish her hard work, she figured she should at least *grasp* one of the cinnamon rolls she'd made first. She reached into the display and grabbed the confection, then put the surprisingly gooey edge of it to her mouth as if a bite was a possibility.

Then, the music stopped. She hadn't done that, had she?

She heard the same tiny ding the little bell over Lyla's door always made when a customer entered the café. It was a damn good replica, after all.

"Interesting place to meet," it said.

Gabriel was an "it." Unequivocally.

Its mouth was vertical. The black lips that defined the orifice ran from the being's chin, past where a nose should be, over its forehead, and stopped a few inches past where the average high hairline starts.

"I hope this café doesn't hold some special significance for you," it said. "It's dreadfully mundane if it does, no offense."

The rows of teeth, one set behind another with a third set behind those, made it difficult to find offense amongst the scattering of more easily identifiable emotions Amanda felt. She reminded herself that whatever Gabriel presented as wasn't something she had to agree to see. She worked quickly to think up an alternative skin for it and didn't need to hear its hyena laugh to know that seeing *it* as anything but what it was had failed.

The beast's eyes were placed at the furthest edges of its head. There were two quarter-sized pits on either side of its mouth that might have been nostrils, but it was hard to tell. Its scarlet skin seemed to crawl, shifting the shapes on its facial anatomy as it did. The head holding together the whole mess of its face—huge and unyielding—reminded her of the prize watermelon she'd stepped to once at a county fair with her folks. All of that head looked like it might teeter right off its shoulders, which, in their own right, might have belonged to a hairless gorilla. But it stopped laughing, and its head stayed put.

"I'll take a latte," it said before putting its belly to the glass cases between them. "Do you do an iced version?"

"You can see it?" Amanda asked. "The coffee shop?"

She was surprised at how that realization squashed all her previous fear.

"Is that so unbelievable?" it asked.

Its voice was ever-shifting, too. Even when it had laughed at her for trying to wish its image away, the sound started male, gave way to something animal, then gave way to female, then turned into a child's giggle before settling into something unrecognizable altogether.

"I didn't think—"

"No, you didn't," it said as it moved away from the counter and eyed an open table Amanda hadn't made. "I was kidding about the latte. Come sit with me."

She found herself seated. Now she was close enough to feel its breath. Was that possible? It smelled like rotting fish one second and a pungent red wine the next. Amanda tried not to inhale, but again, was that even possible?

"For me to see what you've made for yourself to see is as easy as me simply deciding it is so," Gabriel said. "They're lying, you knew that. We wouldn't be meeting otherwise."

She thought she understood, but apparently, Gabriel didn't.

"It's like being a good listener. That's a relatively easy thing to be, wouldn't you say?"

Its tone bordered on mansplaining.

"You listen—listen without doing any thinking of your own—and you get to hear what it was that someone said," Gabriel told her.

No . . . beast-splaining, Amanda thought for a moment, while containing her smile.

"Anyone can do it, Amanda. Nothing magical about it. And yet, there weren't many good listeners where you were before, were there?"

"No. No one listens to anyone," she answered.

True or not, it was what Gabriel wanted to hear. "Exactly, and residency here doesn't grant you anything. It doesn't transform the selfish into the unselfish. Like in the land of the living, you have to work to change. There are not a lot of good listeners in Prior Plane, and so there are not a lot of good listeners here."

"I'm a good listener," Amanda said.

"We'll see."

To her relief, she no longer feared Gabriel. She'd come to think of it as some Key West tattoo artist's idea of a demon. Whatever it'd come here to share with her would've been much scarier if it'd presented as the human it'd been on Prior Plane. Regular people, cloaked in human skin, said the scariest shit—Bundy, Gacy, Holmes, ER doctors—that had always been true. Discussing possession should've been all the theater Gabriel needed, and yet—

Maybe it or he or she wasn't from Prior Plane . . . or *her* Prior Plane.

She decided she didn't care. She was there for answers.

Its tongue exited its mouth. It was neon Crayola green and ran across its black gums.

Did it intend to eat her?

Anything was possible—at least, it had seemed to be suggesting as much.

"Look, it doesn't take magic to see what you are seeing. The Text says something about one resident not seeing what another resident is visualizing, right?"

Her irritation with its pace burned, but she nodded.

"What The Text is really saying is that most residents can't be bothered with listening. Good listeners can't be made. Bad listeners can always be worse listeners. What the council is ham-fistedly communicating through The Text is that they believe most residents can't be bothered with seeing—seeing what's right in front of them. So, why not help residents see less, and then less, and then less still, until all a resident *can* see is nothing."

She understood the gist, but was it fucking with her? The eyes on its head, which had moved inward across its face and toward its mouth while it was talking, looked almost delighted by her confusion. Or maybe all the voices it used had her feeling like it was some cosmic prank.

"The text wants you to be a beautiful little fool. It's the best thing you can be in this world, right? A beautiful little fool."

The beast had her attention now.

Gabriel smiled the kind of smile a person typically saves for a friend that they've finally realized is dumb by definition. The slight was vertical, but Amanda knew the condolence well.

Before she could respond, it turned away to take in more of the novelties around the room. Gabriel seemed to be enjoying the collection, but then its stare stopped and lingered on the print in a small frame on a floating shelf to the left of an espresso-less espresso machine.

Coffee. Because Adulting Is Hard!!!

"Not sure I'd have gone with the three exclamation points, but you do you, Amanda."

"This isn't the coffee shop I used to—"

"Why are we meeting?" it asked, dropping the small-talk rhythm. "Why have you summoned me?"

"I didn't summon you, you invited *me* to connect."

It let her in on its joke with a wink, and God, it was awful to see. She smiled to placate it.

"Why did you decide to accept my invitation?" it asked.

"If I told you, you'd think I was bonkers," she said, twirling a finger next to her head.

"Bonkers? My favorite people are. Maybe I'm counting on it. Try me."

"I don't know what it was exactly about your invitation. Accepting it was a gut-feeling."

It had seemed impossible earlier, but its black eyes somehow lit up. "We all *know* things. Despite the systems created to destroy it, here or in Prior Plane, instinct isn't extinct. Not yet."

"I'm talking about things that can help me."
"Help you do what?"
"Bring my son here."
"Your son?"
"Yes. His name is Ethan."
"And how old is Ethan?" it asked.

Amanda leaned back and crossed her arms. "You already know, don't you? He'll be four in a couple of months." She'd been in Second Plane for the better part of an Earthly year, and still she had not managed to reunite with her son, not in any meaningful way.

"You bring Ethan here, and he'll be twenty-five instantly. He'll be a man. Age acceleration. Happens all the time. And the man he'll be when he arrives won't be anything like the baby or the toddler or the *silly boy* you think you remember."

"That's what I've heard," she said with her best stone-faced expression, hopefully denying Gabriel the pleasure it surely wanted when it'd dropped her endearment for her son.

She'd called Ethan "Silly Boy" so often in Prior Plane and didn't even particularly like it. The two words had come on like an unshakeable tic. Ethan didn't have comedic timing or a robust vocabulary, or any idea what was or wasn't a pun. His slapstick was rarely intentional, and he could be the sourest grape she'd ever met. Even so, no human being made her laugh like her son, and no being ever would again. That belief was unbendable. He *was* a silly boy; he *is* a silly boy. Her silly boy. Gabriel's use of the pet name had her façade flickering from anger.

"I'm guessing you don't believe in age-acceleration, Amanda."

"No, Tag does, but it's too absurd—even for this place."

The mention of Tag's name stopped Gabriel's eyes from moving about its face, a first since its arrival. "Does your husband know you're here?" Its tone flirted with concern, but legitimate or not, Gabriel didn't wait for Amanda to answer. "Let me guess: the gutless type."

"No. He and I . . ." She paused because it was plain to see that all Gabriel had wanted was a laugh. "Gutless," she got it now—all residents were, technically, but its blithe disregard for her situation only angered Amanda more. Its rows of teeth chattered, but she refused to play along.

"Fine. *You* don't believe in age-acceleration," it said. "What proof do you have?"

She managed to still her visage. "There are liars here. It's fair to assume there are lies."

"And *how* do you know that?"

"I've told my own."

"Mind if I ask what lie you told?"

She laughed. "I wish it were only one."

It didn't laugh or smile back and instead held its eyes still on her for the second time. When it stared at her in this way, as it was then, the more playful, cartoonish aspects of its appearance did less well at hiding its menace, like a pufferfish, still ludicrous but deadly lethal.

"I told my first mentor I wasn't going to kill my son," she said.

"That hardly counts. Rebecca wouldn't have believed you even if you had kept on insisting that you were going to kill him. She would have chalked it up to a reverse bereavement of sorts that's common here, even if the feelings it brings on are only echoes, as they say." Gabriel paused, sizing her up in the most obvious way possible. "Then again, I suppose a lie is a lie so long as you know it to be," it said. "But you telling a fib isn't definitive proof that children exist here."

"No, I guess it's not."

"So, I'll ask again: what proof do you have that the council and The Text are lying about how a child's arrival here is handled?"

"I've heard them."

"Bingo," Gabriel said.

It slammed its hulking fist onto the table between them. When it did, the coffee shop around them started to sink into the nothing underneath it. Every mug, every spoon, the photographs and kitsch, all the memories of one place or as many as seven, every last detail along with the building's structure was ripped toward a ground that didn't really exist either.

After the rumble of the shop's destruction faded away, it was just her and it, floating, existing, hearing nothing of each other and hearing nothing else at all until other residents and their noises started to filter in from every direction—the laughter of children.

The laughter alone wasn't enough to make Amanda a believer, but one by one, other residents appeared, many with children in tow. She could not stop her smile, in fact, it felt as if it'd grown cartoonishly large. Gabriel put a finger at each corner and squeezed her mouth back to proportion. She slapped at its hands, connected, but it only laughed again, this time like a gull.

By now, a dozen or more children were running through the chaos of nothing, smiling and shouting, playing and screaming, and ignoring the pleas any adult made to "Take it easy," "Slow down a bit," or "Get over here, right now."

She was crying, and nothing and everything made sense at once. Better sense, anyway.

She hadn't been wrong. She hadn't been crazy.

"No, you aren't crazy. You decided to listen. Really listen," Gabriel said. "You decided to see. *Really* see."

It could read her thoughts. The beast's grin turned itself nearly ninety degrees, tickled with itself for its trick. That it could read her thoughts was less startling than how close it'd come to dangerously swallowing its own eyes. It felt necessary to thank it, so she did.

"Thank you," she said. Saying it felt genuine but uncomfortable after the fact.

Child residents carried on around them, and the swell of emotion inside her, one that must've been mimicking a confidence she once knew if The Text were to be believed, was liable to burst the chest she no longer technically had. It'd come to help her. She'd passed its test.

"Do you know how I can bring Ethan here?"

It didn't answer aloud, but she knew. She couldn't say if the blueprint had been hers all along or if the beast had implanted the details in her thinking to save itself some time. There was a way to bring Ethan home. *Possession.* Not a rumor, but a method. Not just the type of human receptive to possession, but the actual mechanics behind inhabiting the body of a troubled soul. Gabriel scoffed aloud and with emphasis as if it was put off by watching her sudden how-to realization materialize.

"There's a lot of fuck around and find out in Second Plane," it said. "The Life After Death? Death for the dead? The Third Plane.

I'm sure you've heard the whispers. It won't suit you. The council's punishment for possession is not detailed in The Text, and why would it be?"

It was already wandering through the crowd, its back turned, and disinterested in anything else Amanda might have to say. "Think on it," Gabriel said as it left. "I'll be in touch again soon. Maybe even with a candidate for you." As it faded into the nothing beyond the growing scene of parks and playgrounds, ice cream shops, and carousels, it shouted a warning.

"And hey, if you love Ethan—I mean, love-love-love your Silly Boy—you'll keep this new skill I've shared theoretical. For your own good. For Tag's, too . . . if that matters anymore."

THE TEXT | SECTION TWELVE

THE FREE WILL YOU ONLY THOUGHT YOU HAD.

Reading the title of this section probably stings. SORRY! Or maybe you are reading this section only after implementing The Text's suggestions and are feeling no emotion at all. If so, CONGRATS!

If not, TRY AGAIN.

Free will in Prior Plane was only as good as the immediate world around you, which we can all agree was luck of the draw. In the life you once lived, no one chose to be poor. No one chose to be a racist. No one chose to live in a big city or hunker down in a cabin in the woods. You were born into a world where even if you had a parent who performed their responsibilities with the lightest touch imaginable, it still left an indelible impression that affected every decision you ever made before becoming a resident here.

DON'T TURN THE PAGE OR GO CROSSLY LOOKING FOR MANAGEMENT. Sit with the notion that free will, as you knew it, came with strings.

It's also possible you arrived here as a firm believer in fate, destiny, or divine providence. The realization, slow or otherwise, that no such thing exists—that all the Gods of Prior Plane don't exist—must have delivered a sting of its own.

Free will *is* free will here. No strings. No nurture versus nature. A blank slate, but only if you do the work to wipe it clean. With time, with practice, with dedication, you can finally manifest the outcomes you once sought.

13
TAG

Everyone thinks they can refinish a tabletop until they've refinished their first. In a fit of impatience, Tag had started on their dining table just days before Ethan was due, then rushed the project to ensure the mess in the kitchen no longer existed when they brought their baby home. The ta-da moment he'd planned for it had been a dud, too. Amanda wasn't cruel in her critique of the piece but suggested he give it another go after they settled into being first-time parents. The memory was laughable, but in the year they had it, they'd come to love the monstrosity.

Tag was connecting with Amanda soon and had recreated that table for the occasion. A thick cut of pine, stained at least three times in its life, mounted to stainless-steel legs custom-made by a friend. This version lacked the textured detail of the original slab, but there were enough nicks and dents for it to pass in a squint. It had the tiny hollows that swallowed the big-dream schemes they once shared over it. No doubt the desires the table had overheard dated back decades, well before theirs, and it was a good bet it had heard its fair share of disagreements, too.

He ran his hands over his recreation as he waited for Amanda to arrive.

No one here could see it, but if they could, the table would be little more than an uninventive place to hang out. But for Tag, the piece was an anchor to a past he needed to remember: one where Amanda was a doting mother incapable of wishing ill on their son.

He hadn't seen his estranged wife since their very last visit to see Ethan. A year maybe, as defined in Prior Plane. It could've been ten years, but the only way to know would be to observe again—something he hadn't done in, well, who could say? He decided on a month. Maybe this time, it'd stick. By the same inventive math, he'd been dead for well over a year and still had no clue what awaited residents who committed to an existence free of objects, desires, and images they'd once known. The Text called it zeroing out. Conjuring an old kitchen table this deep into residency was a good indication his commitment was lacking.

His mentor hadn't completely zeroed out his past, either. Tag wondered if anyone could. He'd asked Donovan how lengthy a resident's removal from living needed to be for it to happen naturally, and all he offered was, "They say it's different for everyone." Wishy-washy old fuck.

When Amanda reached out, she hadn't offered specifics. She wasn't coming to tell him she'd zeroed out. Whatever her news, Tag didn't think it'd be the good kind.

Ethan's old high chair appeared at his left. Conjuring his son's seat was inadvertent, a byproduct of straining hard to ensure the best kitchen table recreation possible. Amanda wouldn't see the high chair there any more than she'd be able to make out the table he was using as a security blanket. As her dark energy filled the molecules around him, he decided to leave it.

"Our kitchen table," Amanda said, arriving unseen.

He pulled his hands off the slab as quickly as if he'd burned them on the stove. As her façade formed on the other side of the table, Tag made out her fingers running along its top. He wondered if the flat position of his palms over the table had been hint enough for a lucky guess.

"You can see the table?" he asked.

"Very detailed, Tag. Like you'd been to Prior Plane to see it just yesterday."

"I don't observe anymore," he said when she was fully formed. "Haven't been for a while."

"Oh, please. That hint of pride I'm catching from you is on par with a teenage boy who's gone a whole week without masturbating. It's simply not as impressive as you think." She strolled toward him, keeping one finger on the exact edge of the table the entire time. "You did a lovely job. Of recreating it, I mean. Every bit as heinous as I remember."

The absence of a chair had left him standing before her. The electricity in the air between them surged, but Tag had committed to civility. He emptied his form of anger, causing the space between their chests to further pop and hiss. This wasn't a feeling mimicking ire, but real anger, even if The Text said that Prior Plane anger wasn't a possibility. Then again, Amanda wasn't supposed to be able to see what he was seeing either—The Text said that, too.

"Go ahead, conjure something else. I'll wait," Amanda said, then crossed her arms.

Tag conjured a new piece between them.

Amanda tsked. "Ethan's crib was birch, but white oak will do."

Tag let the crib, the high chair, and the table go. He was unsettled but held his ground.

Amanda smiled, then said, "Speaking of Ethan—"

"How are you seeing what I'm seeing?" he asked.

"That's a fair question," Amanda said. "Let's sit, and I'll answer it."

"Sit where?"

"You tell me," she said. She looked to her right.

Tag followed her line of sight. He saw nothing.

"See what's in front of you, honey. See me."

The first indications of a shape materialized. He didn't need the leather or its color to know it was their old couch. A couch they'd given to a friend for free before Ethan's arrival. It was a high-dollar Italian original that made little sense with kids around. As stuffing and cushions filled in the frame, Tag walked toward it. Masterful, certainly better than his work.

"Your face right now—is that supposed to be impressed or livid?" she asked.

"Neither."

"But you can see the couch."

He nodded.

"And yet you still believe The Text's bullshit about not having feelings?" She walked over to the couch, sat, and patted the empty cushion next to her twice. "Come on, you goof. Have a seat. I can't bite." Until she sat, he hadn't realized how much focus he was putting on vanishing the couch. "Don't hurt yourself, Tag. You can see the couch, not set it on fire." He remained standing, which seemed to frustrate Amanda. "If this bit of nothing distorted your worldview, I'm hesitant to start on why I'm here."

She stood and released it. "OK then," she said, "we'll do this rip-the-Band-Aid-off style. Let the record show I was willing to exchange a bit of light chitchat first." She put one hand on each of his shoulders and shook him in celebration. "I know how to do it! Not just know how to do it, I've known how for some time, but now I *can* do it—have been doing it."

Tag didn't have to ask what *it* was. Possession. He never doubted her persistence.

"You don't look excited," she said.

To the best of his ability, he kept his disgust veiled. "You seem too excited."

"It's gross, I know. What kind of mother would kill her son and all that?" she asked, throwing her arms into the air mockingly. "Gabriel told me not to gloat. It . . ." For a split second, she averted her gaze at Tag. It wasn't contrition on her face. No, it was something else. But he hadn't recovered enough from the shock of her glee to say anything logical before she continued. "Your disdain is fair, even if it isn't real here. I won't deny there are complexities, but you haven't sat in the gray area of the deed's morality for the eternity we've been here like I have."

"Gabriel? Is that another mentor?" Tag asked.

"Something like that."

It didn't matter. He needed to focus on changing her mind while she was still there. "Look—for me, it was black and white on day one," Tag said, walking away before she could call him a liar. It hadn't been black and white, but any gray area for him had never stayed long.

An overstuffed chair she'd once used to breastfeed Ethan at a suburban furniture store appeared in front of him. His disgust with the impediment might have been as obvious as the loathing looks he remembered customers giving her that day. The best life possible for her son had always been her priority. A mother's sacrifices are another human's reason for rage. There'd been genuine malice in the eyes of some of the men shopping that day. He'd chalked it up to having taken a field trip outside the walls of their otherwise liberal bastion. But Amanda told him those aggressions happened everywhere, and he'd just never been paying close enough attention.

"When you cheated on me, was that black and white?" Amanda asked. She was in the chair now, and her retort, off-topic or not, drew him out from the memory.

"That was different."

"Was it?" Amanda stood from the chair and it vanished.

Tag started for a horizon. He'd honored the connection with Amanda as required and had stayed long enough to end it if he decided to.

"It isn't possible, anyway," he said.

"You've been led to believe that," Amanda said, without committing to catch up to him.

"So you made a couch I could see," Tag shouted back at her. "That's a far cry from *possession*."

She appeared right next to him.

"Forget the couch," she whispered. "This is bigger than the fucking couch. Jesus."

"Amanda. There are no children here."

Her face soured in frustration. "OK, I stand corrected. Let's go back to the couch for a second. Not for real, just metaphorically."

"OK," he said.

"Until you saw my couch, you *didn't* see my couch—because you didn't want to see it."

"And?"

"We didn't see any kids here because we didn't want to see them. It'd have been too painful to see them. Well, I've seen them. The Text is full of lies."

"I'm having trouble believing that," Tag said. That was a lie, too.

He believed her—just like he always had—but didn't want to sound excited. He must have done a poor job of hiding it because she proceeded to lay it all out for him like she was teaching a 101 on mortality.

"Kids that die with their parents arrive with their parents. It happens more than you'd think. Or more than we would have thought when we were making our own plans around death."

A dark trail of ballast appeared underneath them, a path based on the memory of a park in Morris County, New Jersey, that was once a railroad. They went frequently. If you did it there and back, it was only eight miles, but still worth a day trip from Brooklyn. He finished the creation without much effort, and Amanda took the hint. The crunch was the first new sound.

"Even if I believed you, why would you want to bring a four-year-old here?" he asked.

"Not just any four-year-old. Ethan."

He shook his head. "It's complicated here. I feel more lost now than I did when we arrived."

"That's wonderful news."

"I don't share your optimism," he said, looking away from the only pleasant smile he could remember her making since they'd arrived in Second Plane.

Ducks floated in the wet acres of a nearby pond. The serenity of the scene was off-kilter as there was no grass or land or any other terrain surrounding the body of water. Their quacking was robust, almost as if they were demanding to be seen. Above them, he might have added a few clouds, white puffs tucked here and there amongst the even whiter white of nothing else. Then he saw the first of some birds and the blur of flying insects. They all moved too fast to identify. Plenty to hear now. The echo of other people's steps, the laughter of young couples taking first-date walks, the sound of vendors hawking hot dogs and ice cream. Their carts were scattered amongst tufts of grass hovering in space. The birds grew louder, and then came the barking, dogs running after sticks or balls or other dogs. Some could be seen, while others could only be heard. There was no overall landscape to support the recollections as they materialized.

"Do you remember the video of baby calves being taken from their mothers?" Amanda asked.

A cow was added to the growing insanity of animals and human activity in front of them. Its moos joined a chorus he wasn't sure Amanda was paying attention to. He did remember, though. It was horrific. The panic in the mother cow's eyes was real, and Tag and his family gave up milk the very next day, but what good had that done? It was, like their current situation, perhaps the natural order of things. They were dead, Ethan wasn't. He was in a better place, they were not.

"There is nothing more unnatural in all of existence than forced separation from your offspring," Amanda continued.

The sounds from the sights were deafening, but Amanda's words kept their clarity. He turned up the surrounding volume, but her voice rose with it, as if it was in his head.

"Losing the child you love, even in reverse, is not something you can practice your way out of. That's the part they aren't going to tell us. I don't care how much you follow The Text, your mentor's best advice—I don't care if the council itself pays you a special visit—that feeling of being incomplete, lost, and living as we do without a reason for being . . . it won't go away."

"It sounds like you think I'm not suffering," Tag said. "Or underestimating the impact of our loss."

"You haven't given me much to believe otherwise," she said with a heavy sigh.

"There's nothing to gain by expressing my grief to you."

"I don't think you actually believe that."

"What I believe is that we are two different kinds of crazy," he said. "You want to solve your pain by killing our son. I want to solve my pain by forgetting he ever existed."

The impromptu world he'd created was masterful by now. The path was long and disappeared into rolling hills. Few gaps and holes were left in the scenery, and for the most part, it was the park down the road from where his mother still lived.

Then, the sound of children laughing flared up. They were playing and giggling and having a day of everything they ever wanted. Tag wondered how Ethan would react to this creation, how big he'd smile. He could hear his son say, "Best day ever, Da Da."

"Look at what you've created here," she said, pointing to the playground, then to the beautiful homes tucked amongst the countryside. "Now tell me you still believe we've left Ethan in a better place. Nicole will relapse. Even sober, she's a ticking time bomb. I swear it."

"You don't know that," he said.

She stopped in her tracks. Tag chose to keep going.

"What?" he asked her. "You don't. Last I saw her, she seemed healthy and happy."

"And when was that?" Amanda asked, her face lighting up like she'd just won the lotto. "Taggart Littlefield, I knew you were full of shit that day outside of the pediatrician's office."

He'd been sincere when he told her he was making his Final Goodbye. Although he hadn't delivered it, he'd still felt confident it would be his last visit when he left that day. But staying away forever had proven impossible—but he wasn't about to let her gloat about his failures.

"I'm trying. Can you say the same? Either way, my point stands: Nicole is better."

"I don't have the statistics on first-time sobriety handy, but I'm telling you, it's phony," Amanda said. "She's playing a role. I'm not saying some part of her doesn't love Ethan, but—"

"You are rooting for a friend to fail, Amanda. It's all too much."

She reappeared in front of him. He kept walking, and she returned to his side. "I'm not rooting for her to fail. I'm being realistic. Tell me you'd rather see our son deal with bullying, a relapse by his stepmother, and parents who could never love him the way you and I do. The threat of suffering a horrible death on his way here, rather than something quick and painless, is real. But I could expedite his passage."

He wouldn't admit it, but she had his attention, and his face must have indicated as much.

"You yourself have said how horrible Matthew is with money. They've blown most of what we gave them—rehab isn't cheap. At some point, our boy's heart will be broken, and who will be there to mend it? His new family will always put him last because he isn't blood. We are blood. We can bring him here. I can do it now. We control what he sees here, and eventually, he controls what he sees. It's paradise."

Tag completed the park's unfinished edges and plugged the last remaining holes with grass and other shrubbery. He took one final look. There was nothing left to conjure.

Amanda reached for his hand, and he wanted to hold it. He wanted to hug her, and he wanted to feel that feeling from the last hug the three of them had ever had, the one before they'd boarded their flight. Team Littlefield. The fates had decided to separate them. It was unjust. They had no business pulling them apart. Them or anybody else. Her logic wasn't entirely flawed.

"Why hasn't it been paradise until now?" he asked.

"We haven't wanted it because we were essentially told it couldn't be."

"It can't be that simple," he said as he realized his hand was in Amanda's.

She turned to face him and said, "I think it can be."

Since seeing her last, Tag's feelings for Amanda were uncertain, but he knew for sure right then that he still loved her. They'd never kissed in death. Going back further, he thought about how the sex they'd had after he revealed his affair to her had been awkward and transactional. He had wondered often if, for her, it was a kind of fake-it-until-I-forgive-you style of intercourse. One night, when he'd pushed her too far about where they were at, she basically told him as much.

I'm fucking you because I'm horny, not because I love you. But I do still love you . . . I think.

It was his fault. He understood that and wasn't certain they'd ever come close to finding their way back to the intimacy they'd once had. He hated himself for having ruined them.

The intimacy they once shared—hot, untethered from reality, and soul healing—felt possible again. A kiss here, made as a sort of informal agreement that he agreed with her about what to do with Ethan, might unlock the passion they'd lost. All would be forgiven . . . or at least forgotten. If that were true, Second Plane could be paradise. His son, the wife he loved who loved him back, could be together again—so long as she didn't get caught. He'd forgotten to ask her if she knew about Third Plane and forgot again just as quickly as she leaned toward him.

He aimed his lips for hers, pink and soft. There was a sadness in him as he did, a vague realization that what he was doing was wrong, but then her hand had found his groin. The vibrations it created caught him off-guard, but it was welcome. She was right, The Text knew nothing about feelings. The Text was all lies. Maybe Nicole and Matthew would be better off—

Right before they kissed, that wild buzz of anticipation—no longer dopamine, but maybe even a stronger chemical messenger they'd been told nothing about—emptied abruptly from his being as if it'd been pulverized out with a sledgehammer. Her irises were devoid of color, not clear nor white, but a dark and unsettling gray. Inhuman. At that same moment, while wrapped in her embrace, he felt the charged electricity of the hatred consuming her from within—not for him, but for herself.

Behind her, the aircraft that carried them to their deaths came screaming through the beautiful skies he'd created, crushing half a neighborhood block into a million little blocks and opening a black hole that gobbled up every bit of the paradise he'd created.

Amanda squeezed his hands until he thought they should hurt.

"Stop it," he said. "Amanda, let go of me!"

She pulled him closer to complete the kiss.

"I said stop it. God dammit, I *won't*. I won't kill Ethan for you. Let go! Now!"

And she did. She pulled back from him and ignored the destruction around them. "Don't you love me?" She still had him by the hands. "Don't you love me?" she repeated.

He was still recovering from what she'd asked of him without asking, and though he'd never heard tell of any physical retribution in Second Plane, he was fearful that any answer other than the one she wanted to hear might cause her to do something that *could* hurt him.

"I do. But not enough to hurt Ethan for you."

She held onto him for a moment more. "Coward," she said. Amanda cast his hands back, and they blinked in and out of existence as he recovered his footing.

Then, her body inverted, turning in on itself, but it didn't reveal her brain, lungs, heart, and other organs. She was thick black ooze flowing from jagged bone, and that form disappeared as quickly as it had appeared. She was gone, but the stench of what she'd become before leaving remained—thick and identifiable: feces and rotten meat, in bulk.

He could not go after her.

She would not connect with him again.

He'd not connected with her to win, per se, but it certainly felt like he had lost.

Grief he'd only known as an early resident in Second Plane burned within his existence and grew quickly—a hot red emotion too raw and too crippling to ignore or chalk up to a mimic from his days of living. Who could say that all residents were not just stars in space? There were plenty of them; 2,000 new ones formed every second Tag had once read, and he was now a supernova, burning at one billion degrees. Nothing could be done with that kind of all-encompassing energy other than to release it as a scream. After his wailing had ended, he could not describe himself as hollow or gutted—no, he was something much worse: useless.

She was Death. And for that, he had no solution.

But then he remembered: Amanda hadn't meant to, but she'd given him a name.

Gabriel.

PART II

14

AIDAN

Aidan Schaeffer woke far from his bed. He was standing in the dry goods aisle of a corner market he didn't recognize. His synapses misfired and his legs buckled under the weight he carried above the belt. A complete collapse to the linoleum was halted when his fingers instinctively grabbed for the handrail of a shopping cart parked to his left. He found his balance there long enough to take one deep breath.

The cart was half the size of the ones he used at his suburban superstore, eroding metal instead of bright blue plastic, and held not a single item, top to bottom. He wasn't sure who'd left it here or if it was his, but there was no time to decide as the casters announced a penetrating squeal. His makeshift crutch rolled away, conspiring with his confusion to drop his 185-pound frame headfirst to the floor. He let go just in time. With great strain, he returned his body to a poised posture, at least a posture normal enough to suggest to anyone who might be gawking that he was a legitimate shopper and not there for some nefarious reason.

He regained his balance and checked to make sure he was at least dressed this time.

T-shirt? Check.

Pants? Check.

Shoes? Two out of three would have to do.

The double-sided shelving to his left and right held unfamiliar goods. The store was cramped and dingy, and he could smell the produce rotting an aisle over. The products' names were fuzzy. He squinted into the bright colors of the boxes, bags, and containers. Their shapes, amorphous as they were, were all he had to go on. He had a feeling he was far away from home.

Turning his body in any direction for a thorough investigation was more difficult than it should have been. Without some serious effort to stay in control of his mind and body, he might go dark again. He would be him, but not him at all. The heavy lean on his consciousness felt similar to the sandman's pull. He tilted his head back and went eyes-wide into the fluorescent lights overhead. This episode felt worse than those prior. A short stare into the buzzing bulbs, he thought, wouldn't be enough to keep what had walked his body there at bay.

He knew he hadn't taken something, prescription or otherwise. He'd flushed his stash of Xanax and other benzos last week, but abstinence hadn't made a difference. Whatever this was had moved his body to where it stood and wasn't ready to release him. The empty basket suggested this presence inside of him wasn't there to shop. He fought to keep his eyes open to the light as that inner force tried to pull his chin back to his chest using his own muscles.

"Cut that shit out," he said. "I mean it."

His threat had little effect. The weight of his arms was unbearable and his legs ached. It was as if he wore an invisible, soaking wet greatcoat. He tried to step left, right, forward, or back, but had yet to gain enough control of his body to move from where he stood. The odds of making it out of the bodega of his own accord seemed slim. Aidan decided on a plan of sit-still-and-see, and he forced his eyelids as wide as they would go, keeping his eyes glued to the lights above. The sting of amassing tears might help free him from his captor. It was worth a shot.

"Just try it, fucker. I'm on to you."

A squat man with gray tufts of hair above each ear rounded the endcap of the aisle in time to hear Aidan's dare. From the corner of his eye, Aidan watched as the coward backpedaled, which was a relief.

Aidan didn't want any help, for one thing, but more importantly, he hadn't been entirely sure he was even speaking out loud. That was progress and a reason to smile.

This was the seventh time in three months that Aidan had awoken in a location he hadn't consciously chosen. He thought about the drugs again. He only ever dosed himself with anxiety medications when he was hunting or entertaining himself at home with the most recent victim. The last time one of these loss-of-control episodes hit him, he'd been pretty high. Luckily, he'd already gutted the slut locked in his basement before the thing inside him had taken control.

One near fuck-up was enough, and Aidan hadn't hunted since and had stayed off everything, even caffeine. It was unequivocally not the drugs. He knew that now.

He wasn't actively stalking anyone and had no reason to be in the city.

Weeks ago, maybe after the fourth episode, he had spent some time speculating—hell, go ahead and call it daydreaming—that his sleepwalking fits were part of some cat-and-mouse-like game being perpetrated against him by a victim's friend or family. He wanted the daydream to be true, desperately, but it was a long shot any pimp had somehow picked up mind control.

This time was the first he'd woken up somewhere public. His head was cocked back and his unblinking eyes watered under the lights. He lowered his gaze just long enough to pick up the monotony of brownstone buildings outside the store window—he might have guessed the Upper West Side of Manhattan, but right before he put his eyes back on the light fixtures, he saw a sign that read North Slope Vet. Whatever it was had taken his body to Brooklyn, and that extra distance—even with the ease of public transportation—only made the feat more impressive.

The thrill of waking from these hazes to find himself elsewhere was novel at first, maybe even promising. He'd heard no voices in his head, but maybe being moved about without consent was a precursor of some sort. He wanted to believe he'd been chosen, a vessel for grand carnage, but so far, this thing inside of him appeared to have no plans beyond moving him about. It was no longer exciting, it was a damn inconvenience. It was time to do whatever was necessary to get his life back on track. "Shit or get off the pot," he whispered, unsure if the thing inside heard the taunt. It was worth a try, wasn't it?

Maybe it was a legitimate medical problem: blackouts occurring as a byproduct of a guilty conscience. But that wasn't possible, really. He'd never felt guilty. Like his hero before him, Aidan felt sorry for anyone who could feel guilty, though he doubted he or Ted Bundy had ever truly experienced genuine pity for anyone. Empathy was a prison. He knew that.

Maybe his impatience was irrational. A grand reveal at the end of this wild psychosis could be right around the corner. This wasn't the vacant lots at midnight he'd come to in before. There were people in the store with him. Whatever had dragged him to Park Slope might have business to conduct there. But with whom? And why? And even if it did, he couldn't be sure he'd be mentally present to witness it go down. He'd never been a pawn for anyone. But maybe the force, one he couldn't really peg, wasn't anyone at all—something inhuman, magical.

He could sense the pulse of consumer indecision all around him. It was pathetic. No one had any business being an occupant of the establishment for more than five or ten minutes, tops.

"Are you OK?" a woman's voice asked.

"I'm fine," he said without turning his head away from the lights.

"Is there something on the ceiling?"

He didn't need to look at her to know she was his type: a sweet voice and a warm body poking her nose in somebody else's business. She walked into the reflection of the convex safety mirror to his right. She was on the short side, a drugstore blonde with pink and purple streaks. She had a stroller next to her. The kid stuffed into it was too big to be hitching a ride. The woman was fit, but moms were fit if you traveled far enough. His examination had weakened the tenuous grip he held on himself. Time to return to the lights and the lights alone.

"No," he said. "There's nothing on the ceiling."

"I didn't think so," she said. "So . . . you aren't having a stroke, are you?"

"I appreciate your concern, but I'm fine. Really."

He wasn't, though. This interruption had set him back. The thickness of the thing was still on him or in him. He was losing what little control he had taken back. Staring at the lights wasn't the fix-all he thought it'd be. It had worked once before, but it occurred to him that maybe on that occasion, the thing inside of him had its own reason for leaving.

"It's none of my business, but you don't look fine. I'm Nicole, by the way."

Was this idiot extending her hand now too?

"Pleasure," he muttered, without reaching out to shake her hand. His eyes stayed on the fixtures above, leaving her delicate and pale appendage hanging. He'd lose himself again if he did what he wanted, which was to tell her to fuck herself right off. Hell no. The lights were working. Anything more than calm chitchat was too risky.

"I'm just stretching. It's a whole thing," he said. Without thinking, he rocked his head back and forth, extending his neck. "Work accident and well . . . here we are." He went still again just as quickly, hopeful that the movements to sell the ruse hadn't weakened his grip on himself.

"Would it help if I grabbed what you need?" Nicole asked. "Your cart's empty, and you've been standing here for a good five minutes. We popped in for milk . . . and a lollipop."

"Do you like lollipops?" the boy in the stroller asked.

His question left Aidan nauseous. He was losing control. Vibrations rattled every internal organ. He decided it must be a late-blooming biological defect. The harder he tried to prevent himself from vomiting, the more likely it seemed. The brightness of the lights above him dimmed. The hum of the machinery keeping craft beer cold faded. Fine, he decided. The bitch asked for it. That was the last thought he'd make on his own until later that night.

Aidan, as he knew himself, gave in to the sickness, but it didn't come. Instead, his balance was immediately restored. He hadn't found his footing, something else found it for him. He was sturdy on its feet. His chin came down with a snap, and the visual information on the labels all around him crystallized. The brand names he hadn't been able to read were clear.

He thought it might be time to walk away. He wanted to thank the woman and head for the exit, but he couldn't move either leg to take a first step. It was inside him, had control again, but this time, some part of his brain was along for the ride.

His head turned toward the woman and her child. His muscles performed the move, but he was cognizant of the cerebral disconnection from his actions. He was staring at them now.

"He's adorable," Aidan said. "How old?"

It was his voice, but the inflections were too bright to be him.

"Just turned—"

"I'm in my fifth year of living," Ethan said, finishing the answer for Nicole.

Her cheeks flushed, and why wouldn't they? Nicole was a real-life walking-talking billboard for the success rate of rehab and AA according to Tag—a *perfect* mom now.

The thought was sarcastic, flagrantly dismissive, and definitely not Aidan's own.

"Four, he's four. His dad taught him that *year of living* nonsense."

"He doesn't look a thing like you." It was his voice but the tone was catfight ugly.

The woman rolled the stroller back a few inches. Her face didn't wear regret well. Aidan, the Aidan lost inside of his own body, squirmed at the way Nicole's face had contorted her pixie-like features into something vile and rat-like. That was the way it was with women: attractive until they weren't. His rage was always strongest on the heels of the very wrinkles and lines he caused, carving a woman's face from something caring to one full of disappointment and fear. He felt that same adrenaline now and thought he might have closed his right hand into a fist. Was he stumbling back into having control of his body? The next words that left his mouth removed the hope that he might be returning.

"Oh, of course he doesn't," his voice continued. "He's not *yours*, is he?" His body stepped closer. The mother was only an arm's length away. "He's that little boy who survived the horrible crash last year, isn't he?"

The woman didn't answer. Her fingers tightened around the stroller's handle. It seemed like she was staring through him. Did she know he was in there? No. She was looking over his shoulder for help. That made more sense. Maybe there was another shopper behind him or a clerk who might help her, inadvertently helping him.

"My name is Ethan," the boy said proudly, with a hint of playful defiance. His unexpected declaration focused the woman's attention solely on Aidan again and drained the color from her face.

"Yes, his name is Ethan," Nicole repeated, an admission made with shaky resignation.

"Ethan, that's right. Such a beautiful name. Who could forget it?"

"Sooooo," Ethan started, "*do* you like lollipops?"

Aidan felt his head bend unnaturally to address the child. "You bet I do, silly boy."

His voice had shifted to something more songbird than man. The woman pulled her son back another few inches, but Aidan's body made up the new distance with a stiff shuffle.

"What's your favorite flavor?" he asked.

"Strawberry," Ethan said as he held up the red sucker that'd been in his left hand the whole time. "But strawberry wasn't my favorite forever."

"No, it wasn't, was it?" Aidan heard his voice ask. "Your favorite used to be grape!"

"That's right! How did you know?" the child asked earnestly.

"Oh, I remember," his voice said, leaning in closer.

The mother slid her foot backward and into the shelving behind her. She had run out of room to create any more distance. A few boxes of rice and macaroni fell to the floor, but she didn't kneel to clean up the mess. Aidan caught her hand moving slowly into her purse. His body—or whatever was driving it—didn't seem to notice. Pepper spray seemed likely. Hookers never carried it, but it was a sure bet this

Park Slope mommy had worried herself into keeping the deterrent on her. The haves always have, even when it comes to weapons they rarely use.

He heard footsteps at his rear. His body turned, and he had nothing to do with it. A couple had entered the aisle. For now, their eyes were scanning bottled spices, but their proximity seemed to bolster the mother's confidence. "I'm sorry, did you know the Littlefields?" she asked.

Aidan didn't hear himself answer the mother's question. His eyes bounced from Ethan's head to his toes and back again, and he felt his body drop to its knees in a way he was sure had left him hurt. Whatever or whoever was controlling him never took his gaze off the child. From its kneel, Aidan's body moved even closer to the boy, leaving the woman no choice but to violently jerk the stroller back as if she could absorb it and the boy, who giggled all the same.

"Excuse me, I asked you a question," she said, with more heat and her hand still tucked into her bag. "Did you know the Littlefields?"

If he didn't answer, it seemed certain she'd get to spraying or that she'd drag the couple behind him into this mess, but he said nothing. He was silent because the thing controlling him had gone silent within him. A damn odd thing to feel yourself reenter your own skin. His eyes rolled backward in unison with his head before he caught himself and snapped his head forward. He had full control again, though it probably didn't look it to her or the other shoppers.

"Is there a problem here?" the woman behind Aidan asked. "Is this man bothering you?"

He turned to evaluate this new threat, and this time, the decision had been all his.

She wasn't much taller than the mother, but she came off tough. One arm sleeved in tattoos, a fucking cigarette behind one ear. Weren't all the kids vaping these days? But as so often is the case with human presentation, her authority derived mostly from her military posture.

"We're good," Aidan answered before the mother could. The tone of his voice was familiar again, uncaring and monotone, and that wouldn't do either. He adjusted his pitch to swing his words into something bright and neighborly. "I was just leaving. If I frightened you or your little boy, you have my apologies."

The growing tension was lost on the little boy. His hand had never stopped pawing around the interior of the stroller. At that moment, it popped up with a second lollipop that he held out, stretching his little arm as far and high as it could go so that Aidan could have an easy go at grabbing the treat.

"Want one? We have tons," he said. "Take it."

"I'm all good, my man," Aidan declined.

He'd never said "my man" in his life, not once, but it felt like a light punctuation that would end this scene quietly. After forcing a smile, he stood, then backed away from the stroller. His first step to turn toward the door was uncertain, but he had the control he needed to free himself from the store. As he spun to exit, though, the mother grabbed his shoulder, jerking him violently backward and stopping his momentum. Her collar on him was surprisingly solid. She was all mama-bear now, but her hand was no longer in her bag. The clerk behind the counter was tumbleweed thin, eyes squinting into the screen of his phone. A surge of adrenaline forced Aidan into a split-second fantasy, one where his muscle memory had left the mother and the other woman's corpses beaten, bloodied, and split to the guts to rot upon the store's tile floor.

"You never answered me," he heard the mommy say. "Did you? Know the Littlefields?"

He sequestered his rage and managed to say, "Let go of me."

There was nothing neighborly or sing-songy about his tone now.

Behind him, he heard the other woman put the tiny basket from her arm onto the floor. In the convex mirror above, he could see she'd stationed herself as an obstacle to the exit. There are some headaches a barefoot man simply shouldn't deal with, so he slacked his shoulders and let the rest of his muscles go limp, white flagging-it. Still, the mommy kept her grip tight on him.

He struggled to think of a suitable lie. Anything outlandish would increase the odds that she or the woman behind him would remember details about his face, his height, or even that he wasn't wearing shoes. They were already taking him in. Before he could come up with an adequate fib to de-escalate things, she released her hold and repeated the original question.

"How else could you know Ethan's favorite lollipop used to be grape? Were you friends of the family?"

"God no, miss. All that lollipop stuff? Lucky guess," he said as he left the store. "You two ladies have a good evening now."

Any other night I would have killed one of you . . . or both.

15
NICOLE

Nicole stood in the doorway of the hallway bathroom upstairs. It was the third time she'd walked Ethan to the toilet since putting him to bed five minutes before, and that wasn't an exaggeration. He needed to pee again. This was a new wrinkle to his bedtime routine and their pediatrician had said to keep an eye on it, but not to worry either. Who can do both?

She watched her son push his tiny bare thighs into the bowl's rim as if doing so was crucial to emptying his bladder. He strained long after the stream ran dry. It looked painful, but prior attempts at explaining how the sting of an overused genital muscle tricked a person into believing they still had urine to spend had been made in vain. She'd presented the biology lesson casually, trying not to make it a big deal, Ethan feigning understanding expertly. The boy's assurances were all-adult, but none of the urinary how-to ever stuck. He didn't want to wet his bed, and that made good sense. This was his solution, one that only barely beat the annoyance of having to change the sheets in the wee hours.

Even the best parents vilify the child that dares rob them of what precious little me-time they believe they've earned at the end of the day. Nicole was no different, except now she *was* different. She had the tool-kit to deal with mole hills—to deal with all of life's mole hills—and she'd turned very few of them into mountains of late. Thank God for AA. A true miracle.

Her son had accidentally wet the bed a few nights before. It couldn't have been said a year ago, but in this house, that was no big deal. She'd hardened her resolve already and accepted she could not change the possibility that Ethan would ask to use the bathroom one to four more times tonight. This could be over shortly or it could take another hour. Her empathy for him and his situation was real, but the kindness she deployed was the fakest kindness she could imagine.

"I think that's it, don't you?" She thought her question sounded like a Disney princess who'd taken a job as a bartender in a rough part of town: ill-prepared to be ushering antagonistic barflies to the streets without their car keys and home for the night. "There's no more pee-pee in you. I promise."

Ethan pulled up his pajama bottoms and took Nicole's hand.

From the hallway, she heard a movie that Matthew had started without her downstairs. There was a good chance her husband was already asleep. She needed this trip to the bathroom to be the boy's last. If she had to wake her husband when she made it back downstairs, any conversation, let alone the one she hoped to have, would be worthless.

"I feel like I have to go again," Ethan said as she tucked him under his blanket, battening the corners tightly underneath him into something they'd come to call Sleepy Worm Mode.

No parent wants to admit that they've created too complex a ritual for a child to drift peacefully off to sleep, but Worm Mode qualified, and Nicole resented herself for creating it.

"Can I try one more time?"

"No," Nicole snapped. "We're done."

Her sharp departure from the more helpful character she'd played back in the bathroom was startling, but she simply lacked the energy to reprise the role. "You aren't going to wet the bed, Ethan. Believe me." Her final tuck was aggressive, and the boy winced. "Now go to sleep."

Ethan closed his eyes tightly. There was no additional fuss or tears. It broke her heart, but walking back her attack now was an inch she wasn't willing to give. He'd take a mile. Kids always do. The world revolves around them. She had every right to be mad. Ethan didn't care that she needed sleep tonight. A child wouldn't understand the exhaustion she felt for having put off telling Matthew about the incident at the market. And why had she delayed? Because doing so would open a whole new can of worms with him. And this boy in the bed under her nose—it was always give give give. First Emily, and now a four-year-old she hadn't technically agreed to house. Had she ever signed anything? She had three children now, including her husband. How had putting Ethan to bed every single night become her responsibility? Who had made that decision? It certainly wasn't her fuckin—

Ethan coughed lightly as his body found better comfort against a large pillow.

She was alarmed to find herself still in his room. Remnants of her internal tirade echoed in her head as she backed herself to the door. Nicole didn't remember having closed it, but it was shut. She was breathing, but it felt like her whole retreat had been made in the deep end of a pool.

Once safely outside of Ethan's room, she gasped for the first real hit of oxygen she'd had since barking at her son to go to sleep. It was easy enough to pin the spell on frayed nerves. The run-in with the man at the market wasn't nefarious, but she'd been keeping it a secret as though it alone could unravel everything that she'd worked so hard to overcome.

The conversation with the man—or *men*, as she'd come to believe it'd been—had rattled her. She hadn't slept well since the night it'd happened. The rest her body was begging for might be possible by releasing some anxiety she had about the stranger. At least, she hoped that would be the case; she was grade-A beat. "I'm just tired," she assured herself.

At the top of the stairs, she readied herself to share her story with Matthew. Was that him already snoring? Or was she just imagining the sound to create a dead end, one that would send her straight to bed for another fitful sleep? She looked at the time on her phone. Em was at a friend's house for another hour, easy. Plenty of time to talk.

Her thoughts about what had transpired had needed time to define themselves. If she told her husband the man's aura bothered her, he'd dismiss it. If she said the man had given her the creeps, he'd say Brooklyn had a lot of weirdos. If she repeated the exchange verbatim, she was worried he'd imply she'd read too much into it, that she must have been confused, or accuse her of drinking or using again.

Even now, she didn't have the right words to effectively describe what had happened.

How do you tell someone a stranger's face was not their own?

The man at the store must have been two men. She'd watched the stranger's craniofacial muscles making two entirely different sets of expressions. She'd heard two distinct voices coming from the same set of vocal cords. It hadn't been a person struggling with drug problems, it was far different. Nicole had recently started reaching out to those suffering from addiction when she could. This wasn't that, but even if Matthew really listened, he'd chalk it up to that.

She committed to making it to the bottom of the staircase to look into the family room, but Matthew wasn't there. She reached for the TV remote, paused the film, and was surprised to see it had already been playing for over an hour. With the film's soundtrack silenced, the clink of a spoon against a bowl in the kitchen was easy to hear.

"You want some ice cream?" Matthew asked.

"I'm good, thanks."

"Wanna at least come sit in the kitchen and chat?"

"Yeah, that'd be nice. One sec." She stood frozen and unsure of what he might want to chat about. Even in sobriety, moments like this compressed their already too-small-for-four home around her. She'd yet to die from the suffocation, but when that particular type of panic hit, it always felt like death might be a better alternative than pushing through it. After a minute passed, she took her phone out to use as a prop only. If Matthew peeked around the corner to see why "one sec" had turned into five minutes, texting with a friend from the program was a reliable alibi.

She'd rehearsed the words she would use to describe the man, what he'd said to Ethan, how he'd said it, and the effect the whole experience was having on her. "You've got this," she assured herself, but her weak affirmation only gave way to more doubts and possibilities. She thought about how easy it would be for Matthew to claim she'd once been two women too. If he said her use of alcohol and drugs once had a Dr. Jekyll and Mr. Hyde effect on her, she wouldn't be able to argue otherwise. It had. Even if she was able to clearly communicate the phenomenon she'd witnessed, she imagined he'd congratulate her on having the newfound clarity to identify exactly what she'd been: an addict. He'd call that progress and say so patronizingly.

She wished he'd been asleep.

Nicole was just over a year sober and trying her hardest, but Matthew still had trouble behaving as though he were convinced. His version of a supportive partner came with too much worry, too many personal suggestions, and, as she was coming to realize, no knowledge of what would or wouldn't trigger a relapse—and no real desire to pick up that knowledge either.

She was happier in her new health than she'd been since before Emily was Ethan's age. She understood how important it was to communicate her gratitude for that health and happiness with Matthew and the Administration for Children's Services. Playing up her happiness left little room for sharing her unease, if and when she had any. Matthew didn't want to hear about any distresses, or, if he did, she was projecting her own disinterest in all she found discontenting onto her husband.

In the two meetings a week she was able to make, Nicole could only claim a few minutes to share her problems. She worried that raising her hand at every gathering, going on and on any time a meeting's speaker picked her to share, would classify her as something other than well adjusted. After all, she'd made harsh judgments in the rooms after others had behaved the same.

Whiners, not grateful enough, simply not in it to win it.

Matthew wanted her to continue her recovery journey but also wanted her home. It wasn't unfair. He'd held down the fort solo for her six-week stint in rehab, taking care of Em and Ethan, all while under the scrutiny of ACS and the lingering inconvenience of Ethan's celebrity.

During the ninety days after she'd checked out of the facility, he'd never complained. And in those first three months back home, she'd spent half of their daylight hours attending Alcoholics

Anonymous meetings around their borough. It'd been a great foundation for what they both hoped would be a forever recovery.

Few mothers she'd met in the program had been afforded that kind of leeway and space to build a toolkit and learn how to use it to stay clean. But Nicole's good fortune came with a heavy burden of guilt. While sharing in meetings, doing step-work with her sponsor, and outpatient therapy had lessened the load, their positive effect was always short-lived. She needed—

"Are you coming or not, Nic?" Matthew asked. His head poked into the family room to check on her. "Who are you texting?"

Nicole put the phone in her back pocket. "No one," she started. "I mean, I was writing Em, but I changed my mind. I'm trying to get better at giving her the space she needs, too."

It was a damn fine lie. Even better than the one she'd planned— one she'd have to remember. Another tool in the toolkit.

"You're doing great," Matthew said without committing to the family room or the kitchen. "I'm going to walk Pepper and then maybe you want to finish this movie with me?"

He'd unwittingly offered Nicole the chance to procrastinate. If he wanted to walk the dog, he'd be less inclined to give anything she had to say about the stranger's behavior any consideration at all. The easiest thing to do would be to say "yep." Yep would be so simple. Yep meant he'd walk the dog, join her for what remained of the movie, and fall asleep on the couch. Yep meant no hearing him say she was manufacturing anxiety. A practice he'd already suggested was her way of walking back to drugs and alcohol. Yep might mean she could try for some real rest, too, via Sleepytime tea, though it'd never given her an easy lie-down before.

"Earth to Nicole . . . are you hearing me?" he asked. He whistled for Pepper.

"Yep," she said. The concession was easy. "Finishing the movie sounds good."

16

ETHAN

"Children, it's time to pack your things and line up for Miss Natalie."

His teacher's orders never sounded like orders, at least not the ones Ethan heard at home, and that was part of the reason he always wanted to do his best for Miss Gracey. This time was no different. Besides, this task was easier than remembering which side of a plate a fork went on or cutting paper with scissors. He was good at packing—good, but slow because watching the other kids move their things from their cubbies to their backpacks was more fun. He even had less to grab, but being last in line to leave school didn't make him feel sad or mad or cranky.

Mark, Gwendolyn, and his best friend, Lucas, came to class and left the class with stuffed animals all the time, and not always the same ones. That afternoon, a rabbit, a pink dolphin, and a toy that Lucas had called Baby Groot were dancing across the rug while Miss Gracey reminded them, "It's important to focus on readying yourselves to go home. Your parents are waiting."

His classmates brought bigger lunches, too, packed in colorful plastic boxes that made Ethan think of Christmas. His box was not special. Mommy had lots of Tougherware at home. Tougherware was not fun, but he could *see* the peanut butter and jelly sandwiches

Mommy made him before opening the lid. He pretended it was because he had X-ray vision.

The tallest boy at school took a phone out of his backpack and tried very badly to hide it from the teachers with his other hand. Ethan was pretty sure his name was Liam. His class was Pre-K through 1st grade, and the boy was almost six but still not supposed to bring a phone or lots of other things to class. The boy was so bad at hiding the things they weren't allowed to bring, too. He showed it to Ethan like it was a big secret that would get the class in trouble, which was dumb because Ethan thought both teachers knew about the phone. Was it real? It never rang, and he never let him or his friends hold it, so Ethan couldn't be sure.

"It's not for babies."

Liam didn't share lots of his stuff and always called everyone a baby. Ethan hadn't gone to this school very long, but that didn't make him a baby. He knew that. Babies couldn't be "old souls" or "wise beyond their years," things Em and Mommy had often told him he was. He didn't understand what those expressions meant, but he'd yet to meet an old or wise baby himself. Besides, his school was special. Everyone said so. He liked being there, even if going to a private school might turn him into a big snoot like Emily said it would. She went to a school called Public. He'd asked her to explain what big snoot meant, and she did, but he still wasn't happy about maybe growing a giant nose.

It was called Little Thinkers Academy, and his new dad had picked the school a while back when Mommy was on vacation. Ethan had overheard his dad tell his grammy that Miss Gracey was empathetic to their situation and was the only one willing to forego a waiting list. "Good things are finally coming our way," his daddy had said. And Ethan had been very glad to hear it was *good* things that were coming and not the wild kind from his favorite bedtime book.

"Finish packing, Ethan," Miss Gracey said. "Time to join the others."

The older children were already in line, ready to follow Miss Gracey or Miss Natalie to the front door of the brownstone. He had sat down this time, hoping to prove that he could be first in line any time he wanted—really—but he and the two three-year-olds were the only kids still squatting on the room's rug. No time to be sad about it. He stood to race the real babies and not be last in line again. Running was a no-no, but he wanted to beat them a lot. Two steps into it, his Tougherware fell to the floor. His backpack's zipper wasn't zipped. He always forgot to do the zipping part, and the three-year-olds laughed at him as they beat him to the back of the line.

Miss Natalie got on her knees next to him. Ethan thought she must be an adult to be a teacher, but in a lot of ways, Miss Natalie didn't look a lot older than Em. Her nails were fun, just like his sister's nails, each one had its own color, and the colors that she used were different almost every week. Miss Natalie's hair was brown like Em's and in a ponytail, too, just like hers, but Miss Natalie's horse must have been smaller than the one his sister got her tail from.

Miss Natalie smiled as she tucked his Tougherware back into his bag, and it was the way she smiled that reminded Ethan of his sister the most. Em always seemed happy, even when his new mommy and daddy fought or seemed to be in the kind of trouble that he believed adults got into. Miss Natalie's smile was all he needed to not care about being last for a billion times.

"You're all set," she said as she handed him his backpack, which she'd zipped like an expert. "When I was little, I always wanted to leave school last, too, even if I didn't know it."

"I don't like being last," Ethan said. "I'm going to be first tomorrow." He was unsure if that was the truth or if it just felt like the right answer.

"Sometimes being last is when the really good stuff happens, though," she said.

From the back of the line-up, he turned around to see if anything good was happening. "Like what?" he asked.

Miss Natalie's hand disappeared into her pocket and dug around behind the flowers on her dress. It reappeared with a lollipop. She squatted again and held it out for him to grab.

"Don't tell Miss Gracey," Miss Natalie said without letting go of the lollipop. She looked at the front of the line-up, which had already made it to the door. Miss Gracey was busy handing over Mark to his mommy or maybe his grammy, the woman on the stoop who took Mark's hand looked old like Ethan's grammy did. "Candy at school is a big no-no. Miss Gracey *hates* candy." She winked at him and finally released the lollipop. "So, keep it on the down low, OK, Ethan?"

Ethan didn't think he'd be in any *real* trouble if Miss Gracey saw that he had a lollipop. After all, Liam had a whole phone and hadn't gotten into trouble. He decided to be very careful with it anyway and to try to hide it while they waited for Emily to come and pick him up.

"I will," he said. "Ooh, strawberry." He stretched his arm to hold it as low and as close to the floor as he could, hoping the sucker was "down low" enough to impress his teacher.

"Your favorite," Miss Natalie said.

"Thank you, Miss Natalie. Strawberry *is* my favorite."

"You don't say," she said in a manner he thought was meant to poke fun at the fact that he probably said strawberry was his favorite all the time. "You're welcome, Ethan. But wait to eat it on your walk home with your sister, OK?"

He couldn't promise that he would, but he nodded anyway.

A horrible belching noise came from the middle of the line. Miss Gracey ran from the open front door to the middle of the lineup. She reached for a student. It was the boy maybe named Liam, and there was a big puddle of vomit at his feet. His face was scrunched tight, and he looked like he might throw up some more.

His friends who hadn't left yet were screaming, gagging and coughing and squirming like the mess was the biggest case of cooties ever. It was funny, but Ethan also felt sad for the tall boy. Throwing up wasn't fun, and he wondered if what he and his friends were doing was mean. He considered asking his friends to be nicer, but before he could, Miss Gracey shushed them.

His classmates all backed up and away from the throw-up, forming a big circle around it as Miss Gracey pulled the boy away from the group. They passed him and Miss Natalie on the way to the tiny kitchen that was at the back of the school. Ethan could smell the boy's lunch as they whooshed by, eaten bits of it were clinging to the front of his Mandalorian T-shirt. Maybe he's the baby, after all, Ethan thought. That felt mean, too.

"Natalie, take the children up front, away from the mess," Miss Gracey said. Before she and Liam disappeared into the kitchen, she also said, "I'll be back with something to soak it up."

His teacher sounded kind, even in an emergency. Ethan wondered if the boy was going to be alright and was glad he had a nice teacher to help him get better.

Miss Natalie was already moving his friends forward, walking them away from the cheesy puddle of throw-up, one by one, and to the front door, which was still wide open.

His classmates weren't being very cooperative. Each tried to make a bigger deal about Liam's accident than the last. Watching his teacher struggle to keep his friends still as they all went on with their pretend squirming made Ethan sad. The scene and feeling reminded him of a bucket of caught fish that he saw one day while walking by the river with his sister.

He decided he would help Miss Natalie. None of his friends were, and she looked like she could use a hand, though he wasn't sure what it was he could do while not getting in her way.

There was a roll of paper towels on a small table next to the front door, but to grab them, he would have to push his way through his friends, which wouldn't be polite. It seemed like cutting in line, and like the lollipop, cutting in line was a big no-no at the school. Bigger.

Sometimes you've got to break the rules.

Who had said that? New Dad? Grammy? Probably Em. This had to be one of those times.

He tucked his lollipop into his pants pocket. Then, he pushed his way past the other kids. Miss Natalie was busy putting the backpacks that had dropped to the floor back onto the three-year-olds, and she didn't even notice that he had walked from last in line to very first by the door.

The paper towels were a great idea. Ethan couldn't believe that none of his friends had thought to grab them. He felt warm, and his heart was beating faster. This must be pride, he thought. It was a word they'd discussed at school often, but until then, he wasn't sure he'd ever had the feeling for real. If he was going to get in trouble for shoving past his friends to help Miss Natalie, this new feeling was worth it. Standing as tall as he could, he handed Miss Natalie the towels.

"Here," he said. "I want to help."

She took the roll without looking at him or saying thank you. She stood still and stared way over his head. Her eyes looked mean, and Ethan felt in trouble. This wasn't how he pictured the thank you he imagined she was going to give him for finding the paper towels. He thought he should ask if he was in trouble for leaving his place in line, but a man in the doorway spoke first.

"Looks like you could use a hand."

The voice was familiar. Nice-sounding, but also upsetting, like a broken toy almost.

"Please stay outside, Mister . . . uh, I'm sorry, I don't recognize you," Miss Natalie said.

She looked toward the kitchen where Miss Gracey had gone. Ethan could hear Liam still barfing. It looked like Miss Natalie wanted to call out to Miss Gracey, but instead, she turned back around to talk to the man. Ethan turned with her to see the man, too.

"Are you a parent?" she asked.

The first thing Ethan saw was a very large hand on the door knob. He started there and moved his eyes up the length of an arm until his head tilted so far back that he felt like it might roll backward off his neck. Once his eyes adjusted to the sunlight behind the stranger, he saw that it was the man from the store Mommy had taken him to for candy. The man who wanted to know what lollipop was his favorite. The man who knew grape used to be his favorite flavor.

"No, not a parent," he told Miss Natalie. "I'm a friend of Ethan's family."

Miss Natalie looked away from the man and down at Ethan. He hadn't seen her make this face before. Was this what his teacher looked like when she was confused? "Do you know this man, Ethan?"

He didn't know the man, not really, but they had met, and he wasn't sure what to say.

"Kind of," he said. That was the truth. And so long as what he said was the truth, his new mommy told him he could never be in real trouble. "But I don't know his name."

The man shrugged, then smiled at Miss Natalie.
Ethan didn't like his smile. It felt fake. Like the kind he made when he wanted a new toy.

"Kids," the man said. "It's all in one ear and out the other, isn't it?" The man's hand moved to pat Ethan's head, shaking like a bird with a broken wing.

"Sir! Please, do not touch that child."

Miss Natalie's order was loud. She'd never scared Ethan before. Maybe her shout had scared the man he kind of knew, too, because his eyes went squinty like a snake. He dropped his arm suddenly, it hung weird-looking at his side. It seemed like he wanted to raise his arm again, but couldn't. It was the same as at the store, pretending to be a robot. But it wasn't a fun robot.

"Gracey," Miss Natalie called out. "Can you come out here, please? Miss Gracey?"

His teacher did not answer.

"Mr. Williams, I'd like for you to come out here, too. Right away, please."

Ethan hadn't met a Mr. Williams at school. Hadn't heard of him either. He and a few of his friends looked around as if they expected a brand-new teacher to magically appear from thin air. None came. Not the New Mr. Williams and not Miss Gracey, either.

In the back, the sink was running, and Liam was dry-heaving. The rest of the classroom was quiet. Eerie was the word Em used once to describe that kind of quiet.

Ethan looked through the space between the strange man's legs. Other parents were bunched up behind him, further back on the stoop. He didn't see Emily, but she was always late. That was part of the reason he didn't mind being last in the line-up every day. He was about to smile about that, but Miss Natalie's new tone made smiling right then seem like something you'd get in trouble for.

"Children, I want you to form a brand-new line behind me," she said. "Ready. Set. Go!"

His friends ran the short distance it took to stand behind her, but for some reason, Ethan stayed put. He wasn't sure why. The man smelled like a type of soup he thought he would never ever try—even if his new daddy asked him nicely to have a tiny taste. But it was a soup smell. The icky kind that came from cans, but he couldn't take his eyes off the man he kind of knew.

"Don't be a silly boy," the man said to him. "Get in line with your friends. We've got to listen to our teachers. What would it be like here or anywhere else if we didn't follow the rules?"

The parents behind the man seemed grumpy. Muttering about the "hold-up" and asking where their kids were. Ethan's face flushed though he'd done nothing to anger them. He joined his classmates in the new line, mostly to get away from the mean-sounding voices outside and not so much because both the man and Miss Natalie had asked. From his spot in the line, she looked so much bigger than before. Like she had somehow inflated herself to hide him and his friends from the man at the door. Did adults have growth spurts like he did? He didn't think so.

The family friend turned around to look at the other adults on the stoop, whose questions were louder now and all in mad-voices—they were almost yelling. "Sorry, everyone—I'm new at this pick-up thing. I appreciate your patience," he said. Being polite was important, Ethan thought, and the man had been. Even so, he heard a parent ask, "Miss Natalie, do you know this man?" from outside. She and all the parents still sounded very grumpy. Ethan was glad they weren't cross with him. He didn't think being angry could cause a person to fall over, but the stranger grabbed the doorknob again to keep himself standing, it looked like he might tip over.

When the man was steady again, he turned back to Miss Natalie. He raised his hand to rub his face, maybe, but his hand missed his whole head by a lot. His fingers were rubbing the air to the left of his face, it looked weird, and when the man realized it, his arm dropped back to his side again so quickly that Ethan was surprised it didn't yank itself right off the man's body.

"How about this, young lady: I'll head back to the end of the line to let you get your other kids sorted. Unlike the parents bent out of shape behind me, I've got no place to be. When you've finished, we can phone Matthew or Nicole and square this away. Does that sound good?"

Miss Natalie didn't answer the man right away. Maybe she was distracted by the loud noises still coming from the kitchen. Ethan sure was. Poor Liam. Poor Miss Gracey. Still no Mr. Williams, either. The man cleared his throat, which was only a tiny bit louder than the heaving happening in the back. Miss Natalie turned to the man, and though she was quiet and sounded different than Ethan remembered, her answer lifted the man's eyebrows.

"That's a better plan, sure, Mister . . ."

"Schaeffer. Mr. Schaeffer. I'm a family friend." Then he winked at Ethan in a way that felt familiar. Miss Natalie didn't look happy about it. "I'll be back, silly boy. Don't you worry. Got your favorite flavor lollipop, too." And he did. It was a bright red one, twice the size of the one Miss Natalie had given him. "Strawberry!" He waved it in the air as he turned to leave.

Miss Natalie's face looked older now. This only ever happened when she tried to tell Ethan and his classmates the things Miss Gracey told her to tell them. Serious stuff. Quiet-time stuff. *No talking while I'm reading a story* stuff. But this time, that change in her skin stayed.

As the man and his lollipop disappeared behind the crowd of parents on the stoop, Ethan's classmates whined about wanting candy from Mr. Schaeffer, too. It was very rude. This time, Ethan hushed them before Miss Natalie could, but not in a loud way. He didn't want his friends to hate him later. Miss Natalie didn't notice his help. Her face was confused-looking. It reminded him a bit of when Pepper didn't know who to run to if the whole family called for him to come at once. The parents at the door still sounded angry, but why at Miss Natalie? And the kid maybe named Liam's crying in the back was even louder. It was a lot to hear at once.

Miss Natalie grabbed for his hand and it scared him. "Ethan, come up next to me," she said. He did as he was told. "Do you know that man?" she asked. Her grip was tight, but her voice was shaky. Was Miss Natalie afraid, too?

Ethan wondered if he said yes, did that mean she would let him run after the man? The man who had a second lollipop and was a family friend he had not met but had kind of met at the store. The man who knew his favorite flavor used to be grape. If he said yes, would Miss Natalie release him? He didn't think that he would run to the man even if she did. Did she want him to?

Never, ever leave with anyone who isn't me, Matthew, or Nicole—or maybe Lucinda.

That was what Emily had told him. Many times.

There was a woman at the door and in the way of leaving anyway. Ethan was pretty sure it was Gwendolyn's mommy. Her face went funny. Probably the smell of the throw-up that Miss Natalie hadn't cleaned up with the paper towels he'd given her yet. It looked like Gwendolyn's mommy smelled the bad smell, but then her face looked like it might explode from being too red.

"Ms. Natalie, what in heaven's name is going on here? Where's Ms. Gracey?"

Miss Natalie held up a hand. The woman liked that less than the vomit smell.

"It seems like Mr. Schaeffer knows you and your mommy and daddy," Miss Natalie said as she squatted next to Ethan again. "Do you know him?"

He'd never heard her sound so tired, but being a teacher must be tiring, he thought. He usually napped after school. Teaching might be as hard as learning.

Did he know the man, or was he a stranger? He wasn't sure what answer Miss Natalie wanted to hear him say but he wanted to get it right. He liked getting answers right, especially when it was Miss Natalie asking.

But before Ethan could answer Miss Natalie, his sister Emily shouted from behind all the waiting parents. "Jesus Christ, people! What in the hell is taking so long?"

17

NICOLE

The front door opened before Nicole put her key into the lock. Matthew grabbed her hand, pulled her inside their apartment, and shut the door in a hurry.

It was early evening, still a couple of hours from night, but dark enough to notice Matthew had all the lights off. The curtain in the kitchen window had been drawn, too.

As her eyes adjusted, Pepper greeted her with two gentle licks on the hand. The dog was calm, even as Matthew anxiously locked the deadbolts and slid the other hardware into place—like they once did, back when all possible interlopers threatened to walk up, knock, and insist the family had an obligation to speak with the press about Ethan and the crash.

Nicole hadn't missed those days. Life had been so crazy back then, but past troubles, which had been a useful reference for fashioning a better present, had been easier to forget than most people would have believed. Hiding in your home on the regular, specifically.

The dog followed her into the kitchen. There was no "Mommy's home!" from Ethan. Maybe he was upstairs, but there were no thumps or thuds bounding her way. She pulled the closed curtain over the sink aside a bit, just enough to see the basin was suspiciously empty. She opened the dishwasher, Em and Ethan's lunch Tupperware wasn't neatly tucked between its rungs. Their backpacks were missing as well, and those commercial eyesores rarely made it past the countertop without her reminding the kids to stash them in their room.

"Are the kids at the park?" she asked.

Matthew ignored her in favor of peering out the peephole. When had he removed the putty? Could have been months ago, could have been five minutes ago.

"Kids, Mommy's home," she tried.

"They're with Tag's mother," Matthew said. He hadn't bothered to turn around.

Nicole sat at the kitchen table. It was best to let him explain why her children were at Lucinda's on a weekday when he was good and ready. She didn't need to see his face to understand that he was not. His energy was off, and his concern was creeping into her own.

When they'd first met, Nicole fell in love with Matthew for a half-dozen reasons. His calm demeanor was chief among them. He had answers for problems, and his nonchalance about life's obstacles had been intoxicating. He'd been her antithesis; opposites attract and all that. Even now, when her husband didn't know what to do, he carried indecision and uncertainty quietly until he had solutions. Not every fix was the right one, but little blew up in his face, and he didn't lose his shit when it did. No, he went back to the drawing board and did so whistling.

He finally spun away from the door to join her in the kitchen, but even with the curtain pulled, it was still too dark to read his face. His expression rarely contorted itself beyond a configuration one might read as minorly bummed, but as he sat across from her at the kitchen table, she saw he was capable of communicating genuine panic after all.

She thought she might be in trouble. A great deal of time in sobriety had been spent feeling that way, an emotional relic of her life prior, maybe. Her sponsor had suggested that many spouses—even supportive ones—at times force those in recovery into that space of guilt and self-loathing inadvertently, especially those who didn't attend Al-Anon. She also said it was more likely Nicole hadn't forgiven herself completely and was projecting. Matthew still hadn't said shit, though, and her mind raced too fast to give a fuck if she'd done something wrong.

"Are you going to tell me what's going on?" she asked.

He wiped away the concern by rubbing his hand from forehead to chin.

"I'm sure it's nothing, but . . ." There was a quiver in the deep breath he took as he gathered his thoughts. "Gracey phoned before Em and Ethan made it home. She said a man tried to pick up Ethan from school this afternoon."

Her entire respiratory system felt paralyzed. Other than a nauseating intuition that some in the rooms of AA referred to as newly developed spidey senses, there was no reason to think it was the same man from the bodega. She managed to ask, "What man?" and felt she'd only asked it in an attempt to convince herself that the two men being the same man was a stretch.

"He told Natalie his last name was Schaeffer. Called himself a family friend."

"A reporter, maybe?" she asked. "Or some influencer who *thinks* they're a reporter?"

Matthew squinted and made the hmm sound he always made when he thought she was talking out of her ass. She didn't think her questions had been dumb, but, of course, she didn't believe it was either of those. Even her voice had sounded doubtful. It was true that most people had moved on from Flight 2332 and the Miracle Boy, but not everyone. People obsessed over a lot of insane bullshit these days. Last she'd checked, conspiracy theory videos about why Ethan had been spared had view counts in the tens of millions. It was entirely possible that the two men were the same man and that he was some loon who believed he'd been chosen to play a part in some prophecy outlined by slick hucksters looking to make a quick buck via clickbait videos.

"Where were you this afternoon?" he asked.

Oh, fuck. He hadn't thought her suggestion sounded ignorant after all—he was suspicious. For a moment, her rage overpowered her anxiety and growing worry about the man and the situation at hand. It was difficult to keep the muscles in her face from trembling.

"What in the hell does that have to do with anything?"

"I don't know that it does, but where were you?" he asked again.

She'd been at her meeting. Her whole life now was AA meetings, errands, and mothering. How dare he ask her where she was. She'd lost the battle with her nerves, and her head and arms shook as she swallowed what she really wanted to say to him—and had wanted to say to him for months: *You have no fucking idea what's going on with me, and you don't care.*

"You know where I was. My meeting," she said instead.

His shoulders dropped. "I'm sorry, of course you were. I don't know why I asked."

His contrition seemed genuine, which surprised her. Though this was an absolutely inopportune time, she wanted to stay angry at him. She wanted that anger to lead somewhere productive . . . or maybe destructive. As it was, she added nothing more to his insinuation, and neither did he. They sat in silence until her concern for Ethan and Em came back in full.

"Why did you have Lucinda take the kids?"

"I didn't want them around while we discussed this."

"Why not?"

"Because it's fucking serious. And scary. And they're kids—even Em." He was right. This time, her question had been stupid. She was about to apologize when he added, "Things were just starting to feel normal around here, you know?"

Whether it'd been a dig at her or not, it threatened to reignite her desire to argue and to come clean about how she'd been feeling. If she was going to come clean about anything, it needed to be about the incident at the bodega, though. All she'd left unsaid that week about the stranger and his interaction with Ethan flooded her thinking. Her hand started to tremble on top of the table again, and she put her other one over it to try and still it. This time, Matthew noticed.

"Are you alright? You're shaking."

"Did Gracey say what the guy looked like?"

"She didn't see him. The whole thing happened after another kid threw up and—"

"What about Emily?"

"I wasn't finished. When Em got there, he was already gone, or maybe he'd snaked off amongst the chaos when she arrived, but Natalie saw him."

"Well, what did Natalie say then?"

"Tall, dark hair, large but not unfit, ordinary face, but . . . off."

The man from the store was all those things, but the description also fit a thousand different someones walking around Brooklyn on any given day. Off could mean drunk, high, slow—it never meant a body that didn't seem to belong to them, not like the one she'd seen.

"Off how? Like not altogether there?" she asked. "Like struggling physically?"

"All she said was off. She told Gracey the man felt dangerous . . . also said Ethan recognized him and that for a minute, Natalie thought he might even know him. He had a lollipop for Ethan, too. I mean, candy from strangers—I thought that shit was an urban—"

Nicole jumped from her seat and managed to make it to the sink. It was him. How fucking dumb had she been to not tell Matthew about the man? She tried to hold onto the sick barreling from her stomach through her throat, but her nausea was overpowering. A colorful mix of what had been a salad, a coffee, and natural bile coated the basin. The smell alone was enough for round two.

"I'm sorry," she managed before spitting up a second time, mostly stomach juices. "Did you call the police? We need to call the police. Now." She hadn't meant to sound panicked, but it was utterly impossible to control it. "And the kids. We need to get the kids."

Matthew was at her side now. "Hon, you need to calm down," he said as he handed her the towel he'd grabbed from the oven handle. "I already called the police. They're going to assign an officer to the school for the next couple of days. They said it's all they can do at this point. Just breathe. Jesus."

He put his hand on her shoulder and peered into the sink with her. "What is that? Carrots?"

His attempt at levity sounded particularly strained. Her vomiting was probably unexpected, confusing, and, to him, suspicious for all the wrong reasons. His bullshit calm, her omissions—the kids not being home—only angered her more, and her thoughts conspired to ensure every last molecule from her stomach was ejected. Matthew pulled the curtains over the sink all the way open and stared out the window while she finished.

When she was done, she practically fell back into her seat at the table.

"Are you having an affair?" he asked, still looking out the window but filling a glass of water she assumed he intended to give her. "You can tell me, you know." He was all calm again. Practical. Understanding. Everything she'd once admired about him was ugly now. Inauthentic.

She decided no answer was the only appropriate one. How he'd managed to make this about him or them when Ethan or maybe even both the kids were in danger was just so very expected. When he turned to join her back at the table, though, there was something in his eyes that made her feel like he was legitimately hoping to hear that she was having an affair.

"You'd feel better if I was having an affair?"

He sat, slid the glass of water over to her, and laid out his own bit of insanity. "If you *were* having an affair—met someone in the rooms, maybe—and the dipshit you slept with thought it'd be nice or clever or a good shot at home-wrecking to pop by Ethan's school to pick him up . . . I don't know, Nicole. I realize a jilted-lover prank sounds absolutely nuts, but the alternative is far worse. You and I would have to accept that some brazen motherfucker tried to abduct Ethan in broad daylight. So, I just think—"

"I met this man the other night," she said. It came out easy. Painless. She was still learning that the truth almost always did.

"Met him where?" he asked. His face was surprisingly wrecked.

She shook her head. "Not in a romantic way. Met isn't the right word." She was on a roll now and could not be bothered with hoping to hear he believed her. "He was at the grocery store, just standing in the aisle, staring at the lights in the ceiling and swaying a bit. I thought he might be high or having a stroke, so I offered to help him."

"What makes you think it's the same guy?"

"His interest in Ethan was off-putting."

"I thought you said he was having a stroke?"

"At first... but at some point, he... I don't know... *clicked*. Like went from not being there to being there. And started to talk to Ethan. He or maybe even she—"

"Wait, you're not even sure it was a man?"

"It *was* a man," she said, frustrated. "But when he spoke to Ethan, his voice switched. It was him, but not him."

Matthew pressed his lips into a fine line, ran a finger up and down along the back of his neck, then finally said, "I honestly don't know what the hell you are talking about, Nicole."

"Half the reason I didn't say anything is because I'm still not sure how to describe it." She started to stand, but the nausea was still potent, and she sat back down quickly. "I just want to go get the kids," she said, resting her head against the palm of her hand.

"Not until you tell me what you saw. I won't say another word."

That was unlikely. He didn't know how to stay quiet. A character defect if there ever was one. His ultimatum was shitty, too, but her earlier rage had found all the old nooks and crannies it had always relied on to hide. She was tired. Unsure. Scared. And maybe worst of all, sober.

"He went from gruff and disinterested to sweet and adoring—not only his words but his face. It changed. I thought he was just being overly kind, cartoonishly so, but he knew things about Ethan. He knew what his favorite lollipop flavor was—from when he was two."

"*Ethan* couldn't know what his favorite flavor was from when he was two." Matthew was wrong about that, but Nicole let that slide. "Jesus Christ, Nicole. I can't believe you're just now telling me this."

"I wanted to tell you the other night, but . . ."

"But what?"

"I thought you'd think I was making things up."

"Why would I think that?"

"I don't know . . . maybe insinuating I'm having affairs has something to do with my reluctance to tell you anything that doesn't fit your perfect little family fantasy."

The twitch under his eye would've been imperceptible to most, but she saw it. Her barb had stung, she'd wounded him, and the buzz of nausea gave way to another swift kick of that untamable adrenaline she'd felt before. Just enough to fire one last shot at him.

"Someone tries to kidnap Ethan, and the first place your mind goes is, 'Nicole must be fucking some *loon* she met at one of her meetings.' It's unfair but not surprising."

"You're right," he said. "I'm sorry. It was a shitty thing to think. Let's start over."

Matthew only ever used the word "sorry" when he'd backed himself into a corner. She took another deep breath, already on the third of the ten it took to calm herself. An obvious practice now that she knew it. Breathing correctly—with intention—would have saved her from so many other violent blow-ups over the years. Where would she be now if she'd been taught to breathe correctly two decades ago? It was an odd thought to have, but it came nonetheless.

"Fine," she said between the fifth exhale and the next inhale. "Start over."

"So, you have a stalker."

He'd said it calmly and had tried hard to soften his face to project plausible belief, but it wouldn't take. She pressed on. "I don't think this guy is into me. He was all eyes on Ethan."

"Stalkers do crazy shit, Nicole." He looked down at the table as if embarrassed by her ignorance of worldly things. But when his eyes found hers again, they had changed. His pupils had dilated under raised brows, and there was a slight quiver in his voice when he quietly asked her, "Wait, are you saying he's a pedophile?"

That thought had occurred to Nicole, but on nothing more than a mother's intuition, she'd already decided that wasn't the case with the man. "No," she said firmly, but because she didn't want to give her husband more reason to think her naïve, she added, "I mean, how would I know if he was? But it wasn't like that."

"For fuck's sake. Quit holding back. I'm ready to believe whatever." His capitulation had sounded legitimate.

Nicole and Amanda hadn't really been friends, more like patient acquaintances, entirely different stars, one bright and one dimming, that orbited near each other once in a while within the galaxy of their husbands' best-buddies friendship. She hadn't hated Amanda, but she hadn't quite liked her either. Amanda was pitch-perfect Park Slope material. Everything Nicole wasn't. Being a wasted wreck almost anytime Tag and his family were over never helped her over the hump of shame for being anything but right for mothering in that neighborhood. What they talked about, when they talked to each other at all, must have been held in the brain cells that Nicole shed from using, but she hadn't forgotten one very pertinent thing: the nickname Amanda had used for Ethan with an almost sickening regularity. She knew that Matthew knew it just as well.

"The man called Ethan 'silly boy.'"

18

AIDAN

Aidan sat alone in the waiting room. The smell of elderly ointments and soiled diapers came and went over a baseline hint of bleach. A fine reminder that illness, like death, lands upon people at any age. He himself had sent souls between eighteen and fifty-two to heaven or hell, but reminiscing about those kills did little to distract him from the offending odors. He was no stranger to foul scents—but at home, he used a 3M reusable respirator and vapor cartridges to clean up and dispose of the messes his victims had made. He'd been in such a rush to be on time for his appointment that bringing even a handkerchief slipped his mind. The smell of sickness here was at least less pungent than it'd have been at the Urgent Care in Norwalk, where the average resident was sure to be considerably older, it had to be. This office was less public, too.

The physician he was there to see was a coworker's recommendation, but so far, the promise of reliable appointment times was as flimsy as it had sounded. He picked at his nails, then at the thin spot of denim above one knee. He folded his arms and stuck his hands under his pits to try and keep himself still and presentable. Nerves weren't something he remembered having, but he was definitely rocking a bit, back and forth, in the chair. His swaying wasn't aggressive like that of a mental patient in a movie, but it wasn't subtle, either. It would not do.

He reached for a magazine he'd flipped through already, started on the first page again, and then revisited every page after. A second read-through failed to take his mind off his reason for being there. Then again, *Popular Science* can only do so much for a man fretting about being seen by a doctor, or in Aidan's case, being seen at all. Doctors asked questions. Doctors wanted a list of symptoms. Doctors wanted answers before they would hand out their solutions.

He wasn't sure how he'd respond when the physician asked, "What seems to be the problem?" There was a high probability the doctor would start there. He'd already given it a great deal of thought but could not find an approachable word to describe what he had.

I can't be the only one to ever say, "Hey, Doc, I think I might be possessed."

He chuckled at the thought, but the levity was fleeting.

What started out as something mildly entertaining had turned frustrating. Possession wasn't scary. Possession was damn inconvenient. At least for him. He wasn't actually at the doctor to claim he was possessed. That morning, Aidan had landed on an alternative theory for his two long-distance sleepwalking trips from Stamford to Brooklyn: a brain tumor.

He'd Googled gliomas, meningiomas, astrocytomas, and all the other -omas. Enough of what he was experiencing matched up pretty well with the details online. But it was patently abhorrent how often idiots performed self-diagnoses like that. You've got a problem you don't understand? You go to an expert. So, there he was: waiting to see an expert. If the doctor ruled out the various tumors he'd read about, he'd move on to a priest.

It'd been three days since Aidan took back control of his body in front of that school. He only gained that control after falling into the concrete wall of the building's staircase. Other adults, holding hands with their children, filed past him while he struggled to steady himself. He hadn't stuck around to learn more and considered it lucky to have been able to walk away from the property on his own. His memory of what he'd seen occur while under its spell was fuzzier than it had been with the other episode inside the bodega, but he was pretty certain that he—or rather something using his body—had caused an incident that wouldn't soon be forgotten.

Whatever it was inside of him, tumor or demon, its power was getting stronger.

Around his thirty-fifth birthday, he'd sworn off doctors because the last one tried to get him hooked on antidepressants. Big Pharma was good for a laugh, good for a rest, good for a thrill, but there was no prescription cure for his way of being. Of course, he had never owned up to his unquenchable bloodthirst with them. An inextinguishable flame of black hatred for the deserving wasn't going to be pilled away, anyway. His thinking differed from the rest of the human species, a defect—what one might call it, if they didn't have it—that had been apparent since early childhood.

Mom and Dad knew what he was, and he'd worked hard at honing in on an emotion that could pass as gratitude for their constant worry. Who was anyone to say if that feeling he had for their efforts was authentic or not? They had tried to solve him and had failed. But they tried, and as they say, all one can do is try. Divorce yourself from the consequences of your actions. Trying is plenty. The journey is the reward. Even a shitty one, he guessed. What a load.

Of course, addressing his shortcomings as a member of civilized society was easier these days. There were more theories, more specialists, and more research on the causes, external and peripheral. Plus, it was loads quicker to find the documentation of that research online. If they'd lived only a decade longer, his parents might have stumbled upon a cure. There were legitimate scientific reasons now, some more well-known than others, explaining why some men bent toward a life of killing for gratification. At a minimum, Mom and Dad might've liked to pick a hypothesis just to have some closure. As it was, they were dead, and if it wasn't their constant searching for a fix to him that had exhausted them into their early graves, it was the related heartache of knowing they'd birthed an abomination and could not bring themselves to imprison him. Their love was unconditional. Even from her sickbed, Mom had gone on and on about how there was good in him somewhere; she told him she loved him with every fiber of her being.

"There's time yet to put you on the right path, Aidan . . . to save you from yourself." She closed her eyes the final time, still believing.

His own theory was cut-and-dried: He enjoyed killing, and God, in his infinite wisdom, had seen to it that some of his flock were meant for killing. To be honest, it was more of a belief than a theory, as it was certainly not provable. But he was what he was, and besides, wanting sluts dead didn't make him unique. History was pocked with others. At best, what made him special was that he'd spent his adult life employing far more self-control than the repeat murderers whose stories made streaming services rich. At least he liked to think he was special for that reason. His current situation ran counter to the killer he hoped to die as: proficient, not famous, a reaper of only the deserving, not randoms. And no kids. Ever. No. Kids.

His reasons were his own, making the recent unauthorized trip of his body to the school that much more unnerving. The incident was the second time in a week that he'd quasi-watched himself harass a child. And the same child, which was odd. Bits and pieces of the interactions stabbed at his brain. In both instances, the memories came in like a hangover—a state of being he knew well from his days at Princeton. He'd tried to drink himself to death. His first murder, a hooker of no note, had done a real number on his confidence that semester. It hadn't left him happy or sad. Emotionally, the end result had been so confusing that he talked himself into accepting that he'd been foolish and plain wrong about following his true calling. He had no business doing what he loved. As a student, that thinking probably hadn't made him all that unique either. Thankfully, drinking yourself dead was harder than advertised. Practice, on the other hand, didn't ever actually make perfect, not with murder, but it sure as hell made each kill that followed the last a lot easier. And in time, the gratification came. He considered himself a pro now, but even Michael Jordan had had stuff he needed to work on toward the end of his career. The key difference, Aidan thought, was that should a newsman ever ask him, he was perfectly OK with admitting that he didn't have it all figured out.

Twenty-five years had passed since that suicide attempt. Personal improvement and the acceptance of his personality, beliefs, and his troubled spirit had come easily thanks to the hundreds of self-help books that still made up a good chunk of his personal library at home. The core principles behind authentic self, no matter how they were presented or who was presenting them, made good sense. He'd even mailed a few handwritten and carefully considered letters to his three favorite authors, all of them women, by the way, thanking them for the tools they provided and for helping guide him through some dark uncertainties about who he was meant to be in the world. Only one of those authors—or more likely a member of their PR team—had sent him back a typed form response along with a signed copy of their most recent book. Just their name, though, no personalization. Coincidentally, that expert's twenty-something daughter went missing while attending Vassar just an hour and a half north of Stamford, Connecticut, where Aidan lived. To his knowledge, the girl was yet to be found, and while he hadn't anything to do with her disappearance, he felt there was a certain poetic karma at play. The author hadn't published a new book since, and that was fine. Much of what her book and the others held had long been coopted by corporations and influencers by then to help sell burgers, shoes, nicotine, and shiny lifestyles. The whole world was unwittingly self-helping their way into debt, but not Aidan, because he bettered himself the old-fashioned way: giving up time to actually earn it.

He'd been born a killer. This wasn't a choice he'd made. Every child who leaves the womb faces the same dilemma. Genetics, geography, and the family you had or did not have was not a choice you got to make. To be a child was to be told what to be, where to be, how to be, and what to do. Even when children decided to rebel against that paradigm, the rebellion itself was not a choice, it'd been built in and was expected. His decision to spare children, no matter how petulant, repugnant, or ignorant they seemed, hadn't been made because he couldn't stomach killing them—he simply believed no child could ever qualify as deserving. They'd had no chance to choose—not really. When a child looks up to the heavens above and asks, "Why me," they have every right to do so. They are anchored to a system that was created without their input. If, after turning eighteen, that same child had decided the best they could do was exchange hand-jobs for drugs behind the dive bars behind Anytown, USA, that was their choice. "Why me?" was no longer an unanswerable riddle. It had one, and only one, correct answer now: Because you decided this was who you were, and were therefore deserving of the end Aidan had in store for you. "Why me?" was exactly how all those experts made their millions with those books—not that he'd ever uttered it or thought it. Aidan had never felt that otherworldly forces were conspiring against him—well, that was until now—and possibly against the child, too.

If the child was in danger, more drastic measures might be necessary. His empathy for the boy, regardless of whether it was real or faked or somewhere in between, was considerably less important than regaining control of his body full-time in order to ensure that how he'd modeled his life as a killer remained intact. Eluding capture until he chose to stop killing or died of natural causes was the script he wanted to stick to. His body had interacted with two different women now. One at the store and one at the school. He had spoken long enough to both the boy's mother and a teacher for either of them to provide details about his appearance to the police. Brooklyn detectives had easier crimes to solve and wouldn't take any report made about a man who might be baiting kids with candy that seriously. At least not reports filed by upper-middle-class mothers. It was the most laughable of legends around abduction. Kids were easy enough to grab. You didn't need to coax them with candy or puppies or pretend to be looking for one of their friends. Just snatch and go. That said, neighborhoods like the ones he'd been walked to were as nice as they were due to the collective paranoia of their residents. They reported anything and everything twenty-four-seven. The police rarely gave a damn, but on occasion, some newbie rookie might. They'd ask for security footage. He hadn't done anything illegal at the store—probably he just looked like a junkie coming down hard—but being seen or discovered or analyzed in any way, no matter the interpretation, would be a consequence of a decision his possessor had made for him.

Oh, so you're committing to possession, now?

Either way, any positive identification would be difficult. If the cops knocked on his door, he had perfectly logical answers to any questions they wanted to ask him. It wouldn't be soon. There was plenty of time to come up with a whole set of grand excuses for being there.

Maybe you can tell them it was a tumor.

Reality hit him again. The smell. The magazines. The uncaring buzz of canned light.

A tumor would make more sense.

"Mr. Schaeffer, the doctor will see you now."

In circumstances less dire, Aidan might have taken in the female physician's assistant's appearance, noted whether she had a wedding ring or no ring, and decided to mark her for observation. He might have followed up on that decision by stalking her to see if she was just pretending to be a decent human being or if she, like so many he'd observed before her, had addictions that she could only manage by debasing herself. What choices was she making in the world? But as he followed her through the hallway and to the examination room, his mind was preoccupied with a new idea: He was being punished. In fact, punishment was what he'd expected for most of his adult life. An eye for an eye, as it were. He'd robbed women of their dignity, their personhood, and their lives enough times to believe God's wrath would find him eventually. Even if it was God who'd allowed him to be successful, if not legendary, as a killer thus far. He or she or it was a fickle bitch. But the thing inside him didn't feel holy or pious.

Aidan wasn't like one of these idiots who'd been recently polled and thought they could get the upper hand on a grizzly bear. And whenever he was under, so to speak—when that force inside of him had full control, it seemed far more fitful, unpredictable, and utterly determined than he believed any animal ever could be. It pained him to think it, but maybe he'd met his match, and for the first time since arriving at the doctor's, he found himself rooting for a tumor.

19

NICOLE

Nicole took a seat and evaluated the strangers in the circle. The faces at the AA meeting in downtown Manhattan were as unrecognizable as she'd hoped they'd be when she left the house. In the heat of a moment they were having, Matthew had suggested she take a long walk to cool down. He hadn't had to tell her twice. She let her anger carry her like a tsunami outside of her neighborhood, across the Brooklyn Bridge, onto John Street somewhere north of Manhattan's Financial District, and down the steps of a church into its basement. They say if you don't like a meeting, find another one. Without trying, she had, and the mix of grizzled old-timers in wifebeaters and perfectly coifed banker bros suggested it would be a real doozy at that.

It had been three days since the failed abduction attempt on Ethan. The kids were still going to school, with Matthew insisting that his taking them there and back himself was protection enough for now. During that time, he hadn't explicitly said that he didn't want her to leave the house, but when she tried to leave for a meeting with her home group the night before, he guilt-tripped her into staying home to watch a movie with the family. So far, his idea of the best path forward seemed centered on more hunkering down in that tiny shit condo—hoping that, like the reporters had eventually, this new problem with a fucking kidnapper would just go away.

The hour-and-a-half walk there hadn't quieted her discontent. She desperately needed the meeting to start so that her mind might have a legitimate sixty-minute distraction from the spiraling thoughts about the kids, her husband, and the heated argument he and she had over ensuring Ethan and Emily remained safe and, to put it plainly, were never kidnapped. But so far, the volunteer hadn't shown up to conduct the meeting, and their fight remained front and center.

After an early dinner, Em had taken Ethan to read in the family room. With the kids just out of earshot, Nicole boosted the volume of the Bluetooth speaker streaming NPR's recap of that day's news. She'd started with a reasonable suggestion and did so before Matthew opened his laptop. Because when he made that nightly transition to work mode, talking to him about anything important would have been less productive than spilling her guts to the dog.

"I don't think we should keep sending the kids to school like everything's normal."

He rested his hand on the lid of his computer for a moment as if debating whether or not he wanted to engage. Then, he bent his head to one side until his neck went *crack*, the way he always did when he was about to act put off for having to be the calm one, the sensible one. As a drunk, that sound hadn't bothered her much, but in sobriety, she found the snap to be as repulsive as what it foreshadowed. He hadn't said anything yet, and she already felt sick to her stomach.

"We're not acting like everything is normal. The police are involved; that's not normal."

He didn't bother turning the kitchen chair around to engage with her further, and his hand started back toward his laptop. The frenzied husband from three nights ago was no more. Old Matthew had returned the very next morning. Mister Easy Peasy. Mister It'll All Work Out. Mister You Don't Know What You're Talking About. Mister I'm Too Busy for Your Crazy. There was a time that would have been fair, but this was not the old her and not the old crazy.

"Don't you fucking open that computer," she said.

She was as surprised as he was by the command, but if that's what it took to get his attention, so be it. He was damn well spun around in that chair to talk to her now, eyes on fire between the squint of appalled disbelief, and ready to lose his shit.

"Everything alright in there?" Em asked.

Neither of them answered right away.

"Yeah, everything alright?" Ethan repeated, brightly but thick with concern.

"We're fine," Matthew said. "But thank you for checking."

Before her husband could use the interruption as another out, Nicole added, "Em, take Ethan upstairs and give him a bath, will you? I'll be up in a minute to relieve you from duty." The chuckle she made to help sell the ask was so phony.

"Fine," Em replied. "So long as you two behave."

So much of Nicole's behavior and the things she said and did lately had felt insincere. Like an act. Her love for the kids was genuine, but this new version of her was having a hard time landing on a personality that comfortably matched her renewed enthusiasm for parenting.

"Get after it, thank you."

She and Matthew stayed quiet until they heard the tub turn on upstairs.

"I don't have time for this—"

"Fine," she stopped him. "Don't make the time for me, make it for them, goddammit."

"I am, Nicole. Who's walking them to and from school now? Me."

"That was your decision—not mine. And it's not enough, anyway. Frankly, it's dumb that you are. I know what the guy at the store looked like, not you. How in the hell are you going to stop anything from happening? You don't even know who to watch out for."

Matthew stood, then closed the pocket door between the kitchen and the family room. "Keep your voice down," he said as he walked to the front door to check all the locks. When he was done, he seated himself again, but this time on the side of the kitchen table that was furthest from her. "If we're going to talk about this rationally, can you at least take a seat?"

She didn't want to. But she also wasn't about to give him a reason to cut this short. She took the seat across from him, took a deep breath, and tried to mimic his calm. "I'm just saying that we could be doing more. This isn't a rogue reporter or an inconsiderate looky-loo. Checking the locks twice before bed isn't going to cut it for me. We need to be proactive. Maybe relocate."

"Move?" he asked, shaking his head before even waiting for confirmation.

It wasn't like she'd said to Mars. "Yes. Move."

"Look. What happened at the bodega freaked you out. I get that, and it's not that I'm not freaked out—I am—but we told the cops about that, too. You gave them your description of the man. You were there. They literally asked us to go about business as usual, so what the hell else are we supposed to be doing, Nicole? Besides running away? Tell me. I want to know."

It didn't sound like he wanted to know. It sounded like he wanted her to agree with him so he could put his head back in the digital sand and go on pretending all those extra hours he spent analyzing data were going to do fuck-all for his latest start-up. Her compliance probably seemed like a given to him at this point because, in fairness, she'd spent one-third of her life giving him exactly what he wanted in this type of situation. There was no specific rule or step or expectation in AA that one was supposed to stay calm at all times—maybe a suggestion at best.

"If you're hoping to hear me say you're right, you can fuck off. Because you're not."

"*I* can fuck off?"

"Yes. If you expect me to just go with the flow here, after what I saw—after someone tried to take one of our children from us—you can fuck off. We aren't doing enough."

"You're hysterical," he said. He grabbed his computer from the table as he stood. "I'm done with this conversation. You should take a long walk."

She might have been content to let him leave the room, but he wasn't actually done.

"And if you end up going to a bar instead, I'll know. I'll know, and it won't be good."

Her fist had gone flying, and what do you know? She connected. In fact, now that she'd had a moment to sit still, waiting for the meeting to start, she noticed that her whole arm was still throbbing from the punch she'd landed. She didn't know what he'd meant by "it won't be good," but as the lights dimmed and the other alcoholics in the room quieted, she decided it couldn't be much worse than life with him had been recently.

His efforts to understand how long-term sobriety worked were lacking. He was *playing* the part of an interested spouse, cheering her on, but only when other people were around and it made him look good. He didn't go to Al-Anon like other addicts' partners did. He hadn't stopped drinking wine around her—or even offered—and became utterly disinterested anytime she talked about the progress she believed she was making for longer than five minutes.

In a bid to gain his empathy or at least a more sincere curiosity, she'd let Matthew know the support network at her regular meeting had become more interested in domestic gossip than working the twelve steps. Many of her new friends couldn't let her vent at a meeting without throwing out unsolicited advice. It didn't matter how often the chairperson reminded the group that crosstalk wasn't allowed. Scheming to get him more interested in her sobriety had backfired, and Matthew began to judge the group. It seemed to her that he was getting a little nervous about what real long-term sobriety for her was going to look like for him. She'd never directly told him that her new friends thought she should leave him. Alluded to it, maybe. They were a snarky bunch, as bored as she was but for their own crude reasons. Was leaving him what she wanted?

"Hello. My name is Mike, and I'm an alcoholic."

Fuck. The chairperson had already started the meeting. Had described the program, welcomed newcomers, and introduced the meeting's speaker, who was sitting behind a table on a small stage at the front of the room, all while she'd continued spiraling out.

Breathe.

"Hi, Mike," the room said in unison, even Nicole.

Mike was older than everyone else in the room, hardened, a relic of what South Street Seaport must have surely attracted before billionaire developers figured out a way to condo-ize that part of the island. His appearance was a stark contrast to the other personalities she'd subconsciously heard jockeying for attention from one another under her own thinking while waiting for the meeting to begin. Accountants, bankers, investors, maybe. These were assumptions, of course, but casting aspersions on a group of mostly men was comforting. They all reminded her of what she imagined Matthew wished he was. Wealthy, fit, a more important cog in the machine. Of course, they were here. They were drunks. Money hadn't saved them, but the watches they still wore proved they hadn't given up on trying to find salvation by climbing the corporate ladder they already knew high, high into the sky.

"Thank you, Ogden, for asking me to speak," Mike said. Another volunteer dimmed the lights even further. "It's an honor to be back. These days, I'm rarely down this way, but when I am, I make a point of being at this meeting. It all began here for me, so this place is sacred."

Mike's voice was deep. His words were barely more audible than a good dishwasher's rumble. A meaningful share from an old-timer is like a hypnotic lullaby, and that was exactly the calming effect Nicole needed to reset. Not to focus on his story, but in order to calmly think about her story instead. In the near darkness of the room, she tuned out Mike and the others and decided to get honest with herself.

Her sobriety—well before that week's developments—was shaky. It was time to admit that. She had plenty of excuses to offer for its fragility, but nothing dire—at least nothing a normie would rubberstamp. Sober living had been as stable as advertised. She could spend an entire day with Emily, really present and engaged. Emily was bright, her observations about the world were intriguing, and the years Nicole had left to bond with her daughter before she most certainly bounced for college were less fear-inducing. They still had their disagreements, but now those didn't end in a shouting match, slammed doors and threats, or with Nicole losing the next forty-eight hours to the zombie-like state Xanax and booze created. She was also enamored with the way her daughter had stepped up to care for and connect with Ethan while she focused on her sobriety and Matthew on his business. Ethan was, in fact, an absolute doll. Mothering a young boy was a different ride completely. Or maybe having navigated early parenthood with Em as horribly as Nicole had simply set the stage for a more fun, go-with-the-flow time with a son. He was easier in some respects, certainly more amenable than Nicole remembered Em being, though with a clearer mind, Em's rebellion had become understandable.

She loved them both. That feeling wasn't something she'd had to convince herself was legit. It was a complex wave of adoration and purpose that she found overwhelming at times, a type of joy Nicole didn't always believe she deserved. The only dark itch she could identify regarding the kids was that Ethan was also a constant reminder of how disinterested and passively vindictive she'd been when it came to his biological parents. Making amends to Tag and Amanda through spoken prayer—something her sponsor had suggested—didn't provide the same relief performing Step Nine had with the still-living humans she'd apologized to.

Mothering in sobriety also came with a despicable predictability. The failed abduction attempt wasn't something to relish, far from it, but damn . . . at least it'd kicked her in the gut. The incident, the man, the possibility of chaos—she wanted none of it but could not deny that the adrenaline rushes were welcome. Beyond that physical effect, the mystery of it all had also conveniently distracted her from feeling that even as a sober person, she was coming up well short in portraying the ideal thirty-something Park Slope mommy. During the first eleven years of Emily's life, Nicole had blamed her drinking squarely on the responsibilities of motherhood.

But it wasn't that, was it? Not quite.

She looked around the room, trying to read the faces.

Who else was thinking about drinking again?

Who else wondered if the only reason they wanted to drink again was that they'd finally realized they no longer loved—perhaps had never loved—their spouse?

Her epiphany hit right as her gaze landed on the only other face not attuned to Mike.

She held her stare on the man across the circle to confirm. It was the stranger from the grocery store. Her eyes had adjusted to the dark room, enough to see the pearl-white teeth framed by the same crooked smile he'd flashed while chatting Ethan up about his favorite lollipops. She squinted to try and make better sense of his face. Maybe it was the low light in the room or her imagination, but his eyes were a callous gray, like an angry smoke, trapped and swirling between his lids. She looked away but felt compelled to return. She would stare at him firmly in an attempt to force him to look away. Maybe he wouldn't recognize her.

Too late. He waved his hand clumsily from his lap and then moved a single pointed finger to the center of his lips as if to request she refrain from causing a scene. She remained caught in their mutual stare while she evaluated him and considered her options.

Shlub was the first word that came to mind. An everyday Joe fresh off a trip to a strip mall Great Clips and dressed to mow a lawn. And yet, oozing with an energy that wasn't bad boy so much as bad juju. A kind of dark voodoo no one believes in until that first pin comes for you.

She stood to leave, she wouldn't have been the first to do so during a speaker's share, but it was late, and the dark streets of the financial district would be empty at this time. If the stranger followed her, he'd have her to himself, so she sat back down to wait for the meeting to end. Moving outside with the group would be safer. She could ask any of the other men or the few women there if they'd be willing to share an Uber or a cab. It wouldn't matter what part of town they were headed to; anywhere with anyone would put distance between her and the man.

She glanced at the clock on the wall behind him. The meeting wouldn't be over for another forty minutes. Mike continued sharing his story. When he was done, and the lights came back up for the other addicts to speak, she hoped she would find she'd been wrong. It wouldn't be the man from the deli, only another anonymous nobody disfigured by her overactive imagination. Then again, if it *was* the man, she might learn about him if he chose to raise his hand to share with the group. Maybe he was someone from meetings she'd attended in early sobriety or an acquaintance she'd made while still using. Matthew had suggested that possibility and worse. But if he was a jilted former one-night stand, wouldn't his face have sparked some recollection by now? She hadn't had many carnal indiscretions in the year prior to her last cocktail, but black-out drinking hadn't left her with accurate mental pictures of the handful of men with whom she had one-night affairs. Beer goggles or not, the man did not fit her type.

An acidic symphony tuned up in her stomach. Sitting much longer would be difficult.

She'd meant to take her eyes off of the man but hadn't. In his relative stillness, he had a rigidity to his torso that seemed forced. It was as if he was using every muscle available above the waist to sit still or else his body would crumple, and by now, his grin from earlier had given way to a dark glower she could no longer stomach.

Mike started to wrap up his share. As good a reason as any to turn away from the man to force a few agreeing nods.

"One-day-at-a-time living. It's a simple program for complex people," Mike said.

As he offered a few other suggestions for newcomers, she could still feel the stranger's stare. Out of the corner of her eye, she could sense his body's indecision to stay put. He might have stood at any minute. She tried to steady her nerves in preparation to defend herself should he decide to lunge at her. She felt very much like a gazelle, but one that was keenly aware that the predator stalking her was injured in some way. Making the first move was the right next step.

Mike called on the first person to raise their hand. It wasn't the stranger. "I'm David, and I'm an alcoholic."

She and everyone else, even the stranger, replied, "Hi David."

He hadn't attacked her and was giving his undivided attention to David now.

Fuck Matthew for possibly being right. The stranger being a nutjob she'd banged was starting to feel more likely. But what about his eyes? She dared to look at him again.

The man's head was cocked toward David now, and while his posture was still composed of limbs resting at discomforting angles, it was difficult to see if the irises had returned to normal. She held her stare on him, and he did not return it. It was possible that her own unresolved guilt about her affairs and growing disinterest in having anything to do with Matthew was screwing with her head. She was tired. Angry. Lonely and hungry. HALT. The AA standby just popped into her mind. As good a reason as any for feeling like only going full-tilt into a night of hardcore drinking was the solution to her realizations and an equally good reason for her mind making the stranger out to be something more sinister.

As the next share began, she looked down at her hands that she'd inadvertently put together in prayer on her lap, and got lost in thinking about the work she'd done with her sponsor. She'd left out the affairs, figuring she'd add them when she worked the steps a second time. A second go at working the steps was something many others claimed to have done. "Progress, not perfection" was a motto that made it easy to omit certain misdeeds while making a searching and fearless moral inventory of oneself. Would have been better to have gotten it out of the way. Pretending Matthew didn't know she'd been unfaithful felt equally ignorant. How careful had she ever been, really? She'd fought so valiantly in defense of herself—lying in real-time, again and again, forcing him into contrition, one that she now believed had to have been phony.

I've welcomed a nutcase into our lives in exchange for a night of sex I can't remember.

Her hands were shaking now. She looked up to take the stranger in again—to examine his face for any detail that would confirm this was what had happened—but he was no longer there.

20

MATTHEW

Matthew closed the door to Em and Ethan's room, then slow-stepped his way down the stairs to limit their creaking. Any audible crack was the only excuse his son needed to pop from his bed and demand full cooperation with a late-night investigation into it. To live at all after ten o'clock in a home decades overdue for renovations required a stealth he hadn't yet perfected.

Emily had been easier to put to bed when she was Ethan's age. But maybe that was a bit of revisionist history. Back then, Nicole put their daughter to sleep most nights. Anything he believed he knew about the simplicity of Emily's evening routine at age four was formed via eavesdropping while hunched in front of a laptop at the kitchen table a full floor away, working unpaid hours in the hopes of building a fortune that never materialized.

Regrets. He had a few.

Waking their daughter and readying her for the day had been his job. And he'd always known it was the better half of the arrangement he and Nicole had agreed to.

To traverse the flight of stairs sound-free required a commitment to the act: both hands were needed to practically lift himself off the steps by using the railings, which inexplicably made no sounds of their own under additional duress. What worked one night did not promise to work the next. Adults in larger, newer homes probably didn't have to play these games to score a bit of quiet time.

When they'd taken on Ethan, Matthew suggested they move into something more accommodating for a family of four and one dog. Emily would be a teen soon and deserved a room of her own, but he'd put Nicole's sobriety first. There'd been no talk of moving since those first few weeks of caring for Ethan until that afternoon. Moving was on the table again, apparently. Nicole's big damn idea to keep the kids safe was to pick up and go. Even with their minimal belongings, moves cost money. Moves took time that would cost him money, too. She knew as well as he did what meager savings they had, and most of the funds Tag left them had been spent on rehab. That was a decision Matthew didn't regret. Taking care of Ethan for Tag and Amanda meant having a reliable mother—at a minimum. Yes, ACS had forced the issue, but he was thrilled she was sober. So far, it'd been money well spent. She was healthier and happier, and while they still couldn't seem to ever get on the same page, her loving relationship with the kids seemed genuine. So OK. Maybe he'd overreacted when she suggested relocating, but when you are running from the boogeyman, is there really any place to hide?

He dismounted from the second-to-last step and stuck his landing into the family room without making a sound. Then, he waited at the base of the stairs for a beat, expecting to hear footsteps above. There were none. Success!

Pepper eyed him from his fetal curl on the floor, less than impressed.

The morning after the abduction attempt, if that's even what it was, he'd ordered a pet gate from Amazon. His idea was to keep the dog downstairs all night now for protection. The contraption was on the porch when he got home, and he installed it that evening—had even actually read the instructions. But he found Pepper lying against the kids' bedroom door the following morning. The dog could jump, he knew that, but he'd been surprised to see the gate still standing when he made it downstairs. He'd meant to ask Em if she'd let Pepper up during the night but had forgotten to ask. He'd set the gate up again last night. Same result, but he was too beat to bother with trying to troubleshoot the installation a third time.

As Matthew settled into the loveseat, he pined for the version of the dog he once knew. *That* Pepper had always slept wherever Matthew decided to hunker down. If Matthew made it to his and Nicole's bed, Pepper was there. If it was a night on the couch, the dog squashed him to it for the duration, camping out across Matthew's legs and leaving him unable to move.

Ever since Ethan moved in, though, anytime Matthew woke to use the bathroom, or if he went downstairs to get a snack from the kitchen, or if he moved himself from the couch to his bed, he always found Pepper asleep in the hall, right outside of the kids' closed bedroom door.

"At least *I* still love you," he said before pulling his phone from his front pocket.

It was 10:05 PM, and Nicole hadn't responded to his texts, the first of which he'd sent after he and Emily finished doing the dishes from a prebedtime snack a couple of hours ago.

Hey. Guessing you decided to go to a meeting. LMK.

He reviewed every text he'd sent. He had tried to refrain from escalating, but the last one, which he'd written while Emily read a book to Ethan, read harsher than he remembered.

If you're mad at me, there are better ways to handle it.

He had tried ringing her in between text four and text five but didn't leave a message when it went to her voicemail. What choice did he have now but to try her again?

He hit call and put the phone to his ear, listening to the trill while he kept half his focus on monitoring the silence, thankfully still happening from upstairs.

Hi, you've reached Nicole. Leave a message.

"Hon, why aren't you picking up? I'm starting to worry. The last text I sent . . . I'm sorry. Please call me or text me back when you get this." He should've left it at that, but his anger found an opening before his finger found the disconnect button. "This isn't the week to go AWOL, Nicole. It's not something sober people do—I know that. At least let me know you're alive. This is a really shitty thing to do to us right now."

The hole he'd dug was deeper—maybe it needed to be. He was furious and incensed enough to throw his phone, but he pulled it back before his hand could release it. He couldn't afford any extraneous sounds. He needed to think; he needed the quiet of two kids sleeping.

In the past, he'd accepted that sometimes Nicole was going to be unreachable and elsewhere for the night. Her excuses ran the gamut from "totally wiped, accidentally fell asleep at a friend's" to "just didn't feel like coming home." Her absences were infrequent, too few over a decade for Matthew to ever label her an alcoholic aloud. Maybe he hadn't wanted to, maybe he was holding her performance up against cinema's more tragic portrayal of drunks—it was moot.

Nicole's dismay at his suggestion the stranger was someone she knew had been a believable performance three nights ago. But where was she now? And who with?

When he'd suggested the man who'd come to Ethan's school was someone she'd slept with, it'd felt justifiable—it still did. She'd never come to him to admit having slept with another man or woman, but there'd been plenty of times in the past that he suspected she was cheating on him. Her disinterest in doing anything intimate with him peaked in the weeks after her absences. A few glances at her cell phone over the years, made while she was passed out or sleeping, hadn't ever provided concrete proof. His own forced indifference, something he internally referred to as a live-and-let-live approach, had been as toxic to their relationship as it had been to her disease. And what could he do about it now?

He thought about calling the police again. This time to report her missing. Of course, when she came home hungover or still drunk the next day, they'd just bring ACS back into it.

He considered reaching out to Lucinda, but it seemed likely that she would call the police, and ACS would still be back in the fold.

Leaving the kids alone with Pepper? No. Where would he go looking anyway?

There was nothing to do but wait.

In the morning, there would be a birthday party to attend for one of Ethan's classmates. Unless he was mistaken, Nicole and Em were supposed to be having a mom-daughter day while the boys were at the event. It was still possible both of those plans would come to fruition, but as the minutes ticked by with no return text or call from Nicole, it seemed unlikely.

Matthew decided to ask Emily to go to the party. She was plenty old enough to stay home alone and had done so that year as expertly as any twelve-year-old could, but it was risky to leave her home alone because if Nicole did return home, hungover from a relapse... well, that was too much for him to ask Emily to bear alone.

Not going to the birthday celebration was an option, too, but if Nicole was going to stumble in late or not come home at all, something about his attendance at the party felt like just the right amount of spite.

"I took the kids to the party, hon. Don't worry about it; get some rest."

It would be the ideal knife to twist into what he hoped would be her guilt-ridden guts.

He enjoyed the thought of punishing Nicole for a moment more before it felt ugly and unproductive, then turned on the TV, fumbling with the remote as he lowered the volume as quickly as he could to zero. Closed captioning would have to do. There could be no Ethan-led investigations; he needed his peace.

He flipped from the rom-com filling the screen to the news and then from the news to re-runs of *Seinfeld*. He couldn't count on Nicole, but he'd always been able to count on syndicated comedies to distract him from his anxiety and concern.

Had he slept well the two nights prior, sleep might have eluded him, but as it was, his lids went heavy, no matter how hard he tried to focus on reading the jokes at the bottom of the screen. He struggled to open them even when he caught Pepper heading up the stairs to take his place as sentry outside of Em and Ethan's bedroom door.

21
AIDAN

The thick growl of a garbage truck barreling around a corner didn't wake Aidan, but it had registered. The gusto of its approach passed itself off as a nightmare until the echo of its diesel engine threatened to unearth his bones from his skin. Even then, it took the snap and snarl of its compaction, seemingly happening right on top of him, to drag him from sleep completely.

Two sanitation workers ran to and from black bag mountains on either side of the street. The sun had only begun introducing itself to the avenue and the men bounced between facades tinted in the variation of orange that colored dumps into a temporary nirvana. Not a bright day yet, but that morning had all the tells. His eyes burned. It was too risky to close them, but the sting demanded it. When he opened them again as easily as if they were his own he was relieved.

The ache in his head was a positive sign. His sensory nerves relayed little when his possessor had control. Pain was a good thing. He'd always known that to be true. A deep breath reduced the pulsation of his brain long enough for an attempt at standing, but the smell of himself punctuated the hurt, and he half-expected to pass out again. How was it possible to be so close to busting wide-open, while feeling like all internal organs had abandoned him overnight?

He stayed seated with his hands to his ears until the sounds of the sanitation crew wouldn't interfere with a whisper. Then, with his back pressed into the wall, he put his palms to the bricks on his left and right side to help shimmy his body into a posture resembling upright. Free from the heat of the urine he'd been sitting in, he settled into his precarious lean. Breathing was painful. Seeing was painful. Hearing was painful. Again, all welcome news.

He rolled his tongue over the grit on his teeth. Filthy.

His watch said it was Saturday. He'd had no control of his body since Friday afternoon when he'd felt—whatever it was—sliding his body on like a pair of jeans a mother many times over pulls from a forgotten trunk in the attic. He'd been happy for his new awareness of its entering him when it happened, but not knowing how long ago it had left him here pissed him off.

A simple cross over an otherwise inconsequential door caught his eye. He cursed his intruder for having left his body to rot in an alley outside of a church for God knows how long.

Guess God does know exactly how long, doesn't he? Fuckers, the both of you.

Aidan tested his balance, taking one hand away from the wall carefully while leaving the other put. So far, so good, so he removed the other. His limbs were quivering, but it felt more like routine low blood sugar than a lack of mental control. Whatever dragged him into the city again hadn't bothered to feed him.

To be sure the thing wasn't just playing possum, he opened his eyes as wide as he could and set his stare on the sky. He held it there, doing so through the tears it caused, which added a shimmer to the beautiful orange color leaving the city to fend on its own. His commitment to staring himself blind wasn't tied to an intention to remember anything, but flashes of what he'd seen while out the evening before and not in control of his body popped in and out of his head.

His first recollection was of the woman from the grocery store sitting across from him, inside what he assumed was the church to his right. So long as he didn't blink, he thought it might be possible to recall or relive everything that had occurred between the two of them while he'd been out.

The woman looked scared.

Scared for all the wrong reasons, he thought.

He chuckled when he realized he'd been at an AA meeting.

Aidan had experience with the rooms of AA, but only because he once stalked a young prostitute from his hometown who frequented them. The memory of the meeting he'd attended with the fit mom from the grocery store last night made it clear that not much had changed with how the "Friends of Bill" conducted business. Had any of the babble in those meetings stuck, that prostitute might still be alive today. Second chances and all that. He wasn't above it.

No time to daydream about how I killed that whore.

There was a new woman in his life, the one with the boy who loved lollipops, a petite busybody chasing her higher power that he hadn't chosen to pursue, at least, not technically.

These memories were of the woman and not the boy, a potential relief. If the thing haunting his insides had plans for the child's mother, Aidan could get into it. He would welcome the opportunity to kill the bitch in a partnership of sorts with what he'd come to believe might be a demon or the devil itself. He wasn't sure what that looked like exactly. The sin of a snuffing done at the behest of some beast from hell was hypothetical, an oddity that hadn't ever crossed his mind until now, but even in the abstract, the idea and its possibilities set fire to his groin.

If you want to kill the woman, count me in.

He hoped it was listening or hearing his thoughts.

But I'm not about killing children. I want no part in that.

Aidan had no evidence his possessor wanted to murder either of them—just a hunch. But as the memory of staring at Nicole during the meeting went on, Aidan wondered if the demon he was dealing with had changed the game plan. Otherwise, what was the point of being at the meeting at all? Whatever it'd been, leaving him here was a waste of his full potential.

"You all right, buddy?" a man's voice asked.

Aidan continued staring into the nothingness above him. Whoever it was, it was damn inconvenient. He wanted to see more from the past two days and had no intention of breaking from the film of memories that had just started playing.

"Did you hear me, sir? Are you OK?"

I'm standing, aren't I? In pissed pants, but last I checked, that isn't a crime.

From his blurry periphery, he took in the stature of the interruption approaching and held up a hand to signal the man to keep his distance.

The day's light was an assault on his retinas, but there was more to remember, more to see. At some point, his possessor stood with the meeting still in progress—ah, yes! He remembered now. There'd been a moment where he'd resumed partial control and could feel the entity inside of him panicking. It had lifted his body from his seat abruptly and stumbled into the bathroom in the adjacent hall. Using the mirror over the sink, they'd both taken in his reflection, but seeing the lines on his face that shaped his expressions moving under something else's control had spooked Aidan, and that was that—he'd gone back under.

It was worth noting that it had been possible to fight the force within.

He let the memory proceed and watched as he cracked open the door in time to see Nicole standing midmeeting while some banker-type droned on about the pressures of his seven-figure existence. She hesitated, stared long at the seat that he no longer occupied, then rushed right past the bathroom—and them—on her way up the stairs to the street-level exit.

Come on now. Surely, we didn't let her get away.

His body struggled to move and pursue its prey. The demon had lost its control, and his limbs were quaking, each like a fish thrashing about a boat's deck, trying like hell to flop their way to the relative safety of the sea. It managed to shut and lock the bathroom door before Aidan's body collapsed to the tile floor.

Get up, dumbass. Follow her.

Aidan felt nauseous. He didn't know if it was happening to his stomach in the alley right then or if the pain was an echo of a sickness his body had endured while trying to stand up to go after the woman. Before he could get a beat on the *when* of the biological inconvenience, he felt the hand of the concerned stranger land on his present-day shoulder.

"You don't look so great," the do-gooder said. "Come into the church with me, and we'll clean you up and get you some water."

Aidan's lips mouthed *leave me alone,* but no sounds accompanied the demand. Water and dry pants for the trip home sounded good, but he had to see the ending to the story playing against the flicker of his eyelids, which were fighting valiantly against the sun to remain open.

At least the man's grip on his shoulder was strong. Aidan welcomed the help in keeping his body erect. He managed to buy himself some time just by mumbling utter nonsense at him.

Aidan recalled that in the bathroom, his body finally rose from the floor. They were leaving, good for them! He doubted his invader had done so in time to catch up with Nicole but found himself rooting for his possessor with the same blind lunacy of a die-hard fan who's certain a Hail Mary will succeed. He was to the stairs now. His body lurched to climb the first step. The woman's fragrance was in the air—or his brain was only adding that delicious detail. His legs navigated each next step with caution, and it was hard to say if the adrenaline he felt at that moment was any more real than the perfume scent that his body was chasing. He was halfway up the stairs.

"I don't have all day," the stranger interrupted. "Do you want some help or—"

The speed with which his knife went from the sheath on his waist into the do-gooder's throat surprised Aidan. He'd barely been able to move his mouth seconds ago, but his body had effortlessly drawn the blade and punctured the stranger's aorta in a flash. The thing was back.

Blood gurgled from the gash in the man's neck as he gasped for air. The sounds gave Aidan no immediate pleasure. The weight of the victim's hand grew tenfold on his shoulder as it tried to keep the do-gooder from dropping to the ground. His other hand was wrapped around his throat, trying in vain to keep his life inside where it belonged.

It was a spectacle, but the kill had been out of character.

God dammit! What the hell have you done?

This kind of very public kill might give the impression Aidan wanted to get caught. What this thing inside of him had done was rookie, a true disappointment.

As his consciousness dimmed, he felt the warm splatter of the churchman's blood as it decorated his arms. One last flash of the memory hit him: his body made it to the street, then turned into the alley, but the woman from the grocery store was long gone. A few steps later, it collapsed, sending his head into the corner of the dumpster before settling on the ground.

Whatever you are, you're stronger now.

Aidan had no idea if the entity within had heard him, but he shared until he couldn't.

Whatever you are, clean us up before we kill again. There's bound to be some pants in a donation bin that fit. If we're going to do this, let's at least try to be professional about it.

22

NICOLE

Blackout blinds don't amount to much if you haven't shut your eyes in the first place. Though it bordered on abstract, thanks to Nicole's blurry vision, the fit of the automated covering over the window in room 1335 was the best she'd ever seen. But no man-made sun-blocker is ever perfect, and the morning outside had already found the only breach it needed to help her count the bottles at her bedside. There were many, but many was still too few.

This Radisson was on the same block as the church she'd fled twelve hours ago. She'd checked in with what she thought was enough booze to guarantee a different kind of blackout. Corner liquor stores were a real thing, and what did Manhattan have if not corners? The darkness she was seeking was one far more effective than any space-age polymer could ever deliver. She'd given it a real run, too, but the welcome embrace of a Nicole-made void built on booze had yet to squeeze the life out of her completely.

Other people in meetings shared all the time about their romanticized hopes for a big night out after putting together a significant day count. Sobriety, it seemed, gave every former addict and alcoholic the clarity they needed to outline a kind of forbidden grand plan that would put their lesser angels to the test. The Radisson north of the Financial District hardly fit the bill.

Some of those same people hadn't been bluffing. Relapse was common. Those who returned to the rooms to start their day counts over often reported, with a clearer clarity than ever before, that the liquor or the drugs or both—done full-orgy—had failed miserably at creating the bliss they'd once known. Of course, some of those diehards had died, too. Death was never the objective, but everyone understood that death was on the table when concocting these plans.

You can put the drinking aside, attend the meetings, work the steps, and confide in a sponsor about most of your shit, but if you don't identify the root cause of your disease—beyond the convenient excuse of your genealogy—then start to address it in earnest, the idea that a good, long, no-holds-barred drunk might actually deliver salvation it never had before doesn't just become hard to shake, it steels itself. It is an idea that will kill you . . . eventually.

John, a rehab therapist, had said basically that. It was a message Nicole had largely ignored.

Nicole had left the six-week program knowing in her heart she'd drink again. There'd been simply too much at stake to believe otherwise. But until her reason for wanting to live permanently sauced crystalized in the church basement, those stakes had been vague. It was a legitimate epiphany, and any good drunk runs like hell from those.

The root cause of the mess she'd become was Matthew.

She was capable of being a mother to one kid or two—or ten if she someday wanted. What had left her unhinged was having to parent her children with a partner she resented. She'd tackled and resolved so many resentments recently, but not with him. Not directly.

It wouldn't have mattered who she told or how she'd told them. It wouldn't have helped to workbook through the reasons or turn her guilt over to God as she understood him. To admit aloud to a sponsor, a friend, or anyone else that she was unhappy meant possibly starting a new life, one without Matthew. That was a future too optimistic and fanciful to be deserved.

The idea of an authentically happy version of herself was scary. Friends in her home group had shared their own stories of overcoming their fear of the same—it didn't matter, she still felt isolated and trapped. Defective. No one disliked her husband—at least, no one she knew. In fact, they all loved him. A consummate buddy. Tag and Amanda had held him in such high regard that . . . well, they certainly hadn't picked them to be Ethan's backup family because of her. She'd spent nearly a year believing that if she continued to fix herself, someday soon, she'd see Matthew the way everyone else did. The opposite had happened. Physically, she'd never been this healthy, but internally, she was infinitely more disingenuous for having quit drinking.

The red digits behind a large vodka bottle flipped to 11:25 AM. There'd been no new texts or calls from Matthew since his last voicemail the evening before. *Boundaries.* The word popped into her mind—not just the word but how he'd often said it. "This is your journey, Nicole. I'm here to help, but you know, I have to set boundaries." His smug image made her spit. Fine, Matthew, set your boundaries. See what that gets you.

She grabbed a lukewarm beer from the nightstand and gulped for salvation, but it did little to ease what was stabbing at Nicole's heart even more: Emily, who had her own phone, hadn't reached out to check on her missing mother, not once. Nicole's body shook from her hatred of them both and shook further still as her hostility shifted— she hated herself for hating them both so completely.

Part of what had always made her relationship with Emily so tenuous was her daughter had sensed from a young age that she didn't love Matthew. It could have been projection, all in Nicole's head, save for the fact Emily had once, and only once, asked about her feelings directly.

You don't really love Dad all that much, do you?

Em was only seven when she'd asked. Nicole lied and tried to punctuate it by telling Emily it was a ridiculous question. Her daughter never brought it up again, but Nicole knew it wasn't because she'd convinced her otherwise. Not everyone fakes love well.

As her daughter got older, Emily's antagonism toward Nicole grew. When Nicole was a drunk, Emily's anger was justifiable. But with Nicole sober and attentive, Em could still be quite caustic. Her epiphany last night revealed more than knowing it could never work out with Matthew. Emily still loathed her because she knew her mother had picked up the lie where she'd left off. Sober, stronger, capable, and still with Matthew. She was a coward.

She reached for the open pack of Camel Lights on the floor, a brand-new sin she'd added to her self-destruction repertoire. She'd smoked three of them, and they weren't doing much for her anxiety. Were they supposed to? The clerk at the liquor store had recommended them.

"What's a good cigarette to smoke?" she had asked him.

He squinted over an intentionally puckered lip as if the question was too dumb to answer. It was the type of disapproval that can sometimes turn a relatively plain man into forbidden fruit.

She tried to grin the question away, but the heat in her cheeks was uncomfortable, and speaking seemed like the only way to effectively squash her embarrassment.

"I mean, what do you smoke?"

"Camel Lights," he said. His face had dropped the faux stupefaction. He was decidedly unremarkable again.

"OK then, give me a pack of those."

He'd already grabbed and tossed them next to the liquor and beer. "That it?"

"That's it. Yes."

"You headed to a party?" he asked as he rang her up.

"No. Sadly, this is all just for me."

His face went sideways again. It was far less sexy than the first time.

"It *could* be a party," she hedged.

"Oh yeah?"

She'd already mentally committed to bringing him along for her tragedy. "Yeah, why the fuck not."

"Cool. I'm off in a little bit."

He'd arrived far earlier than she'd imagined he would, and she was only one drink in—ten too few to fuck a liquor store clerk. So, they drank together for a while, but the chit-chat was stilted. When he veered into questions about her home life after spotting her wedding ring, not even shot-gunning warm vodka made sex with him more appealing, so she pulled the plug.

His exit had been uneventful. Half of her had hoped he'd get angry, maybe even physical. She was ready to be broken, and violence might've been the quickest means to that end.

Nicole's phone vibrated for the first time that morning.

ICAL EVENT: ETHAN'S FRIEND'S BIRTHDAY PARTY—10 MINUTES

A calendar reminder ushering in crushing pangs of regret might have been good for a chuckle had it not been happening to her. The ping on its own was devastating.

Her stomach couldn't hold any more liquor, and the blackout she'd hoped for—a days-long, unfeeling detachment from everything real—remained out of reach. Dead to the world had been the goal. Or had she been wanting to die. To be dead. She wondered just how thin the line between the two feelings actually was. Either way, she cursed herself for not having put in the extra legwork the evening before to secure the drugs capable of packing just such a punch. A real walloper that didn't give two shits about how sober you'd been, what you'd learned in the program, or how your brain had rewired itself to be impervious to its mind-altering credentials.

She hurt—bad. Her whole being was cloaked in a deeper distress than any she'd ever experienced, and she'd brought it on herself. Maybe *that* had been her plan. To work herself into a darkness so bleak and self-destructive that Matthew would have no choice but to leave her instead of the other way around. It was a coward's plan, ripe with guilt, paranoia, and bordering on hysteria, not at all a best foot forward.

If there was a way to reverse course, Nicole would have to find out later. Her body finally succumbed to its agony and exhaustion. Call it passing out or going to sleep, it didn't matter, Nicole was grateful for her brain's insistence on shutting down. Booze had failed, perhaps rest would succeed and there'd be time to right wrongs tomorrow—but the hurt was too thick to drift away, and her eyes wouldn't close, not in the way she remembered eyes closing for sleep. Was it tiredness at all? Something heavy invaded her body, and it felt like second breaths were being made by another using her lungs. Inhalations she was not in control of were going in and out around the slower breathing she still had a grip on. She thought it might be a stroke or a heart attack or both, but the panic it created did nothing to help her lift herself from the bed.

She tried to reach for her phone, but her limb stayed put. When she kicked, no kick came. She'd had dreams where she'd tried to run only to stay still or move like she was in quicksand, but this was ten times worse. No thought led to any action from her body—and then, her body started moving with no thought on her part. Her eyes had remained wide open the entire time, but her vision darkened with each passing second. As she fought to stay present in her body and to keep her eyes her own, she heard a voice, faint but familiar.

I'm sorry, Nicole, but there's no other way to stop Amanda. I'll take good care of your body so that you still have a chance to take better care of it yourself down the road.

It was Tag.

PART III

23
MATTHEW

Matthew sang "Happy Birthday" with the other adults and children. His contribution felt hollow, so he raised his volume above the others to legitimize his good wishes for the birthday girl. Across the table, Em might've been trying to set him on fire by thinking about it. "Stop it," she mouthed. She didn't embarrass easily, but she did have a zero-tolerance policy for anyone full of shit.

She'd put up only a light resistance to joining him and Ethan for the party that morning. The past was no barometer of what she might do in the present, but he'd been thankful she'd made it easy and had leaned on her frequently already as he navigated toddler-party politics.

Matthew used to tell his friends their daughter had her mother's short fuse. Only those they'd known since college ever laughed at the comparison. The adults they'd met through parenting groups and Em's early schooling had no point of reference to *be* amused. It wasn't a good joke, but its success relied on an intimacy with a version of his wife they'd never met.

Somewhere along the way, after Emily's birth, Nicole had lost her lust for fighting, for love, and maybe for living. He had hoped when she got sober, some of that old Nicole would come back. Maybe it had, or maybe it would, but who'd had the time to find out?

Before Emily's eyes could finish crucifying him, Matthew forced a smile to let her know he'd read her loud and clear. He dropped his singing to a hush as they belted out the tune's final line. His fluctuations hadn't seemed to bother anyone. They were preoccupied with holding their children back from destroying the three-tier cake prematurely. Seeing their intolerant grips made him ease his own on Ethan, which had probably been tighter than theirs.

Matthew was exhausted. He'd fallen asleep mad enough to hope Nicole might never return. A tired brain presents simple solutions to a problem, and he'd faded out on the couch, believing her permanent absence might be the best thing for him and the kids. It'd made sense at that hour and only a bit less sense now. When it came to their family, she seemed disinterested.

Emily tapped his arm. He hadn't seen her walk around the melee to his side of the table. Though her touch was gentle and she was grinning, it startled him, and he released his clutch on Ethan. The boy took advantage of his freedom. He hopped to the floor from his chair and joined the children campaigning for bigger slices of cake at the end of the table. Ethan's manners were noticeably mature compared to those of the other preschoolers. He said please. He said pretty please, too. But his son's civility didn't garner a slice any faster, and Matthew wondered if he'd spent too much time preaching the virtues of playing by the rules to his kids.

Then, the host handed his son a plate holding the largest slice she'd served so far. He smiled at the woman's kindness, and she smiled back. It was a near ear-to-ear bend made of color-corrected teeth, too straight to be natural, sure, but the smile's effect was pure light. There was true joy in her, Matthew could feel it. She seemed authentically delighted with the chaos of dozens of hands that knew nothing about waiting their turn. If it was an act, it was deserving of an Oscar. Her patience with the children turned him on.

His sudden attraction to a woman he'd only met two hours ago was unexpected, and the timing was utterly inappropriate, but there was something sexy about how her enthusiasm rose to the challenge of matching the little monsters' fervor. He wondered how much she'd had to drink, how she'd found the right balance of champagne and food to stay calm but not uncaring. He considered offering to help her do the dishes later for the chance to flirt with her more directly.

He'd fallen under the spell of other mothers before. Women who seemed immune to the intentional and negligent destruction happening around them, like it was right then.

Four children at the party, all under seven, belonged to the host. He'd been introduced to them all. Her kids and no less than fifteen others, from twelve months to twelve years, were actively bum-rushing the house, armed with chocolate icing the white walls could not defend. Matthew had already accidentally smooshed cubes of cheese and other bite-sized snacks under his feet and into expensive rugs in every room. A casual surveillance of the event turned up dozens of marks and smudges on furniture and walls, which weren't there when they'd arrived.

How this woman had held her composure thus far was mindboggling. Hers was an equilibrium to lust after. He reassured himself this was what he was attracted to, not the woman herself, but making that assertion didn't quiet his anticipation of getting to know her better later.

He and Nicole had never hosted a party this large. For the first time, Matthew wondered if the decision to keep Emily's parties a more manageable size had been a mutual one. His wife's nerves frayed easily, so they never had more than two of Emily's friends over at once. It was what they always did—put his wife's needs above Emily's and even his own. And now Ethan's too.

Emily poked at him again. This time, it was hard and into a love handle.

"What a nightmare," she said. "Don't you think?"

Her tone was light. It sounded like she'd fashioned the question just to end his spiraling.

"You don't wish you'd had parties like this?" Matthew asked, eyes still on the host.

She grabbed his hand firmly and dragged him away from the table. As she navigated them from the dining room to the living room at the front of the house, he wondered if she'd set out to save him from making a mistake or just wanted his undivided attention for a while. She hadn't had it in over a year. It was an odd place for that to sink in, but better late than never, so he went with her willingly. She settled them near a bay window and patted for him to sit.

"Do you think that brat is going to remember any of this?" she asked.

He took it all in again: Hundreds of pastel-colored balloons covered every inch of the ceiling, and intricately decorated cookies and cupcakes modeled after popular children's show characters were on every available surface. There was laughter and music, and, well, they hadn't brought in a live pony or anything, but it seemed like a possibility. This was a celebration he knew he would remember. For no other reason than never having given Emily one like it.

"The birthday girl just turned four," Emily said. "Four! I don't remember my party from that age, and it's not because you guys forgot to stuff the house with every kid from the block."

"You honestly don't remember anything from that day?" he asked.

"My fourth birthday?"

"Yeah."

"If I say I definitely don't, will it hurt your feelings?"

"No," Matthew lied as he steeled himself for the impending hurt.

"Who can say what I remember and what I only think I remember? I've seen the pictures of my fourth birthday on Mom's Facebook page, you know what I mean?"

"Well, I remember it," Matthew said lightly, happy she'd handled her response delicately. "Every detail. There were only two other kids, but we *did* hire a clown. He scared the crap out of you, but I still tipped him."

Her expression offered no clue as to whether he'd jogged her memory, but his recollection of Em's fourth birthday party had eased his growing concern for Nicole, which had merged with his guilt for wanting to sleep with the birthday girl's mother. For a moment, he was present and only thinking about his little girl. Not so little now. He thought he might actually leave the party in a better mood than the one he'd arrived in, but the reprieve was short-lived.

"Are we going to talk about Mom?"

He acted like he hadn't heard her question.

They'd talked about Nicole already. Both the kids had wanted to know where she was when she didn't come down for breakfast that morning.

He told them she'd left early for a meeting and that sometimes when you are working out the hard stuff, you need extra help. If it had been only Emily, he'd have told her the truth: your mom went out last night, didn't come home, and hasn't called, texted, or responded to mine. But with Ethan all ears, too, he had lied. "She'll join us later this afternoon, I promise."

Save Santa Claus, the Easter Bunny, and the Tooth Fairy, Matthew had always worked hard to ensure that whatever he told his daughter was the truth. He'd also made the same promise to speak the truth to Ethan when he'd first arrived. But if he ever sat to count, he knew the number of fabrications he'd made up to protect his son this past year would stack up quickly.

As it turned out, Matthew had been ill-prepared to talk with Ethan about Tag, Amanda, and the accident. His son had so many questions about death, and the convenience of Heaven was too easy to ignore. Ethan, though, often protested his descriptions of a fluffy cloud afterlife inhabited by winged angels going about their good deeds—protested as best as a four-year-old could, anyway. That made sense. Ethan was bright and it all sounded too stupid to be believed. He didn't like lying to Ethan, wasn't about to start lying to Emily, and would have put it all out there about Nicole for Emily right then, but as it turned out, he'd misunderstood her question.

"Sure," he said. "I think you know that she didn't have a meeting this—"

"No, Dad. I mean, she's just been hiding outside on the sidewalk. For like an hour."

He looked through the bay window, expecting to see Nicole lean out from behind a tree. "Why didn't you tell me?"

Emily turned to look for her mother, too. "I figured you knew and were ignoring her."

"Are you sure?"

"Well, I don't see her now," Emily said, shrugging it off like a thousand times before.

God help him if Nicole was outside, hiding, or doing who knew what else. Matthew jumped up to go out front to look for her. As he did, he spotted Ethan in a large circle of other children on the floor.

His son's face was covered in chocolate icing, and he was laughing happily at the cartoon playing on the giant TV hung over the fireplace mantle.

Emily had stood too, and his pause gave her time to reach the front door ahead of him.

"No, Em. Please stay here and keep an eye on your brother."

Surprisingly, she returned to the living room and plopped into the only available chair without any backtalk. However, she did open her eyes extra wide before exaggeratingly looking at Ethan. "Like this," she said without blinking. "If she's out there, don't make a scene."

"That's rich, coming from you," he said with a chuckle as he opened the front door. Then again, Emily had treated Sober Nicole more affectionately in recent months, relatively speaking. "You got it," he corrected himself before stepping onto the empty stoop. He scanned the sidewalk from left to right and pulled his phone from his coat pocket. There were no new texts.

"Nicole," he said in a hush. "If you're out here, just say so. I'm not angry."

As he put the device back and started down the stoop's stairs, a huge crash came from the rear of the house. The impact was too heavy to be a wine glass or glass bowl, and it was followed by a smattering of "Oh my Gods," "Are you alright?" and one "Someone call 911."

From inside the house, Emily shouted, "Dad! Come quick, come quick!"

He ran through the foyer and back into the living room, where he'd left her to watch Ethan. She was no longer in the chair—she, Ethan, and everyone else had left the room. As he entered the dining room, he heard Ethan crying somewhere beyond the crowd of other parents and children now blocking the entrance into the kitchen at the back of the house.

"Daddy!"

Em hadn't called him Daddy since she was three. Her voice was fighting back tears. He pushed his way through the gawkers who, moments ago, had been stuffing cheese and booze into their already swollen guts. Together, they made a decent blockade.

On the other side of the group, he found Emily holding tight onto Ethan. To their right was Nicole, splayed out face down and bleeding on the floor, with the host holding her hand and telling his wife over and over again to hang in there, hang in there.

Matthew dropped to his knees beside Nicole and put a finger to her neck to check for a pulse. Behind her, there was no longer a window in the floor-to-ceiling frame. What was left of the glass was scattered all around them. She was alive but unconscious; the cuts on her body were deep, and the blood spilling from them grew to puddles on the tile quickly.

Another parent said an ambulance was on its way, and he started lifting Nicole to examine her torso. As he caught a glimpse of another gash that had just missed her jugular, she coughed. He welcomed the sign of life, even as it blew the contents of what smelled like a whole moonshine still into his and the host's faces. He held his wife's head gently above the mess so that she would not choke or suffocate.

"What the hell happened?" he asked the host, who'd lost all her allure.

"I don't know for sure. I saw her enter the backyard through the alley. She was stumbling horribly. I didn't know she was your wife. She hadn't come with you—I mean, we didn't meet her when you introduced yourself, and so I didn't recognize her, and I don't think I've ever seen her picking up Ethan from the academy. Something was off—it freaked me out, and I panicked."

"She doesn't do pick-up," Matthew said quietly as he tried to look past the part of the group still lingering around the trainwreck. No EMS, just strangers already gathering their things while trying to coax their children toward the front door to dress for leaving. He turned back to the host. "What do you mean you panicked? She's obviously drunk. What did you do to her?"

"Some people never change," another guest said under their breath.

"Fuck you," Em said, her body threatening to lunge.

He grabbed his daughter with his free hand before the fight in her got physical. "Don't. It's not worth it."

She stayed put, and Matthew looked back at the host for an answer.

"All I know is I asked her several times who she was. When she didn't answer, I ushered the kids who were back there into the house and shut and locked the door."

"It's true," another guest said. "I mean, I know who your wife is, but she didn't answer."

"We *all* know who your wife is, mister," said another.

"Is that what this is?" he asked the host. The room suddenly felt ten degrees warmer. "You recognized my wife and what? Got scared? Thought she would beat you up unprovoked?"

"I have no idea what you are talking about," the host replied.

There wasn't anything acrid in her tone, and her face appeared genuinely contrite.

He hadn't calmed, but forced his face to look it. "OK, I'm sorry. I just—"

"I know what drunk looks like," the host said. "This wasn't just drunk. It was more off than that—like her joints were strapped on backward. Anyway . . . she lost her balance on the patio and fell head-first through the window like something threw her into it. I'll swear to it."

As the sounds of an approaching ambulance grew, it hit Matthew that Ethan had long stopped crying. His son had not moved. He was puffy-eyed and seated at the feet of the remaining gawkers. Matthew tried to break his son's stare with a wave, but it never deviated from Nicole's broken body.

No other parent there had thought to pick up his son and move him to another room. Matthew didn't know what he'd expected anyone else there to do to help. Their inaction and sudden silence were grimly understandable, if not deeply disappointing. After all, Nicole's incident with Claire Bear hadn't really ever faded. Not locally. What Nicole had done was practically rebranded as a cautionary bit of folklore in their neighborhood. Until now, the faces huddled around the room had done a bang-up job of pretending they'd forgiven Nicole for bringing shame to Park Slope. Matthew's shame flared up. When he looked back at the host, who was technically helping by holding his wife's hand, his anger flared up, too.

He felt his face flush, and Emily stood as if she'd read his mind. As the ambulance screeched to a halt in front of the building, she picked up her brother, tried in vain to tuck his face into her neck, and said, "Come with me, little man. Mom's going to be fine." Still, the adults did nothing to help, save shuffle a little to make way for her.

"Fuck all of you," Matthew slipped. Then he looked the host right in the eye. "Even you."

24

AMANDA

Amanda had spent a good chunk of her Saturday morning in Prior Plane simply walking Aidan's body around Lower Manhattan. She fed him a pepperoni pizza slice for an early lunch, took him for a pleasant stroll along the East River, and rested his body on the occasional park bench. No one ran away terrified when she politely declined their attempts at conversation, and she had even managed to take him to urinate in a relatively clean bathroom inside the National Museum of the American Indian. She'd never been to see the exhibits while living, but it was free to enter, and even with the seemingly endless concrete steps at its entrance, it'd been far less hassle than negotiating a pop-in use of the toilet at a local eatery. Within Aidan's body, she managed to see it all in under two hours and had an espresso from their café to boot. They say practice makes perfect, and so far, she'd held her possession of Aidan without any interruption from him.

Not to get cocky, but by that afternoon, riding the Q train over the Manhattan Bridge to Park Slope inside Aidan's body felt secondhand. She had control now, and it felt complete.

She stared at the map of the transit system on the wall across from her. The various color lines sprawled out in every direction, and she regretted the lack of effort she'd put in while living there to see more of what each borough offered. When she returned her attention to the Manhattan skyline outside the window of the racing train, she couldn't help but wonder if, in time, it would be possible to possess Aidan's form forever—to mother Ethan through him.

Just stick to the original plan.

Whether it had worked or not, trying to spook Nicole into a relapse in the hopes that she would make some grave mistake with Ethan had been an unwise decision. When she'd hatched that idea, her own commitment to causing an accident or killing her son had been faltering. Being directly responsible for bringing Ethan to Second Plane had started to seem like an act she wasn't sure she could live with, so to speak. She understood that to grieve at all was actually a gift. You could not despair as she was without having loved someone very deeply. There was an argument to be made that one could actually be grateful for grief—but it was so intense of late.

Unlike The Text suggested, the passage of time had not weakened her desire to hold Ethan. Unlike The Text suggested, she was affecting things in Prior Plane with ease. Unlike The Text claimed, children *were* children in Second Plane. The Text was an index of lies as far as Amanda was concerned. Through rumors, the council had most assuredly planted the biggest lie of all: a punishment known as Third Plane, a banishment of sorts for any resident who succeeded in altering the course of a nonresident existence. Lies and more lies in the service of control.

But there was also a new wrinkle: seeing Ethan begin to thrive the past year with a newly sober Nicole had made her jealous. Amanda was no longer sure if she was acting out of grief or resentment. She could not deny that there was some part of her rooting for Nicole to fail spectacularly. The complexity of those feelings—emotions The Text and other residents wanted her to pretend she could not have—had eaten almost all that was left of her sanity. At a certain point, a parent's torment, if left untreated, will ignite and burn their whole home to the ground.

If she loved her son, his death would have to be her doing. Targeting Nicole to set off some loosey-goosey chain of events had always been a long shot—and more important, Aidan got off on it. Last night, she'd lost her grip on the possession because she'd inadvertently excited whatever little bit of him had been along for the ride.

That was her hypothesis, anyway. For that reason, she would have better luck maintaining control of his body if she kept him unsettled. Somewhat ironically, inhabiting him worked best when she kept his brain tethered to the very possibility that he feared most: that he'd lose control of himself at some point and kill a child.

If he ever got caught or turned himself in, Aidan would be instantly labeled a serial killer. Prior to getting to know him better, she'd have agreed with any chyron that said as much. But she wasn't sure the moniker fit. Not neatly. It shouldn't have come as a surprise that, like all walks of life, killers couldn't be grouped under one umbrella. Many killers in the living plane of existence probably murdered anything and anyone of any age and felt no remorse. Aidan, though, had feelings, maybe not empathy by definition, but something close enough, and his soul had been battling the complexities of his atonement for decades.

The self-loathing he adroitly hid from the world was neatly documented in hundreds of journals shelved in his home library in Stamford, Connecticut. The collection was a true-crime treasure trove. In those early days of possession, while honing her control of Aidan's body, she cautiously kept him home and would seat him at his desk to read his hand-written tomes.

He hated humanity. He hated adults. He hated himself, too, at least enough to once try suicide. The books may have numbered in the thousands and they had no dates, nor had Aidan shelved them in chronological order. There wasn't time to read them all, but Amanda had counted only ten of the hundreds she'd read or scanned that were focused solely on the gratuitous details of his murders. His affinity for children was intriguing. He was sympathetic to kids because, in his experience, few boys and fewer girls ever got a real shot to define their lives, at least not until they were adults, when much of their independent thinking was actually the thoughts and actions that had been molded by their parents, both good, bad, and indifferent. He considered himself some sort of protector of the innocent, and only the young *could* be innocent, he'd written—many times over. With children, death by his hand was self-forbidden.

Recalling his ramblings as the train rumbled through the darkness underneath Brooklyn threatened to lull Amanda out of her possession.

She stood quickly from her seat and caught Aidan's reflection between the etched graffiti on the window. Looking away proved difficult.

He's not wrong, of course. Ending Ethan's time here will only give credence to his belief that children have no real control. Their destinies are built on the whims of broken souls.

"Pull yourself together," a voice said.

The sharp directive broke the reflection's hold on her.

"Excuse me?" Amanda said as she turned to address the meddler.

It was a man in his thirties, seated across from her, phone hanging awkwardly in hand with the browser still open and playing a porno clip featuring a woman at the center of a bunch of paunchy male bodies unloading their semen in turn on her face. He'd been at the other end of the car for most of the ride, and she hadn't seen him get up to move or noticed the cigarette burns that pocked the skin up and down both of his too-thin arms. Under closer scrutiny, his irrelevance to her earlier was even more justified. She started to tell him to mind his own fucking business when she noticed a familiar gray swirl of smoke dancing about in both his eyes.

"Don't get your panties in a wad. It's Gabriel."

Years of commuting on high alert had instinctively caused Amanda to put Aidan's body into fight-or-flight mode. She eased his muscles and sat back down.

Gabriel had never shown up in Prior Plane during a possession before—at least as far as she knew—but the way the muscles underneath the man's face undulated vertically from one side to the other removed all doubt.

"I'm confused," Amanda said.

"A byproduct of the amount of time you've been in Aidan today, I imagine."

"No . . . I mean, why are you here?"

"To make sure you don't fuck this up. If you haven't already."

In the past year, Gabriel had asked her for nothing. Why it had been willing to identify Aidan as a candidate for possession remained a mystery. The connections they'd made while Amanda familiarized herself with possession rarely strayed outside the lines of friendly chitchat.

"How are you doing with Aidan?" it would ask. This was always its lead.

If she answered in detail, the beast would shush her as if it had realized they were on a hot mic during a segment of an interview not meant for broadcast. Was it afraid, or was it because Gabriel simply didn't care? Or didn't care yet? The only answer it ever wanted to hear when it asked how things were going was, "It's going good."

"Going good, is it?" Gabriel asked.

"Better than expected. Tonight's the night."

Before she could retract it, she gave it a thumbs-up with Aidan's hand. It wasn't amused.

"That's not what I observed," it moaned.

"You've been watching?" she asked.

"Killing that fella at the church this morning is your idea of 'going good?'"

"That was Aidan, not me."

Amanda wasn't sure if that was a lie. She wanted to believe it had been Aidan. True or false, the stranger's mouth curled in disgust.

"Aidan wouldn't have killed that man," Gabriel said in a tone that almost sounded like it had taken her accusation personally. "Not there, not like that."

Amanda rolled Aidan's tongue over his lips as she considered the truth. "OK, maybe I did. What does it matter?"

The man's body jerked forward violently from the waist, and his phone dropped to the floor. Gabriel kicked the device under the row of seats, but it did not retract the man's forward lean, which seemed to stretch over the aisle further than was possible. Under the inward tilt of the man's brows, its eyes went deep-space black.

"I realize it's a Saturday, Amanda, but did you really think dragging that poor soul's corpse behind the dumpster was a long-term solution?"

"No."

"No," it shook its head as it leaned the man's body back into the seat. "Of course not."

It would make no difference to Gabriel, but Amanda didn't remember doing that. In the minutes after the kill that she'd made using Aidan's body and his knife, she'd been utterly shell-shocked. After she took back control of Aidan, she'd heard his thoughts. His frustration was a lot to process and so, yes, maybe she'd fucked up hiding the body. It seemed trivial—not the man's death, that had weighed on her quickly, but how she'd gone about cleaning up didn't matter. Objectively, stabbing the man in the throat still seemed like it'd been the right thing to do, but the thought of possibly meeting that same man at some point as a new resident in Second Plane had been uncomfortable. Convincing herself the do-gooder's murder wasn't her, or at minimum that it'd been a cooperative effort had been easy because doing so was necessary to move forward.

"There was a witness, too," Gabriel said. "NYPD has a description. Don't shoot the messenger, but you are running out of time, my friend."

The train pulled into the station. She was the next stop. They sat in silence as they waited to see if anyone else would board the car.

Gabriel had once called Aidan a very unique possessee and told Amanda that what made his mental state weak enough for her to inhabit his body was that as a very young boy, he'd become infected with an insufferable sadness that all his kills had not cured—would not cure and could not cure. Being inside his body hadn't proved Gabriel's claim one way or another. The books he'd penned seemed to support its assertions, but oddly, when Amanda had once brought up Aidan's journaling, Gabriel swore it knew nothing of the vast library or the man's ramblings. "Either way," it had assured her, "his dark sadness is our bright fortune."

The only new passenger to board their car had chosen to put as much distance between them and herself as possible. A mouse of a thing, and neither considered her a threat. The train lurched into motion—a jolt that in the weeks past might have been enough to wake Aidan. Even Gabriel's face went slack in anticipation of seeing Aidan resume control, but Amanda felt no inner-rumblings and heard no extraneous thought and moved from her seat to sit next to Gabriel.

"I'm on my way to Ethan now," she whispered. "To bring him home."

"Good," Gabriel replied in a snarl, though it didn't turn its head to do so. "Try not to kill anyone else on your way there. As twisted as

Aidan's legacy is, it isn't yours to fuck up . . . at least not any more than you already have."

It had said it so loud that Amanda cocked Aidan's head a bit and looked to the end of the car. The other passenger had her attention buried in the book she had propped on her pregnant belly. It was a book Amanda remembered ordering once from Amazon, but she'd never bothered to crack it open: *The Overparenting Epidemic*. She grinned an ever so subtle self-admonishing smirk and felt Aidan's face do so in kind. The control she had over him was thicker than ever.

As the train pulled into Amanda's station, she turned confidently back to Gabriel and said, "I realize I've asked before, but I have to know . . . why are you helping me?"

The man's head turned with uncertainty as his very regular eyes simultaneously struggled to locate his phone. When he registered how close Aidan's body was to him, he managed to say, "Ever heard of personal space? Get the hell away from me, man!"

Gabriel was gone.

"Stand clear of the closing doors, please."

Amanda jumped from her seat and ran for the train's exit. The body's leap and sprint were impressive, and she made it out of the car before the doors slid shut.

Though the visit from Gabriel had been troubling, physically she felt steady. She felt grounded. She smiled wide and Aidan's mouth smiled. There was no tremble or glitch between her commands and his body's actions. Her amusement with that development continued when, for the first time in dozens of tries, she walked Aidan through the station as comfortably as if his body were her own, practically dancing up the stairs and into the street.

Park Slope had always had a scent. All the boroughs did. Maybe it'd been her imagination, but this part of Brooklyn always smelled sweeter than the other neighborhoods. It was the scent of knowing you were home. She'd arrived—in Aidan's body—and was too strong this time to give running back to Second Plane to get into it again with Gabriel a second thought.

25
MATTHEW

"Keep an eye on your brother," Matthew said. "This will only take a minute."

He and the kids had just walked through the front door, but if he was going to catch Lucinda before she was asleep, he needed to make the call quickly. As he climbed the staircase, Em stopped short of removing her puffy black jacket and slid it back over her shoulders. She grabbed the remote from the coffee table and practically pushed Ethan onto the couch, who was still in his blue parka, hoodie drawn tight around the exhaustion on his face.

"On it," she said, with a zeal unbefitting of a family who'd spent the whole afternoon and most of the evening at the hospital, bedside with Nicole. "Who wants to watch some Minions?"

Since Ethan's arrival, his daughter's preteen angst had largely regressed to a more youthful, playful disposition, especially when her new brother was in the same room. That change had been heartwarming to witness and was no less so, even with next steps for Nicole on his mind.

His children had seen their mother bleeding and unconscious, hurried away by EMS amid the disquieting innuendo spoken in cruel whispers by supposed friends. They then sat for hours next to Nicole, who'd done little more than mumble to them and her doctor between bouts of fitful sleep. Nothing he planned on telling Ethan's grandmother would traumatize the kids further, but keeping whatever conversation happened between him and Lucinda private was the responsible thing to do. His side of their talk, at least, so Matthew closed his bedroom door.

Over the past year, Lucinda had been reasonable, even kind. She clearly loved Ethan and had occasionally taken in Emily for a few nights. They were both her grandchildren at this point.

When Nicole was in rehab, Lucinda always ended every in-person get-together, phone call, email, or text with "Call me if you need anything," though sometimes her voice-texting translated the message to "Call me if Eunice gets filings." Always good for a laugh. She remained eager to lend a hand even after Nicole came back home. Slightly suspicious, maybe, but eager nonetheless. Tag never went into much detail about his father's alcoholism or the abuse Lucinda withstood until he passed, but Matthew knew enough to put up with Lucinda's doubts.

"Hope it sticks," she said once to Nicole. "The kids are counting on you."

Asking her to watch the kids a second time that week didn't feel like an imposition, but Matthew reconsidered reaching out to her as he scrolled to her name on his phone.

For a moment, his ears tuned back into the kids and the TV downstairs.

"Oh, hey! Looka!" he heard a Minion say. "C'est un banano!"

"C'est un banano!" Ethan repeated, laughing extra hard as he often did just to get his sister to laugh with him. Emily didn't leave him hanging. Their resilience was admirable.

With his thumb floating above CALL, he considered the consequences of reaching out.

The Lucinda he'd grabbed Ethan from a year ago wasn't the woman Matthew knew now. If she held out some hope of bringing Ethan home to live with her permanently, she'd never told him. The legal battle he once suspected would come never materialized. Even when he had shared the situation regarding ACS and their investigation into Nicole and their family, Lucinda offered half a dozen contacts she believed could help Matthew steer through the process.

Since then, maybe the few times she'd watched Ethan over a weekend had left her weary of caring for the boy full-time. Aging parents do a slick job of forgetting the trials of full-time parenting.

He clicked CALL, and as the phone trilled, Matthew couldn't discount the possibility that Ethan's grandmother had always been waiting for the right time and an obvious tragedy to make the necessary legal fuss required to become the boy's custodial parent. Would that even be bad?

"It's late, Matthew. Is everything all right?"

He hadn't expected a hello, but it put him off kilter when she skipped the pleasantry.

"Hello, Lucinda, yes . . . everything is OK. How are you?"

OK? It wasn't exactly a lie. Emily and Ethan were unharmed, at least physically, and watching cartoons downstairs. Their durability in the face of their mother's self-inflicted misfortunes was old hat by now. What each might say about Nicole and him to future therapists was easy to guess. But that was a black hole to fall into some other day.

"Everyone's OK? You sure about that, Matthew?"

It sounded like she somehow already knew, some sort of Grandma intuition.

"Yes, we are *all* OK."

Technically, Nicole was stable. She was in the capable hands of the staff at New York-Presbyterian Brooklyn Methodist Hospital, bandaged and banged up but asleep when they'd left. She'd arrived with some internal bleeding. "Nothing fatal," the attending physician had said.

Nicole was OK. They were OK. He was OK. He was doing the right thing, he thought, by phoning Lucinda for help. All of these facts could be neatly housed under the very definition of OK. He'd self-vindicated the use of the word. They *were* OK.

Lucinda let out a long sigh, more tired than annoyed.

"I'm OK, too, thanks for asking. Reading in bed, though, I think I nodded off a few pages back. Book club is brunching tomorrow to discuss this catastrophe, and I'm sure the other biddies will take a cruel delight in realizing I'm many chapters behind. I'll fake it, best I can."

Matthew felt she was expecting a laugh, so he forced one through his growing anxiety. It barely made a sound. The children's giggles downstairs had more volume than his manufactured amusement. Whatever the Minions had done, it was enough to cause a second bigger laugh from the kids, one that penetrated the walls of his bedroom.

"Is that the kids I hear? Kind of late for Ethan to still be up, isn't it?"

On the way back from the hospital, Matthew had committed to getting right to the point—he wasn't surprised by his second thoughts, but his brain struggled to come up with alternative believable excuses for having phoned at 10:30 PM on a Saturday.

"I don't mean to be rude, Matthew, but there *is* a reason you rang me, isn't there?"

"Nicole's had an accident," he answered and chewed at his lip after he had.

"Oh my, is she hurt?" The sleep in her voice vanished. "What happened this time?"

This time. She made it sound as if she'd been tallying their problems all along. Nicole had created more than her fair share of problems in the past, but lumping in this accident with those—an accident the old bitch didn't even know anything about yet—sickened his stomach.

His regret for sharing the news was instant, but there was no turning back now. He desperately needed the kids out of the house the whole week if he was going to be of any real help in helping Nicole get well enough to navigate her reentry into recovery successfully.

"I didn't see it happen," he answered. "But she either fell through a window or walked into it . . . maybe she threw herself into the pane. No one knows for sure."

"I don't understand. Threw herself through a window? How? Or . . . why?"

According to the doctor, Nicole's blood alcohol level measured in the range where a loss of consciousness had been possible. He hadn't needed a hematologist's results to know she was loaded. Her stink of booze and perspiration probably still lingered in the host's kitchen.

"Stuart? Makalino?"

"Banana . . . banana!!"

"Bob! Stopa!"

There was no laughter from either Em or Ethan this time. It made sense they'd crashed so quickly after the day they'd all had.

"Matthew," Lucinda said sharply, snapping him back to the call. "Why it happened doesn't really matter, does it? Is Nicole home with you now? Are the kids hurt?"

He'd phoned for help and had no right to be angered by her concern, but a furnace went on inside of his gut. Containing the heat, preventing his insides from boiling out and through his mouth in the form of expletives, would be difficult. Best to try and back out.

"It's fine . . . she's at a hospital a few blocks from here—"

"I'm coming over. Don't say another word."

There was a legitimate ringing in his ears, one he knew was possible any time all the blood rushed to his head and found no exits to relieve the pressure. Underneath it, he heard the woman shuffle out of her bed and to her closet. This was what he wanted, wasn't it? Her help?

He needed to focus on Nicole. A week would barely make a dent. He needed time to find out what had actually happened with Nicole, outline a plan with her and her doctors, and do so without worrying about what the kids were hearing, how much they were eating or not eating, or who was trying to pick them up or not picking them up without his permission.

"Lucinda, coming over right this minute isn't necessary," he said.

"Mmmhmm" was all he heard back. The woman had made up her mind, and inexplicably, her commitment to helping them immediately only angered him more.

She had the means to get there safely. She had the means to care for them both. She had the means to watch them indefinitely. Her help was going to make everything easier. He needed it. He couldn't deny that. There was no one else in the world more trustworthy than a blood relative. She wasn't his blood, but she was Ethan's, at least. Fighting her arrival was dumb.

His thoughts stacked quickly, blending into one another and making too much sense. They were interrupted briefly by what sounded like Lucinda talking to someone else at her home. Like she'd cupped the receiver and grabbed a landline to reach out to someone else while dressing. Even if she wasn't now, who might she alert once she found out Nicole hadn't just had an accident but had disappeared the night before and gotten filthy drunk?

The year so far had been calm relative to the clusterfuck this week had become, and it'd gone tits up not long after the anniversary of their last clusterfuck. He believed Lucinda liked him. She'd remarked positively on the connection he'd fostered with her only grandson a handful of times, but how much additional slack would she be willing to give?

He heard a conversation; it was faint through what felt like plugged ears. What was the old woman saying to someone else as she dressed to come to their rescue? She lived alone. His mind was spinning out on the possibilities now—charging ahead on absurd postulations while remaining oblivious to the sound of Pepper barking violently downstairs.

"Who are you talking to, Lucinda?" He'd practically screamed it.

"I'm not talking to anyone," she said, still calm on her end. "The TV is on."

"I thought you were reading." He sounded less angry but no less suspicious.

"What are you implying, Matthew?" she asked.

"If you've called someone, I have a right—"

"And what's got the dog so riled up?" she interrupted.

All the blood stuck in Matthew's head flushed back toward his chest, overloading his heart. Free from their obstruction, his ears keyed in on the repetitive boom of Pepper's worry. It was a shrill barking that Matthew had never heard before, and it grew more and more haunting as he raced down the stairs to the otherwise quiet family room below.

26
TAG

Tag had left the hospital well before Matthew and the kids. While there, Nicole had been unresponsive to his attempts to possess her a second time. Now, he was just a ghost again, standing on the moonlit sidewalk outside Matthew's home in case Amanda showed up in Aidan's body, and utterly uncertain of what to do about her if she did.

He decided his failure to occupy Nicole's body properly had been a lucky break. Had it worked, anything he said through her to Matthew in front of that kind of supervision might have seen a nurse or doctor administer a stronger sedative. She was already zonked. If a decision was made to put her in the psych ward, the eyes on her and the body he needed would surely double.

Then again, maybe possessing Nicole the *first* time had been the lucky break.

"Putting a body on isn't for everyone," Gabriel had said. "Especially the meek."

He hated how *it* had phrased the act of possession. Of course, he hated a lot of what Gabriel had said to him when they'd connected.

As the noises of the city, near and far, faded in and out on the wind, Tag thought back on the conversation he had with Gabriel and wondered if, in truth, he'd had no luck at all. Everything since their meeting had felt more like a curse. Plus, as the beast had said, maybe

Tag didn't have the guts to see possession through. "Not like *her*—not like Amanda."

Curse or no curse, the connection itself could have been categorized as divine intervention.

* * *

When Amanda left him, Tag had only the name Gabriel. How many residents in Second Plane also went by Gabriel or Gabe or even Gabby? At a minimum, many centuries' worth of residents had to have arrived with that name or some variation of it. Others may have taken on the designation as a nickname for whatever reason, religious or kooky. Tag had no last name, and even if he had, there was nothing in the way of a phone book. He didn't know where to start.

Then, he remembered how Rebecca, Amanda's first mentor, had once taken a chance on him. She had tried to warn him—in her ass-backward way—about what lay ahead for Amanda. She'd spoken of the symptoms of something darker happening within Tag's wife. Though, as he recalled it, Rebecca had been vague, almost cryptic, about what she thought Amanda was up to.

She's seeking an answer to a question no decent resident here will answer.

Perhaps not understanding her insinuations at the time had been his fault. Maybe he hadn't really been listening to the woman, or maybe he hadn't wanted to believe her. He hadn't been all that pleasant, either, and she might have held a grudge against him . . . or his wife.

With only the name Gabriel in hand, he reached out to Rebecca, hoping for nothing and expecting even less than that. It was a long shot, but better than no shot. All he could do after was wait to see if she'd accept his invitation to connect. To his surprise, she did.

When they met, Tag hadn't bothered with conjuring scenery for the visit, but what Rebecca had created around herself was a perfect recreation of a 1980s suburban kitchen. Hers, no doubt, and a stunning effort either way. It was a claustrophobic galley-style layout with white laminate cabinetry above a ceramic tile counter with a thick gray grout that looked difficult to keep clean. The wood veneer on the tops and sides of the microwave was the first tell, but it was the faux brick linoleum floor that gave the era away completely.

As Amanda had insisted, Tag saw what Rebecca had created because he had chosen to see it. Rebecca waited for him behind the living room side of the kitchen counter, perched on an overstuffed barstool that might have passed for chic during that decade. Her smile was still bubbly, but unlike their original meeting, neither made any benign pleasantries to start this conversation. Tag would never know if Rebecca knew why he'd come to see her beforehand because, as it was, he'd been unable to keep the name and reason for being there under wraps.

No hello. No how have you been? Just out with it:

"Do you know someone named Gabriel?" he asked.

Her smile snapped flat, and he thought he had caught a few of the appliances disappearing in his periphery. She wasn't quick to respond but eventually said, "Yes. Unfortunately, I do." Like the first time they met, she did most of the talking from there.

Rebecca knew Gabriel because, at some point during her residency, Gabriel had wanted to know her. It had sent the requisite invitation to connect, "It's about your husband, Henry." Although Rebecca had observed Henry in Prior Plane recently, she had hurriedly agreed to meet.

Once she revealed to Tag that she knew who Amanda had been talking to and could point him to Gabriel, it became difficult for him to feign interest in the rest of Rebecca's story. He wanted to leave. He wanted to get on with it. Ethan's life was on the line, and he assumed that only Gabriel had the answer to his question. The same question Amanda had once sought. He needed to connect with Gabriel. Thankfully, perhaps sensing his urgency, Rebecca kept it brief.

She told Tag she believed Gabriel had sought her out because of how long her "one true love," Henry, was taking to die. Rebecca admitted that, at times, she couldn't understand why, like her, Henry hadn't taken his own life by then. Gabriel had offered to help Rebecca kill her husband or cause an accident to get Henry to Second Plane sooner.

"After all," it had told her, "Your husband has had a good long go of it, love."

That was true, she said. By Rebecca's estimation, Henry had beaten the odds countless times thanks to Big Pharma. But what had been untrue was the claim Rebecca had made when she first met Tag about no longer tracking the passage of time. Her laissez-faire "he's meant to be joining me soon" attitude about his eventual arrival in Second Plane had all been an act.

She admitted she'd been desperate, said she must have reeked of it, and so wanting of her husband to be by her side that she might have gone ahead with a plan to kill him. But as it turned out, that wasn't all that Gabriel wanted. What it did want, Rebecca could not say, not exactly, because as she had done with Tag, she got the sense that Gabriel kept its proposition vague on purpose. After all, in Second Plane, one never knew who might run to squeal to the council.

Gabriel had told her, "If we succeed, perhaps, in turn, you might be kind enough to do something for me." Though Henry was all Rebecca wanted, all she ever thought about anymore, she'd still taken a hard pass on the opportunity and stood by her decision until Gabriel vacated.

"It wasn't so much what it'd said," Rebecca told Tag. "But how it'd said it—or maybe even what Gabriel looks like when it speaks. Honestly, Tag, as a resident, I hadn't felt anything close to scared until its visit. What Gabriel is, I do not know. Demon? Former human? It is a foul thing. I know that much. Horribly foul, unconscionably so. With plans of its own, I'm certain."

She hadn't been wrong about those last two details, though even after meeting Gabriel, Tag would remain unclear about its objective for wanting to help any of them.

When Tag connected with Gabriel, he realized that beyond the look it presented, it also put off an energy he struggled to identify. It wasn't just that Gabriel was a living nightmare; it was that Gabriel was a nightmare that somehow still made you feel like if you would only play ball with it, it might be your best friend. And why any resident would want that, including Tag, when he'd been near it, Tag could not say. It certainly hadn't tried to charm him with words.

"Nice of your wife to name-drop me," it had said.

"I don't think she inten—"

"Funny enough, your wife didn't have much to say—maybe nothing at all—about you when she and I met. In and of itself, that says plenty about what kind of man you are, *Taggart*."

It'd dropped his full name like Lucinda used to when she was disappointed in him, probably not all that different than other mothers did with their sons when cross. His name left the beast's mouth with a harder-than-necessary T to start a scoldingly elongated version, one that sounded more motorbike than maternal.

What followed were other barbs—some sharp, some whiffs—and it had spoken each one in a different voice, punctuating them all by leaning into his full name in that way.

"You have snitch written all over you, *Taggart*."

Fine.

"Is this who you were back in Prior Plane? All skin and bone with no bulge under your belt. How did you ever land such a gorgeous, intelligent woman, *Taggart*?"

That one had been a fair question.

"She's going to succeed, you know. Your boy . . . he will die. And I'm not going to help you. You can beg, you can plead, but you brought this all on yourself, *Taggart*."

That last bit had been hard to sit through—too much truth in it—but Tag did not waver. Its facial composition made it hard to say if Gabriel was disappointed by its failure to provoke him. As its form faded, it said, "Useless, that's you. Useless from day one. A mother knows."

But then something happened. Gabriel's eyes went stock-still, and it returned fully. The two dark pits stayed motionless on Tag, and for a moment, the creature said nothing. Tag wondered if whatever Gabriel was had glitched. Its form had been lively prior, moving about as it made those jibes at him. Now, the dark mass of scribbled black mess that it presented itself as appeared to be stuck, like a Zoom meeting attendee frozen in a presentation smile, except in this case, the smile featured rows and rows of teeth that filled its vertical mouth well past its gullet.

"On second thought . . ." it finally announced, "They—the council and just about everyone I've ever met here—say being dead doesn't mean you can see the future. I wonder, Tag, do you agree?"

Its question came from so far left field that Tag spat out the first thing that came to mind.

"I've heard of a theory about confusing the future for the present in an observation—"

"Of course," Gabriel interrupted. "But I'm not talking about that. Anyway . . . I agree with what *they* say. I've tried to see the future from here. There's a lot that's possible in Second Plane, *that* I know, but precognition isn't one of them. If it were, maybe I wouldn't be so sad myself."

Tag wanted to know what had made the thing in front of him sad, but he dared not ask.

Gabriel stood there, mumbling under its breath. Maybe it wanted Tag *to* ask.

It rambled on for a while, debating itself softly about what sounded loosely like options, though Tag could not ascertain whose. He worried it was considering leaving. It hadn't told him anything of value, and if Gabriel broke the connection, Tag figured that'd be it. No help, no solutions. No additional meet-ups. Gabriel was under no obligation to ever connect again.

"Buuuuuut . . ." Gabriel said, breaking the silence and letting the word flow from its mouth longer than necessary. "That doesn't mean one should belie a hunch, does it?"

It crept closer to Tag now. Put a stringy black arm around him. Its touch was unpleasant, like maggots crawling on skin, and as it leaned in, he picked up Vieux Boulogne on its breath.

"When intuition kicks in—be it a mother's or otherwise—maybe it's best we listen." It was speaking now in a sweet voice of maternal permission. "Yes. When we have a strong inkling, we must listen to it with everything we've got as if we know it to be the future ahead."

"At the end of the day, isn't that just a gamble?" Tag asked.

"Not in my opinion," it said. "The trendy call it manifestation."

Tag stayed silent and wondered if Gabriel's heavy grip would prevent him from leaving.

"Who knows?" it said, far more gleefully than it had been the entire time. "Maybe possession is a gamble—for *you*, what with Third Plane being the punishment." It tsked loudly. "Horrible thing to be banished there and unable to see your boy when he arrives. Whenever that may be." Then, its eyes closed, disappearing from its face, though not wholly, as it softly added, "I know I couldn't do it." For a moment, through all the Burtonesque bells and whistles of its repugnant appearance, Tag thought Gabriel looked almost wistful. As if caught, it shuddered its sadness off just as quickly and said, "But a gamble for *me*? Well, I guess with what I'm about to tell you, we'll find out one way or another. But I like my odds, Tag. I really, really do."

* * *

Back on the street, there was a sudden burst of laughter as a group of teens passed through Tag. The disturbance of their trespass was enough to shake him from the memory of his meet-up with Gabriel. In the end, Gabriel gave Tag the secret to possession and only said, "I have my reasons." But it'd sworn up and down and backward—and in its case, its mouth had traveled behind its head—that it did not know of a person Tag could possess in Prior Plane.

"You're on your own with that part," it had said. "Good luck."

And so now, Tag was back to where he'd been just moments ago: observing Matthew's house, feeling lucky his possession of Nicole had taken the first time, and wondering if he'd ever have that opportunity again. Even if he did get that chance and it worked, he doubted with a crippling certainty that he'd fare any better at moving her body, when and if he ran into Amanda.

Taking Nicole to the birthday party had been a mistake. In hindsight, Tag wished he'd spent a little more time working with his possession of her body in the hotel room before trying to warn Matthew about Amanda. Or about Aidan. He didn't know how he'd have framed it.

His fall through the window could have killed Nicole, and what then? Tag knew of no other inhabitable soul, and there wasn't time to run around trying out people willy-nilly.

Not long after Tag arrived at the house, Matthew and the kids had returned home. He'd followed his friend upstairs but left while Matthew was on the phone with Tag's mother in order to act as a sentry out front—an inept one, sure, but he foolishly hoped that when it mattered, there might be something—*anything*—he could do.

Amanda had never admitted to having caused a piece of Ethan's broken cereal bowl to drop to the floor a year ago with Matthew, nor to making their son's waffle plate fling from the high chair tray when ACS was incessantly ringing at the door. Still, Tag had yet to let go of the idea that she had somehow affected Prior Plane on those occasions. With the right motivation, he might be able to cause a tangible act in Prior Plane, as well. But he recognized it was quite a leap from nudging a dish off a tray to, say, shoving a window air conditioner onto a killer's head.

There was no telling how Matthew's call with Lucinda was going. Being in two places at once wasn't possible, even dead, but he'd heard enough of their conversation before returning to the street to believe that his mother would be there soon to grab Em and Ethan. State lines wouldn't stop Amanda, but moving the kids to New Jersey would create more distance for Aidan to travel. Construct or not, it would create time. Lucinda just needed to beat Amanda to Ethan.

The foot traffic on the street was thinning. It was mostly people walking their dogs and the occasional single or couple returning relatively early from a night on the town, sometimes loudly. Tag imagined if he could be seen, the intense scrutiny he was putting on any human being within fifty yards would get him arrested—or at least reported by the neighborhood watch.

If Amanda didn't show up soon in Aidan's body, he would head back to the hospital to see if the effects of the drugs they'd given Nicole were waning. Returning there could happen in a blink, but walking her body to the house would take time. Fighting Amanda in Aidan's body using Nicole as a vessel might end disastrously—his wife had more practice. Possessing Nicole successfully had surprised him, even if using her when he did had been an educated guess.

Thanks, Dad.

There was little to like about his dad, a hardworking man who had first put his career ahead of his family and then later his addictions for as far back as Tag could remember. He'd never been particularly cruel to Tag or his mother; his father wasn't physically abusive in any way and was known to disappear for long spells, but never forever. Even so, he'd been emotionally absent from anything that was important to either of them and had been fundamentally missing from their lives long before they'd had to put him in the ground.

When Dad died, he was glad. Good riddance. Childish behavior maybe, given that Tag had been his own man by then, but ten years later, and dead himself, his feelings hadn't changed.

Early on in Second Plane, it occurred to Tag that it might be possible to see his dad again. In fact, if he so chose, he could have visited his old man without needing it to be consensual.

Only blood relations are excluded from making a mutual commitment for a connection to occur. You may ask why, but the only answer we can offer is that it's never not been this way.

Tag had never asked why it was that way, and he had also never seriously considered making a connection. His dad never showed up unexpectedly in his space, either, so he guessed the hard feelings they'd both gone to the grave with about each other remained mutual: Dad with a deep resentment for Tag's constant badgering, and Tag with an ambivalent hate for his father.

But after Tag discovered that Amanda was using Aidan's body and on the loose in Prior Plane, he felt he had no one else to turn to. When he asked Donovan for help, "I am not my brother's keeper" from The Text was all the excuse his mentor had needed to "sit this one out."

Tag wondered if his father had been observing his life before death and had "met" his only grandson, perhaps even relished having one. Anything was possible in Second Plane, or so he'd been told. There was no booze in Second Plane, and while that didn't mean Dad was free of newer addictions, it could mean he was at least sane enough to want his grandson to live.

Tag decided a visit with his father was worth a try. He thought it, and nothing happened. He tried willing himself into what was supposed to be that sure-fire connection with his father, over and over. Eventually, it became clear that no connection could be made, but thinking so hard about his dad in order to see him brought up a lot of uncomfortable memories. One of those recollections was a striking misfit, a fondish memory of something his father had said to him once in a rare moment of clarity a few days after a relapse that was just like Nicole's.

I'm done, son. Not with drinking but with living. Don't act so shocked, and no, I don't mean I'm going to off myself. What awaits us in death is too uncertain for me to put myself there. Yes, your old man is scared. But I can't say I wouldn't welcome the silence . . . if that's a part of it. Not from you or your mother—I love you both, in my way—but a permanent break from myself. Should the Grim Reaper take my hand today, I'd go willingly. I'm not looking for pity. Just know that I'm sad, even though sad is an imperfect word for the darkness I find myself in.

It had seemed to Tag that Nicole had walked herself into that same darkness. When he managed to place himself into her physical being at the hotel, it had removed all doubt.

Bad things and bad people do not happen for a reason, but a person can choose to put their trauma to good use.

Like Second Plane, New York City was a place where anything could happen, and while standing as a dead person only blocks away from the building that he once called home, Tag finally found some peace with his father. He wondered if his dad had been banished, and—

Right then, Aidan arrived, too free of panic to be anyone other than Amanda.

27
TAG

When Amanda arrived in Aidan's body, she went straight for Matthew's front door. Tag tried to move into the man as he ran down the stairs to stop her. No luck.

The skill with which Aidan's fingers entered the code to the lock on the door was impressive. The punching of keys and the click of the bolt were a Pavlovian pattern that Pepper had come to expect from family. No barking. And just like that, Amanda had subdued the dog.

"Mom?" Emily said from the family room.

It made no sense. Had she forgotten her mother was laid up in the hospital?

Aidan didn't answer.

Emily stood from the couch, leaving Ethan there, his eyes sleepy and struggling to remain focused on the cartoon playing from the TV. Tag put himself in her way to stop her investigation, but she went right through him. She crossed the threshold into the dark kitchen, reaching for the light switch as she entered. Before it clicked, Aidan and Amanda grabbed Emily and held her in a choke-out grip until her eyes rolled back into her head and her body went limp. The girl dropped to the floor, and the damn dog didn't bark once. An open bag of beef-flavored snacks had seen to that. Pepper didn't yelp, whine, or growl to alert Matthew upstairs. He went from treat to treat, several dozen that Amanda and Aidan had spread around the kitchen.

As quiet as the assault on Emily had been, the melee had still grabbed Ethan's attention, but Tag's son never left his roost on the edge of the couch. Even when Tag had tried screaming into the ether, "Run! Run, Ethan! Run and hide," his son had stayed put, eyes wide and in wait.

Everything Amanda had done with Aidan's body thus far had been lightning quick, but now, she walked the man from the kitchen into the family room and toward Ethan in an impressive display of casual familiarity. Ethan sat frozen as she approached, though there was a slight hint of recognition on the boy's face, maybe even awe, like a child who'd just busted Santa Claus after the jolly stranger had come down the chimney—or was Ethan's reverie all in Tag's head?

"Where is Em?" Ethan asked with a concern that didn't seem possible from a voice so small.

"Your sister is fine, Silly Boy, just sleeping for a bit," Aidan said in a timbre that wasn't quite Amanda's but with a lilt that Tag knew well. The man's eyes shifted to the staircase and the mumble of Matthew on the phone somewhere overhead, then quickly to the sounds of the dog still eating his way around the kitchen. "We haven't much time, I'm afraid. This will be hard to understand, Ethan, but it's me, Mommy—your Mommy from before, do you remember?"

Tag thought about trying to possess Matthew, but knew it was unlikely to take. He shouted again, "Ethan, run upstairs! Scream for your daddy! Please!" It made no difference.

"My mommy is at the hospital," Ethan said quietly, but his tiny shoulders went back as he said it, suggesting he had confidence in his answer. "She fell."

Aidan, or rather Amanda inside Aidan, smiled at the news but not too big, catching her amusement in time to refashion it into something more effective on their son.

"You are such a smart boy. So, so smart. But I know if you try—really *really* try—you'll remember me: your *real* Mommy."

Right then, Tag swore Aidan's face contorted into Amanda's, like she'd somehow managed to use every mimetic muscle to fashion a mask of herself over Aidan's head. Her face came and went in a flash that lasted only as long as the bright, brilliant pop of a firecracker.

Ethan scrunched his nose up to his eyes and thought for a moment. "Dead Mommy?"

It broke Tag's heart to hear those two words together, glitching Tag's view, but he managed to steady himself within the observation.

"Not dead, Silly Boy . . . just different now. Come with me and I'll show you," Amanda said. She put Aidan's hand out for their son to take. Ethan still didn't seem so sure, so she added, "We'll get lollipops and maybe even see Dead Daddy, too. Would you like that?"

"Amanda, don't do this!" Tag cried, but if she'd heard him, she ignored his demand.

She didn't force herself on Ethan. Aidan's outstretched hand hung patiently in the air, steady and inviting, waiting for Ethan to accept it. Then, the man quietly hummed the first several bars of Puccini's "O Mio Babbino Caro." It was not the only song Amanda had ever sung for Ethan while changing his diaper, but a favorite. It repulsed Tag, but the melody was enough for his son, whose eyes went comfortably wide over a knowing smile.

The pain of watching Amanda's trick so easily put Ethan's trust in a stranger sent Tag's observation vision into an imbalance between Prior Plane and Second Plane, half in the kitchen and half in the nothing of his space, but he managed to reground himself in the observation in time to watch his son firmly take Amanda's hand—a stranger's hand—and walk with the possessed body toward the front door.

"I told you not just any dog was good security, Tag."

He couldn't talk back and shouldn't have been surprised she knew he was observing.

"I told you: You've got to train them," she said.

Three months after Ethan was born, he'd pitched her the idea of getting a dog on the premise of security. Now, he saw first-hand how right Amanda had been when she'd argued that a dog could be useless as fuck when it mattered. The alternative, at least for Amanda, had been self-defense classes. A better return on investment, she'd said, and the hold Aidan and Amanda had used on Matthew's daughter was proof his wife had been right about that, too.

The door shut behind Aidan and Ethan; only then did the dog finally start barking.

Emily was already stirring, and seemed to be OK, so Tag followed them outside.

Amanda wasted no time walking Ethan in a rush toward the avenue at the end of the street. She made a game of it. Skipping with their son and saying, "Hurry, hurry, Silly Boy."

"Where are we going?" Ethan asked with genuine curiosity.

"Home. Our new home," she answered. "A place with everything you could want: puppies, candy, beautiful parks with the best playgrounds you've ever seen. Doesn't that sound fun? Best of all, when we get there, I'll look like Mommy again."

Ethan glanced up at the man's face. It'd returned to a visage that was all Aidan—hard, foreign, and cruel despite the broad smile Amanda was forcing through it. "Promise?" Ethan asked. He sounded uncertain but not mistrusting enough to change his mind.

Amanda's grip on their son's hand tightened while she used Aidan's free hand to draw a large X across the left of his chest. "Cross my heart and . . . well, I promise. You'll see, Ethan."

Tag screamed—hollow and unjust—as he moved along the sidewalk with them.

"I don't know if you're following us, hon, but if you are, you might want to stop," Amanda said to him through Aidan.

Tag tried bouncing into Aidan, then he tried imposing himself on Aidan. Neither worked. He hadn't expected it to, but to observe idly was no different than killing Ethan himself. He shouted, again and again, looking up desperately to the lit windows of brownstones as they hustled down the street, hoping for someone to hear him. "He's got my son! Help! Somebody, help me! Help my son. Please!" The one pedestrian Aidan and Ethan passed as Amanda raced them down the sidewalk, an elderly man out late with his French bulldog, unleashed, actually looked delighted to see the two of them. And why not? A father and son gleefully skipping somewhere together, despite that absurd hour? Of course. Only in New York.

The possibility of possessing Ethan came to Tag's mind. There was absolutely no reason to believe it'd work, but before he could give it a try, they were at the intersection. Aidan's body stopped, Ethan's hand still firmly in his own, then he looked left and right, then left again where Amanda held her gaze.

Tag saw the approaching box truck half a block away at the same time Amanda did. Without any hesitation, she picked up their son, one hand under an armpit and one hand grabbing his tiny thigh. The roar of cars moving in both directions on Fifth Avenue wasn't enough to mute Ethan's scream. Joyful at first, but it quickly turned distressed. As the box truck advanced from their left, she pulled Ethan's whole body to Aidan's right side, winding up big to heave him right into the truck's grill or to throw their son under the tires.

"Please, Amanda—don't!" Tag shouted. "Don't do this!"

Tag tried to snatch their son from Aidan. His arms just went through.

"Mommy, what are you doing?" Ethan cried, eyes too wide to tear and squirming as best he could to set himself free.

"Don't worry, Silly Boy. I'll see you back home."

"Oh my God!" a pedestrian on the opposite corner shouted as he and Tag watched the forward momentum of Aidan's toss. "What the hell, man? Don't do it! Please don't. *Stop!*"

At its apex, Amanda's swing toward traffic ended abruptly. As it did, Aidan's fingertips dug into the boy, a squeeze strong enough to make Ethan wince and holler.

The box truck driver blared on the horn as 25,000 pounds of steel, aluminum, plastic, and glass on wheels raced past, just inches from the top of Ethan's head.

"What the fuck?" Tag heard Aidan's voice utter under his breath. "Let me do this!"

Tag didn't quite understand why, but Amanda had been unable to release their son.

"Goddammit, you're just delaying the inevitable," she said—to whom? To Aidan? Could he be fighting back somehow? She struggled to cock Ethan back for another attempt at tossing him into a passing coupe. For a moment, the man's body held a wailing Ethan in the air, arms frozen and stiff, a perverse statue.

The pedestrian had their phone to their ear. "I'm calling the cops! Stay there."

"We're just playing a game," Amanda shouted back at him, still holding Ethan in the air.

"I don't give a fuck," the man said. "Stay put."

"Ethan, wave to the man across the street so he knows you're OK. Mommy was just playing a game. Tell the man it was just a game."

She put their son on his feet. He did as she'd asked, waving to the man while holding back the tears in his eyes. A siren blared up a few blocks away. A few other people staring from every corner of the intersection seemed to be too confused or too scared to come to Ethan's aid.

As the concerned pedestrian started into the crosswalk, dodging oncoming traffic as he did, Aidan's hand went high into the air to hail a cab. Amanda managed to deliver a spectacular whistle using Aidan's mouth, and Tag saw that a cabbie half a block away had already angled his car to pick them up.

He threw his energy into Aidan's body again, hoping it might be possible to knock Amanda out of him. It didn't work, and the effort he'd put into trying to dislodge his wife was too much. The pull from Second Plane had him—he fought to stay, but the effort only strengthened its hold—and as he started his full return, all Tag could do was watch a fading picture of Aidan casually putting Ethan into the back of the cab.

"Manhattan via the Manhattan Bridge, thank you," he heard Amanda tell the driver.

The door slammed shut, and though the pedestrian made a valiant effort to run after the cab, Amanda had Tag's son to herself. Until he could return, all Tag could do was hope she'd come to her senses now that her plan to kill Ethan was no longer theoretical. As he left Prior Plane, Tag had a thought that made some sense, but only a little: *Or maybe Aidan comes to his.*

28
AIDAN

Somewhere within himself, he resided. Alive, so to speak, cognizant to a degree. Aidan hoped that whatever or whoever was possessing him wasn't aware of his stirrings. He lacked the strength to force his abductor from his body. Still, there was no point in tipping the entity off.

I'm on a train. I'm on Metro-North.

He wasn't a frequent passenger, but Aidan had ridden the Metro-North lines enough times to recognize the unique buzz and echo that accompanied the departures it made, running north and south between his home in Connecticut and Manhattan.

Now, no vibrations accompanied the sound of the train's momentum. He felt no pressure on his posterior or feet and had no sense of attachment to limbs he hoped he still had. What he heard indicated he'd been seated in a coach car, but he wasn't able to use his eyes to verify the hunch.

He worked to wake more of his mind. The last twenty-four hours came and went, featuring memories that were quick and bright. If he held onto any one image long enough, trying to learn more about what his body had gotten up to while he was out, it felt as if the vision might split his head right down the middle.

It might have been his conscience that ached.

"Next stop, Stamford Station," a male voice said.

The speakers seemed shot. Or maybe his current shortcomings had added extra crack and pop to the announcement. Regardless, Aidan understood the recording and congratulated himself on being right about where his body was currently sitting.

He also had a destination now. Home.

His eyes felt open, be he still couldn't see. Blinking created no blink at all.

He weighed whether it was real or a dream. No dream he'd ever had was blackness and blackness alone.

It had him. The silver lining: at least he was still in his body . . . somewhere.

Best to stay still, until I'm stronger.

It didn't sound like much of a plan—very un-Aidan—but what could he do?

His vision was tuning up but buggy. What he heard came and went as if the connection from his ears to his brain was made with a cable that required a few wiggles from time to time to keep the cord coupled to an amp's jack. A glitch that reminded him of the time he'd tried to teach himself how to play the guitar as a kid. He had one shitty cord. If he'd had others, his destiny might have been very different. He liked playing guitar—or wanted to like it, at least.

He nearly floated away again on that memory, a memory of his own. It was peaceful and less painful than trying to remember more recent events. He didn't need to see what had happened in the last twelve hours to know he'd had nothing to do with it. Ignorance was bliss, that was a better plan, but then, he heard the boy's voice. The boy was seated right next to him.

"If you are my Mommy, why are you a man?"

The thing in him had found the kid. Whatever it was, it'd convinced the boy that it was his mother, too. Hadn't Aidan made a deal with his captor? Hadn't he told *her* that he'd have no part in the kidnapping of a child? He was livid, but it was a rage with no place to go.

"Silly Boy, there's a lot about the world that doesn't make sense. Let's use our indoor voices, OK? Not everyone wants to hear about things they can't quite understand."

It hurt Aidan to hear himself speak. His voice stringing together words he hadn't chosen was a new kind of grating. The routine act of his mouth moving on her command was physically painful, too. Pain was a good sign. If speaking aloud had hurt him, it meant he was feeling again.

"Mommy has missed you so much—so, so much," he heard himself say in a sugary hush he'd never used. "Do you remember the plane crash? The one that killed Mommy and Daddy?"

The child did not respond, or if he had nonverbally, Aidan could still not see.

"Well, ever since then, Mommy's been working nonstop to be with you again. And this is going to sound terribly funny, but you know what Mommy had to do to get you back?"

"No," the child whispered. "What did Mommy do?"

"She had to *borrow* someone else's body. A man's body. Like magic. Isn't that the craziest thing you've ever heard?" Aidan's arm raised and she had pointed a finger at his own face. He heard the boy giggle softly. "Inside here is your real mommy, Ethan, but when I get you home, you'll only see Mommy's face on Mommy again, not *this*—I promise."

This. It was heavily emphasized and louder than the rest of the words in the secret promise. A cruel critique with an inflection that left Aidan wondering if his possessor knew he was listening.

The child—Ethan was his name, he remembered now—laughed harder, and Aidan caught a hint of his own facial muscles relaxing. Maybe she hadn't been mocking his appearance to insult his prying mind. It was possible she'd made a cartoonishly ugly face to humor the boy, a simple spontaneity to put the child at ease. Maybe he could think freely without worrying—

It'd be a really bad idea for you to take your body back over right now, Aidan. You have no idea what it is you've done. It won't be good. I can promise you that.

It was the mommy's voice, making a very different kind of promise than she had to Ethan. Less sugary. He thought about asking the woman if she could hear him but thinking about the question was all that was necessary for her to answer.

Yes, I can. No idea how. I haven't had that problem before. If I thought it was possible, I'd put you back to sleep. I know you don't want any part of this. I've read your journals, a good chunk of them, anyway. You don't have the stomach for murdering children, you made that quite clear not thirty minutes ago. Best to sit this out until I finish what I came here to do.

Without a solid attachment to his body and only a minor connection to his brain, it was difficult to categorize what he was feeling. It wasn't ambivalence. No hit of adrenaline arrived. There was no fight-or-flight at all. If anything, he was pissed off. He'd always wondered who'd be the first to read his journals. A cop with more balls than brains, a crime scene detective, a clever abductee who'd escaped their bindings . . . it certainly never occurred to him that it'd be some rando mom inside of him. As pissed off as he was and kept trying to become about the injustice of it all, pissed off was just a thought, and to think it came with none of the bells and whistles of a physical response that he could galvanize.

He sensed he was falling back into the coma of being hidden within his own brain. It was the damnedest thing to experience feelings born only from thought. Free from the distraction of external sights and awaiting sensations. Some of his thinking had become kind as a lullaby. He was almost out again, drifting away on thoughts—a single question, really. It was a need-to-know that his possessor couldn't help but comment on.

That's an excellent question, Aidan. Why haven't I already killed my son?

A memory exploded in front of him. He had tried—no, *she* had tried to throw the boy in front of traffic in Brooklyn, but his grip had gone tight, and she couldn't release the boy. Had he done that? Or had she found herself incapable of murdering her son after all? It couldn't be easy.

He was hit with another echo. From his point of view, he saw himself swinging Ethan toward an approaching subway train, dangling him over the track, only to snatch the kid back to safety right before the lead car had a chance to deliver its death blow.

You are wondering, did I stop this woman from killing her son, or did she stop herself?

And, of course, he was wondering just that and also wondering if he'd been seen.

Of course you were seen. It's New York City. So, here we sit, riding peacefully to your home, all three of us. We lost the pitch-fork mob for now, so we'll try again when we can. We will succeed. Because I'm good at inhabiting you, Aidan. We can agree on this. Not escape-from-jail good, no. Being in you is taxing, but we will get this done tonight, then both move on.

Yet again, she answered him without his having spoken.

Oh, please. I'm sick? That's rich. This is my son. What's your excuse?

"How much longer until we get there, Mommy?" Ethan asked.

Aidan was relieved the child had interrupted. He needed a break from the pain the conversation with his possessor was causing. If he ever had the chance to journal about the experience, he wasn't sure he would be able to find the words to describe the torment of being held captive within himself. It was like being held underwater until finding out one could breathe it in and still live, but even that didn't do the occurrence justice.

Wait. That was it, wasn't it? Fighting her wasn't going to work. Giving in completely to her control might be the most ridiculous way through the power she held and to an ending that saw him back in control. He fought hard as hell not to think about giving his theory a try. He didn't want to tip off the woman while she was distracted by the boy.

"Not much longer, Ethan," he heard himself say. "Did I already tell you where we're going? A place where you can dream up anything you like, anytime you like. Puppies, candy—oh, I said that already, didn't I?" His voice—her voice—it was growing lethargic, even confused. "You'll see, Silly Boy. It's going . . . going to be . . . wonderful."

"Will Daddy be there too?" A beat. "Mommy?"

Aidan somehow forced his eyesight to return. Until now, every time he'd come to, in his bedroom, in his home, at the store, or in an alley or field, it'd felt like tripping through an open window while sleepwalking. Accidental with a touch of luck. Or maybe, he'd only ever taken back control of his body because the spirit had grown too tired to keep her control over him.

As he regained authority over his right arm, it felt like the limb was under attack by hundreds of hornets stinging his flesh. The woman was inside him still but had gone silent. Perhaps thwarting his return to bodily autonomy required her to focus on his cerebellum.

"Mommy?" the boy asked. "Mommy, are you OK?"

Aidan's eyes were his own again. Fully. No one else in their train car other than Ethan. From his periphery, he saw through the windows of the doors at the car's front and back. In those cars, passengers stood as the train began to slow itself for its stop at Stamford Station.

His eyesight dimmed. Staring into the lights overhead, as he had to shake free of his possessor in the past, was a good way to draw unwanted attention—a definite no-go—he was fortunate not to have already attracted any other strangers to their car.

Before the train stopped, he managed to stand, creating a sway that threatened to collapse his body onto the boy. He was winning. The woman who had been more than happy to jaw with him inside his skull was silent. There were no grunts or exasperated breaths. Even his lungs seemed frozen, though Aidan was sure he must be breathing if he were still standing.

"Come back, Mommy," the boy said. "Come back, please."

Could the child see something on his face or in his posture suggesting his mother had left? He wanted to believe she was gone, but his motor skills were weak. He might be holding onto the luggage rack above, or she might be holding onto it. He had no way of knowing.

If she hadn't vanished, her inaction might have been intentional. Resting within him for more power and a better chance at success the next time she took control. It was what he'd do. With her son still alive, she'd return. He'd had no success at preventing her possessions before, though he wondered if he'd ever actually tried to prevent her from entering his body.

Until that week, it'd been a perverse thrill to feel he had been possibly chosen by something bigger. A welcome deviation from his otherwise steadfast routine. Killing people had become a bore, but killing people at the command of another who'd possessed you was a grim fairytale that he'd let seduce him. All of that was before he realized its prey—or *her* prey was the boy who was running to the doors furthest away from him now.

"Ethan! Don't run, I'm going to help you. I want to help you, Ethan!" The boy's name left Aidan's mouth easily, like a byte of information that had accidentally been copied onto his brain while the intruder was at the reins. His declaration was sincere, but the boy did not turn around and charged unsteadily through the slowing train car toward a door. Another attempt at hollering fell short. Opening his jaw, barely enough to mumble, stung Aidan's nose like he'd been clocked by a professional boxer.

The train had stopped, and the doors would be opening soon. Through its windows, Aidan saw a uniformed police officer leaning against a pillar on the platform. The boy stood on his tiptoes, saw the officer, too, and his stare was determined. No doubt he'd been told to find a policeman anytime he felt threatened or had, in fact, been kidnapped by a stranger. Whatever the mommy had been able to present him as using only his facial muscles and his voice must have been long gone.

Jail seemed likely, and maybe that was fine. It'd be easy enough to hang himself in the first holding cell they put him in if he committed to it. The authorities didn't know anything about him, it'd take them long enough to learn. An immediate try was his best shot. Hung, before they had what they needed to search his home, and before any qualified prison shrink could declare Aidan a risk to himself, and his incarceration became less manageable. There was no death penalty in Connecticut; there would be no death row. Save a hunger strike, there wouldn't be much he could do to end his run here if he didn't kill himself quickly when imprisoned.

Aidan thought about destiny. It wasn't the first time, but this felt different. He came to believe in it, and he wondered if life in prison had always been in the cards and wondered loud enough to be heard, he guessed, because the woman inside him broke her temporary silence.

Let me speak again, Aidan. He will hear me, not you.

What choice did he have?

As the train's doors opened, he heard himself say, "Silly Boy, don't go. I'm just having a little trouble moving, that's all. Can you please come back and help Mommy? Help Mommy."

The doors shut, and Ethan stumbled when the train lurched forward, but his walk back seemed certain. Aidan watched as his own arm moved toward the boy to help him come closer. Ethan's face was calm and serene, indicating Mommy had resumed control. Perhaps she was using his Zygomaticus major muscle to smile at the boy in a way unique to her—she'd convinced the boy again, it didn't matter how, really—the child grabbed for her or his open hand, and the last thing Aidan felt was his fingers wrapping around Ethan's tightly.

As the sound of the train picking up speed left his ears, Aidan went dark once again.

29
TAG

Other than her eyelids, Tag found Nicole's body unresponsive to any suggested action. He was able to use her eyes, though, to see with them. The clock he'd spotted on the hospital room's wall, an ancient thing, had already ticked away an entire half hour. They'd been alone that whole time. Nicole's ears weren't relaying the sounds of its second hand, but as Tag lay frozen within her stillness, thinking about what he'd already watched his wife try to do to their boy, its relentless rhythm was easy enough to imagine. In Nicole's body, time was not on his side.

After Amanda fled Park Slope in a cab, on sheer will alone, Tag was able to return relatively quickly from Second Plane to find her and Ethan going into Manhattan across the Manhattan Bridge. His wife ditched the taxi on Canal Street almost immediately and ran with Ethan down the stairs of the nearest subway station. He'd thrown himself at and into her several times to no avail, screaming uselessly the entire time at other commuters to stop her. Like her previous attempt, throwing Ethan in front of an approaching train had halted last minute. Even so, to think about what she'd tried anymore threatened to upset him right back to Second Plane.

Tag had followed them all the way to a train station one stop north of Stamford, where he'd watched them get into an Uber without incident. He had no idea who was in control of Aidan, but he or his wife still had Ethan—and no matter who was in charge, there was no good reason to believe things would end well if he didn't get Nicole up and onto her feet immediately.

He tried to stand Nicole's body again, but his conviction made no difference.

He considered something simpler: roll Nicole off the bed. The impact on the linoleum might free some piece of her brain from the sedative's effects, but if her body landed the wrong way, the fall might break a bone, leaving her body unable to execute his escape.

He focused on hearing again. Silence. A white-hot heat threatened to bounce him back to Second Plane, and his vision of the room through her eyes started to fog over. Every decision he'd ever made led to this. He was livid with himself, but none of his agitations had an effect on Nicole's body. His phantom movements moved zilch in the physical world.

He needed to calm himself. He needed space away from his memories.

Sounds had returned, but it wasn't until a pair of orderlies passed outside Nicole's room, talking about how patients didn't listen like they used to, that he realized her ears were his now. That was progress, but it'd come on so slowly, and when he tried to move her again, it failed.

He considered jumping from Nicole back to Second Plane to tell the council—if he could even find them—that he'd observed his wife possess a body on Earth. Of course . . . it was reasonable to assume they might know he'd done the same with Nicole's by now. Not as successfully, not as repeatedly, and not with the same dexterity Amanda had done it, but he doubted his incompetence at possession thus far would matter. Even if the council excused his behavior, they'd ask why he hadn't told them about Amanda sooner, and the only answer he had was, "I didn't think she'd ever go this far."

But how had *he* let her go this far?

He had listened intently to Martha and understood her warning—and yet he had done nothing. Even after connecting with Gabriel, it wasn't until he'd observed Amanda taking control of Aidan's body—using it to walk, read, and talk—that he accepted he'd been in denial.

And even then, he could've reported her immediately, but no. Instead, he'd stood by as she honed the skill, and though he'd already been thinking about who to possess himself, the real reason he hadn't wanted to tell anyone was simple: the consequences for residents caught possessing the living—rumor or not—meant never seeing Amanda again. He still loved her.

His thoughts spiraled out on what awaited them both until a more optimistic idea anchored him back to the moment itself. If the council knew, he hadn't been summoned.

They had time, and for a moment he wondered if he could make a good case for himself—for them both. Something along the lines of an insanity defense. Temporary, at that. After all, he was in good standing. He knew the suggestions inside and out. But there were no report cards, no gold stars or other types of scoring systems for a resident to track how they were doing. Second Plane was the antithesis of the way beings lived prior. All a resident had to go on in determining their success was to deem themselves successful. Very progressive.

Asking a mentor for their opinion on how you were doing wasn't expressly forbidden.

"There's no way for me to know," Donovan once said. "I appreciate that we meet frequently, and I take everything you say at face value, but if we're being honest with each other, you could be up to all sorts of things during your stay that I'd have no idea about."

"But they'd know, wouldn't they?"

"The council?" Donovan asked.

"Yeah."

"They're not God, Tag. At least not the God we grew up on."

If that was true, the only way the council could know he was in Nicole's body right now, or that Amanda was possessing Aidan's, was if he abandoned his plan—right now—and found a resident who *did* know how to contact them. There was only one resident who would: Gabriel.

When intuition kicks in—be it a mother's or otherwise—maybe it's best we listen.

Tag could end this now, but not without *it*. His intuition told him that seemed unlikely. After all, Gabriel had taught both of them.

First Amanda and then Tag, but only because it had its own agenda. Whatever it hoped to achieve by setting them both loose on the living, it certainly wasn't about helping his family. Tag might have gone back to spinning out, this time on Gabriel's real motivations, had he not realized that he'd managed to move Nicole's left arm.

He committed to rolling her off the bed. This time it worked. He heard the heavy thud of her body but didn't feel the impact. She didn't stir on her own, and he didn't try to move her again until he was certain no one in the hallways or nurses' stations had heard her fall. There were no audible signs of concern and no sounds of footsteps approaching. The cords running to her body had stayed connected to the machines monitoring her vitals at the other end. The steady beeping noises they made suggested Nicole's biology wasn't aware she'd tumbled out of bed either. If he was able to stand and then able to walk, he wasn't sure how long he'd have to leave unseen before the interruption in the reporting of her vitals sent nurses running to her room.

He sensed nothing new suggesting he'd have a better go of controlling Nicole for having sent her to the floor, but before he could verify his doubts, he heard a voice . . . it was Nicole's.

I'm here, Tag. I don't know how this works, but maybe I can help. I want to help.

He said nothing in return—had no time to think about her offer, what it meant for them both—but moving Nicole's body was instantly easier, as if her form had always been his own.

30

EMILY

Emily sat alone in her bedroom. It was where her father had asked her to go, and she hadn't protested. The police had heard her version of what had happened. Most of that version had been sobs. She'd told the same short and useless story in between hysterics, over and over, hoping new details would emerge just by repeating it.

"I heard the door open, and I thought it was Mom. But then, that didn't make much sense. We left her at the hospital, but Pepper wasn't barking, and he went into the kitchen like everything was totally normal—I figured it was her, and she'd been let go, or maybe that she'd left on her own. A man grabbed me and choked me. I tried to yell but couldn't. I promise I tried."

By her seventh retelling, only Lucinda seemed to be listening.

"Your little girl might want to get some rest," the older of the two detectives said.

Her suggestion sounded rehearsed. There was a rhythm to it that made Emily wonder if the cop had modeled her whole vibe on some policewoman from the crime shows that Lucinda sometimes made her and Ethan watch when they spent weekends at her place.

When her dad didn't respond, the detective acted like she had a psych degree too and pushed the suggestion, "Things like this are a lot to process for a kid, you know?"

Emily pushed her face deeper into her pillow, wondering how many times the detective had told other parents their children needed rest to "process" horrible crimes. And then heinous crimes were all she could think about. Emily didn't mind. Thinking about other violent assaults might help her resume crying more about her own. She'd once read the glands above the eyes produced fifteen to thirty gallons of tears in a year, but no more tears came, and no other crime she dreamt up was as sad as the one she'd played a part in. She'd gone very dark, very fast in imagining the worst events possible, but her sadness was spent, and she went numb.

Pepper lay next to her, and though Emily had already vowed to hate the dog forever, she shuffled from the top of her bed to the bottom and put her head on his belly. No one hates a dog forever, except people who hate dogs from the start.

Lucinda had promised to check on Emily after she gave her own statement. She had no idea what the old lady thought she had to offer the detectives but wished she would hurry up about it. Waiting to hear Ethan's grandmother knock on the bedroom door was an additional anxiety Emily could do without.

Lucinda had arrived after the police, which was good. Had she gotten there before the detectives, Emily was sure she would have killed her dad on the spot. The old woman came through the front door furious, screaming at everyone there. According to her, they were all to blame: Matthew, the police, Nicole, and "that damn dog." She had calmed herself eventually, and after staying quiet for longer than anyone in the room might have expected, she said her piece.

"It's my fault, really. My fault for not fighting tooth and nail to stop you from ever taking custody of my grandson in the first place. My fault for helping you navigate things with ACS when I knew damn well all along that Nicole wasn't fit to be anybody's mother."

Lucinda might have gone on laying blame and taking blame, but her own grief dropped her to the floor. Her ire made sense. Emily had doubted her parents were up to the task of taking on Ethan when they did too. At that time, Nicole was more like a sister to him, and that was a kind comparison.

She hadn't spent a lot of time thinking about how Nicole had mothered her when she was Ethan's age; she had better memories of that time than she cared to admit. Nicole had never been a bad mom. It was more like she hadn't been a mom at all. She couldn't wait to get away from Nicole, and Emily had spent a fair amount of time fantasizing about that.

The day her family picked up Ethan, Emily stopped counting how many days it was until she could legally leave home. How could she? Matthew was an OK father, she knew nobody was perfect, but in and of itself, being an OK father didn't mean he was an OK husband.

Emily was no psychologist, but she'd read enough books to make some assumptions: Matthew doted on her in a way that made Nicole jealous. She and Dad married young and had her too soon thereafter. There hadn't been a whole lot of time between meeting each other and parenting for her mom and dad to fortify their feelings, find out if those feelings were real, or realize they hadn't had any attraction to one another that went beyond the carnal variety.

Privately, Emily had given the whole Ethan experiment two weeks. Maybe three. And that was before she knew what a nightmare it was to house the only survivor of Flight 2332. Few people, even the most put-together and level-headed of the species, would survive that grind.

The fucked-up thing about those first few weeks was that she'd liked it.

She'd stopped counting the days until her exit because she loved Ethan. It was undeniable and immediate. Before, whenever their families got together, she'd played with him and he'd been fine. She couldn't have foreseen feeling as connected as she did now to her little brother. If her parents weren't up for the task, she would be. It'd been a conscious decision. Necessary. She woke up one morning and knew that taking care of Ethan was what she'd been born to do. When ACS initially got involved, she might have been the only one happy about it. It was a chance for both Matthew and Nicole to evaluate their situation—and fuck if it hadn't almost worked.

Nicole's sobriety had whitewashed things for a while. Its positive effect on some day-to-day issues had been genuine. Like Matthew, like Lucinda, and maybe even as her mother had, Emily convinced herself that Nicole's new way of living was all the family needed to ensure they lived up to Tag and Amanda's expectations. Ones they had surely had when they'd picked them.

There was a knock on the bedroom door.

"It's me, sweetie," Lucinda said softly. "Are you awake?"

"It's open," Emily replied.

She came in, and her hand went straight for the light switch and flipped it on without asking for Emily's permission. She'd flooded the room with the reality Emily had been hiding from, if even unsuccessfully.

"I'm sorry, dear, but my eyes are too old to traverse a young girl's room in the dark."

"It's fine," Emily said, recoiling as she adjusted to the light.

Ethan's grandmother looked old now. Frail and weak and of no help, really.

She was rich, or at least her house and the way it was decorated had made it seem like Tag's mother was rich, but unless her brother's kidnapper was planning on asking for a ransom, what good would Lucinda's money do? A large reward for information on Ethan and his whereabouts would get the phones ringing, but there was no reason to believe any of the callers or their tips would be legitimate.

"What are the police still doing here?" Emily asked. She could hear them still talking with her father downstairs. "They should be out looking for Ethan. We all should."

Lucinda's eyes were seeking permission from Emily to sit on the bed.

Maybe Emily had given her the OK, but she hadn't felt her face move.

The old woman looked at the dog, and her prior disgust with him and his failure to prevent the assault and abduction returned. Her mouth curled at one side of her lips, then went higher, as if she was trying to fashion something more like a smile, but you can't grin away that kind of loathing.

"It's not Pepper's fault, Lucinda."

The old woman sighed. With her new proximity, every wrinkle she already owned was deeper. Her sort-of-grandmother's face was typically warm and soft looking given its age. It'd always been a peaceful place to gaze, but she looked like she was wearing the witch masks pop-up Halloween shops sold for under twenty dollars now. Her edges were hard, and the color left on her face was only variations of gray and blue.

"Of course not," Lucinda said. "No one is blaming Pepper."

Her tone was always so phony. The only adult who still talked to Emily like she was three instead of almost thirteen.

"But it's not your fault either," Lucinda added. "It's no one's fault, and I was wrong to come into the house screaming otherwise. That wasn't very helpful of ol' Grandma, was it?"

"You're wrong, though. It *was* my fault," Emily said.

"I know you feel that way. But *my* grandson's well-being wasn't ever your responsibility."

Emily didn't like the way the woman had said the words "my grandson." Maybe Lucinda had spit it out nasty inadvertently. A Freudian slip made by her subconscious to help stop her from lashing out at Emily, her father, or even the dog.

An hour ago, Emily thought her brother's grandmother would have killed the whole family if that was what it took to bring Ethan home. She thought about asking Lucinda if she knew anybody who might want to kidnap Ethan, but she never got the chance.

Then Lucinda said, "Your father and I think it'd be best if you stayed with me for a while." She stood and looked around the room as if she was already trying to decide what she'd allow Emily to pack for however much time "a while" meant.

"Do you usually come to my place with a suitcase? Do you have more than one? I can't remember. I'm sure we'll come back here tomorrow, but let's grab what we can now and—"

Lucinda's search for items to pack or suitcases to pack them in went cold.

Ethan's toys were on his side of the room. Twenty-two stuffed animals, other than the elephant which was probably still in the family car, were posed in a group just as Emily had left them for Ethan when she'd made his bed. When the old woman saw the stuffies, it was like she'd thrown a rod. There was no more go in her, and that didn't seem fair to Emily. She was angry, too! This was no time to panic, freeze, or run away. She had no plan of her own to get Ethan back, but what the old woman was suggesting felt like everyone was giving up completely. Now, with Lucinda sad and possibly rebroken, Emily had been robbed of the opportunity to campaign for any other option besides leaving with her sort-of-grandmother to hide out and hope for the best. She felt like fighting but knew that doing anything other than the right thing wouldn't help the situation. The right thing to do was ask Lucinda if she was alright.

As it turned out, Emily's phone buzzed, and she didn't need to say anything to bring Lucinda back from the brink. She put a hand over it, trying to muffle the sound, but the old woman turned around as the phone vibrated a second time and stepped toward Emily like she'd every right to grab it without asking.

"The police should have your phone, sweetie."

"I doubt Ethan's kidnapper is reaching out to me—"

"Give me the phone," Lucinda demanded. She looked even older, if that was possible.

Emily shifted her butt to sit on the phone. She understood why Lucinda wanted it. The possibilities the adults had discussed after she'd gone upstairs had been loud enough to hear.

The prevailing theory was Ethan's kidnapper was someone who knew him. A family member or a friend. The other premise Emily had overheard, though it seemed a distant second, was that her brother had been kidnapped for ransom. The officer who spoke most had also wondered aloud if all the interviews, TV appearances, and the like had made her family a bundle and, therefore, a target. It hadn't helped when Dad told them Nicole had once wanted to get rich off the spectacle, but then again, that was Dad, wasn't it? Sharing too much was his tell. He was anxious, it happened, even to him. To his credit, he had worked quickly to assure the police the family had made very little from all the PR, but the detective told him that hardly mattered. The kidnapper only needed to *think* they were rich.

"Fork it over," Lucinda said, grabbing Emily by the wrist.

The firmness of the old woman's grip was impressive, and Emily shifted her weight to one buttock, hoping it'd be enough to stop Lucinda from grabbing the phone. Her sort-of-grandma was stronger than she looked, though, and before Emily could settle on a more strategic posture, Lucinda grabbed her by the neck and threw her to the floor.

"You fucking bitch," Emily heard herself shout. "Give it back, or I swear you'll regret it."

"My God! The attachment your generation has to your devices is sickening." Lucinda spat. "It's an addiction. Worse than your mother's, if you ask me. Now just settle down."

The fake sweetness the old woman deployed when first entering Emily's room was long gone. As Lucinda stood over her, clutching the phone in one hand like it was a carnival prize, the kind few dupes ever win, Emily considered delivering a swift kick to Lucinda's ankle—it might be enough to take her down. But Emily's thud to the floor had someone, likely her dad, coming up the stairs. A kick like that could wait. The best bet now was to play the role of the victim.

Her dad would come up, take her phone, and give it to the police. Then, the adults would all huddle around her device and his for days, hoping for a ransom call that Emily didn't believe would ever come.

Lucinda held Emily's phone in front of her face. The old woman's brows were uneven, one high and one low. Even so, she was squinting into the screen, studying the caller's name. "Who's Nicole?"

"My mom," Emily capitulated. "Duh."

"Your mom. Of course. Of course you don't call your mom 'Mom.' Why *would* you?"

"Why?" she asked. "What does it matter?"

"It says you missed her call. There's a message, too. Give me your password."

"No."

"God dammit, child! Give me your password!"

Matthew appeared in the doorway. "What the hell is going on in here?"

As the old woman turned to no doubt lie about what had transpired, Emily sprung from the floor and snatched her phone back. With Matthew there, Lucinda seemed to lose a bit of her nerve and dropped herself defeatedly onto Ethan's bed. "Nicole just rang, and the little brat won't give me the phone."

"Is that true?" Matthew asked her before looking back toward the staircase.

If either detective was on their way up to see what the fuss was about, they would've had to have been capable of floating. There wasn't a sound, but no one said anything else or even moved until they all heard the female detective cough downstairs.

Matthew took two steps into the room. "Is that true? Did your mother call you?" he asked, much quieter this time.

Emily wondered if he and Lucinda had been able to pick up any part of her mom's voicemail that she was already playing to her ear. Mom had asked for Dad, so she held the phone face-up in front of her chest, put it on speaker so they could all hear it, and then moved the slider to the left to start her mother's message again from the beginning.

"Emily . . . it's your mother. Sort of, anyway—maybe that's obvious right now. I can't really say, and I don't have time to try to act like I have any idea how to sound like her."

It was Mom's voice, but it was true: the rhythm of her words was different, and the vocabulary she used wasn't common for Nicole. There was no rational reason for the message itself to cause a chill, but Emily's skin went prickly and ice cold. Her mother's tone was dull and broken, and hearing it should have frightened everyone, but Lucinda rolled her eyes like only old women who've seen it all can, then offered her two cents.

"Has your wife gone completely bat sh—"

Matthew held out his hand to shush Lucinda, then pulled the door shut. "Start it over," he said as he sat next to Emily.

"I was going to call Matthew—your dad, I mean—but then, Amanda already has Ethan, doesn't she? So, I imagined that by now, your dad had gotten the police involved. And that makes sense. I'd have done the same. If I call him, I think they'll hear this. Leaving a message on your phone seems like a bad idea, too, but there's no time to ring you again and hope that you pick up. So . . . find your father, Emily, and play this for him, please. Both of you . . . you're going to have to trust me on this: telling the police or anyone else what I'm about to say right now will be of no help. Ethan's still alive, I'm sure of it, but if you drag the police into this,

or even my mom—Lucinda, I mean—I don't know what Amanda will do with him."

Hearing what she'd already heard, now a third time, didn't diminish its hypnotic hold. As they listened to the rest of Nicole's message—or something using her voice to leave a message, anyway—Emily hoped her father would do everything her mother was asking, save the part about leaving her home while he followed the instructions. If either he or Lucinda thought for a second that she wasn't going to leave with them to help Tag, too, it was going to get ugly, fast.

31
TAG

Tag hid in the shadows the suburban-urban mix of Stamford afforded.

This is what the living always claimed to want: buzzing bistros and Manhattan-like cocktail bars just a short drive from safer, white-picket-fence neighborhoods. That perfect mix of city convenience balanced with rural inconvenience.

"Stamford's a safe place," he remembered hearing.

It was an odd time to recall that they had once talked about making a move to the Connecticut town to escape the yuppie influx in Brooklyn. Not as safe as advertised, he guessed.

It didn't matter how he'd traveled there from Manhattan, but the short-term memories he'd made while using Nicole's brain came and went as he walked her body into Aidan's neighborhood. One minute he was thinking the block was ritzy, and wishing he and Amanda had had the chance to move there. The next minute, the scramble to get Nicole's body to Stamford would grab his full attention. If the memories were legit, the trip up had been shockingly lucky.

He remembered being awful at moving her body through the hospital's halls. Even with the "help" Nicole had promised, there'd been stumbling and a zombie-like quality to the escape they'd made, first into an elevator and then through the lobby on the ground floor. *How in the hell did we pull that off?* He could only imagine he had the routine dysfunction of America's medical-industrial complex to thank. Outside the building, the reflection of Nicole's body in a plate glass window had caught his eye; a punishing amble is how he'd describe it, one he thought would definitely hurt the next day, at least for Nicole.

Had he been running from a hospital in any place that wasn't New York City, it was a good bet a barefoot fare, dressed in a blue medical gown, arms and face dotted with bandages, standing on a corner of a block with a hospital, and doing so after midnight, would've been a hard pass. The city that never sleeps had seen it all, though, and the Uber driver he'd summoned using Nicole's phone was accommodating, maybe even too eager to help an awkward stranger he'd never met.

Zombie walk or not, the driver unlocked the doors, no questions asked. When the man didn't drive Nicole's body back to the ER immediately, Tag relaxed, which caused him to lose control of her altogether. Maybe it seemed like she'd passed out? It was also possible Nicole had regained control of her faculties and made passable chit-chat and excuses for her appearance.

"Dark days left me running a lot, too," the driver had said.

Oh, that's right, the driver had told Nicole about his own experience with substance abuse. Tag remembered that now. He "got it," the man behind the wheel may have said. For all Tag knew, he and Nicole had bonded with the driver over addiction war stories, and that was the only reason he was in Stamford now waiting for Matthew to show. Shockingly lucky, indeed.

At some point during the ride there, Emily texted Nicole's phone back. It'd been a notification on Nicole's locked phone screen when he resumed final control, right before their driver pulled the car alongside a curb to drop them two blocks from Aidan's address. Nicole had either missed the message or she'd left its notification for Tag to find.

A few houses from Aidan's, Tag stopped to reread the message again. Emily's text back was the response he'd asked his best friend to leave. If he took the single sunglasses-smile emoji on the screen at face value, it meant Emily had not only listened but that she'd followed his instructions and played his message for her father. Its delivery was timestamped. Based on the time the phone showed now, it was safe to assume Matthew wouldn't arrive for at least another twenty minutes. And that was only if he was on his way at all.

Operating Nicole's cell had taken a lot of effort, but paled in comparison to the effort it took to create coherent sentences about a plan he formed on the fly with a mouth that wasn't his. Matthew might have listened to what the message outlined and shared it with the police solely out of his confusion. If that was the case, the authorities were on their way, and that inconvenience would not have taken another twenty minutes.

Only Matthew would understand what Tag meant when he'd finished the message.

"If you are willing to help, send me the emoji sign-off you used with Tag."

Optimistically, that single sunglasses-smile emoji on the screen indicated Matthew was on his way, alone. No police. It meant his friend was willing to put disbelief on the back burner and take a chance on something unbelievable if it meant saving his—no, their son.

"Fuuuuuuuuuuuccccck!"

Aidan's shout startled him. Tag had barely registered that he'd made it into the man's yard. He flopped Nicole's body under a bush and looked toward the house to see if the cuss had been made because he or she had been spotted. It looked bigger than when he'd visited the inside.

His observations there had been brief, but only because Tag suspected Amanda had known he was there observing her as she honed her possession of Aidan. The exterior and landscaping were all very John Q. Public. What Tag had cataloged inside wasn't completely abnormal, either. It had fine couches, expensive chairs, beds in most of the rooms, and the types of knick-knacks that typically signal an occupant has too much time on their hands. But it also housed the stench of death. Tag had smelled it, but wondered if it was only because one of Aidan's victims had remarked as much the day before her corpse became a part of the odor.

The one lamp on in the living room went dark, but the fixture in the next room lit up right after. There was no way to tell if it was Aidan or Amanda moving from one room to the next. The man's cuss could have meant he'd stubbed a toe under his own power as much as it might have indicated frustration with being unable to stub a toe even if he pleased.

He had no visual on Ethan. Leaving Nicole's body to perform an observation inside crossed his mind, but possessing her again, even with cooperation, might have proven impossible.

Human bodies weren't gloves, at least not for Tag. Amanda had given the art of possession her full attention. She was better at it. Par for the course, alive or dead, never not better than him at anything they both tried.

Leaving and coming back, even if done efficiently, was risky. Ethan was still alive, he felt it, then again, hunches of any kind were only how the living rebranded wishful thinking.

The scheming to escape from the hospital, to get Matthew to Aidan's, to retrieve Ethan from Amanda—to say nothing of how hard it was to move another body, even one as spiritually damaged as Nicole's—had kept Tag occupied. No space for emotion, no time for anything except decisions, but as he walked Nicole's body to a window to peer into Aidan's home, he was afraid.

Tag was terrified for his son. Not an ethereal mimicry of a fear he once knew, the real deal: panic and worry, trepidation, and no certainty he'd be able to overpower Amanda *if* he was even able to keep his possession of Nicole going. He'd lost control of his son's welfare a second time.

On day one of his residency, Tag committed to the literature. After all, it was the easiest way forward. In particular, the council's suggestion that feelings of any kind were echoes of emotions residents had experienced while living was particularly comforting. If he worked at it, he wasn't supposed to feel anything. All decisions in the afterlife could be made in a vacuum.

In theory, that attribute would keep residents from straying into tasks like the one Tag was engaged in now. What could be better than feeling nothing at all? A second existence free from anxiety, sorrow, anger, and grief might also be worth never feeling love, admiration, joy, or pride. But it'd all been bullshit. Not echoes or mimics, but real. Gabriel had told Tag as much.

Residents claiming to have mastered feeling nothing were lying to themselves or lying to the recently deceased to gain good standing with the council. What's worse, no resident had any actual idea what the council's good graces might ever provide, lead to, or help them achieve. There was no *official* mention of any punishment for affecting the living in The Text, but there didn't need to be. Every resident understood how the rumors of that punishment made them feel.

The threat of a fate worse than death existed. It wasn't bandied about by residents, but as innuendo, it was well-known. Death for the dead was real, and that's why almost no one talked about it. Not because they didn't know what would happen if their residency in Second Plane was terminated by the council, but *because* they didn't want to know for sure.

"What do you want from me?" Tag heard Aidan ask. His shout was closer to the window this time and loud enough to wake the neighbors. "I swear to God, I won't let you do it!"

No new lights from any nearby homes popped on.

A hand lost in the darkness of the room flipped a switch, illuminating the study on the other side of the pane. There, Aidan steadied himself, putting both his palms down on the desk. The man's face continued its bend into terror as he did his best to reason with Amanda.

"Ask anything else of me," Aidan said as he looked out the window, past Tag, and seemingly unaware he had Nicole's body standing there. "There are many more deserving of my cruel hand. I've spent a lifetime working within a religion of my own creation, and I won't let you fuck it up. I can't. This could've been amazing, you and me—that's what's so screwed up."

The rage on his face collapsed as if his expression had stepped on a trap door. He was less than ambivalent, just a body in between souls with empty eyes that stayed open on muscle memory alone. When life returned to his face, he said nothing. Aidan walked from the living room to the hallway, leaving the light on behind him. She had him again. Tag was sure of it.

Waiting for Matthew was no longer an option.

32

MATTHEW

"Mom asked for you to come alone, I get that . . . but let's be honest: I know Nicole a hell of a lot better than you. I have a way better chance of talking her down."

His daughter popped off her bed and headed for the door. Having a headstrong child had always been both a blessing and a curse.

"No," Matthew said, reaching for her hand from behind to stop her. "And keep your voice down." She wasn't happy about his grip but seemed settled enough to at least hear him out.

"If she has my grandson, I'm going too," Lucinda said. "You can't talk me out of it, Matthew, so I suggest you quit wasting precious time."

What he'd been about to pitch them was pointless. Both their eyes said as much.

After concocting a plan, they headed downstairs. Matthew had Em's daisy-print suitcase in one hand. It was heavy, but only because he'd dumped the dirty clothes from the kids' laundry basket into it in case the lone officer left in their kitchen insisted on helping them to the car.

"I've decided to drive Emily to Lucinda's . . . to drive them both. Safety in numbers."

Matthew's lie was solid, even if his delivery was flimsy.

The officer hmmed as he reached for his cell, and Matthew glared at Lucinda.

"I don't need *you* to get us home safe, thank you," she said.

Her tantrum was enough for the cop to forget about his phone. Really sold the ruse.

"I can have a cruiser do it," the officer suggested. "Or take you myself, maybe,"

"I just said I don't *need* any help," Lucinda repeated. "Not his, not yours."

Lucinda's castigating stare came naturally. She had friends in all the tentacles of law enforcement, and Lucinda never spoke kindly about any of them. She donated to their causes, but only to stay in good standing with a community that expected public sacrifices from its wealthiest members. She needed their help now, and that probably pissed her off even more.

"It's not far, thank you, Officer," Matthew said, hoping the man wouldn't insist. He put a hand on Lucinda's shoulder, unsure he'd ever get it back. "Honestly, Mom, I think we all need the fresh air, wouldn't you agree?"

He'd never called her Mom. The ire on her face came for him, but Matthew didn't care. Her intensity kept the cop quiet.

"Is that all right?" Matthew asked the detective with his eyes still on Lucinda.

"Are you talking to me now?" the cop asked.

"I'm sorry. Yes, I am, Officer," Matthew said. "Can we go? Or do you need to call one of the detectives who was here earlier to ask if it's OK?"

"Suit yourself."

Whether the cop left behind to babysit them had been flustered by that final line or had just been blasé, it had worked.

Now the three of them were racing north on I-95 in the family Subaru. Matthew wondered if keeping the police in the dark had been the right thing to do. It wasn't. How could it be? The right thing would have been to tell the police that Nicole had lost her mind. Heading back to play his wife's voicemail for the detectives was still—

"You're going to miss the exit!" Em shouted.

Matthew swung the steering wheel hard right, swerving dangerously from the fast lane to thread the offramp leading into Stamford. With a heavy foot on the gas, he looked into the rear-view mirror to evaluate their situation. Had he said "Hold tight"? He'd meant to.

"You see anything?"

Lucinda had her head cocked over her shoulder to make the same investigation. "You are giving the NYPD way too much credit . . . we're fine."

Matthew eased his foot off the accelerator. The rash move hadn't seemed to fluster Emily, who sat in the passenger seat with her eyes plugged into Google Maps, but he was overcome by the heat of his irresponsibility. The detectives weren't on their tail; Lucinda was right.

Nicole leaving the hospital undetected wasn't that surprising. A big city ER at that time of night is its own unique brand of chaos. He'd watched the doctors dose her to calm his wife, and they'd left her sleeping, effectively moving Nicole to the bottom of the hospital staff's to-do list.

Eventually, someone would check on her and find that she was missing, though, and when they couldn't find his wife, wouldn't they be calling him to share that news? And if the hospital phoned Matthew to report her missing, the police would hear that news, too. He'd agreed to let them monitor his cell and computer. Any calls, texts, or emails were as much theirs now as they were his. At some point, a doctor was going to ring him to say Nicole had disappeared, and when that happened, he and Lucinda would no longer be the only two people wondering if it was possible his wife had somehow managed to abduct Ethan.

"Take a left here," Emily said, pointing at a sign that read *Ledge Lane*.

As Matthew made the turn onto the street Nicole had given them in her rambling voicemail, he considered going dark. No headlights might raise suspicions, but it might let him see Nicole before she had a chance to see them.

Her instructions had been clear: Matthew was supposed to come alone. It was the only part of her message that made good sense. He had no idea what Nicole was capable of at this point. The whole voicemail would take the bejesus out of the most hardened. The scariest part was that she hadn't sounded drunk or high, not for her, anyway, which left only insane.

"*I know who has Ethan and what he's planning on doing. Or she, I mean. She hasn't killed him yet. I've seen that they haven't, but I don't know how much longer the guy who took Ethan will be able to keep Amanda from murdering him. Not even sure that's what's happening, to be honest. Fuck, I sound crazy. This sounds crazy. It's a lot to hear. It's a lot for me to say. I mean, physically, it's difficult to use a mouth that isn't yours. I hope the important parts make sense. Maybe I've lost my mind. Either way, I need your help, Matthew. I'm not as strong as she is . . . she's just . . . it's Amanda, you know? 'Doesn't fuck around.' Remember when you said that? It's in Stamford, 1345 Ledge Lane. I'll be there soon. Come alone. I mean it. This guy, even if it's not Amanda . . . things could go bad fast. No police. Just you.*"

They'd listened to the message over and over on the way to Connecticut. It'd never sounded anything other than utterly mad. Maybe the fall had given her a concussion, some tiny structural defect the doctors had missed. That was the best-case scenario Matthew could imagine. He'd sent the damn emoji anyway. What other choice did he have?

Ever since the turn onto Ledge Lane, Matthew had kept his eyes on the street numbers. He'd left the headlamps on, too, and had not thought to ask either of his passengers to at least duck their heads. Now, the address Nicole had given him was only four homes up the block.

He stopped the car and killed the lights. He'd walk the rest of the way alone, and if they didn't let him do it alone, there was no choice really, he'd have to call the cops himself.

"Em, I want you to stay in the car."

"Not going to happen."

"Em, this isn't up for debate. Your mother is unwell."

"You don't say?" she said flatly.

"For fuck's sake, Emily. Can you just trust me this once?"

"I'm not staying in the car either," Lucinda said.

Punching the old woman was an option, but he gave the thought time to pass. "Lucinda, you are pissed. You blame me. You have every right to blame me, I get that."

The edges of the anger on her face didn't soften with his attempt at an apology.

"I know you are going to do whatever you want," Matthew pressed on. "All I can do is ask you to *want* to do what's best for your grandson. And, maybe more so, to want to do what's best for my daughter. Who is still here, in front of us both. Please, Lucinda, stay here. Stay with my daughter and make sure she's safe."

Lucinda looked past him like she couldn't be bothered to hear him go on. "Someone's coming," she said. "Turn the car back on, Matthew. Turn it on. Do it now!"

He heard his daughter scream "Daddy!" as he turned to see who was approaching. The driver-side window burst, and the opposite end of the gun that had shattered the glass pushed hard into Matthew's temple. His hands instinctively went up and flat on top of the steering wheel. He was instantly blind. Their attacker had a small tactical flashlight in the other hand, bright as hell. The figure pointed the beam at Matthew's face. He couldn't make out much more than a form, but there were enough details to know it wasn't Nicole.

From his periphery, he sensed Emily might open her door and try to make a run for it.

"Em, it's going to be all right," he said. "Stay put."

He wanted to lay a hand on his daughter's leg to keep her from bolting but feared the tiniest movement would be all it took for a bullet to enter his brain through an eyeball. He managed a peek in the rearview. Lucinda sat frozen in the backseat, finally at a loss for words.

"Let's everyone just take it easy. Relax. I'm sure this is all a misunderstanding." He turned slowly against the pistol's tip, not even three degrees, in an effort to connect with the man holding it. "Right? Wrong place, wrong time type thing."

His assailant left the question unanswered. The homes around them stayed dark. There were no neighbors shouting about the noise or asking what the hell was going on. For a moment that felt like an eternity, only the crickets spoke, and then the figure moved the flashlight's beam off of Matthew's face and onto Emily's.

It *was* a man. He saw that now. Only the P in the "please" came out, because the tip of the gun pushed harder against his head, and

Matthew swallowed the rest of the word as his amygdala prepared for the worst.

"Your daughter's OK," the man said. "That's good. I'd never perform a choke-hold on a little girl on my own." He sounded sincere but resigned all the same. "Unfortunately for you three, I haven't really been me lately. I don't expect you to believe that, but . . ."

The pause might have meant an unlikely apology was on its way, but it never came. Instead, the gun went vertical, and the man punched Matthew with the blunt side of its handle, hard enough to stun him. Matthew's chest fell into the steering wheel. He wasn't unconscious, but his vision dimmed, and the shapes of familiar things turned blobby and uncertain.

The driver-side door opened as Lucinda asked the man to rethink his situation. Despite her commitment, Matthew felt his feet swing out from under him as the man yanked his body from the car and onto the street. The gun to his head was replaced with a boot to his back. With nothing to focus on underneath the car, his vision couldn't correct from its blur.

Lucinda's failing pleas were loud. She was screaming when she threatened to call the police, and Matthew wanted to tell her to stop, but his mouth was more unavailing than his eyes. The *POP!* overhead left his ears ringing, but he still heard the second shot that ended Lucinda's whimper. Between the first shot and second, Emily's feet dropped to the ground, and her possible escape had him too excited or too worried to know if he was feeling anguish for Lucinda at all. With his head firm to the ground, Matthew watched his daughter's feet take the first few steps of a sprint, and when the echo of the gunfire had subsided, there were no sounds of her sneakers pounding pavement to fill its void. He had no idea how far Emily had run. Another possibility started to form in his head, one where the second shot had targeted Emily. Thank God the man spoke before the idea could take root.

"I pray your girl stays hidden. Truly I do. At least until this is all sorted."

The man grabbed Matthew's hand, pulled him up, and stood him stomach to the car.

Lucinda's body was slumped against the rear passenger window. The hole in her head was spilling blood down the glass, her mouth was agape, caught in a scream she'd never finished, and smushed flat against the pane. The fog of her last breath hadn't yet dissipated.

Matthew hadn't meant to, but he heard himself tsk. It felt wholly inappropriate.

Eternal rest grant unto her, O Lord, and let perpetual light shine upon her.

He must have mumbled the prayer, but his captor offered no condolences.

"I'd tell you I was sorry," the man offered, "but I don't do lies. Simply no sport in it."

33
TAG

Tag balled up Nicole's hand to punch through one of nine tiny panes on Aidan's back door. Breaking into the house would alert Amanda, but he still had the element of surprise.

He cocked the fist, midtorso and to Nicole's right, ready to unload, but it hung there as he considered the possibility that throwing the punch would cut her wrist, leaving them bleeding out on a psychopath's back porch. Just then, the only lit lamp downstairs went dark.

It felt like he'd been caught, but scrambling Nicole's body backward, away from the rear door, was more difficult than walking it forward. Before Tag could turn her body around to run for the bushes, he caught the outline of a human moving toward the entryway of the house. Then, through the window he'd meant to break, he watched Aidan slowly open the front door.

Aidan's silhouette filled its frame, headlights illuminating his body from somewhere down the street. He seemed bigger than before, like an impossible enemy to vanquish, but only for a moment because the beams went dark. Then he or Amanda—if she was in control—shut the door behind them.

With Aidan in the front yard, Tag worried less about the sound the shattering glass would make if he punched through it to break in. Even if Aidan heard it from the other side of the home, the opportunity to run inside to find and grab Ethan was too good and unlikely to improve.

Go for it, just angle the punch down when you do. I'm good with it.

Nicole hadn't spoken to him since the hospital.

When the pain from the punch through the glass started to set in, she said nothing.

Once inside, Tag navigated Nicole's body through the darkness of the room, using the memory of prior observations of the home, until he had Nicole standing near the basement door.

He reached for the knob and noticed her hand was bleeding. He couldn't tell if it was fatal, but her fingers were unresponsive, and the dangle of her index and pinky was unsettling.

Her left hand was an option, but as he went to use it, he realized everything he'd done that needed hands—at the hospital and while in control on the way there—he'd done with her right.

She might have been right-handed, or she might have been left-handed. He'd never paid any attention to which one held her fork when their families had dined together. She'd almost never eaten anyway. At least, nothing solid. But Nicole's left was as useless as her right hand had become.

He called out Ethan's name. Nicole's mouth moved to deliver the shout, but her vocal cords hadn't received the same message. It was all croak. Too many actions at once created a glitch in his possession of her body, or maybe all he'd put her through so far was reason enough for his control to wane.

He propped Nicole against the wall and focused on shouting to Ethan, but the pop of a gunshot outside spoiled the effort. What had come out of Nicole's mouth was pure zombie-hum, and if Ethan had heard her at all, Tag couldn't imagine his son had found any salvation in it.

A second shot rang out before the echo of the first had finished.

Tag didn't realize it yet, but a picture of what was happening outside started to form.

The four living room windows he'd used to see into the house earlier had black velvet curtains drawn over them now. He considered moving Nicole closer to investigate.

The knob on the back door started to turn, and by instinct, Tag threw himself and her body to the other end of the hallway and into the open pantry.

Nicole hit the hardwood over the hollow of the basement below. The thud was ten times louder than 111 pounds seemed capable of. The back door slowly opened.

Had Tag been able to move Nicole, he might have closed the pantry door, leaving only a small gap to spy from, but as it was, he'd lost the necessary motor skills to perform that simple task. As a possessor, he was very much an amateur, and he counted himself lucky that her ears and eyes were still working for him, and luckier still that whoever had entered through the kitchen hadn't bothered to turn on the lights.

He heard footsteps, too soft to be booted like Aidan's, with a silence between them that was too short to be an adult's stride. They'd started in the kitchen, had been cautious through the hallway, and though Nicole's mind might be playing tricks on him, were headed his way.

"Ethan," a young girl said in a hush. "Ethan, it's me, Em."

In death, Tag had felt many things, even while working hard not to. But as a resident, he hadn't once been struck from head to toe as he was in that moment by an actual flood of dopamine and serotonin. Whether it'd been his or Nicole's neurotransmitters didn't matter. Joy. She'd felt joy, and he'd felt joy, goddammit! The happiness he'd only wandered into from time to time in Second Plane was indeed an echo—nothing he'd experienced there had come close to the living version of it.

If Emily was here, though, that meant Matthew was, too. And if Matthew was here, that meant the shots he heard outside may have killed his best friend, and his best friend's help was the help he'd needed, help he needed desperately now that he could no longer run, fight, walk, or even crawl Nicole's body out of the pantry to help the best mother Ethan had ever had: Emily.

He'd felt joy, for only a second, then rage, then despair, and then fear—a fear that rivaled the one he'd known in the last minute of Flight 2332. None of it had done a damn thing to get Nicole moving again.

Time may have very well been a construct, there and in Second Plane, but the way people used that notion while living had mostly been a cynical snipe. As a resident, perhaps it *was* a construct, but if you were alive in Prior Plane, there was a definitive end waiting for you. A termination tomorrow or maybe fifty years from then. Everything before death was time—your time—to appreciate joy, to be grateful for love, to understand that while the world wasn't perfect, the emotions and feelings that came with living were a gift absolute.

Tag could feel Nicole experiencing the same epiphany while also contending with a deep dissatisfaction with how she'd spent her life so far, coupled with what felt like the self-immolation of her very soul for being unable to spring to action and protect her daughter or his son—tears were running down her cheeks. And fuck The Text, fuck The Text, fuck The—

The front door opened, and this time, the footsteps were heavy. Two sets of steps, too.

Emily raced through the darkness, past the open pantry, and Tag could not grab the girl. He was stuck, and as he tried to shake Nicole herself back into action, he heard nothing from her.

From the living room, one of the two people who'd entered was breathing hard and fast.

Tag heard Emily's footsteps finish their race through the dark, up the last of the stairs, followed by their soft and slower patter on the floor above him. He didn't remember moving Nicole himself, but her body had shifted to the right side of the pantry. The new angle created a thin line of sight into the living room.

A small lamp went on, and in the dim light it created, he saw Matthew . . . then Aidan behind him with a gun pointed at the back of his best friend's head.

"I'm not going to harm the girl," Aidan told Matthew. "*She* might, but I'm trying. For real, I am, but this thing inside me . . . well, she can be a real bitch."

Aidan seemed to be Aidan at the moment, and Matthew was alive. Maybe the shots earlier had been a warning. His best friend had believed him or had believed the message he'd left through Nicole. Tag's regret was immediate. In his rush to save his son, he'd endangered the very family Ethan would desperately need if he was ever going to survive the trauma unfolding.

"What the fuck are you going on about?" Matthew asked, sounding discomposed.

Aidan stepped closer to Matthew and put the tip of the gun to the back of his head.

"You wouldn't understand. You don't need to understand," Aidan said. "Head to that door on your left."

Aidan grabbed Matthew by the collar with his free hand and shoved him until he was in front of it. Tag had the element of surprise, but that would only matter if his attempt to rush Aidan moved Nicole's body. It looked to be about eight long steps to where the men stood.

"Open it," Aidan said.

Matthew took a deep breath, but before he could do anything with it, Aidan kicked him in the back.

"Goddammit, Matty . . . Open it! I won't ask again."

Matty. It was Amanda now. It was what she'd always called him. More than that, for the first time, Aidan's voice resembled hers, like she'd managed to shorten and tighten the man's vocal cords on sheer willpower alone.

As soon as the opening was wide enough, she shoved Matthew. The impact his body made at the bottom of the stairs was more crack than thud, and that sickening pop was the last sound to come from the basement before Aidan shut the door.

Even with all he'd witnessed, Tag had trouble believing his wife was behind the shove.

A rumble upstairs caught Tag and Aidan's attention. It was a guess, but it sounded like a run for it. Four feet, not two, and maybe the bravest attempt at an escape he'd ever heard.

Pride. Long misunderstood and maligned when the feeling was about oneself. But when felt for a child, or in this case, their children, no synthetic stimulant's effect could come close.

Tag ran out from the pantry, charging toward Aidan with a speed he hadn't anticipated—an effort that had only been possible because

Nicole had turned control of her body over to him completely, he'd felt her do it, right before their sprint, full possession, but it still wasn't enough.

Aidan spun around and pointed his gun at Nicole's chest.

The man's advantage froze Tag immediately. He raised Nicole's hands above her head, hoping Aidan would decide to let Nicole join Matthew in the basement.

"Don't do it," he pleaded. "Don't shoot."

"It's *me*, Tag . . . your wife. Do you have any idea how stupidly lucky you are right now?" Aidan's face lightened as Amanda took his body a step forward, enough to press the muzzle into Nicole's sternum. "Aidan is unstable. I mean, why wouldn't he be? We don't see eye to eye on certain things. One very specific thing about killing kids, if I'm being honest."

She motioned for Tag to put Nicole's arms down with Aidan's free hand. He did. Slowly.

"I'm not going to shoot Nicole, honey, but *he* might. So, you've got a big decision to make. Are you going to walk Nicole out of here before Aidan's back in charge, or take your chances with trying to talk me out of killing Ethan—all while hoping a fucking serial killer doesn't regain control and kill your best friend's wife? Use your head before you lose hers."

Tag couldn't look his wife in the eyes anymore. Black now. Holes really. It was a hate that could not be faked. No longer a window to the soul, at least not the one she'd once been. She had the upper hand. Nothing new about that. The control she had over Aidan's body wasn't all that different than the control she'd had over him since the night they first met. He remembered a time before they were married or even engaged. They'd stayed out on the Lower East Side of Manhattan until 4 AM and found a relatively safe-looking bench along the East River to sit and wait for the sun. Though they'd been together for six months, that was the first time they told each other "I love you." They were drunk, sure, but more than that, they were mutually smitten, and not long after, "I love you so much" became a sort of game.

I love you so much it wouldn't matter if it turned out you were an alien.
I love you so much it doesn't even matter that you fart a lot in your sleep.
I love you so much that if I could, I'd put you in my pocket forever and ever.
I could eat you. I'll tolerate your mother. I'd happily stay broke as long as it's with you.

They'd played off and on for the entire walk back to DUMBO. On the short elevator ride up to his apartment, Amanda asked, "Do you love me so much, you'd kill for me?"

And while she'd not been serious, Tag said yes. Meant it at that moment even. And, of course, she never asked—but if she had asked him to kill for her at any point up until the pregnancy, he might have. Amanda may have never been totally cognizant of the power she had over him; he didn't believe she'd ever intentionally manipulated him by leaning into his affection for her, but at some point, Tag felt a rebellion of sorts was necessary if only to prove to himself that he was still his own man. So he cheated on her. People sleep with other people for a whole host of reasons, but for him, that one night with her best friend had been nothing more than an experiment in free will. Amanda could not be his God, Amanda could not be his everything, she could not be his sole reason for living—especially after Ethan had so quickly become hers.

"Look at me, Tag. See me. Please," Amanda said.

More running thumped from upstairs, but this time, neither of them looked up.

"I'm proud of you, hon," she continued. "Never thought of you as a fighter. I underestimated you."

Tag felt Nicole's lips curl as he smiled. A fake, but maybe Amanda thought they were having a moment. It might buy him a few seconds to look around for a piece of furniture or a vase or a table clock or anything to use to disable his wife, or at least the body she was in.

"So, what's it going to be?" she asked. "Are you two leaving, or are you two staying?"

"I'm not leaving," Nicole's mouth said. Tag hadn't said it. "And you aren't killing my son. You or the psycho you possessed. He's *my* son now. Not yours."

"Oh Nicole, it's you now, isn't it?" Amanda asked, shaking Aidan's head as she did. "That's just grand, really it is. Just. Grand." Then she let out an exasperated laugh, one that suggested nobody, living or dead, had ever felt more put out than she was right then. She quickly recovered, steadied the gun again, and said, "Good. There's a better-than-average chance that you're still the most reasonable person in this room."

Despite all the harm Nicole had done to herself, over the year he'd spent observing her recovery from addiction, he'd come to understand her motivations. Rightly or wrongly, she'd lashed out like many before her, feeling forever trapped with nothing graceful on the table to free themselves. They weren't so different. And if they survived, she'd remain a great mom.

"I'm assuming that's Emily upstairs?" Amanda asked.

Tag felt Nicole's instant nausea. He wondered if she could feel his empathy for her and his guilt for having put her, his best friend, and their little girl in this situation in the first place.

"Lucinda too, Tag. He brought your mother, or I'm guessing she insisted."

"You're bluffing," Tag said, momentarily recovering control of Nicole.

Amanda was cunning, she'd spent enough time in Aidan's body to know that certain intense emotions, buttressed by the very real chemicals within the possessed, could eject the possessor. It'd almost happened to Tag several times while there inside Nicole already.

As if she sensed he was slipping back to Second Plane, she said, "I'm afraid she won't be coming inside, though. Aidan killed her, not me. I tried to stop him, honest. I've been doing this a lot longer than you, I know, but I'm still no expert."

And he was. Slipping. The pull was there the moment his grief hit. He could not talk himself into believing it was a con. Lucinda was dead. He didn't know his mother was dead because he could magically feel her missing. He knew it because for as long as he'd known his wife, she'd never lied. In death, she'd been the same. Brutally honest. For better or worse.

"You're lying," he tried, but the diffusion of the room around him continued.

"I'm not you, Tag."

That was true, too.

Before they'd died, Tag's guilt over his affair and the lies he'd told Amanda to try to hide it had punched him in the gut plenty. But not like this.

Any one of the ill feelings he was experiencing might have bounced him back to Second Plane on their own. But this . . . everyone dear was either dead or in danger of being dead soon.

His soul was adrift, somewhere between the living and the dead, when he heard Nicole's voice say, "He's not going anywhere, Amanda."

He felt his consciousness wholly return to Nicole's body once more.

The gun remained aimed at Nicole's chest, but Aidan's hand started to shake.

"Don't hate me for wanting what's best for our son," Amanda said, her voice more Aidan's again than her own. "It's horrible here . . . just horrible."

Aidan's face bounced between Amanda's expressions and expressions of his own.

His eyes went gray and back to blue just as quickly.

Tag hoped Amanda might be having her own difficulty staying put but dared not ask.

"Why didn't he die with us, Tag?" she whispered.

"I don't know."

"Don't tell me you don't know. I need an answer."

"Come back home, and we can talk about it."

There were no tears coming from Aidan's gray eyes.

"I'm sad, Tag. I know that's not poetic or even unique, but I've just been so very sad." The shake in Aidan's hand had moved to his body now, and a collapse looked certain. "Just so, so sad, you know?"

Be ready, he said to Nicole.

Though he believed his wife might return to Second Plane, that'd still leave Aidan.

Nicole made no responding thought. But he felt it. She understood and was.

The best chance of overpowering Aidan's body would be in the second of space between Amanda's faltering control and Aidan's recapture of it. That opportunity looked imminent.

"If we had to do it again, would you make the same decision—GET THE FUCK OUT OF MY HEAD, IT'S MY HEAD NOW—would *you* name Matthew and Nicole guardians?"

He'd been wrong. She wasn't going to give up. Something akin to a premortem surge thrust Amanda back. Nicole's fingers twitched as Tag thought about the iron poker next to the fireplace.

We can do this, he thought.

We can do this, she agreed.

"We've put too much on their plate now, and it was already so fucking full. And with Lucinda gone, who gets Ethan now?—I TOLD YOU, IT'S MY HEAD NOW—Don't you see, Tag? There is no other choice here. Help me do it. Help me—NO, YOU GET THE FUCK OUT OF ME, BITCH!"

Aidan's eyes went gray. The irises, pupils, and sclera looked like a stormy sea from which there was no navigating back home. There was no choice but to take them both out at once. If they could kill Aidan, Amanda would have no vessel in the fight.

They jumped for the fireplace, grabbed the poker, and spun back around with it already cocked for the blow, but before they could swing, there was another gunshot, louder than the two Tag had heard before, and this time he could smell the gunpowder.

Toe to head, Aidan's body was steady. Tag moved Nicole's hand to where the bullet had ripped through her abdomen. The glow of the living had returned to Aidan's eyes. He was himself again, for only a bit, or maybe forever.

Nicole's body dropped to its knees. Tag didn't feel their collision with the hardwood floor this time. What vision he had out of her eyes flickered like a wick wet with wax.

Nicole, are you alright? Nicole?

Her body fell face-first to the floor, and Tag was expelled, maybe for the last time.

Before he was fully removed from Prior Plane, he got one last long look at Aidan's face. The man didn't look happy about what he'd done—the control he'd lost. Whether it'd been Aidan or Amanda who'd shot Nicole, Tag could not say. But if Aidan was Aidan right then, there was still hope. Despite all the man's brain had to be processing in the moments after he'd shot Nicole, Aidan might still fight for his life, and maybe in doing so, would save Ethan's too.

34

AIDAN

Aidan woke in his living room, sitting cross-legged and barefoot on the couch. His hands hurt, but each was blood-free and resting palm down on a knee. He figured he'd dozed off midmeditation. The decision to contemplate, or pray, or to even hum away what was in his head, a cognitive marauder more literal than spiritual, had seemed like a good idea around 2 AM, but in truth, he knew nothing of the practice.

Still, this awakening felt real, like it belonged to him, as if it were the result of a solid sleep instead of a temporary repossession of the body he'd owned and had run solo for so long.

The heavy curtains around the room were drawn. The sun had yet to intrude. He didn't need a clock to peg the time as 6 AM or 6:15 AM at the latest. He was a man of few marketable talents, and his lifelong sense of where he existed in a day wasn't one of them.

He'd had visitors last night, he remembered.

Unexpected ones, unruly ones, old and young, a man he'd dragged from a car, others that had broken into his home on their own, and even the woman within him. She'd certainly worn out her welcome. But what of the woman they'd shot?

He looked over his shoulder to the floor behind the couch. Aidan didn't need the sun's rays or the light from the table lamp, which he didn't remember turning off, to see the woman's slumped form was no longer where he'd left it last night.

A memory washed over him. He watched himself shoot a single shot, watched the slug bury itself into the woman's gut, and the intimacy of his or her kill made him scoff. It hadn't been him, had it? Surely, he didn't fire the gun on his own. After dwelling on the memory a bit more, though, Aidan decided the decision to shoot her had been his, but at this point, he couldn't know for sure.

"Amanda," he said aloud. "Your name is Amanda."

Amanda was the one who'd been bouncing in and out of him for months now, and her frequent infestations of his brain had to have severely impaired his ability to think straight.

His eyes investigated the shadows, beyond the floor behind his couch, past the pantry from where Nicole had rushed to assault him, and stopped at the closed door to his backyard. It was only then that he saw the hanging shards of glass in one rectangle of its nine-paned window.

One of the younger guests or the now missing woman must've broken the window.

"Nicole."

He knew her name, too. He knew it because she'd introduced herself at the market the first time they'd met. Her name had been twice-baked into his brain now because either he or Amanda, possibly some combination of them both, had called her Nicole a bit before killing her.

But *had* he killed her?

The woman—Nicole—might have survived the shot to her midsection and crawled elsewhere. Her body could have been moved by the littles who'd been hiding upstairs. That seemed unlikely. An adult corpse was heavy. Aidan knew that better than anyone. Still . . .

Cries from his basement began, but it didn't unsettle Aidan. Screams and pleading were common from that direction, but this wasn't an invited guest, stuck and begging for release from their chains. He remained seated until the growing moans sparked a memory. This was . . . *Matthew*. The man he'd walked at gunpoint into his home was Matthew.

Whether he'd heard Amanda use the name last night or had learned it simply from her having known it while she was inside his head, it didn't matter. He had an urge to reach out to anyone who'd believe him to let them know that he'd played no real role in nabbing the man.

That said, if Matthew didn't stop yelling soon, Aidan would do something about it.

Aidan looked to his left and then to his right for his gun. He unfurled his body from its yoga-like position and pushed his feet into the white shag rug on the floor, then wiggled his toes. Thus far, all of his movements felt like decisions that he'd made. It was enough for a smile, and as his forty-three facial muscles came together to make one, the smile felt like his decision, too.

His grin stayed put as he looked for the gun. It wasn't on the couch or the coffee table, and there was no sign of it at his feet. The house was brighter than it had been minutes ago, but what little light the sun cast through the crack between the curtains was of no help.

He wasn't ready to try standing. Not yet. Staying seated while his eyes did the heavy lifting would have to do. He ran them over the living room, mostly scanning the rug, then the hardwoods on either side of it, then back across the shag until they hit a dead end in the form of little girls' shoes. Two purple sneakers that looked like someone had vomited silver and sparkly star stickers on every square canvas inch, perhaps twice. And, of course, it was the sister.

Something about the way her legs were crossed, tight but casual, an ankle over an ankle, told him the girl had been there the whole time he'd been awake. Aidan had simply not noticed. His brain had been elsewhere.

"Hello," he heard her say. "How's it going for you?"

The girl pointed his gun at him. She held the weapon between two hands, with its butt resting firmly on her lap, and both index fingers laced tightly over its trigger. By definition, it was a predicament, but at least the gun's present location had something to do with the physics of the reality he and the girl inhabited. There was some solace to be had in knowing that whatever came of that situation, he was in control of his body. He could only presume that she was, too.

Aidan had always been good at finding the silver linings in the worst situations imaginable. Just ask the body that had once inexplicably exploded in his trunk on the way to bury it in Black Rock State Park. That day trip turned into an overnighter. Cleaning up chunks of muscle and flesh and organs and goo takes time, but in the end, he had removed every bit of evidence and had done so under more stars than he'd seen since he was a kid. He could have eaten breakfast on that trunk's polypropylene and polystyrene surfaces, but he didn't. No. He'd had waffles, smothered in soft butter, drowning in syrup, with a generous shake of rainbow sprinkles at some joint off Route 8 on his way home.

When Aidan met the girl's stare, the memory of having participated in choking her out in her kitchen before running off with her little brother hit hard, forcing a bit of stomach acid through his esophagus that he quickly caught and swallowed for the benefit of the couch.

"Sorry," he said. "It's all a bit much, isn't it?"

"Is it *you?*" the girl asked. "Are *you* in control?"

He had to admit, she wasn't so little at all. Not when they'd kidnapped Ethan, not when she'd run from the car after he'd ambushed her daddy and shot the old lady they'd brought along, and certainly not now. She was not little or tiny or small or at all insignificant, sitting in the chair right across from him with his gun in her hands and intent in her glare.

"If you are asking if it is me, Aidan, then yes, it's me."

She narrowed her eyes. "How can I know for sure?"

"You can't, really," he said.

He pulled his legs back into the crossed position from before, glancing at the gun as he did to gauge her strength. There was no perceptible tremble or twitch, so he pressed on.

"That's the really fucked up part, isn't it? If you'd told me a few months ago that the deceased were capable of possessing us . . . well, I might have believed it, if I'm being honest. But I still wouldn't have believed that it could ever happen to me."

"And why's that?" the girl asked. "Do you think you're too tough?"

"God, no," Aidan said. The suggestion almost made him laugh, but he caught it before it could escape. "I'm about the least tough guy I've ever known, I'll swear to that."

The screaming from the cellar hadn't stopped. It was intermittent, and the howls from the trapped man were more pained, yet several degrees weaker with every new shout. Aidan looked at the door and then back to the girl. She'd not bothered to follow the shift in his attention.

"That's your daddy screaming downstairs, you know that, right?"

"Mmhmm. He'll live," she replied, as calmly as her dad might have, but Aidan could only know it'd been as calmly as Matthew might have said it if Amanda was still lurking.

The girl's nonchalance caught him off guard. It seemed genuine.

"OK, then," he said. "What's the plan here?"

The urgency in him was an unfamiliar feeling. He'd spent a lifetime letting everything play out in the timeframes his victims dictated. Panic and insistence were no friend to a man like him. So, why was he feeling anything other than the usual "things will be what they'll be?" Even with a gun pointed at him, he could honestly say he had no desire to hurt her or her little brother.

He felt words forming in his head. Words that weren't his own.

"Listen, I don't mean to be rude, Emily. But Aidan's right. *Do* you have a plan?"

Amanda's effect on his voice was back. He sounded like her, and the girl stiffened.

"How'd you know my name?" Emily asked.

"I heard your daddy say it . . . silly girl. Where's Ethan?" God, her voice as his was a migraine in the making.

"Not here," Emily said. "Somewhere far, far from you." There was sharp recognition in the girl's eyes but her hold on his gun had gone unstable.

"Come on now, this asshole shot your grandmother," Amanda said.

Aidan felt himself standing, and he could do nothing to sit himself back down.

Emily raised the gun from her lap, it looked like the piece had gone hot potato on her for a moment, and if it'd fired right then, it wouldn't have been a surprise. She managed to still the weapon in her hand again, and some part of Aidan was rooting for the girl. Even so, he'd seen enough guns in people's hands over the years to know who was and wasn't going to end up pulling the trigger.

"And then he shot your mother," he heard Amanda tell the girl.

His body was a few feet from the girl now, and she stood. Then, as he expected she would, Emily pushed the gun out too far in front of her chest.

Amanda was going to grab it. He could feel her thinking about it and knew from his own experience that it'd be easy enough to do.

"And now he's going to shoot you!" Amanda finished.

Aidan's left hand grabbed the barrel of the gun as his right hand swung into Emily's wrist. In one lightning-quick move, Amanda had turned the weapon on the girl, who quickly let it go. Now his hands held the gun and were pointing it at Emily, who already had her arms crossed over her face, pleading for him not to shoot. Pleading for Amanda not to shoot.

"I'm sorry," Emily said. "Please don't. Just let us go. Just let us live!"

His index finger tightened. Amanda would pull the trigger, and if she did, the small shred of humanity that Aidan had used to define himself as less than a monster would be no more.

Halfway through its action, with the finger too far into its destiny to reverse course, Aidan turned the gun backward, then up, and pointed it at his own head as it fired. A single bullet entered through his left eye and tore through the fat of his brain before striking the back of his skull and embedding itself in his meninges.

He or Amanda or both put a hand over his eye. It wouldn't keep him alive; why had they bothered to do it? Instinct, maybe. In the moments before the shot, he'd felt fully present and in control. He was cold now. Distant from the form he once owned. As his body collapsed, his head collided with the marble coffee table that had always been so easy to clean. It should have hurt, he thought, worse than the shot he'd fired into his brain, which had stung more than he'd expected given that he'd hand-delivered it and had braced for its impact when he'd fired the gun. But as the pointed corner of the table opened more of him to the world, he felt nothing.

Had he ended Amanda's life, too? Was the boy going to be OK?

From the floor, he caught a last glimpse of Nicole standing in the throughway to the kitchen. Her blue smock was bloodstained but she was upright, Ethan gripped in her arms so very tightly.

Maybe they were all ghosts—Nicole, Ethan, Emily, even the man in the basement whose screaming had stopped. Aidan hadn't believed in ghosts, but as he died, it didn't feel permanent.

The past fifteen minutes hadn't offered a reason for a smile, but his grin went ear to ear. He felt it growing—or imagined the sensation—as his vision of life and material things ended.

Would he be back too? Wasn't that a distinct possibility?

Who might I kill, when I am no longer trapped in my own skin?

It was Aidan's last living thought, and it came to him in the last moment of his living life, here in the existence he knew . . . or in the existence he had known . . . right before somewhere else, right before somewhere as blank as he wanted it to be, though he didn't know yet that it *could* be as blank or as black or as dark or as endless as *he* wanted it to be, and then that last living thought ended, right before he read the first words of a small book that had appeared in front of him as a new resident in Second Plane . . .

WELCOME, AIDAN!

. . . and right before he met Gabriel, a hideous and foul creation—the spitting image of an inky-black nightmare he'd drawn on a piece of paper as a young boy. Back then, for a period of time that had to be longer than he remembered, that very beast hung by thumbtack on the wall next to his bed. Here—wherever here was—the monster looked nothing like the mother he'd known, the mother who'd loved him, or the mother who while living had sworn to Aidan over and over again that she'd never stop trying to help him get well, at any cost. But Aidan knew the creature's true identity intimately and immediately. As the beautiful spectacle approached him over a vast white sweep of nothingness, he went warm. It was if he had a fever—not just in his head—all over a body he was sure he didn't have anymore. Gabriel had connected and had come to greet him in his new space, and Aidan awaited its embrace with open arms, because while it'd given him no name one way or the other, Aidan understood it was his mother just the same.

35
TAG

The chair was an original creation with a tall back, high enough to be throne-like, though that had not been Tag's intent. He had overly and overtly stuffed its comfy cushions to the point of caricature, then squeezed them between armrests the size of surfboards. From its two-inch peg legs up, he'd wrapped it in a multi-colored fabric too offensive to be in stock at Rooms To Go.

The chair was perfect, and he'd built it as he had for no other reason than to piss off his wife. As he took it in, Tag didn't mind thinking its design was about as petty a thing as any he'd ever attempted, but didn't Amanda have at least that coming? Of course, his wife would only notice if she cared to notice. That's how it worked. They knew that now, they both did.

Tag didn't think the woman, who *might* have killed his mother but had failed to off his son, would be much longer. He'd requested an immediate connection the moment he observed Aidan hit the floor, and his wife had always been prompt when it mattered to her.

It was possible that upon her return to Second Plane, she'd stew alone through the infinity of space it offered, and do so forever. She might also ignore Tag's request to meet, and it was also possible she'd run straight to Gabriel, hoping it had a lead on another body, one soured and ready to go, so she could again try to bring Ethan "home."

All those things were possible, but none seemed likely to Tag.

For now, he'd won. Indirectly, but a victory nonetheless.

What *did* seem likely was she'd be very emotional about that fact.

He leaned back, searching for the comfort of the chair he'd created. He couldn't find it.

He'd had a body again, for not even twenty-four hours, but he'd felt—truly *experienced*—breezes, smells, sounds, excitement, doubt, and pain through Nicole's nerve endings and cerebral mechanisms. What The Text had to say about feelings being mere mimics of what a resident had once known wasn't entirely untrue. Save the love for his son, no sensation he'd known as a resident had ever come close. The possession had made that painfully obvious.

If there was going to be anything easy about the conversation he was planning on having with his wife, the love they felt for Ethan would be the only reason.

Love, it seemed, was as real in Second Plane as it was for the living.

Love distorts.

Love corrupts.

Love empowers . . . and eventually, love means loss.

His and Amanda's grief over the past year played out differently. That it had didn't make either of them all that unique, no matter if they resided in Prior Plane, there, or even in the next existence, an existence that awaited them both.

His wife would want to regroup, but Tag knew the one thing he could do—the one thing he *would* do at all costs—the one thing possible that would give Ethan's life the space it or anyone else's deserved—he knew that this one thing would ensure Amanda never got another chance. So, he felt no anxiety about the future—their future—because his decision was made.

Amanda used to say choices were Tag's kryptonite, and that was true. For his short duration in Second Plane, there'd been plenty of vexing options, as well. Anything a resident wanted to see or do was a possibility of a sort. He'd found comfort by leaning into The Text's suggestions, which helped eliminate choice. He didn't need the help now. There was only one path forward, and for him, there was an absolute freedom in deciding to pick Life After Death.

Life After Death, aka Third Plane, was no life at all. At least, not one where your life, the very first you ever had—what you'd had, what you'd known, who you'd loved—was in any way viewable anymore. Life After Death meant a total blackout, no more observations, and it was no longer a suggestion. To be blunt, it was a punishment, and no resident of Second Plane had ever returned after they'd been banished there.

The play on the familiar colloquialism of the living, Life After Death, was probably coined by a resident eons ago. A softer way, humorous to some, that gave Third Plane a codename that residents could use to weaken its punch. At least, that'd been Martha's theory on the origin of the next existence's nickname. Tag found it believable enough.

When Amanda returned, Tag would tell her all about Life After Death, even if she, too, already knew exactly what it held for anyone banished from Second Plane. He would report himself and Amanda to the council and was considering throwing out Gabriel's name when he did.

I am not my brother's keeper.

He decided against it. What he and Amanda had done was a black-and-white violation, and Tag wasn't sure Gabriel's tutelage on possession was as explicitly forbidden.

For Tag and Amanda, though, the council's verdict would be swift. Not only had they knowingly possessed bodies on earth, his wife had used Aidan's to commit murders. Even if she had been telling the truth and Aidan had been the one to shoot his mother, Amanda set off the events that had led to it. Lucinda was a resident now, too, but it'd be a while—if ever, should the council banish him—before Tag and his mother could discuss whether or not she thought it had been Amanda or Aidan or both their doing. A fun conversation to look forward to.

If the story of Ethan's survival were ever told, no doubt Aidan would seem the hero.

Emily might have even seen it that way.

The serial killer's dedication to his own bizarre set of rules—suggestions, maybe—and a single bullet from his own gun ultimately thwarted Amanda. Technically speaking, that was true. But for Tag, the only memory worth holding onto for dear life was of the role Emily had played.

* * *

A few minutes after Aidan had shot Nicole, he had removed his shoes and socks and then plopped himself on the couch. He crossed his legs, but it appeared to Tag that Amanda was simultaneously trying to stand Aidan's body back up. From within the man, it was like she was kicking with all she had, in every direction, to pop Aidan from his liberation pose and back onto his feet. For the better part of an hour, while fighting to stay in that pose, Aidan's eyes opened from time to time. Gray, then blue, blue, then black, then back to blue. Eventually, he stilled.

Tag left the living room to look for his son. He found Ethan and Emily hiding in a closet on the second floor. His son was sleeping soundly, his body covered by a thick wool coat. His eyes were tight, and it was not a peaceful sleep, but he was alright. Emily had stationed herself between Ethan and the closet door. Her eyes were open, red from tears that were no longer there.

At that moment, Tag hoped she might be waiting for the right amount of silence to try using a phone to call for help or to rush to a neighbor's home nearby. He could not help himself and tried in vain to lift his son from the floor. When Emily turned around to do the same, all Tag could do was watch as she clutched Ethan tightly against her chest and headed for the stairs.

Once in the living room, Emily did not stop to observe Aidan's malfunction, but she did stop for only the time it took to turn off the lamp on the side table to the man's right. Dark got darker, and Aidan's head never made the full turn necessary for him or Amanda or both to watch the girl extinguish the light, or catch her walking carefully behind the short length of couch.

Even when Emily found Nicole's body at her toes, her brief pause and recovery were masterful. She simply stepped higher, widening her stride, and she didn't miss a beat as she and Ethan passed over the stillness of the dark mass that was her mother on the floor.

She put Ethan into a comfortable chair at the furthest corner of an adjacent room that looked like a reading nook, then Emily came back and grabbed Nicole by the hands.

Sliding Nicole's weight across the wood floor would have been an easy move for an adult, but it wasn't going well for Emily. She had her mom by both arms, pulling gently at her toward the kitchen. Each new tug only moved Nicole's body an inch. She'd done all this while Aidan's body shook in short fits as if he had a violent fever. He looked like a defective bear trap, and Tag worried that any next move Emily made would spring him.

Emily eyed the blood stain on her mother's gown, mouthed, "I'm sorry," and then, with a heave better suited for a sack of cement, managed to get the momentum she needed to succeed.

On the kitchen floor, Nicole coughed. Her bark was bloody and loud, and unexpected. Em was unfazed. Nicole opened her eyes, and the fear in them did not spark any in Emily's. She patted her mother on the head lightly, dropped to a knee, and leaned in close for a whisper. "I'll be right back, Mom. I promise."

Nicole's hand reached for her daughter's, and Em took it, squeezing it gently.

"But I need you to be as quiet as possible until then," Emily said.

With Aidan still fighting Amanda on the couch, the girl capably disappeared back up the stairs, was gone for less than a minute, and then returned with a first-aid kit in hand. She put it next to Nicole, who was breathing steadily by then and seemingly alert enough to tend to herself. Without saying another word to her mother, Emily turned and marched to the basement door.

Aidan's spasms now were that of a death row inmate, perpetually frying upon a cushioned electric chair, with a vacancy in his eyes that made identifying who had control of him difficult.

Before Tag could check on Emily, she returned from the basement. She closed the door quietly, then walked up to Aidan's body, which was still trembling in its pose on the couch.

The man's hands had yet to move from his knees, and Tag appreciated his commitment. They stayed put as Emily removed the gun from the denim basket his crossed legs had formed. In the split second that it took for her to grab it, Aidan's eyes opened, and Tag could see that they'd become every bit Amanda's eyes instead. Not gray or black, but green. Not swirling like smoke, but intent and dead set on attacking Emily. If eyes alone had been capable of killing, the girl's life would have ended right then and there.

Aidan kept his body his own, and he did so long enough for Emily to cross the living room, gun in hand, to take a seat in a chair. She sat, put one leg over the other, and steadied the gun for shooting on her right thigh. Its stubbed barrel, which was aimed at Aidan, showed not even a quiver. Aidan's body had gone completely still, and his eyes were closed.

Emily could have fired it over the coffee table right then, but she didn't.

While living, Tag had not known Emily well. At the dinners Matthew hosted, his daughter always seemed a touch sad and, if not sad, quiet. He never thought of her as shy, though, because if he asked a question, anything from "How's school?" to "Who's your favorite band?" she animated quickly. She was a vibrant speaker with strong opinions, and Tag remembered once remarking to Amanda that he hoped their child would be similar. Who she would become for what they'd put her through wasn't something he wanted to speculate on.

The girl kept the gun on Aidan, waiting for the man or his wife to wake, and all Tag could do was bear witness. Emily's motivations were her own.

Though Nicole would come to later, she had, for now, passed back out in the kitchen. Ethan still slept undisturbed, which didn't surprise Tag, given how often his son had conked out in the thick of New York City's roar.

Then, Aidan or Amanda or both woke.

* * *

As much as it'd been hell to watch what transpired after that, Tag remained in awe of Emily's resolve and courage. He was also happy she hadn't had to be the one to pull the trigger.

He felt Amanda arriving now. Unlike the last time they spoke in Second Plane, the molecules offered no indication of what mood she might be in. He braced himself for the worst.

"Well," Amanda said. "That was something." The last part of her façade to form in front of him was her face. She looked calm.

"Aren't you upset?" he asked.

She didn't answer for a while. The silence could have been five minutes or five years.

Time itself is a construct.

"There'll be other opportunities," she answered. She may have even believed it.

"Yeah, could be, I guess," Tag said.

The next pause between them speaking was thicker than the first, the product of an actual distance growing between Amanda and Tag that he didn't yet realize.

"I'm sorry about your mom," Amanda said.

"Don't be," he said. "You should be, but don't be. It won't make much difference now."

"Is Lucinda here?"

"Yep, she's a resident, alright."

And she was, and somehow Tag had already spent years with his mother there, and he knew that his mother understood, and he knew that she relished the minor role she'd played in saving Ethan's life, and Lucinda had already told him that knowing that she'd helped prevent her grandson's death, in a small way, was enough for her to move on as a resident. All was forgiven.

Besides, she didn't give a shit what the suggestions outlined. Very Mom.

She'd also told him she would always and forever check in on her grandson—she would keep tabs on his son.

"It wasn't me, you know," Amanda said, "I mean, I get that she died because of the things I was doing, but—" Her voice wasn't her own, not quite.

"Amanda, I need to—" His voice wasn't his either.

"You don't sound so great, are you OK?" she asked.

"You sound like shit too, hon, if I'm being honest."

In fact, she looked worse than she sounded, looked as bad as he felt. Yes, felt.

"Oh shit . . . Oh shit," Amanda said, not panicky but resigned while wanting to disbelieve.

"What?" Tag managed to ask.

He thought about trying to hold her hand to tell her he was reporting them to the council, but when he moved his hand to take hers, it wasn't there.

"Oh . . . yeah," he said. "I guess we fucked up. Like, we really, really fucked up."

"Did you say something to someone already about what I did?" She didn't sound as angry as he thought she'd be. Tired, but not angry.

He hadn't said something to someone, but it didn't matter.

"We're dying, Tag. Goddammit, we're dying—dying again, aren't we?"

"Maybe, but we'll be alright."

There wasn't much of Amanda left to look at, but her eyes were there and were hers again, from before, no longer gray or callous, but emerald green and part of her glow.

"But what about Ethan?" she asked.

He didn't have an answer for her.

"Tag?"

Or maybe it was because he couldn't answer her.

"Tag, answer me. What about Ethan?"

Her voice sounded like she existed galaxies away. Maybe they were stars after all. He wished he'd told her he loved her, not that he'd forgiven her—even dying a second time, he wouldn't have said that he forgave her. He didn't think he ever *could* forgive her.

Then again, they'd have far fewer distractions where they were headed. Total blackout. Forgiveness was a possibility. Like love, forgiveness could be real and always a possibility, and he imagined that would be true in Third Plane and anywhere else he and Amanda ended up.

She said Ethan's name one more time. "Ethan."

Was it her?
Or was it him wanting to hear her say it?
It didn't matter.
Ethan.

His son's name was the last thing he heard right before somewhere else, before a place as blank as they *needed* it to be, before he remembered he'd never see his son again. His son, whose life he loved more than his own and certainly more than what his existence had become. He wouldn't see him now, not in Prior Plane, and not when Ethan was an old man and a resident in Second Plane, and then . . .

Tag's thinking on Ethan ended forever, right before he read the first words in a book that appeared in front of him as a new resident of Third Plane.

WELCOME, TAGGART!

ACKNOWLEDGMENTS

Save for a few sociopaths I have known personally, I can't think of anyone from my life that doesn't deserve thanks on this page for the part they played in my arrival at this destination. That said, as it pertains to this specific text, I'd like to convey extra appreciation to the following indomitable forces: my Higher Power, Ariele Rosch, Karmen Wells, Johnny Compton, Elle Nash, Danielle Vinson, Ally Wilkes, Jess Verdi, Benita Conde, Jake Lovell, Mom, Dad, King Baby (not the real one, but the one who knows who he is), Jeff and Meredith Clark, mothers, teachers, Ari Weiss, Crooked Lane Books, Tom Nugent, Reid Miller, and my son, Bodhi, who I will love deep into the next plane.